A gift from NESFA.
If you enjoy this book,
visit us at www.nesfa.org.

D1550444

Double Feature

Emma Bull
Will Shetterly

The NESFA Press
Post Office Box 809
Framingham, MA 01701-0203

FIRST EDITION
Second trade paperback printing, March 2004

Library of Congress Catalog Card Number: 93-086987

International Standard Book Number:
1-886778-11-6

Copyright Acknowledgments

For Robert Ray,
who taught us everything we know about
B-grade fiction.

Contents

Introduction

Patrick & Teresa Nielsen Hayden

The trouble with too many introductions is that they come at the beginning of the book. Discussions of The Significance Of This Story, or how the prose style does thus-and-such singular and very memorable thingamajig, are all very well; only, they don't make much sense if you haven't read the stories yet. If you put it all at the end of the book, it might actually be useful.

Another school of intros tries to come up with a clever, pithy but usually just irritatingly coy blurb for each of the stories. These also should be placed at the end of the book, where they're easier to ignore and may even wind up being replaced in the mass-market edition by an ad for the publisher's other books.

But there's no help for it; something called an introduction will perforce wind up at the beginning. We'll try to limit this to things that are actually useful to know.

The stories "Bound Things," "Badu's Luck," "A Happy Birthday," "The Well-Made Plan," and "Six Days Outside the Year"—by Will, Emma, Will, Emma, and Will, respectively—first appeared in the Liavek series, edited by Emma and Will. Liavek was one of those shared-world anthology things "in the best-selling tradition of Thieves' World," as the sales copy on the first volume hopefully announced. The one essential thing to know here is that these stories are perfectly comprehensible even without the rest of the series wrapped around them. Here at Staten Island Consumer Laboratories our technicians tested this proposition by reading them before reading any other Liavek material, ever, and they were just fine. So don't worry.

"Danceland Blood," which was originally published as "Danceland" in Terri Windling's second Borderlands anthology, *Bordertown* (1986), is Will and Emma's only published collaboration. In another sense, though, it's a collaboration still ongoing. The cast of characters spun out from "Danceland"—Wolfboy, Orient, and Tick-Tick, among others—went on to dominate their later separate Borderlands work, including both of their most recent novels, Shetterly's *Nevernever* and Bull's *Finder*. Furthermore, seven years from the first appearance of "Danceland," *Nevernever* reframes the original tale as an unreliable narrative, a work of propaganda and deception devised for a specific purpose by some of the Borderlanders themselves. Never mind. To understand that you'll need to read *Nevernever.* You'll like it.

The other material in this volume explains itself. So enough of fact; let's get down to utilitarian fancy.

What you really need to know about Will Shetterly and Emma Bull is that they're fictional. To be specific, they were invented by Dorothy Dunnett, and no doubt started life as characters in one of her highly satisfactory dramas of murders and manners, politics and enterprises. How Will and Emma came to be running about loose, writing their own books (and short stories and comics and essays), tending their gardens and their theories, is a matter for some conjecture; but it does not disguise their obvious provenance.

Emma Bull on her own is a portrait by Gainsborough or Sir Joshua Reynolds: tall and elegant, all poise and balance and excellent line, like an egret; in person the same, only like that egret, she can suddenly dart, with great speed and accuracy, after something that takes her interest. She is a fine singer and guitar player, an admirable gardener, and incurably tidy.

Will Shetterly, on the other hand, is of course a Holbein—one of those busy, earnest, worldly Renaissance men of affairs whose worktables are covered with inkstands, astrolabes, notes, charts, quills, seals, awls, calipers, correspondence, celestial globes, extra gloves, and any number of small mysterious scientific instruments made of wood. (Life will never be long enough for all these pursuits; life is too short not to pick up yet another absorbing interest.) He has a tenacious way with a notion, and will chew and worry at it until it surrenders up some insight or rule of thumb.

The final thing you need to know is that if you watch Will and Emma long enough, you will find them watching you. They are both great observers. We find this makes us want to do and say entertaining things in their vicinity. This seems, after all, only fair.

Double Feature

Poems seem to be perpetual works in progress, at least for me. This is no exception. I wrote the first draft when I was going to Beloit College. Chad Walsh, poet, professor, and science fiction fan, was very kind about it, as I remember. But then, he was by nature very kind.

—*Emma*

Visionary

Emma Bull

You say that star-furred hunting wolf packs prowl
The black glass, cut stone, asphalt city night.
You hear their triumph in the squad car's howl,
And smell their kill's blood in a bus stop fight.

You claim that hoofbeats ring out in the street
Where no horse for a century has gone,
And that a dragon, *gules,* sinks taloned feet
Into a field of *vert* suburban lawn.

You are unwise, who dream upon this hill.
You bring home nothing, no reward or fame.
You thread your loom with mist, and waste your skill;
This weave will fail, and with it fades your name.

But now the silver strands slip from your hand
And you must catch them, quickly, if you can…

I was invited to speak to a meeting of southern Minnesota librarians, in my capacity as a Genuine Minnesota SF Writer. When Kristine Kathryn Rusch asked me to write a Pulphouse *introduction at almost the same time, and on a particularly suitable topic, I recognized the hand of Fate, or at least, Economy, and produced this essay.*

—Emma

Why I Write Fantasy

Emma Bull

It was not long ago that my father asked me The Question. We were on the phone, talking about my second novel, which was due in the book-stores practically any minute. And he said, politely and cautiously, as if he were bringing up the deficit to a presidential advisor, "Have you ever thought about…do you have any interest in…do you think you'll ever write something that's not science fiction or fantasy?"

It is, I thought then and think now, a perfectly good question. I just hadn't been asked it before. So I gave him a less-than-inspired answer, something on the order of, well, I was still having fun at it, and as long as I was, I'd keep writing fantasy.

The fact is, if fun were my only motivation, I could be having fun writing anything. (Or not having fun not writing anything, which is the other part of the job, and the main cause of writers behaving badly at parties.) But every work of fiction I've finished has been fantasy, and everything I want to write next is, too. It seems I owe my father some more explanation. Well, here it is.

I'll start off with a brisk and potentially annoying clarification: when I say "fantasy," I also mean "science fiction." I believe that science fiction is fantasy's offspring, and remains one of its parts. I write both science fiction and fantasy, and I think I write them out of the same impulse.

They're both part of the literature of "What if?" even when the ifs can be separated out into the categories of improbable magic on one side and probable technology on the other. (And mind you, it's not always that easy.) They often work toward the same goal, though their methods may be different—but I deal later with the purpose of fantastic literature, so when we get there, substitute "science fiction" for "fantasy" and see if you agree that science fiction does the same jobs with different tools.

To some people, fantasy is entry-level literature. It's written for children, to entertain and excite them, and to get them hooked on the thrill and power of reading. Or it's written more or less for adults, but best used to lure jaded teenagers into a book habit, accompanied by a speech like, "If you're into Dungeons & Dragons, you might like this...." Or substitute "Star Trek" for "Dungeons & Dragons," if the book being gestured with has a rocket ship on the spine instead of a dragon.

Now this is perfectly respectable work for fantasy to do, this business of introducing kids to the delicious addiction of reading. But some people think that's its only work. Or maybe they don't think so, but they can't, under pressure, defend themselves when parents or teachers or the library board suggest that there's a time to put aside Fairy Tales and Escapist Junk. By these standards, the proper ambition of every young reader is to graduate to realistic fiction, and the duty of every teacher and librarian and parent is to help them do it.

I'm using "realistic" as a label to identify any fiction I'm not calling fantasy. It's not a good label; it says things about both fantasy and non-fantasy that I don't want to say. It suggests that a book that's set in real 1989 New York, that has no magic or supernatural elements or technological trappings, can be depended on to tell you the absolute truth about the present and the people who live there. John M. Ford, author of *The Dragon Waiting* and Growing Up Weightless, will tell you that Judith Krantz's *I'll Take Manhattan* is demonstrably a fantasy novel. The relationship of events in that book to New York magazine publishing is roughly equivalent to the one between Dorothy's trip to Oz and a ride in a Boeing 747.

And if I say that non-fantasy is "realistic," then I seem to be saying that fantasy isn't. But fantasy is based in truth, fact, reality. It has to be. The writer and the reader have to have a common language, or there's no point in telling the tale. And the common language is the fields we know, whether it's homely details about cooking over a wood stove, or a woman's distaste for a man who's courting her for her money, or a fifteen-year-old's desperate need for some strange new item of clothing.

So "realistic" is a rotten label for the kind of fiction that isn't fantasy. But I don't think we have the word I'm looking for, so I hope you'll forgive my temporary redecoration of the language.

I know why I write fantasy—I know it somewhere down below and behind my lungs. But I can explain it somewhat less well than I can explain why breathing puts oxygen in my blood. I know I *don't* write it so that someday teenagers will grow up and stop liking my books. No, there's something I want to get across—to both adults and kids—that just won't take root and grow in the otherwise fertile ground of realism.

I know that other writers have felt the same way. The tradition of fantasy is as old as literature. Western literature begins with fantasy, with Gilgamesh and the *Iliad* and the *Odyssey*. *Beowulf* pits a mortal man against ghastly supernatural foes…and if you respond that this is literature from the "childhood" of civilization, I'll warn you that you're badly underestimating your ancestors.

Fantasy has an unbroken lineage from then until the present, as a vehicle to amuse kings and queens, to uplift the spirits of men and women, and to make harsh political statements in such a way as to keep the writer out of prison. It had a breathtaking flowering in the '60s in this country with the publication in paperback of J. R. R. Tolkien's *The Lord of the Rings*. I'm going to use a lot of examples from Tolkien in the next few pages. First, because the success of *The Lord of the Rings* prompted Ian and Betty Ballantine and Lin Carter to create the Ballantine Adult Fantasy series, which resurrected many of the classics of fantasy, like the work of E. R. Eddison and Lord Dunsany, and gave us new works of the fantastic, like Peter Beagle's *The Last Unicorn*. I'm also going to conjure with Tolkien because there are few other works of fantasy that have become so much a part of our culture. Even here, where I can expect my readers to be familiar with the literature of fantasy, it's the one book I can be sure almost all of you have read, or heard of, or seen a horrible animated singing cartoon of. (Sometime late in the 1960s my brother, in the army and stationed in Korea, sent home an airmail letter with "Shadowfax Fast!" written on the back of the envelope. Shadowfax is the name of the magical horse that the wizard Gandalf rides in *The Lord of the Rings*. As I remember it, by the time the envelope arrived in Illinois, someone along the line had written "Yeah!" next to Jim's original comment, and drawn a little cartoon horse with speed lines behind it.)

People who dislike it will tell you that modern fantasy consists of the *Dragonlance Chronicles* and Star Trek: The Silly Generation and an army of Middle Earth wannabes (former *Twilight Zone* editor Tappan King refers to them as "Elfy-welfy" books). Yes, modern fantasy includes these. Just as modern realistic fiction includes the complete works of Harold Robbins and Jackie Collins. But modern fantasy is also Gabriel Garcia Marquez's *One Hundred Years of Solitude,* Gene Wolfe's *Book of the New Sun,* Barry Hughart's *Bridge of Birds,* Margaret Atwood's *The Handmaid's Tale,* Jane Yolen's *Cards of Grief,* John Crowley's *Engine Summer.* These people, all of whom are smarter than I am, felt a pull in their guts toward the voice of fantasy, toward a form that, according to many people, puts their books outside the literary pale.

Why is that? Why is it all right to invent a New England college town, and people it with invented professors and invented spouses and their invented kids, to fling these invented people into a struggle with other invented people over non-existent tenure and imagined promotions...but to deny to adult imaginations the business of myth-making and metaphor, the created world and the character big enough to live within it? To many of us, working for Control Data or running a family farm or stocking shelves in bookstores, that New England college town is almost as strange a place as Oz or Perelandra. We value imagination in children. We encourage it. Why don't we nurture imagination in adults? Why don't we urge them to dream fantastical things, conceive of strange futures, emphasize the wonder in the world around them? We're all in a bad way here: choking on our own emissions, wading through our own trash, cringing in a brass-knuckled, hit-him-before-he-hits-you world. The solutions to these and all our problems can only come from the unfettered imaginations of adults. How can we make a better life if we can't imagine it? When we insist that growing up means living only in the real world, we're shooting ourselves in the collective foot.

Creating fiction—any kind of fiction—is a wild, uncontrolled, bizarre activity, a thing many people see as outside the normal range of experience. They don't understand "where you get your crazy ideas," or why, if writing is so hard and pays so lousy and produces such a lonely, misunderstood lifestyle, anyone would sit down and do it. So writers themselves must be a little crazy. Now, if you admit that, what do you say about writers who deal in fantasy? In elves and shape-changers, in talking animals and trees that walk, in sentient beings of pure energy, time travel, psychic powers, galactic civilizations? Put like that, it sounds like a collection of headlines from the *Weekly World News*.

In self-defense, a rational society that values control, order, logic, and citizens who know their place *has* to devalue fantasy. The moral order of the corporate raider and the Harvard MBA dictates that it's a hard world, where you have to do hard things to survive. Accountability is for suckers, and doing the right thing regardless of the profits is for wimps. That moral order can't afford to encourage respect for literature that tells stories like this:

One small, ordinary person makes a long, terrible journey to destroy a ring, a source of great evil. He knows that, instead of destroying the thing, he could take its power and wield it for good, to help his friends, to destroy an even greater evil. The great and wise people around him say that would corrupt him, that he couldn't use that power without becoming evil himself—but what if he could? In the course of his journey, he is warped and twisted and hurt beyond recovery, and he thinks he may die—though all he has to do is use the ring, and he will never die at all. He knows all of this, but he keeps on, because *it's the right thing to do.*

No, the people who believe that whoever dies with the most money wins can't afford to have us read and love Tolkien's *The Lord of the Rings*. It's subversive literature, and the only way they can be safe is to convince us all that it's only fit for children. Because who'll take notice if a child stands up, and points at them, and says, "Mommy, those people are lying"?

I suggested that fantasy was subversive. It might be more honest to say that it's seductive. Fantasy can make an end run around the reader's preconceptions and prejudices; realistic fiction will—pardon the seasonal metaphor—hit that defensive line and very likely lose yardage. The realistic novel might deal with race or class or gender; and its author might hope that whichever subject he or she has chosen will serve as a metaphor for all the rest of the diversity of the human creature. But real-life assumptions and conflicts, set in a place meant to be the real world, are hard to turn into metaphor. They're not elastic enough.

Imagine a reader, child or adult, who firmly believes that African Americans are inferior to European ones, that women aren't as smart or as strong as men, and that homosexuals are a fit subject for dirty jokes and nothing else. If that person reads a book about a black lesbian struggling to prove her worth in a heterosexual white male's milieu—assuming such a reader would pick that book up at the newsstand or library—he or she will get nothing out of it. The wall of preconceptions goes up, saying, Blacks are like this and so, and, Lesbians don't this or that. Anything in the story that runs counter to those preconceptions—well, easy enough to dismiss it as preaching, politicking, or even bad writing.

But that same reader, the one who had firm opinions on women, gays, and blacks, might instead happen upon Isaac Asimov's *The Gods Themselves,* with its three-sexed, very sympathetic, completely alien aliens. Or Ursula Le Guin's *The Left Hand of Darkness,* set on a planet where all the inhabitants are male and female by turns. Or Jane Yolen's *Sister Light, Sister Dark* and *White Jenna,* where the characters are warrior women, king-makers, sorceresses—and very real and familiar people, for all that. These books have the potential to sneak around the wall of preconception, to ooze through the cracks in it, and deliver their message: diversity in humanity is no threat. There are things in the universe stranger to you than anything you've yet seen. Don't be afraid of them, because amazing things are coming, unbelievable things are already here, and if you accept them, they will bring you joy.

Fantasy can do this because every story about aliens or elves, vat-grown humans or werewolves, is really about ourselves. We're the only sapient creatures we know, the only model we have—and the only audience we're likely to get, for a long time, anyway. Much of the proper business of fantasy is to examine the strange condition that is humanity, to explore the natural world's most enduring mystery: ourselves. Ignore those bits of cartography at the beginning of so many fantasy novels; what fantasy maps out for us is the country of our subconscious, the home of our potential for transcendent greatness and profound evil.

Realistic fiction, by its own rules, is only playing fair when it explores the lives of realistic people, living in a world where the scale, and the stakes, are the ones we know—that New England college town, say. But Tolkien's hobbits, whose natural concerns are their gardens and their dinners and a bit of pipeweed and gossip by their front gates, confront evil on a scale that a realistic novel can't encompass. From somewhere in their profoundly ordinary little selves, they have to produce the strength and courage and sheer cussedness to face that evil down. Their ordinariness, in fact, is much of the source of that strength: the knowledge that, whatever the notions of kings may be, the world isn't set right until regular folks are left in peace to grow potatoes in their gardens.

But there's no such thing as hobbits. What use is there in knowing how much courage they can dredge up, and under what circumstances? That would be a very good question, if *The Lord of the Rings* were really only about hobbits. But the hobbits are stand-ins, in that great and terrible conflict, for us. The land of fantasy is in the kingdom of metaphor—it shares a boundary fence with poetry—and its inhabitants may be birds with human voices, or wizard-kings, or little people with furry feet and a passion for six meals a day when they can get them—but they're all us, really. Our kings and warriors and wizards, our servants of evil and our bearers of good, our bitter heroes and altruistic villains…and our gardeners and gossips and cookers of dinner.

I remember the first time I read *The Lord of the Rings,* in high school sometime. I read the last few pages, in which the hobbit Frodo sails in his old age for the lands of the West where heroes go, the awful price of carrying the ring and breaking the back of darkness paid at last. I went out onto the patio of my parents' house, and I stood for a long time, looking at the sunset. No story, no history, no instructive biography or sermon had ever made me feel the way I felt then: that humanity had an infinite capacity for nobility, for goodness, for strength used with wisdom and informed by mercy, and that I was part of that.

J. R. R. Tolkien once wrote, "By the making of Pegasus, horses were ennobled." Humanity is illuminated in the same way by the heroes of fantasy. They may take longer steps than we can, but they take them in directions we're free to choose, and the consequences of that choice, while perhaps larger than the ones we can expect in real life, are at the heart of it the same consequences our actions will have.

Fantasy's purpose can change; it has, as our need of it changed. Once it was part of the job of fairy and folk tales and mythology to explain where deformed babies came from, what was under that hill down the road, why toadstools grew in circles. We don't need fantasy to explain the mechanics of our world anymore. We have physics and chemistry and biology and astronomy. The sun is not a beautiful god who drives his chariot across the sky each day, and the moon is not his sister.

But the sun *is* a natural power plant of unimaginable heat, that in periodic outbursts we can't yet explain can reach across millions of miles of emptiness to whisper in our radios and dance on our TV screens. And the moon, dead ball of stone and dust though it is, still catches and flings back the sun's light like a reckless, heedless sibling sharing some cosmic game of catch, bringing beauty and mystery to the night. How can we record and communicate that sense of enduring magic in the world? And having recognized it, how can we reconcile it with the notion that that great, silver-white face *is* a ball of stone, and men have *walked across it?*

Both of those feelings, those wonders, are the proper food and fuel of the fantastic. Remember what I said earlier, that fantasy's boundaries lie along those of poetry? Once, poetry was our vehicle for communicating wonder. Everyone read it—every literate person read poetry for recreation. Now we read fiction in the same way, and poetry has become a rarer passion. But not all fiction is in the business of communicating wonder. Fantasy is. It transforms the way we see the world by connecting familiar images with new, strange ones. It calls wonder out of the commonplace. It restores to all us grownups the childhood notion that around the next corner, there could be…anything. Infinite possibility. Infinite futures. Infinite capacity for hope.

I suppose it's just as well I didn't have all that at my tongue-tip when I talked to my father; I couldn't have afforded the phone call. But I'm glad he asked what he did, because I needed to know the answer. What I want to do—poetry and seduction, heroes and myth—is best done in the country of fantasy. What I want to learn is best taught there.

But what are you doing still hanging around with me? The country of fantasy is only a page-turn away. Here, here's your coat; put it on and go exploring. And be proud to bring a little wonder with you when you come back.

Minneapolis, October 11, 1989

This should've been my first published story. It never sold, because, well, the plot isn't very original. But I like the things around the plot, and I still think it should've appeared back in '83 or so as A Promising First Effort By A Writer To Look Out For. I've touched it up a little since then, but if I were to sell it to a magazine now, it'd be An Obvious Case Of An Established Writer Making A Quick Buck By Cleaning Out His Closet. So I include it here, to give the curious a hint of the things that concerned me when I first wanted to be a writer.

—Will

Captured Moments

Will Shetterly

I remember Papa's stopbox generator, a teal blue kitchen model Tiempo Capturado that Mama brought home for his birthday. It was huge and inefficient, and she should never have spent so many pesos on a toy, but Papa would not let her return it. He used it to preserve baby tomatoes, cucumbers, and strawberries in translucent cubes that he stored in the pantry for springtime meals in the middle of winter. Mama kept her mink jacket, a family hand-me-down, safe from further aging in a stopbox, and lent the capturador to my uncle to protect his stamp collection. Sometimes they would allow us little ones to seal a treasured toy or a last piece of birthday cake in a block of frozen time until we begged them for its release, usually a few hours after enclosing it.

When my father died, a year or two after my mother, my sisters and I cleaned out their apartment. We found our baby shoes perfectly protected in stopboxes. I took mine home, where they sat above my computer while I worked on my first play. One night when I felt melancholy and did not believe love had ever existed for anyone, I used my own capturador, a sleek titanium Sanyo Tardar Ahora, to undo the stopbox. Bringing my face close to the shoes, I breathed deeply of air that my parents had trapped while closing up that symbol of their love for me.

(The instant would have been improved had my baby shoes been cleaned before they were encased, but as soon as I coughed, I laughed, and I did not try to kill myself that night.)

Let me begin again.

I rather like life on the resort worlds—always have and, after the up-coming mindwipe, always will. Last year, I rented a small house on Vega IV, a sea world, all islands and reefs and archipelagos, turquoise waters and aquamarine skies, sunrises like symphonies and sunsets like stars gone supernova. There's only one city: called Nuevo Acapulco in *La Enciclopedia del Empirio de la Humanidad*, it's N'apulco to the locals. The N'apulcans are mostly Latin emigrants from Polaris II; the only difference between them and their Caribbean ancestors is that the ancestors fleeced NorAm tourists. Now the N'apulcans profit from their Hispanic siblings.

I don't mean to sound cynical. I suppose I wish to show that I'm still capable of a certain authorial distance, a semblance of dispassionate observation. The following events may indicate otherwise.

In fine tourist tradition, most homes on Vega IV are named. Mine was The Dying Flamingo, and its outer walls were coral pink. Were they mood-sensitive, they would have changed as I first viewed them. The rental agent, an attractive N'apulcan named Natasha Cortez, also was not mood-sensitive. She said, "It's beautiful, is it not, Señor Flynn?"

My first instinct was to gesture curtly with a cupped hand that she lift the wind boat and take me elsewhere. But she was young and attractive (as I have said and may say again) and eager and so happy to be assisting the infamous Bernardo Flynn that I merely raised one eyebrow in mild skepticism. And then, because a playwright cannot resist a promising line, I said, "Your Flamingo is in need of a mercy killing."

To say her face fell would do a disservice to Tasha and to literature. (Allow my self-indulgences as you would allow those of a dying man—when I have convinced my mindsmith to permit the wipe, there will be another Bernardo Flynn, one who knows no more of Natasha Cortez or Vega IV than he reads in this file.) Her brows drew together, creasing the lovely, caramel-colored skin around her eyes and showing the pattern for an old woman's wrinkles on her forehead. Her lower lip (a trifle too narrow for her face, perhaps her only physical flaw) thrust forward slightly as she started to speak. She caught herself, slid her jaw infinitesimally back into place, and said, "You don't like it?"

I laughed. What else could I do? I clapped Tasha's shoulder to show I was not laughing at her. "Like it? I hate it, despise it, abhor it! It's gaudy, graceless, pretentious—A house like that is an affront to taste and intelligence. I should buy it in order to raze it, but I am not so kind-hearted. I might, however, rent it."

I think she only heard the last words of my speech. "You will?"

"I might. It amuses me. Show me around, and then I shall decide."

"Of course, Señor Flynn."

"And stop calling me 'señor.' Not even *Los Mundos* is so polite. Call me Bernardo."

"If you wish."

The compromise is inevitably to call me by no name. So it seemed it would be with her. "Tell me, Natasha. Do you have the house controls?"

She patted her briefcase. "Here, Señ…Bernardo."

"Good. I beg you, change the color of the walls, please?"

"But of course!" She fumbled in the case with a flustered ineptness that I found endearing. "Here!" She adjusted dials on the control box. I looked at the house. Nothing happened. "Oh, sorry," she said. "These were all labeled, but now…"

"That's all right."

"I know it's in here somewhere." Twisting another dial on another box, she said, "I'm usually more organized, but…" The house walls shifted from pink to lavender.

I stared.

"How's that?"

I looked at her.

"Worse?"

I nodded. "I would never have thought it possible."

She frowned, studying The Lavender Flamingo. "It is rather ugly," she admitted.

"Disgusting," I corrected, but I was laughing.

"Obscene," said she, laughing too.

"No, no." I pointed. "It has no spires."

"Hmm. I can fix that." She reached for another dial on the house controls.

"Don't you dare!" Her wrist, when I grabbed it, was smooth and strong and warm in my fingers. "I'll take the house. Exactly as it is."

"You will?"

"I must. God knows what you might do to it next." Reluctantly, I released her hand.

The interior of The Flamingo was a delight; perhaps its designer had made the exterior ugly so the interior would astound the visitor. Native cloudwood had been used in a Mediterranean manner, making the house seem primitive and civilized simultaneously. The kitchen and the baths had every convenience that I, at least, desired. From the living room, the view of The Flamingo's beach struck me with such intensity that Tasha asked if I felt ill. All I could say was, "No. I'm in love. " We both thought I referred to the vista.

It's strange how one can write delightedly of the happier moments of life, forgetting the things that one would forget by remembering fully the things one would remember, and suddenly the forgotten, in revenge, rears up to savage the unwary. So it was as I wrote the preceding. My heart convulsed, and I left this manuscript for a three-day spree. Apparently I was so successful that it lasted a week and a half. Not bad for an eighty-three-year-old, even for one who has his rejuve every month. And if I can brag and digress so easily, all this must not be painful enough to merit a mindwipe, yes?

No. I abandoned these notes to my future self to have the wipe done immediately, thinking that Bernardo Flynn should receive such services when he needed them, even should the need arise at the third hour after midnight. My mindsmith was not so understanding. She says I am emotionally a child, to which I reply, "Of course. Why else would I come to you?" My logic does not soothe her; she says I must wait three weeks (three!). Such is the law. I say I do not care about the law, I care about service and she should care about money. Enough. I went on a spree, and it must have been a good one, and I hope the wipe is as successful with my time on Vega IV as my spree was with what I did during it. I dimly remember bed partners who were probably human, and one that I hope was delirium. I will not answer the phone for a week, no matter whose face appears on it.

I continue to evade the issue. But which issue? The issue of why I am evading the issue, or the issue itself? To deal with the first: it hurts to remember. If I am capable of love, and I think I am, I loved her, my young Natasha Cortez. If I am not, as so many have maintained, then I lost the best mirror for my narcissism that I have ever had.

As for the issue itself, I'm no longer sure what I want to record here. The playwright in me demands every scene of our time together. The editor says no, only those that are relevant. The hurt self says no, only those which cause no pain. And the artist says no, only those which cause the greatest pain; in that way only can we recognize the truest memories.

So I shall seek to soothe my quarreling selves with a compromise. I will not talk of the first time Tasha and I tried any act of sex or sport together. Not that these are not worth noting, but I can remember similar things with others. Tasha's witchery lay in making ancient acts new. Is that love? Probably not. But it is something marvelous and rare, and it is surely a sign of love.

If my love for her were the only important thing, I would leave a holo of her with a note: "Future Self, this is Natasha Cortez. You loved her. Affectionately, Your Past."

Enough. To return to my interpretation of the facts: We walked through The Dying Flamingo together, and I decided to buy it. Then…

This is not easy.

I'll try again.

I stand up, I walk around, I pretend someone makes a vid about a writer and I must enact every cliché. I cannot decide what's important. But I have learned something from this: writing trivializes. The Natasha who was is not the Natasha in this file. The Natasha in this file is not even the Tasha I loved (and thought I knew). The Natasha in this file would walk through a net show in half an hour, including commercials, and die just before an ad for Figuero's Flash Diapers—Keeps Baby Driest!

My mistake lies in trying to talk of Tasha. I loved her, but she is not the whole of what happened on Vega IV. I must also write about the villain of this piece, one Emiliano Gabriel Malaquez. And I should decide whether I played Othello to his Iago, or he to mine.

Future Self, you know our style well enough to tell that time has passed between the last sentence and this. Not another spree, at least, not like the other. I have been re-reading all our favorite books…

…and neither of us cares to dwell on such boring subjects, do we?

I would like to pick up with Tasha and me walking about The Dying Flamingo, and then, for the sake of literary convenience, to say that from one corner of the yard I saw a neighboring house, and the sight of it filled me with dire forebodings. But the truth is that Tasha pointed it out from the one place where it could barely be seen, and my only emotion was envy that it had been designed by someone with a sense of understated good taste. "Who lives there?" I asked.

"No one," Tasha replied. (You see? Truth is always more boring than fiction. For Malaquez did not move into Dream's End until some four or five months after I—we? how does one speak to one's future self?—occupied The Flamingo.)

I do not intend to write a book: this narrative must move more quickly. Tasha and I became lovers that evening, after dinner at her apartment. I made some small joke afterward, about approving of her firm's business incentives, and she cried. Consoling her, I first began to suspect I loved her. I moved into The Flamingo on the next day; she gave up her apartment three weeks later to live with me. It was the sort of romance that happens so rarely that most people believe it does not happen at all, the sort of romance that sustains the hopeless billions who regularly watch "A Wandering Star Called Love." (Which is to say, you and me, Future Self.)

Who was Natasha Cortez? She was a twenty-four-year-old (Terran Standard) N'apulcan who left university training in hydroponics to work for her aunt's real estate firm. Her family said she did it to support her father, who was dying of a particularly painful degenerative disease. Tasha said she woke up one morning convinced that if she spent another day studying vegetables, she would become one.

She did not enjoy my plays. I had first impressed her because I was famous and amusing and not, as I had hoped and expected, because I was a great artist. That bothered (yes, and intrigued) me until I realized that she was bored by most plays, movies, and vid. She did not enjoy being a spectator. I frequently told her that she should have a bio-check to see if she suffered from some metabolic imbalance.... I frequently told her too many things.

If, as I hope, I am not the villain of this tale, that role is played by Emiliano Malaquez, master of the "captured moment" school of sculpture. Not even *The Terran Times* has quibbled about his work. To compare his pieces to those of his fellows is to compare mannequins to living models. (Were this for publication, I would abort that metaphor, but I shall let it stand.) Malaquez accented the illusion of reality (I paraphrase his entry in *La Enciclopedia Humanica*) by doing life-size scenes in "the full round," never the easier frontal or three-quarters view. Moreover, he did not do portraits of famous people; his works were thus the reality and could never be compared to it. As is typical of his school, all of his pieces are sealed within stopboxes. The play of light on their surfaces eternally reminds us that we're looking at a made thing, an instant snatched from beneath the hooves of time. I have read that the cubes will outlast planets and suns, that when the universe dies, the works of Malaquez and his followers will be the last things perceived in the final wink of God's eye. (Yes, Self, I am also bothered that this observation ignores half-eaten cheese sandwiches, incomplete insect collections, and locks of infants' hair, forgotten in their stopboxes in closets, basements, and warehouses while humanity evolves into something alien to us, or dies.)

You see the inspiration for my latest play, *Captured Moments*. The mindwipe will separate its creation from my future self—but time too often does that without aid. The play's second act concludes with the last fight between Natasha and me. I have disguised us in the play, and I deleted one brief melodramatic interchange. Now I will mention it, in case I/You decide to restore it. Shortly before she left, Tasha said, "You steal from life for art, Bernardo. You'll impoverish yourself." I only snarled at her and—

My story leaps ahead of itself. Let me retreat and retrench:

One night during N'apulco's mild winter, Tasha returned to The Flamingo, saying, "Nardo! Nardo! Guess what?"

My mind was on other things. "You wish to become pregnant? I suppose I could assist a friend. Purely for the sake of the race, of course..."

"Ever the altruist. Still, if I *do* decide, we could practice..."

Much later, I said, "You've been chosen to succeed the Emperor."

"What?"

"My guess."

She batted at my nose like a cat. "Silly Nardo."

"Then I give up."

"Emiliano Malaquez is buying the house up the hill."

"Oh."

"You don't know who he is?"

"Well..."

"Nardo!" One of the many things I liked about her was that she often thought me shockingly ignorant.

"That's, uh…" I am rarely so quick-witted in person as I am on the page. Especially when someone thinks me shockingly ignorant.

"You know, the sculptor. He's had shows in Brazil and New Madrid and everywhere! He may be more famous than you."

"Imagine that." I remembered an article in *The Medusa* and a photo of a piece in which 100-peso notes fell like confetti onto a small Undersider, sexlessly prepubescent in grimy, oversized clothing. The child's face was a warground for wonder and mistrust. Imprisoned light from forgotten street lamps snagged itself on metal threads in the fluttering pesos; the stars themselves might have fallen on the Undersider and the event would have been no less strange, no less miraculous. "A great artist will live among us, then?"

"Nardo!" She was never tolerant of my ego.

"Well. What's this more-famous-than-me person like?"

"I didn't meet him, jealous old one."

"Too bad. If I thought he could free me from you—"

"Hah!" She wrapped her arms around my stomach. "You'll never be free of me, old man!"

The next evening, she arrived with a stack of glistening stopboxes containing sushi, sashimi, oysters in their shells, and Terran vegetables preserved instants after being plucked from their hydroponic beds. Wondering about the reason for this extravagance, I asked how work had gone that day (how boring we seem at home!).

"Emil came in. He's taking Dream's End."

"Emil?"

"You've no memory left, old one. Emil Malaquez."

"Ah. You did that to test my affections."

"What?"

"Referring to him by his first name. I did something with that in a comedy once. *My Nights with Karl and Groucho*. It was before your time."

"Oh."

"The critics liked it."

"I'm glad." A moment later: "That's not why I called him 'Emil.'"

"No?"

"No. We lunched together. He's very nice."

"Oh."

"It wasn't like that."

"You're free."

"Of course. Still, it wasn't like that. You think I sleep with every famous person I meet?"

As you may have guessed, we had talked about such things before. I do not claim ours was a perfect affair, only a wonderful one.

"Tasha…"

"Do you?"

"No."

"Good. I've invited him to dinner tomorrow."

"Oh?"

"He'll be our neighbor. You say we're becoming too insular, that we need to socialize—"

"I've socialized for sixty-three years."

"Nardo?"

"Yes?"

"How should I reply to that?" Her voice had grown quiet, and I began to feel some guilt. I had, it is true, told her that we needed other company than our own. I said this from years of learning that romances consume themselves without other fuel. But knowing this did not mean I wanted it.

I said, "Reply truthfully." It was the statement of a younger and crueler man than I.

She screamed, "I haven't socialized with Terra's elite for most of my life! I haven't socialized with hardly anyone for hardly any of my life! And I invite a neighbor, one nice, lonely man—"

"I'm sorry."

"—who took me to— What?"

"I'm sorry. Truly."

"Oh." She studied me as a suspicious puppy might, then said, "I'm sorry, too."

"I suppose I sound like I'm bragging when I talk of the things I'm tired of."

"Only because you always are." She smiled.

I had to grin, so I did. "True."

"He may come to dinner?"

"If you wish, he may be dinner."

"I love you."

"And I, you." Months earlier, we might have sought a bed, a couch, or a comfortable chair at this point. Instead, I asked, "Is he handsome?"

"You're jealous."

"A tiny bit. Extremely."

"Content yourself, old one. He's four inches shorter than I, his nose is big and broken, and…"

"This is cosmetic?"

"I don't think so. He's not that ugly. I think they're his natural features."

"Interesting."

"You could write a play about someone like him."

"Perhaps."

"I think his face is his form of vanity. It's the reverse of you with those ridiculous stomach muscles. Old men should be fat."

"Is Emil?"

"Yes."

"I am jealous. I'll eat two dinners tonight. Five desserts."

She giggled. And then we did make love.

I've been thinking about the mindwipe, now two days away. Who said that those who forget the past are doomed to repeat it? I fear that may be true for me, for my personal history. Add this to the reasons I write now: to remember something, perhaps even to learn—

Emil Malaquez arrived immediately after sundown in the finest vampiric tradition. His evening dress was formal, expensive, and slightly stained, as that of all forgetful artists should be. He was a jovial man with an easy laugh, and even uglier than Tasha had suggested. I liked him immediately.

"Emiliano Malaquez?" No other of such an appearance could be at our door.

"Please. Call me Emil. You must be Bernardo. Natasha's told me much about you."

"All of it outrageous praise?"

"All of it."

"Ah, she is wonderfully perceptive."

He raised an eyebrow, then guffawed. "Has she said as much about me?"

"She thinks you are a genius. Do come in."

"Thank you." Stepping into the living room, he said, "A beautiful house."

"I'm glad you came after dark." I noticed that he carried a small package, wrapped in what appeared to be real paper.

Tasha, by accident or design, had found an innocently erotic posture on the couch, where she lay with a book of M'duvian prints. "Emil!" She leapt up. "I did not expect you—"

"So early?"

"—on time. It's unforgivable, but you're forgiven." She nodded at the package. "What's that?"

"For your kindness in inviting a stranger into your home." He held it out, and with a delighted "Oh!" Tasha snatched it from him to rip away the paper.

I stopped here, where this history truly begins, and only the thought that I might miss the mindwipe kept me from another spree. I went walking, but after N'apulco, the megalopolis of Rio seems no fit abode for a creature of flesh. I walked from this hotel to the old city, past the end of the slidewalks, past the softwalks to the hard, cracked pavement of City Park. But the Undersiders left me alone. Perhaps they recognized a fellow ghost. So I returned, and slept, and now the mindwipe is thirteen hours away.

The side of Malaquez's parcel gave way to reveal a greenmunk caught in a shimmer of immobilized air. Bits of leaf mold flew from under his feet as he raced forward, recognizing a friend or a bringer of food. Tasha oohed in awe. I said, "So Frodo's been visiting you, eh?"

Malaquez said, "Your pet?" He sounded jealous, which made no sense to me.

"Hardly. Frodo lives around here somewhere. I suppose he was attracted to the commotion up the hill."

"Ah," Malaquez said. "Why 'Frodo'?"

Tasha said, "A tiny fellow with big, furry feet. What else could he be called?" She handed the sculpture to me.

I almost dropped it; I expected it to weigh no more than a Kodak Hol-gram. "Heavy," I said, as if he might not have known.

Malaquez laughed. "My last piece was of four old Undersiders crouched around a trash fire. Be glad someone didn't toss that to you." He spoke of his art with the enthusiasm of a seven-year-old. I understood how Tasha might find him attractive. "Um, I should wait to importune you, but…"

He grinned shyly. "A confession, first, and then a request. And then you must forgive me for being so forward. It's not easy for me to ask a favor."

"Relax," I said. "It's easy for me to turn one down."

He glanced at me and decided that I was joking. The surprising thing is that I was. "Good. I…I've become aware that my future is floundering."

"You'll forsake sculpture for a fishery?"

He smiled weakly. "Perhaps I should. My last show—"

"—was glorious!" Tasha said.

"—was kindly received," he said. "But an artist who would stay first among his fellows can tell when he begins to fail."

"Oh?" I hoped no one would mention my last three plays.

"I must change my subject matter. No more street urchins, dopers, vagrants, or whores. I want to do more traditional portraits." He spoke quickly, prepared to be rejected. "Would you permit me to do a portrait of you? I would pay—"

"Never," I said.

"Ah." He shrugged.

"Nardo!" Tasha said. "It's an honor—"

"Of course," I said. "That's why I cannot accept payment."

"Oh! Thank you!" Malaquez turned to Tasha. "And you as well? Perhaps the two of you together?"

Her eyes became circles at the idea of being, as she undoubtedly thought it, immortalized by Emiliano Malaquez. Catching herself, she said casually, "Oh…" And then she smiled, laughed loudly at herself in the way that always reminded me that I loved her, and said, "Of course! My God, yes, yes, yes!" For one perfect moment, Emil and Tasha and I were one entity, laughing together until our lungs hurt.

This is torture. I had not considered that I might not write to learn, but to punish myself. No matter. Let me abuse my playwright's self and dismiss the penultimate scene in a few sentences: After crediting a disk giving Emil full rights to a sculpture of Tasha and me, we had a pleasant dinner of curried clam chowder, lobsters boiled on Terra that were released still steaming from their stopboxes on N'apulco, and cinnamon custard for dessert. Then we went out for a late swim. I had drunk too much with dinner, I confess, though we all had. Somehow, Tasha and I began to argue the worth of Solevgrad jazz, as inconsequential a topic as I can imagine. She had studied it in school, so she thought she could speak as an expert. I had once had a neighbor who played it constantly, loudly, and badly, so I thought I knew it better. Malaquez attempted to mediate, but I saw him as siding with Tasha. So, I think, did she. The subject shifted from music to Tasha's obsession with fame, undoubtedly by some leap that I made, and she had no choice but to follow. (I do not remember any of this well, just now, nor do I care to. Those who are truly curious may look at the last act of *Captured Moments*.) I remember suggesting, with characteristic tact, that Tasha add Emil to her small list of major accomplishments.

Malaquez glanced away, embarrassed. Tasha looked at me as though to say, "I will." She only said, "I feel sorry for you, Nardo. I'll see Emil home."

"Yeah," I said, "do that," and did not care what she did, or why.

Emil asked, "You're all right?" I muttered something he must have interpreted as assent. They both walked up the hill to Emil's home while I watched the scarlet moonlight ripple on distant waves. Disgusted with Tasha but primarily disgusted with myself, I finally realized she would not return that night and went into The Dying Flamingo to drink myself to sleep.

She had not come home when I woke in mid-morning. I waited, and drank a glass of Morning-After and several cups of coffee, and wondered whether our affair could survive the events of the night, and whether I wanted it to. Perhaps I should have invited Emil to stay over, but even then I knew that the issue of sex was not the problem between Tasha and me. The problem was that old people do not like to change their ways, have trouble distinguishing between compromise and capitulation, are too aware of symbols and too blind to substance. Shortly before noon, I climbed the sandy path to Dream's End, rehearsing my apology as I walked, slowing only to pluck burrs from between my sandals and my feet.

Malaquez answered the door in blood-red pajamas and a black silk robe. Sixty years ago in a similar situation, I had broken my knuckles on someone's face. I merely said, "Is Tasha here?"

He pursed his lips slightly, then nodded. "Yes."

"May I see her?" When he hesitated, I said, "Last night was my fault. I hold it against neither of you. Please. Let me talk to her."

"I…"

"Please."

He looked me and at last said, "Very well."

We walked through his house in silence, and I saw that he had done nothing to make it his home. It was as attractive and as impersonal as a decorator could prepare for tenants of unknown taste. A tall, narrow stopbox stood in the center of one room; sand trickled forever downwards while beads of water splashed across the sand's path. If that was Malaquez's work, it was a very minor effort. But then, I was in no mood to consider art. I only wanted to despise the man who had slept with my lover. That was easier than despising myself.

He paused before a bedroom door. "I should go in first. To prepare her."

I smiled. "Tasha handles surprise surprisingly well."

"What would it hurt?"

"True. Go ahead. Tell her…" I shrugged. "Tell her I love her."

He studied me, then said, "I'm sorry things happened this way, Bernardo. I didn't anticipate last night—"

"Neither did I. And I'm very good at making things happen this way. But if Tasha will forgive me—"

He nodded, said, "I am sorry," then slipped into the next room. I waited in his dark, carpeted hall. A warm breeze came from silent vents above me. I heard no voices until Malaquez said, "Enter."

I blinked when I opened the door; sunlight filled Malaquez's bedroom. Tasha lay before me, sprawled nude on a rumpled bed. Her skin appeared as smooth and as polished as the bed's teak frame. She was looking slightly to my left, smiling with trust and satisfaction like one sexually content. Malaquez stood near her, pointing something like a camera at my chest. Though the morning sun shone fully on both of them, it shimmered around Tasha.

The part of my mind that remembered four months in NorAm during the Great Cleaning sent me rolling across the floor. Malaquez was not prepared for me to react so quickly, or perhaps he waited too long for an expression I would not have, a gesture I would not make, a poignant moment of repentance, wonder, despair, or love. Had he been faster, he could have had rage. I threw a chair at him, and as he fell, I scrambled onto him, my knees pinning his arms, my fingers probing his neck.

I shouted, "Where is she?" I thought he was keeping her prisoner elsewhere. Foolish me. "Tell me, or I'll kill—"

He began to cry. "She left. Earlier this morning—"

Her clothes lay beside the clear cube enclosing the sculpture. I hit him with the back of my open hand. "Tell me, Malaquez."

"She wanted to be famous. She did! Now she will be."

He seemed to expect me to understand. "Where!" I demanded, squeezing until he began jerking his head madly at the sculpture.

"There!"

I stared. Most of his story I have pieced together since, but I understood enough as I knelt on Malaquez's chest with my hands about his fleshy throat. He had used a capturador to make his name. He began with animals and moved on to derelicts and Undersiders, people who would never be missed. And now he had thought to use vacationers like Tasha and me, to do our sculptures and, when someone came looking, say that we had gone island-hopping in our windboat. Our boat, of course, would disappear into the ocean to be found or not as the wind and tides decided. His story would stand in either case.

I wanted him to tell me more, but he babbled, begging me to forgive him, to understand. I did not listen. I took the capturador, a matte black Tiempo Capturado, from his grip and studied it, not really thinking about it or Malaquez or Tasha. I think I was wondering what it meant, that he could say a thing was a camera, so we accepted it as a camera, that a thing was art, so we accepted it as art. Or perhaps I was thinking about the things that humanity made that would outlive our species. But I was probably only looking at my reflection in the capturador's lens. Had he said then that I should use it on myself, I might have.

That moment passed. I looked at Malaquez. His eyes opened wider while we watched each other, and his lips contorted as if they had lost their ability to shape sound. I turned away to approach the cube that was Tasha's crypt. She smiled in trust or pleasure or pride, an erotic Mona Lisa who would smile forever, and I could never know why.

The controls of Malaquez's capturador were more complex than those of a kitchen model, but I recognized the deactivation switch. I could free Tasha. If I did, three things might happen. Most likely: she would be dead—there is a reason why stopboxes are used to preserve meat. Less likely: she would live the rest of her days with a mind as free of care and worry as a slug's. And the tiniest chance of all: she would emerge as though she had blinked when Emil took her holo. She would frown as she saw that I had somehow materialized in Emil's bedroom, and then she would laugh and tell me that she was going to be immortal.

As I reached to place my hand on the impervious surface of her tomb, I heard Emil run toward the door.

It is strange to know that we can do acts of unrepayable kindness to those we should hate. Know this, my future self: Thanks to us, Emil Malaquez's name will live as long as his masterpiece, "A Self-Portrait: Anguish," endures.

And Tasha? I could say that I did not dare to take responsibility for her fate, but I would lie: To decide not to act is still to decide. I could say that I chose as I did out of consideration for her desire for fame; some critics already say "Waking With Tasha" is Emil's finest work. If science finds a way to safely free the subjects of Emil's art, perhaps the "I" who reads this file will know that my decision is the prudent one. But I cannot stop thinking that I was never afraid of losing Tasha to death or brain damage. I think my fear is that she would live, and I would learn that I had lost her long before Emil Malaquez translated her into a thing that can be kept, studied, admired, and loved.

For in my way, I have done the same thing.

I am ready for the mindwipe now.

This was my first published fiction. I want to point out the things in it that seem to be recurring themes in my work, but I'm the writer, so I won't. You, on the other hand, are the reader. Have fun.

—Emma

Rending Dark

Emma Bull

Marya tightened her reins and turned in the saddle, squinting against the snow thickening in the twilight air. She grinned at the short, cloak-muffled figure that rode up beside her. "You know, I thought I heard you swear just now."

Kit snorted. "I said, 'Mother of little pigs!' You promised me that Sallis was two days' ride from Lyle Valley. We are now two days' ride from Lyle Valley. And I am cold. And wet. And getting more of both. And I don't see a town."

Marya laughed. "Why did I ever call you Woodpecker? You scold like a jay."

"Marya, blast it, where's the town?"

"Over the next rise, oh ye of little patience. And if you'll be good, I'll buy the first round when we get there."

"Yes, and I'll buy the second and third as usual, so where does that get me?" Kit scowled.

"Quite a way into a drunken carouse. Hallo, there!" Marya raised her left arm, pointing, and snow-reflected light slipped off the gleaming black of claw and tendon.

Below them, barely visible through the falling snow, gas lamps glowed like sparks in a feeble row.

"I'm never wrong," Marya said.

"You're lucky I'm tired."

"Oh? Why?"

"Because if I wasn't, I'd remind you of that pack beast you bought in Hobarth."

"Oh. Well, everyone gets one free mistake."

"Motherlorn wretch! C'mon, let's go!"

Kit booted her mount's ribs, and surged downhill through the piling snow. But Marya hesitated. Had a shadow quaked under the boughs of the pines? She shook her head. *I'm tired,* she decided. *There isn't enough light to cast a shadow by.* The wind wailed behind her as she followed Kit down to Sallis town.

When she reached the gate, Kit was already there, cursing elegantly.

"So use the knocker," said Marya.

"I *have* used the knocker. Twice," Kit snapped, then reached and yanked the rope again. The iron arm boomed against the wood.

The gatekeeper's look-see slid open. "What do you want?" a man called out.

"*In,* dearie," Marya replied. "What do *you* want when you knock at gates, hmm?"

"I…I only meant, it's late, and the weather's poor—"

"And that's all the more reason to let us in out of it," Kit snapped. "This must be one fine town, if you're afraid of two riders."

"I only meant to say—"

"Here, maybe this'll make you happy." Kit rode close to the look-see and pulled her cloak back, showing the red-and-blue of the Songsmith patch on her sleeve.

"Your pardon, Songsmith, I didn't—"

"Please, just the gate," said Kit, and Marya reflected, not for the first time, how remarkably well a trained performer could make a sigh heard. Ice cracked loudly as the bar was pulled back, and Marya and Kit trotted through.

The large, soft-spoken type, Marya decided upon seeing the gatekeeper. *My favorite.* She pushed back her hood and smiled down at him. "Thank you. And I apologize for my companion's sharp tongue."

Kit blinked and stared at her as the gatekeeper said, "No, no, it's for me to—"

"We've been riding all day, you see, and the weather…"

He looked sympathetic. "Early for this," he said, kicking his boot toe through the powder. "The wolves are down from the ridge already, and there's stories… It'll be a bad year."

"It's been a bad year for the last half-dozen of them," Kit drawled.

Marya frowned at her, and smiled again at the gatekeeper. "We'd better find her some dinner, before she eats one of the natives. Is there an inn
close by?"

"There *is* only one. Left at the green-shingled house there—" he
pointed, "—and down the lane some ways. It's Amali's Halt."

"Thanks. Um, when are you through here?"

"Hour and half-a-turn." He looked up at her.

"Come by when you're through. She'll probably sing something."
Marya smiled and jerked her thumb at Kit. "And she'll Give News, of
course."

His smile was shy and charming. "I wouldn't miss it."

"Come on, Marya!" Kit called. "If I sit this animal much longer, I'll
freeze to the saddle!" She had turned her mount and started down the
street.

"Thank you again. Oh," said Marya, "something to get warm with."
She drew her left arm out of her cloak at last, holding a coin.

The gatekeeper's face went slack as he stared at her left hand. Marya
looked down at it herself, and tried to see it without familiarity: lean
bone and tendon and long, curving, cruel claws, all black and shining,
cupping the coin like a cage of black iron. Bitterness twisted in her stomach unexpectedly. She watched his face as she flexed the fingers, and saw
terror in his eyes when the tap of a talon made the coin ring. After a still
moment, she tossed the coin to him. He made no move to catch it. They
both watched as it made a little hole in the snow; then she turned her
mount and rode down the street after Kit.

"Well," said Marya as she caught up to the Songsmith, "so much for
my evening."

"Huh?"

She held up her left arm and wiggled the black fingers.

"It bothered him?"

"It bothered him."

"Creeping, superstitious, Motherlorn provincials." Kit sounded as if
she were warming up to something. "Unwashed, unlettered, sheep-screw-
ing, bear-buggering, backwoods—"

"Oh, pipe down," Marya interrupted. "You're only burned because
you think if I can't get laid, you shouldn't either."

"That's not true!" Kit shrieked.

Marya grinned wickedly. "If I could get fish to take bait the way you do, I could be a rich woman on the coast."

"Hah!" said Kit, and then, perhaps because she couldn't think of anything else to add, "Hah!" again.

The gatekeeper's directions were good. The inn was an immaculate little place, and seemed to radiate welcome like heat from an iron stove.

"Bless us all," Kit sighed contentedly.

"I'll take 'em to the stable," Marya offered, swinging out of the saddle.

"You're a dear. I'll order you a wonderful dinner."

"Don't eat it all before I get there."

Kit made a face at her and disappeared into the inn.

Marya found the stable easily. It was clean and well-lit, and the coal-burning Fireproof in the harness room kept the biting edge off the temperature. She looked on approvingly as the stable hand unsaddled their mounts and rubbed them down.

"I'll bet you don't have much to do in weather like this," she commented.

"No'm," said the boy, and flashed her a smile before he bent to brush a long haired fetlock. He ducked under the animal's belly and stood up. "But we're lively come summer."

"What's your name?"

"Gerry, mum." He looked up and grinned. "At your service." He swept her a road-show bow, the currycomb flourishing wildly with his arm.

"Good," Marya laughed. "If you can get the burrs out of that beastie's coat, that'll be service indeed."

Gerry grinned again and turned back to his work.

She watched him out of the corner of her eye while she wiped down her saddle. She was careful to keep her cloak draped over her left arm. At last she said, "You're very good with them."

"Um?"

"With the animals. How did you learn so well, so young?"

"Oh!" A wistful smile tugged at his face, flickering there on and off. "My dad taught me. He's the best...was the...best..." Suddenly he turned his face away from her.

"Did I...say something dumb?"

His brown hair flurried with the force of his headshake.

"You're lucky," Marya continued. "I wouldn't recognize my dad if he kicked me."

"I...gotta get something." He bolted into the feed room. When he came back shortly, empty-handed, Marya looked a question. "Couldn't find it," he said, too loud.

A throttling silence followed. Marya broke it at last with, "I'm sorry. I guess I did say something stupid. Want to tell me about it?"

He shook his head again, and Marya saw her mount flinch away from the force of the currycomb stroke.

He worked his way around to the animal's other side. Then he said, "My dad was...killed."

"Umm." Marya felt as if she'd been holding her breath. "Recently?"

A nod. "Last week."

"Oh."

"He was up on the hills, hunting strays. They went out to look for him the next morning. He was...he was..."

She heard the quivering in his voice, and headed him off. "Was he caught in a storm, or—"

Gerry shook his head. "There was something...clawed him up. Something big."

"Wolf? Cat?"

"Bigger."

There's something familiar about this, Marya thought. She finished with the tack, wished Gerry a good evening, and hurried into the inn.

Kit waved furiously at her from a table by the dining room hearth. "Just wait till you see dinner!" she crowed, grinning.

"Food always lifts your spirits, Woodpecker. The only time you're ever civil is when dinner's imminent."

"Sheepcrap."

"Must you always make a liar out of me?"

Kit snorted. "Fingerfish in wine sauce, venison pie, baked squash and apples, new bread, greensprouts, and cider. Ah, here it comes!"

The innkeeper was a big woman, still flushed from supervising the kitchens. She set the tray down on the table and smiled at Marya. "I know what traveling in this kind of weather does to an appetite, dear, which I told your friend the Songsmith. Nobody goes hungry in Amali's Halt."

"I take it you're Amali?"

"That's me."

"Delighted to meet you."

"And your venison pie," Kit added.

Amali chuckled. "Eat it all, dears—I don't want to see any comebacks from this table. And if you fancy it," she went on, suddenly shy, "we'd be pleased to have you in the taproom after."

Marya shot a look at Kit and found her smiling. "I think we might do that," Kit said. "And if you wouldn't mind, I might even feel like singing a bit."

"It'd be an honor!" Amali beamed. "Thank you, dear. Enjoy your dinner."

Marya waited until Amali was out of earshot before she said, "Tsk. Another year of this and you'll be spoiled rotten."

"Not with you along to keep me in my place."

"A heavy responsibility."

"Shut up and eat."

Marya obediently forked a mouthful of squash and swallowed it before she went on. "Just heard a bit of an odd thing."

Kit looked up, then put her fork down. "That's your 'I think we ought to do something' voice. Spill it."

Marya told her about Gerry's father.

"Bear?" Kit said when she was done.

"That's what I thought, at first. But aren't you carrying news from Lyle Valley about a bear in these hills?"

"Yeah. They killed one two weeks ago."

"That's what I thought. So, two bears in the same range of hills? And both out this late in the year?"

"Unlikely."

"Very. Then what *is* out there?" Marya stabbed a piece of pie for emphasis.

"I dunno."

Marya sighed. "Is that all you can say?"

"Of course it is. Look, I'm on my way to Samarty to pick up a manuscript for the Guild. On the way, I'm delivering news. I am not fighting dragons, rescuing golden-tressed idiots locked in towers, or knocking down windmills. What do you want, to organize a hunt?"

"Well...yes."

Kit leaned her chin in her palms and looked at her. "I guess you do. Marya Clawfinger, you're hopeless."

"No. Hopeful. You're using your 'I can't reason with her, so I'll have to give in' voice."

"We'll talk it over in the morning. Eat."

The guitar's last chord clung to the air in the taproom, making the listeners reluctant to drive it off with applause. Marya smiled as Kit lifted her head and blinked, as if coming out of a trance. The subtle cue touched off a storm of clapping. *Wonderful thing* Marya reflected, *the symbiosis between performer and audience. Is that instinct, or does the Guild teach these things?*

Then Kit set the guitar aside and stood slowly up, and the room plunged into silence. Everyone in the room had waited for this, the moment when the Songsmith would Give News. Marya leaned back to enjoy it.

"From the north and the east," Kit's voice reached out, enfolding the room. "From silver-roofed Sandyn and the Firehall I come. I am the voice and the bearer of the past. What will you have of me?"

Kit's delivery warmed the traditional words. Someone in the crowd shouted, "Lyle Valley!" and his neighbors murmured assent.

Kit nodded slowly and closed her eyes. The whole room seemed to tip forward a little with expectation. Then, clear and bright, tuneless and tuneful all at once, Kit began to chant:

> "Allysum Gredy bore a boy
> With the first snow of November.
> Ere the snow had come and gone again
> Pneumonia took old Francis Berne
> And balanced birth and dying.

> "Etin Yama's grocery burned,
> And Etin blamed Jo Hurlisen.
> The council fined Jo three months' wage,
> And bid him quit cigars.

> "Protecting flocks on Canwit slope,
> Rey Leyne and Winsey Wittemer
> Slew a winter-colored bear,

But something still kills sheep and cows
Along the southern ridge.

"Nil Sabek and Margrete Durenn
Have sworn the Binding Promise,
And Hary Lil, in his best boots,
Walks daily out with Mother Pent.

"Life, death, commerce, and love: Lyle Valley is well."

The room hummed with talk when Kit finished—neighbors laughing and gossiping over the news. Marya smiled and waited for the next town to be called out, and for Kit to start again.

And the taproom door slammed open. "Hey!" somebody yelled, then stopped.

The boy in the doorway was the stable hand, Gerry; the young woman he was almost-carrying was a blood-spattered stranger.

"Nan!" Amali cried. The tray in her hands hit the floor with a clang, and she ran to catch the woman around the waist. Marya elbowed her way to the door. Someone leaped out of a chair and pushed it toward Amali, who lowered Nan into it. "She's my daughter," Amali said wildly to Marya, who wondered why it mattered.

"Are you hurt?" Marya asked, finding the pulse in the bloodstained wrist, peering into the woman's eyes, noting evidence of shock. Nan shook her head.

"Get her closer to the stove and wrap a blanket around her," Marya ordered. "Give her mint tea or water. No alcohol."

"And then ask her what happened," said Kit, appearing out of the crowd at Marya's side.

"At the gate," Nan said, still breathing hard. "Cal. He's dead. And Jimy."

Marya heard a noise in the back of the room, a little cry.

"How?" Amali asked, her voice tight.

"Cal...Cal was opened up from neck to crotch. Just opened up. Jimy's throat...was ripped half away." Nan began to sob weakly.

Sudden motion made Marya look toward the door. Gerry had taken a pace into the room, and his lips still held a half-formed word. He clutched

at the door frame, his gaze leaping around the room. Then he turned and
darted out the door.

"One of you," Amali shouted, "hand me that blanket from—oh."
She stared down at Marya with the blank look of panic. "Oh, no. Then
someone—something—must have come through the gate."

"What? Why?"

"Cal's the gatekeeper."

"The...gatekeeper?" Marya whispered, and looked up, wide-eyed, at
Kit. "The one who..."

Kit reached out and gripped Marya's shoulder, her left one. The singer's
fingers were warm through her shirt, and the contact seemed to trickle
strength into her.

"Let's go see," Marya said, hearing her own voice like a grim bell in
the silence.

Outside there were two sets of tracks through the drifted snow: Nan's,
floundering wildly toward the inn; and another trail, straight and certain,
pointing away, toward the gate. Marya scowled and crouched down for a
better look, balancing her scabbarded blade across her knees. Then she
swore.

The prints were of heelless boots, ridge-soled for good traction on
damp and dirty floors, boots for a farmer or stable hand...

"What is it?" Kit asked.

"Gerry," Marya said, dropping the name like a stone down a well.
"He's after the thing that killed his father. Come on."

And they ran.

Marya drew her sword as she bounded through the snow. She heard
Kit cursing, "Marya! Blast you into darkness, wait for me!" But she was
afraid to slow her pace. The gate court was only a turn away...

She made the turn—and stopped, her sword half-raised, dread and
disbelief freezing her limbs. Gerry stood in the middle of the court. His
face was twisted with horror, and he held a length of timber thrust out
before him with both hands. He might have thought of it, moments
before, as a cudgel. Now it was the only solid thing he had to keep between him and the creature before him.

The creature... Black shreds of it seemed always to be stripping away,
like black steam, in a wind that blew nowhere else in the street, yet nothing ever fell to the snow, and there was never less of it. It walked upright,
and was tall as a bear and gaunt as a half-burnt tree. She heard Kit's voice

weak beside her. "Oh, Mother's Pigs… How can I describe that at the next town?"

A dark arm-shape swept out, swift and easy, and slapped at the boy. The timber hit the snow in two splintery pieces.

"Gerry, get away!" Marya shouted, and leaped at the thing, sweeping her sword in a cut at the dark midsection.

Gerry was screaming and screaming, and suddenly not screaming, falling out of the shadow-thing's embrace with his throat and chest blooming bright and shining red, red bubbling at his mouth. He was dead before he met the snow.

Marya's blade sliced into shadow—and stopped, as if stone had formed around it. Stone was filling the veins of her right hand, calcifying her nerves, brittling her bones, and devouring its way into her shoulder and chest. She wanted to draw a breath, and hadn't the strength. Her sword fell to the snow as she staggered backward, fell to her knees, her human arm limp and swinging wide. She stared at it blankly.

And the shadow turned toward her. The mouth gaped, the eyes glowed with decay—she wanted to shut her eyes, kneel down, and wait for it to go away.

The black arms reached out, obscene parody of comfort, to gather her to it.

"No!" Kit shrieked behind her, and darted past, her dagger a sliver of light in her hand.

"Get back!" Marya yelled, but Kit drove the bright steel up into that thing of tattered darkness—

—and stopped. Kit's mouth opened round with shock. Around her folded the impenetrable shadow of the creature.

"Kit! Get back!" Marya shouted again. Kit seemed to come awake, and flung herself backward. The black thing lashed out. Blood stained the snow where she fell.

"Kit!" Marya slid to her side.

"It's pulling my soul out through a hole in my arm," Kit mumbled.

"What?"

"I can feel it go. Not much nutrition in souls…" and Kit's head slipped sideways.

The creature leaned like a black flame over them, seeming to swell and pulse. Marya grabbed frantically for her sword. Or tried to grab. Her human arm wouldn't obey her.

She lunged up from the snow, to the being's other side. "Here!" she screamed. "Over here, pig feed! Short-shaft!" She scrabbled up a fistful of churned-up gravel and flung it left-handed at the dark thing. Its nightmare mouth opened in a hiss that cut into her skull, and it surged toward her. *Wish that hadn't worked quite so well,* Marya thought as she struck out with her taloned arm. Her fingers sank into shadow.

Heat rushed through Marya's bones as the hiss became a sharp and sudden snarl. *I've hurt it!* she exulted. Her skin was hot and prickling. She clenched her claws in the shadow-stuff of the thing, and it slashed wildly at her head, shrieking like steel on stone.

Her body flooded with more-than-fever. *It's burning me*—then her terror was swallowed up in awe. *No…but I'm burning.* She was not the fuel, but the fire itself; the world lay before her as kindling and coal. Huge with strength, she flared up to scorch the stars, feeding on their power…

The black thing flung backward, howling, leaving flickering darkness fading in her fist. Suddenly she was only a little cold beast kneeling in the snow, and all power had fled. She wanted to scream out for it, to rend flesh, shatter stone, in search of it.

She lunged for the writhing shadow. It swung again at her, missed, then turned and hurtled like some dark driven leaf through the gate and into the night beyond.

The power was gone from her. She looked wildly around the street, envying even the flaring of the lamps. But she had to remain human; there was something a human needed to do…

Then she saw the sprawled red-haired figure in the snow. "Kit!" she cried. "Woodpecker—"

She sank to her knees, cradled the Songsmith in her dark arm, and listened for Kit's breathing. Warm air stirred against her cheek; yes, she breathed. Now the shoulder… She searched her clothes and Kit's for something that was neither blood- nor snow-soaked, and cursed aloud when she couldn't find anything.

"Oh, bright Mother. Here," someone said softly above her head, and a clean cloth napkin appeared in front of her face. She grabbed it and made a pad, tied it against Kit's wound with her own sash.

"I need a cloak for her, a blanket, something…" Marya muttered. A bright blue wool cape swung into sight. She tucked it under and around Kit. *Why isn't she conscious?* Marya wiped the hair out of her eyes. Before her the street lamps showed darkened snow, the gate closed at last, and three people she was clearly too late to help… Her head hurt, and her body felt too heavy to move.

"Should we take her to the inn?" she heard behind her. She turned.

"Amali!"

"I've been here for…a while, but you were…" Amali fluttered her plump hands.

"The word you're looking for is probably 'rude.'" Marya shook off inertia and lifted Kit, letting her snow-sodden cloak swing forward to hide her left arm.

"No harm done," Amali said with a little shrug. "Medics are always odd when they're working."

"Hmm."

"But I hadn't thought a Payer of the Price could take the medics' training."

Marya's foot came down a little too suddenly, and her teeth clacked shut. "A what?" she said.

"A Payer of the Price. I saw your arm, while you tended the Songsmith."

"You did." *Surely,* she thought, *the wretched woman will shut up…*

"You shouldn't try to hide your mark, you know. You bear it to show us our Mother's anger at our tampering with Her holy secrets…"

"That's enough!" Marya hissed. Amali's mouth opened and closed. "I'm sorry," Marya said. "I'm not…religious."

Amali stared at her warily. "I'll pray for you," she said at last. "Let me go ahead and get a bed ready for her."

Marya nodded, and Amali waded away through the snow.

"She means well," croaked Kit's voice near her shoulder. "Just misinformed."

"Woodpecker? How d'you feel?"

"Like I got hold…of the wrong end of a lightning bolt."

"There's a right end on a lightning bolt?"

Kit opened one eye and frowned. "Are you hysterical?" she said faintly. "You're not making any sense."

"You should talk."

"No, I shouldn't. I should rest. If you weren't hysterical, you'd know that."

Marya snorted. "Never try to speak rationally with someone who's lost blood."

"Not blood." Kit shook her head weakly. "More like...strength."

"That's what happens when you lose blood."

"No. That's what I meant about...about a lightning bolt."

"Huh?"

"Instead of getting a blast of something...that—that thing sort of took something out of me."

"Something out of you..." Marya repeated. Her right arm had felt that way, as if the strength had been sucked away from it.

"My shoulder hurts," said Kit, almost firmly. "And I'm cold. Don't just stand here."

"Piglets, you're fussy," Marya smiled, and took long strides in Amali's tracks.

Sunlight poured like a liquid through the door as Marya pushed it open a finger's width. "Kit? Are you awake?" she whispered into the inn bedroom.

"The place is lit up like the damn Ship come to harbor, and she wants to know if I'm awake," Kit grumbled.

Marya stuck her head into the room and grinned. "Your body I can cure. Your disposition is beyond me."

Kit laughed. "Oh, c'mon in."

Marya settled on the end of the bed. "So otherwise, how do you feel?"

"Pretty good, actually. Much better than I ought to, considering how bad I felt out there in the snow."

"Hmm," said Marya. "Let me look at your arm."

"It was as if..." Kit paused while Marya unwound the bandages, "as if I could feel myself dying—which is ridiculous, since it isn't much of a wound."

"True. It's not. It's also clean, and doing all the things it ought to be doing."

"So I suppose it was just fear. A literal example of being scared to death."

"Maybe." Marya sat back and folded her hands, twining flesh with polished black. "Maybe not."

"Maybe not?"

Marya got up and shot the bolt on the door.

"Marya?"

"I've got something I want to show you."

"My mother warned me about women like you…"

"Very funny. Watch this."

Marya crouched down by the iron stove near the bed, and opened the fire door. "It's lit, right?"

"If it hadn't been," said Kit, "I think we would have noticed."

"Yes, but you can see the flames, can't you?"

Kit sighed. "Humor her. Yes, I can see them."

"All right." Marya stretched out her left hand, through the iron doorway, and spread long clawed fingers over the fire like a black-ribbed net. She felt the heat billowing past—and nothing else. *Am I crazy?* she wondered, suddenly afraid. *Was I crazy last night, when this worked?*

Then her shoulder began to tingle. Fever-warmth swept up her left arm, fever-dizziness engulfed her. She was deafened by her own heartbeat.

Between her fingers, she saw the flames struggle, sink; the coals darkened, orange to crimson to wine, then black and ash-gray.

"Urk," Kit said behind her.

Marya sat back on her heels and rubbed her eyes. "That's what I like about you. You always know what to say at times like this."

"Mother at the Helm—"

"It isn't magic!" Marya snapped. "Calm down. It's part of the…the change. You know perfectly well it is."

Kit set her hands firmly on her knees and took several deep breaths. "You're right. I'm calm. Perfectly. Did you know you could do that?"

"I tried it last night, in my room. I don't think I could before last night."

"So where did it come from?"

"I have a theory…"

Kit closed her eyes. "I hate it when you say that."

"You want to hear it?"

"I'm sorry."

"All right. I remember an experiment my mother had me do when I was a kid, with a family of snow hare kittens. I raised half of them in pens outdoors. The other half stayed indoors. The rabbits outdoors changed coloring the way snow hares always do, brown in summer and white in winter. The rabbits raised indoors were never anything but brown."

Kit frowned. "You must have botched it. Snow hares don't do that— and what does that have to do with putting out fires, anyway?"

"I'm getting to that. She explained that my little project showed how living things can sometimes be born with characteristics that don't appear until they're triggered by something outside themselves."

"So?" Kit gestured toward Marya's arm, and the stove.

Marya flexed her dark fingers. "I think, last night, I had a characteristic triggered."

Kit shook her head impatiently. "You've been cold before. And scared before. What—" Her eyes widened. "Triggered by...that...thing?"

Marya nodded.

"No."

"What's your theory—coincidence?"

"Why should it have any effect on you?"

"Because," said Marya, her voice sounding flat even to her, "that thing and my arm are...related."

"Sheepcrap. A big, steaming—"

"I can use my arm to absorb heat, you saw that. I think the thing we went up against last night can do the same. I think that's why it tears its victims open. It sure as day isn't eating them."

"You're wrong." Kit's face was pale and set.

Marya asked softly, "How do you know?"

"Because you're not like that thing! If you're trying to tell me you are—"

"No, no, no. I'm human—I was, I still am. Just because those rabbits never turned white didn't mean they weren't rabbits."

"Shut up about your Motherlorn rabbits."

Marya wanted suddenly to scream at her, to make her believe by volume alone. She bit the inside of her mouth instead, and took a deep breath. "All right. I'm just saying—"

The door bolt clacked against its socket. "Songsmith?" came Amali's voice from outside the door. "Is everything all right?"

"Oops," Marya muttered, and leaped to unlock the door.

"Is everything all right?" Amali repeated, her plump face full of cheerful concern. She carried a pair of copper-and-brass cans. "Here's hot water. Did you sleep well? Does your shoulder hurt you?"

Kit graciously acknowledged the hot water and followed Amali into the bathing room, letting all the rest of the innkeeper's speech go unanswered.

"Her shoulder's fine," Marya said when Amali came out with the empty water cans. "I looked it over. Has there been any more news?"

"News?" Amali said, straightening the covers on the bed Kit had left.

"Of that thing last night."

"It's certainly not been seen again."

"Certainly?"

Amali frowned and plumped a pillow before she said, "Such things can only walk among us at night, while the Mother sails in dream."

A god who goes to sleep when you need her most, Marya thought. *Wonderful.* "You're sure the Mother herself isn't responsible for little treats like that?"

"The Mother does not create evil," Amali lectured mildly. "Evil comes from us. But She allows evil to walk among us to teach us our errors. When we've learned and corrected ourselves, She will rid the world of such terrible things."

"So all we have to do is be very, very good and the creature will go away."

Amali blinked. "Disrespect doesn't become a Payer of the Price, dear."

Marya clenched her teeth. "Isn't someone at least organizing a hunt for the monster?"

"Wolves come down from the hills in winter." Amali smiled. "Do you go out hunting them every time, or do you simply take sensible precautions?"

"We aren't talking about wolves."

"There are many dangers this far from the cities. We live differently here."

"And die differently, too, if that creature is any indication," Marya snapped.

Kit strolled out of the bathing room, dressed and drying her hair with a green towel. "What's this about dying?" she asked.

"Nothing to be concerned with, Songsmith," said Amali. "Will you want to travel on today? The weather is good—"

Someone tapped furtively on the door. "Amali?" came Nan's voice, very soft. "Come quick. The whole town's down there. They're going to go out and—" She'd opened the door and slid through. At the sight of Marya and Kit, she pressed her hand to her mouth. "Oh. Oh, Mother."

"I have things to do downstairs," Amali said in a rush, and turned frantically toward Nan and the door.

"And something to do up here first." Marya stretched out her arm, black and shining, and pushed the door closed. Amali turned, and Marya saw that the jolly innkeeper mask had crumbled. The woman's eyes were full of fear. "The truth, please," Marya finished gently.

Nan made a strangled noise. Amali closed her eyes and gulped air.

"Wait a minute," said Kit. "What did I miss?"

"I don't know yet, Woodpecker," Marya replied. "But something out of the ordinary is going on here—" she raised an eyebrow at Amali and Nan, "—and I think these two can tell me all about it."

Amali shook her head. "No. I'm sorry. You should have the truth; you of all people should be trusted with the truth. But not now."

"Why not?"

"There are people downstairs who are ready to murder what they should only pity. I may be able to keep them from finding...what they hunt."

"The creature," said Marya.

Amali looked away, and nodded.

Marya watched her for a moment before she said, "It killed three people last night."

"It couldn't—" Amali began, then nodded again.

"We've got to go!" Nan hissed at Amali. "Downstairs—"

"We might be able to help," Marya said.

Amali bit her lip. "If I tell you...promise you'll let it live."

"If we can," said Marya.

"Now, *wait* a minute—" Kit began, but Marya gestured her quiet.

Amali looked from Marya to Kit. Then her gaze turned downward.

"The...creature we hunt," she said at last, "is my child."

Marya was too stunned to do more than blink. *You knew it was a mutation,* she told herself. *It had to be child to something. But not to this pudgy, red-faced, normal little woman...*

Amali continued, "Nan was my first-born. Then I had...this one. He was simple, he had to be fed and cleaned—" Her voice cracked and faded, and she pressed her fingers to her lips before she spoke again. "I thought She had judged me strong enough to raise a Payer of the Price. May She help me, *I* thought I was strong enough." She turned to Marya and lifted her head, in pride, or defiance. "Nan and I cared for him for fifteen years. We kept him locked away, for fear the townsfolk would do him a mischief."

Or was it, Marya thought, *that you didn't want Sallis to know you had a mutation in the family?*

Amali hesitated, then plunged grimly back into her story. "A few months ago—things began to happen. I was afraid. I... Nan and I... Mother forgive me, one day we locked the door of his room and went to Lyle Valley. We came back two weeks later."

Tears began to roll down Amali's cheeks. "We buried him after dark, here in the foothills. He was so...he must have been dead, he must have! The Mother has brought him back, to punish me for not trusting Her, for my fear, for...not loving him." And Amali buried her face in her hands and sobbed.

Kit reached a hand halfway out to Amali's shoulder, paused.

"Could the thing be caught, and confined?" Marya asked finally.

"What?" Kit's voice squeaked a little.

Amali replied, "I think so."

"Why?" Kit wailed.

"Then you have until we find it to convince me that we ought to," said Marya, and started for the door.

"Hold it right there!" Kit said in a voice that rattled the window glass. "Are you going crazy?"

"No," Marya said patiently, "I'm going with the hunting party."

Kit opened and closed her mouth. "Then so am I," she said at last.

"But your shoulder..." Marya and Amali said almost at once.

"Where's my cloak?" glared Kit, and Marya recognized the voice of The Last Word.

The foothills were sullen around them, red-washed in the setting sun, thickly clotted with pine groves. Marya squinted in the lash of the bitter wind, switched the reins to her clawed hand, and tucked the other into her armpit to warm it. *Somewhere in all of this,* she reflected, *there's a demon that eats souls. No, somewhere there's a pitiful mutated something that lives on pure energy.* She looked down at her black hand. It reflected sunset like a bloody knife. She concentrated on it, trying to draw heat from the winter sunlight as she had drawn from the fire, but it stayed profoundly, fiercely cold, and still.

She clenched her legs on her mount, and it trotted forward through the snow to where Amali was riding. Behind her she could hear Kit's beast surge forward to Amali's other side.

"All right," said Marya. "We've diverted the rest of the hunting party for you, and we've followed you from spot to spot for the last hour. What are you going to do when we find it?"

"Amali!" Nan's voice rang out. Marya looked up to see her topping the nearest ridge, around a great plume of frozen snow. "He's nearby! There are tracks here, and a dead—"

Marya flung herself out of the saddle to the ground before she quite knew why. A slight, heavy motion in the pine boughs, a shadow... Her mount screamed, and the snow around her steamed with blood. "Get back!" she yelled, but Kit and Amali had already lunged away from the twisting, dying animal with the black monster on its back.

Marya drew her sword, then realized there was nothing she could do with it. *If it will only stay interested in its kill long enough that I can find a way to stop it,* she thought. But the hell-window eyes turned to her, and it rose and faced her. Her stomach wrenched. *The mind of a retarded sixteen-year-old,* she realized—*I hurt it. It understands revenge.* She raised her sinister arm before her, and thought about death.

The impact of the creature's leap drove her down to the snow. Her shoulder jarred against ice and rock, and she cried out, but her dark arm held steady against the weight, held the nightmare face at bay.

Suddenly her hand coursed with heat, and the creature hissed and struck out at her. She felt a line of freezing pain at her temple and knew it had cut her. The world seemed to be separating into fragments, which in turn began to drift apart from each other.

She heard a thud, and cold showered her face. It happened again, and the demon shadow was gone from above her.

"Marya!" she heard Kit yell. "This way!" A lump of snow whizzed past her head.

She looked wildly in the direction of the voice. "You're throwing snowballs?" she shrieked.

"Come on, will you?" Kit howled back, and grabbed another handful of snow. Amali was crouched at her feet, and seemed to be trying to force both her mittened fists into her mouth. "This won't work for—no, here it comes! Move!"

Marya dived for Kit, and reached her side just as the Songsmith fired another snowball. The creature staggered back a step, then came on again.

"Snowballs?" said Marya.

"Well, they're slowing it down!"

"But why?" *The thing absorbs energy,* Marya realized. *Snowballs have energy of motion. Like my sword, and Kit's knife, when we used them last night. But snowballs don't have someone hanging onto them...*

"Snow!" Marya shouted.

Nan was struggling up to them through the drifts. Behind her, Marya saw the towering snow-plume that topped the near ridge, arching in a heavy half-tunnel.

"This way!" She pulled Kit toward the ridge. Behind them, Amali and Nan floundered aside as the monster swept forward.

"Take my sword," Marya panted, and thrust it hilt-first at Kit. "You're going to drop this—" she pointed up at the curve of snow, "—on that thing. As soon as I've got it underneath, chop through the ice near the point of the ridge."

Kit looked dubious. "This'll work?"

"I don't know," said Marya. At the corner of her vision, a shadow grew quickly larger. "Go, go!"

She dodged aside as the creature lunged at her. If she could keep her footing, and keep moving back... She could see hints of humanity now in the wild visage—in the shape of temple and cheekbone, in the motion of the gaping jaws—and the terror made her want to huddle whimpering in the snow. She kept moving.

The shadow of the snow-curve cut the ground beneath her into sections of dying light and blue dusk. The black shape crouched, her only warning of its sudden spring. Marya flung herself aside barely in time. She hit the snow hard, and tasted ice and grit in her mouth.

"Kit!" she gasped. "Now!" She rolled fast and came floundering to her feet in the deep snow, ready to leap out of the path of the avalanche of snow and ice...

...that didn't fall. "Kit!" she yelled again. "Knock it down!" The creature was stalking her once more.

"It won't fall!" shrieked Kit.

Marya spared a glance toward the base of the ridge. Kit was hacking furiously. It was not enough to break down the arch of snow. Marya looked back at the nightshade face all too close to her, and heard a strangling cry she couldn't keep back.

"Jump!" shouted a voice somewhere above her.

The monster crouched to spring.

"Jump clear!" she heard again. "Hurry!" She jumped as far as she could, slipped, fell, rolled. Behind her she heard a wooden groan, and a sudden roar. Her mouth and eyes filled with snow.

"Marya?" Kit called wildly. "Are you all right?"

Marya sat up and shook snow out of her face. "What happened?"

Kit knelt down next to her and looked her over critically. Then she pointed back toward the ridge.

The snow-plume was gone. At the foot of the ridge was a small mountain of snow and ice. Near it lay one of the riding animals, still saddled. Nan was at its head, patting it, talking to it. It tried to rise, and failed.

"Nan saw what we were trying to do, and that it wasn't working," Kit said. "She drove the critter out onto the arch, to bring it down."

Marya nodded, and dragged herself to her feet.

"You're sure you're all right?" Kit asked.

"I hurt all over," said Marya. "A mere nothing." She trudged over to Nan.

"Its leg's broken," Nan said.

"I thought so. I'm sorry."

Nan smiled at her, though the smile was a little lopsided. "It was you or it."

"True. But I'm still sorry."

Nan knelt by the beast's head and took a hunting knife out of a sheath at her belt. Marya looked away quickly, out over the mound of broken snow. Was that a bent, black arm? *No,* Marya realized, *just a tree branch swept down. The creature is buried. By the time it can dig its way out, if it can, it'll be too weak to fight back. And Amali can have her mutant captive back. I wonder how long it will be before she tries to kill it again?*

As if answering her thoughts, Amali appeared at her left shoulder. "Is he dead?"

"I don't think so. It's a hard critter to kill, you know."

Amali looked away. "Even you can't understand."

"I admit, weird, coal-black children who suck the life out of things are difficult to empathize with."

"I loved him at first," Amali murmured.

Marya frowned and looked at her.

"That's so hard for you to believe? Mothers love clubfooted children, they love their simple children. My son was no different."

"No different?" Surprise added a squeak to Marya's voice. "A withered, demonic—"

"He wasn't always like that," Amali said. "That's why I thought you could… He was simple, and his left foot was black and twisted and hard as stone. It was only last year that he began to change, and he began to kill things. Before that, he…"

Marya felt her eyes ache from staring. Her tongue seemed stuck in her dry mouth. She turned away from Amali, and found Kit, wide-eyed, watching her.

"Don't look at me like that," Marya rasped. "It's not true." But she remembered suddenly the wild, bloodthirsty rush of power she had felt in the courtyard at the gate, when she ripped energy away from the mutant child.

"Marya—" Kit reached toward her. But her hand stopped halfway between them.

Marya stared a moment at that hand, before a sob bruised its way out of her throat, and she turned with a wrench and ran.

Her foot caught in snow suddenly deep and uneven, and she fell forward. She stared for a moment at her arms sunk to the elbows in a slope of snow, before she remembered: the avalanche. *If it had just fallen on me, too,* she thought.

A little well appeared in the snow before her. Loose powder sifted into it. It grew larger. And suddenly the mass before her shook and shifted, and knotted black twigs, four of them, poked out of the snow.

It wasn't until they clenched that she recognized them.

She wrenched her left hand out of the drift and grabbed the mutant creature's fingers, yanked at them until the arm was clear of the snow bank. Then she scrabbled until she found the face. It seemed even more human now that weakness had shrunk it. It struggled, twisting its head and free arm. She reached down and plunged her talons around and into its throat.

The blistering heat that raced up her arm was almost familiar. Under her, the creature bucked and writhed, screaming thinly. She heard a human scream, too, behind her, before the roaring in her ears deafened her and dragged her into the dark.

She seemed, after some time, to be waking up. Something about waking struck her as inappropriate; the place, perhaps… Someone was sobbing drearily. Marya felt a nudging at her shoulder. "Huh?"

"Mother at the Helm. You're still alive."

"Kit? Where…what are we…"

"Doing here? Never mind, you'll remember soon enough."

And suddenly Marya did, as she recognized the desultory weeping as Amali's. "Oh," she said. "Oh, oh, oh, oh—"

Kit's slap stung her cheek. "Quiet. It's all right. You're all right. Someone would have had to kill it eventually. Can you get up?"

"I don't know."

"Well, try. I want to get out of here."

Marya nodded. It hurt her head. Kit half-lifted her, and they stumbled to one of the remaining riding animals.

"We're just leaving?" Marya said. "Shouldn't we help—"

"Right now, neither of us is likely to be much help. Nan will get Amali home. I want to get back to the inn, pick up our stuff, and go."

"Travel at night?"

"There's a moon."

Marya shrugged and let Kit boost her up to the saddle. The Songsmith scrambled up in front and urged their mount into a fast walk.

For half an hour, Marya watched the moon-cast shadows of trees deepen and stretch blue-black across the snow.

"D'you want to talk about it?" Kit said finally.

"Well…no. Not really. What I want is for it to have never happened."

"Then it's a deal. It never happened."

"Huh," said Marya. Then, "What if that happens to—"

"It won't happen to you," Kit said.

"You don't know that."

There was a long silence. "No, I don't. But what am I supposed to do about it? Hand you over to the peace keepers? 'Got a dangerous mutant here, Officers,' " Kit grated. " 'Well, no, I guess she's not dangerous yet. But she might be, someday…' No, thank you. I'd feel stupid."

Marya looked for something else to say, and couldn't find anything. They rode half a kilometer before she murmured, "Thank you."

"Mmm," said Kit.

"For trusting me, I mean."

Kit turned in the saddle, and their mount stopped. "Are you going to keep brooding over yourself?"

"What? No."

"Good. You're a pain when you brood. I don't suppose you brought anything to eat?"

"There's dried fruit in the saddlebag," Marya said.

"Dried fruit. I ask for food, and you talk about dried fruit. The cold has addled your brain," Kit grumbled. "Hand me a Motherlorn raisin." And they rode on.

Emma and I are members of the Interstate Writer's Workshop, a.k.a. the Scribblies, a group that has included Steven Brust, Patricia C. Wrede, Pamela Dean, Kara Dalkey, and Nathan Bucklin. Terri Windling, editor extraordinaire, *bought most of our early work.* When Thieves' World *made publishers think there were a lot of bucks to be found in shared world anthologies, Terri asked us to create one of our own. We came up with Liavek, which ran for five volumes and contained stories by writers like Gene Wolfe, Jane Yolen, Megan Lindholm, and Walter Jon Williams.*

This is the first short story that I ever wrote and liked.

—Will

Bound Things

Will Shetterly

One sunny afternoon in Buds, three wizards sat in a quiet room. The youngest, a small man with grim features, said, "You can handle this alone?"

The eldest, a very dark, very handsome man whose black goatee hung midway down his chest, smiled and said, "Of course. After you do your part."

"There must be a reason," the youngest insisted, "why he is called The Magician."

The tallest, a woman who might have been a sister to the younger man, said, "Yes. Because he is vain. Because they do not know what magicians are in this uncivilized place. Because he is the most powerful of the village witches who live on that gaudy lane they call Wizard's Row."

The eldest laughed. "Don't underestimate him. Would we be here in Liavek, if he was weak?"

"Then why does he hide his name?"

The youngest said, "To keep us from gaining power over him?"

The woman sneered, then laughed. "If so, Liavekans are all superstitious savages! Do other magicians in Liavek hide their names or their parentage?"

"No," the eldest answered. "They are like most sorcerers. They only conceal their birthdays and the vessels of their power."

Frowning, the woman said, "Then why does The Magician hide his name?"

"He does not," the eldest answered. "It is said his name is Trav."

"Trav?" the young man asked. "As in *trav?*" He almost barked the word; it meant "spider" in Tichenese. "Or *traav?*" Drawling its syllables, it meant "lefty" in Zhir. "Which hand does he favor?"

The eldest smiled at them both. "Does it matter?"

"No," the woman answered, returning his smile. "Not now."

Trav lay on his stomach on a carpet on the floor of his study and idly flipped through the most recent edition of the *Cat Street Crier.* A half-eaten biscuit sat on a green porcelain plate beside him, which interested a fat, shaggy black cat. Next to the plate was a cup of the same green porcelain, holding the dregs of some pale tea. On the small of his back was a sleeping silver-blue kitten.

Trav wore a long blue robe over tight black trousers, and his sandalled feet were crossed as he scratched the outside of his left ankle with his right foot. His only jewelry was a plain but heavy polished-brass bracelet on each wrist. His sandy hair was cropped close to his skull, his jaw was cleanly shaven, and his eyes were yellow, maybe brown, perhaps green. His face bore no more lines of age or experience than that of a pampered youth.

A voice filled the room like the striking of a gong. "Two prospective clients seek audience with you, O noble master."

The cat leaped away from the biscuit and fled guiltily out of the room; the kitten did not wake. Trav looked up from the *Crier* and said, "Who're you trying to impress, Gogo?"

"I shall ask their names as you request, O mighty Magician." Trav sighed, reached around to transfer the kitten from his back to a pillow, and received a swat for his effort. Gogo spoke again. "They are Sessi of Candlemaker's Street and her companion, the bold Sorel, O wise one."

He did not recognize either name, but he knew that Liavek grew faster than he could learn every person of consequence. He said, "Fine, Gogo. Let them in. And I don't care how rich they are, you needn't fawn so."

"I obey as always, O Magician of Magicians."

Trav sighed again, then stood. He set the cup and plate on a low ebony table by a wide wicker couch, popped the remaining fragment of biscuit into his mouth, glanced at the window which looked out on a sunny beach by a calm sea, and snapped his fingers. The scene beyond the window changed to the bright awnings of the Street of Scales. Hearing footsteps in the hall, Trav stepped to the door and, bowing low in the Tichenese manner, swung it wide.

The first thing he noticed was that the hall beyond was paved with glistening diamonds set in gold; Gogo was doing her best to impress these clients. The second thing he noticed were small, dirty feet which, he saw as his gaze traveled upwards, were attached to a small, dirty child. Her eyes were bright black beads beneath tangled hair, and her dress had been a sugar sack that still bore the imprint of the Gold Harbor Trading Company. The girl smiled shyly, saying, "Hello, Master Magician. Can you find my doll?" In the palm of her outstretched hand was a very thin half-copper coin.

A boy, little taller than the girl though his gauntness and his swagger said he was twice her age, stood behind her. A silver knife was stuck through his sash as though he dared anyone to take it. He pulled a faded cloth cap from his head and said, "I came so's Sessi wouldn't get lost, Your Magiciancy."

Trav whispered, "Gogo..." The guardian did not answer. The children watched him with expectant eyes. "Your...dolly?" he said at last.

"Yes!" said the girl, beginning to cry. "My dolly!"

"Gogo..." Trav whispered. When he saw that the boy studied him with his head cocked warily, Trav shrugged and said, "Enter."

Sorel took the girl's hand and led her into the room. "C'mon, Sessi. The Magician'll find your doll."

Trav bit his lip, then spoke carefully. "This isn't my usual sort of commission. You understand that, don't you?"

The girl nodded. "Yes. You'll find my dolly."

"That's not—"

"I got money. Lookit!" She thrust the copper coin at him. Her voice quavered as though more tears were imminent.

"That is a great deal of money," Trav said gently. "Still—"

The door from the hall opened, and a short woman with hair the color of brass stepped into the room. She was barefoot, and her tunic was a simple white garment, but her hair was elaborately coifed and her copper-dark skin was very clean. "Trav...," she said. Her voice was husky, promising pleasure if he pleased her and trouble if he did not. Her eyes were as green as emeralds.

Trav glanced up. "Who's watching the front door, Gogo?"

"Didi, of course."

"Then who's watching the back?"

"No one's dared to go there in seventy-five years. And Didi's not so simple that he can't handle both."

"You want something? I'm in conference."

"No." Gogo smiled. Leaving, she added, "I'm glad you've agreed to help them." The door closed on her last word.

"Gogo!" Trav raced after her, but when he entered the hallway, it was quiet, shadowy, and empty. "I will never be rich," he whispered.

Gogo's voice rang in the hall like chimes. "Look again at the girl's coin, my wise master. And ask the boy to describe the doll, and how it was stolen."

Trav's eye flicked wide. As he hurried back into the study, the children stared at him. "That's all we got," said Sorel. "Unless..." The boy's voice saddened as his fingers touched the hilt of his silver knife.

"No," Trav said. He took Sessi's half-copper piece and saw that it bore the stamp of Nevriath the Unlucky, the last ruler of S'Rian before Liavekan nomads came almost seven hundred years ago. Tel Jassil of the Street of Old Coins would pay a small fortune for such an antiquity, for His Scarlet Eminence, The Levar's Regent, would pay Jassil a larger one to add it to his collection. Trav allowed himself a tiny smile. "If Gogo thinks we've made a fine bargain, I could hardly alter it now." He nodded, and the coin disappeared from his fingers. "Tell me about this doll."

"It's my dolly," said Sessi. "Some bad men took it."

"The Titch took it," Sorel explained.

"The...Titch?"

"Yeah. The one that's got that big house on the Levar's Way, just past Temple Hill."

Trav stared, then laughed in delight. "The Tichenese ambassador?"

Sorel nodded.

"He stole a doll?"

Sessi sniffed, nodded, and said, "Bad old Titch."

"Not by himself," said Sorel.

"Of course not," said Trav. "There's a Tichenese saying: When others act for you, you pay for success; they pay for failure."

"Huh?"

"Who took the doll?"

The boy squinted nervously. "Some sailors. They snatched Sessi's doll, and she came and got me. I followed them to the Titch's house. I didn't actually see the head Titch. But that's where they went, the Titch's house, and they didn't come out again."

"And you didn't try to go in?"

"You know how well they guard that place?"

Trav nodded. "Describe the doll."

The boy looked at the girl, then said, "Well, it looks like a Titch, and it's about a foot long, and it's carved out of wood. Not very well carved, either. And it's got a little beard made of camel hair, but it was wearing a dress—"

"A long robe?" said Trav. "Golden, like the ambassador's? Or dark blue, with some silver trim?"

"Blue and silver, mostly."

"Gogo was right to admit you."

"What do you mean, your Magiciancy?" Sorel asked.

"Never mind." Trav stopped to face the girl. "Where did you find your dolly?"

She looked down, then whispered, "Sorel gave him to me."

"Oh?"

Sorel bit his lip. "Yeah. I didn't think anyone at the markets would want a Titch doll. 'Specially not a badly carved one."

"And where did you find it?"

"Um, I was in this house—"

The Magician's eyes narrowed, and he said, "I don't care that you stole it. Tell me from whom."

"Deremer Ledoro."

"On Pine Street? Dances at Tam's Palace?"

Sorel stared in surprise or fear. "How'd you know?"

"I'm The Magician. I'm amazed Deremer's home wasn't better guarded."

"It used to be. But all she's got now are a few locks on the windows and doors." Sorel shrugged. "Cheap ones."

"Yes," said Trav. "So someone suspected that Deremer's luck had been freed or stolen, and you were sent because you're dispensable."

"Because I'm good!"

"Did you find the S'Rian coin there?"

"I—"

"You want me to seek the doll?"

Sessi clutched Sorel's arm and said, "Yes!"

"Then tell me what I need to know."

Sorel glanced at Sessi. "The coin was in Deremer's house."

Trav nodded. "Thank you." He glanced at the ceiling. "I think we'll have refreshments now. And then one of my servants will call upon our ambassador from the north."

When Gogo entered with a tray of wooden mugs and a pitcher of pineapple juice, the children were sitting on the wicker couch facing The Magician. Trav sat on the corner of his desk, folding a sheet of paper into the shape of a bird. Several paper birds already flapped around the room, much to the annoyance of the black cat, which crouched beneath the desk, and to the delight of the kitten, which bounded into the air, swatting at the birds. Gogo glanced at Trav, who blushed and came to help her with the drinks.

"My," she said. "You are in a good mood."

The Magician shrugged, then laughed. "I've heard interesting news. Someone," he said, still grinning, "has been *very* careless."

Shortly thereafter, the two children emerged from 17 Wizard's Row. That day, the house was a white cottage that would not have been out of place on Kil Beach or Minnow Island, except perhaps for a tiny brass gargoyle's head set into the center of the front door. As the children left, the gargoyle called, "He said not to come back until tomorrow! So stay away until then! Or longer!"

Sessi whispered, "I liked the other one better."

Sorel said, "You mean that door-thing and the serving woman are the same?"

Sessi nodded. " 'Cept somebody else is the door-thing, right now."

After an instant, Sorel said, "I knew that."

The tiny brass gargoyle snickered maliciously. The white fence gate closed behind The Magician's clients. When they had left Wizard's Row, Number 17 opened again. A small balding man in the gray and blue of the Levar's Guard looked in either direction, then stepped toward the street.

"You needn't hurry back," the gargoyle said.

The balding man laughed. "I like the other one better, too." He strode briskly to One-Hand Lane, where a young woman waited by an empty footcab.

She glanced at his uniform and his flintlock pistol, and said, "Afternoon, Captain. Where to?"

He sat in the cab. "The Tichenese embassy. And don't spare the horses."

The woman frowned as she lifted the shafts to draw the cab away. "If I have to hear more jokes," she mumbled, "I expect a good tip."

The officer was silent for the rest of their trip. The footcab traveled north on Cat Street, passing the flatboats and barges that plied the river and the canals, and then passing the boats' destination: Fisher's Market, the Old Town Market. Hawkers shouted their wares with glee, except for one sad-faced fellow crying plaintively, "Camel stew! *Very* cheap!" and the crowd slowed their passage until they neared Temple Hill.

The homes along the Levar's Way to the west of Temple Circle were walled as though they were fortresses, to keep out invaders in forgotten times and thieves in the present. Two very dark women and a man stood before the iron gates of one, with their arms crossed and no weapon visible. They wore the blue and silver robes of the Guild of Power, which proclaimed them to be among Tichen's most skillful sorcerers.

The footcab stopped by the three foreigners. The Guard captain stepped down, counted out his fare in shiny coppers, and walked toward the spiked fence as the footcab hurried away. The tallest sorcerer blocked his way, smiled down at him, and said, "Does the ambassador expect you?"

"No," the captain answered calmly. "But he would do well to see me, if he did not want the City General to inquire about his dealings with Deremer Ledoro."

The sorcerer's grin widened. "Come, Captain. We shall take you to the one you seek. You will surrender your pistol?"

"Of course."

The smaller woman accepted the weapon and sneered slightly.

Two of the sorcerers, the man and the tall woman, stepped back for the captain to lead, so he took the cobblestone road into the embassy. The grounds beyond the granite wall were elaborately gardened in Tichenese fashion, with small, shaped trees and streams that ran over beds of colored pebbles. The embassy stood several hundred yards beyond the gate.

The captain glanced back at his escorts. Though the young man's face was somber, the tall woman smiled. Her teeth glistened like marble. She said, "Do you have doubts about your mission, Captain?"

"No," the Liavekan answered quietly.

Both sorcerers extended their fingers toward the captain. "You should," the woman said, laughing as the captain disappeared.

Naked of clothing and jewelry, he stood on cold limestone before a wall of polished black rock. Something cast light from behind him, and as he turned, he heard a polite cough that said he was not alone.

A handsome, middle-aged man with Tichenese features stood five paces away. His goatee hung as low as his sternum, and his hair was worn in many long braids. His robe was almost entirely indigo, with only a thin piping of silver at the hem and on each sleeve. The man bowed low and said, "Greetings to you, Trav The Magician. Do not step from the place where you stand, or I must burn you until you are but ashes. That would be a waste, don't you think?"

"Rather," Trav answered cautiously. The lack of window and the cool, moist air suggested they stood in an unfinished basement, probably beneath the embassy. His disguise of the little balding man had disappeared with his clothes, his freedom, and, he noted, all his carefully prepared protective spells. His skull felt naked. When he passed his hand over it, he learned that his hair had been taken, too.

"You needn't trouble yourself about the vessel of your power, Colleague Trav, whatever it might be. All that you wore is far, far more than three paces away from you." The sorcerer smiled gently. "I'm sorry about making you bald. I've never known anyone to successfully invest power in hair, but I take no chances with one of your skill. Please, accept this as a gesture of respect."

Trav shrugged, wondering what other precautions the Tichenese had taken, and sat cross-legged on the chilly floor. "Surely this is an excess of respect, Chiano Mefini."

"Oh!" The sorcerer pursed his lips in pleasure. "My fame precedes me?"

"Who doesn't know of the Guild of Power's Young Teacher, who some say intends to replace the Old Teacher soon?"

"In this uncivilized city," said Mefini, laughing, "no one but Trav The Magician. I enjoy playing the ambassador."

"You do it well. Why've you troubled to lure me here?"

"Ah, you come to the point, Colleague Trav." Mefini patted his goatee, then said, "And since you do, I'll tell you honestly that another war between Liavek and Ka Zhir would ensure that Tichen remains strong. Our Guild has done a few subtle things to hurry such a war, yet several of our agents have failed. We are not familiar with failure. When I suggested to the Old Teacher that Trav The Magician might have intervened, she laughed and said you were too concerned with your wealth and your safety to take sides. And then she suggested that I reassure myself." Mefini took a roll of yellowed parchment from his robe and opened it. "You recognize this?"

Trav studied the sigils. "Yes. The Scroll of Truth. You have much power, Chiano Mefini."

"Thank you." Mefini set the scroll carefully on the ground before Trav. "Place your hand upon it and swear on your luck and your life never to interfere in Tichenese matters. Then you may return to your house and your business."

"I don't suppose you'd accept my promise?" said Trav.

"I'm sorry. It must be the Scroll."

"I'd rather not."

"And I'd rather not kill you."

Trav nodded. "Good. Tell me, is the doll here?"

Mefini glanced at a dark corner perhaps ten feet away, where something small sat atop a crate. "Why?"

"Your ruse was well done." Trav propped his elbows behind him and leaned back as though he lay on the rug in his study. "I imagine you promised the boy a great deal of money to let you alter his memory for a few hours. Since he believed what he said, he couldn't give away your trap. Did you also bewitch the girl, so she believed she had owned the doll? Or did you fail to tell the boy why you had him burgle Deremer Ledoro's home, and he gave the doll to the girl as he said?"

"Does it matter?" Mefini asked.

"I suppose not," said Trav. "But you did have the boy burgle Ledoro's home."

"Yes." Mefini watched Trav as though he suspected there might be more to The Magician's speech than curiosity.

"I thought so," Trav said. "For me to believe his story, most of it had to be true. That was rather risky, Chiano Mefini." The shadows about The Magician seemed to grow blacker. Though his tone was casual, his eyes never left his captor's face.

"A risk worth taking," Mefini replied, smiling apologetically, "as you are now my prisoner." A hint of suspicion crept into his voice. "If you hope to regain your magic, I must confess that all your clothes and jewelry were sent into a volcano's womb. Whatever may have been the vessel of your luck, it is destroyed and you are powerless." Mefini coughed a command in Tichenese, and a ball of fire flared and died above Trav. As its ashes fell on Trav's naked form, Mefini said, "As you see, I am not. Tell what you think, Colleague Trav."

Trav laughed lightly. "I think that Deremer Ledoro seduced you in order to study Tichenese magic. She must have learned your weakness and stolen it. When Ledoro's luck was freed by a friend of mine, you learned she was powerless and sent the boy to take back your doll. And then you thought to use these events to lure me from my home."

Mefini frowned. "My weakness, you say? You think you know what the doll is?"

"You expected its description to intrigue me and doubted I would guess its purpose?" The Magician smiled gently. "You are old, Chiano Mefini, perhaps older than I. Magicians wonder about other magicians, especially those who live for many years. It is the Master's Conundrum, I believe you call it in Tichen, yes? A magician must invest birth luck every year, and it cannot be used for any purpose while it is being invested in a vessel. A magician may stay magically young throughout the year, but eventually, we all grow too old to survive the weight of our true age during those few hours of investiture. Yet a magician who binds birth luck to create a talisman to stay young forever will have no more magic to use. Such a magician with enemies or covetous friends will soon be dead by other means than age. Still, solutions are available, as both of us have found."

Mefini gestured sharply. "Go on."

"A magician loved you," Trav said, "a magician whom you convinced or forced to bind his or her luck into an object whose only purpose is to keep you alive." Trav leaned back further and crossed his legs in perfect ease. "The doll, of course. Rather embarrassing when your Liavekan dancing girl stole it, I imagine."

Mefini shrugged. "I have it back. No matter." Then he grinned. "I appreciate your wisdom, Trav The Magician, yet here you are, my prisoner. Your luck has been freed, all your spells have failed, and two of my students are searching the famous Seventeen Wizard's Row at their leisure. But nothing shall be disturbed if you swear never to meddle in Tichenese matters." He pointed a ringed finger at the Scroll of Truth.

"I told you before," The Magician said carefully. "No."

"You have a rather foolish confidence, Colleague Trav."

"That's probably true. But let me tell you a story."

Mefini snorted, then smiled. "Very well, Colleague Trav. If you think it pertinent, I wish to hear it."

"Decide when I finish." Trav cleared his throat. "In 2947, while Liavek warred with Saltigos, there was a young Liavekan named Marik whose luck was such that he had learned the ill-luck periods of seven of the mightiest Saltigan wizards. He stole the vessels of their luck and destroyed each vessel during its owner's ill-luck period, thus freeing each wizard's luck for all time. The Saltigans, reasonably enough, believed Marik's death was vital to their cause. The leader of these Saltigans thought further, and decided that to strip Marik of his power and parade him before Liavek's walls might so dispirit the Liavekans that they would surrender. So the Saltigans hired three Tichenese sorcerers of your Guild to aid them. Perhaps some form of the tale has come down to you?"

"I almost recognize it," said Mefini. "Speak on."

"The three sorcerers studied the stars and the tides and the entrails of many rare animals, and then they got one of Marik's servants drunk and learned the time of Marik's birth. But they could not learn what vessel he used to keep his luck, so, at the hour when Marik's luck returned from its vessel to his body, the sorcerers used a spell to cast him naked into a prison of their choosing, much as you have done with me."

"Which is why you tell this story, I assume."

"Yes. Their purpose was different from yours, and they had more time to prepare, or so I assume. You will not be insulted if I say that their prison was far cleverer than yours, Chiano Mefini?"

"Oh?" Mefini frowned.

"Indeed. They sent Marik to a place beyond our world where he floated in something like mist. His luck was within him then, full and powerful, yet there was nothing for him to invest it in, not even ground beneath him, and nothing for him to employ it upon. After the time of his birth had passed, the Tichenese sorcerers brought Marik back to our world."

Mefini raised his arms cautiously. "You are not saying we brought you here on your birthday? The odds of that are—"

Trav laughed. "No, Chiano Mefini. I swear it on my luck. I have not been telling you tales to lull you while I reinvested my magic."

"I see," Mefini said, though his shoulders were visibly stiff with tension. "Out of curiosity, Colleague Trav, was your luck in one of your bracelets? Wearing two is a common precaution."

"Not the bracelets," said Trav. "But let me finish my story. It is almost over."

"Very well."

"The sorcerers had complimented themselves on their cleverness as they called Marik back from that dimension of perfect emptiness. They had heard, of course, the rumor that a very rare individual could invest his luck in his own body, but they did not believe that was possible, no more than I believe it today. And so they imagined poor Marik would arrive magicless until his next birthday, ready for delivery to the Saltigans, who would pay a premium for a service perfectly performed."

When Trav said no more, Mefini said, "And?"

Trav smiled. "And Marik appeared before them, as naked as he had been imprisoned. as naked As I am now. In his left fist, he held his severed right hand, the hand that he had cut from his arm with his birth magic and invested with his luck. They say Marik laughed as he slew his captors. Liavekans remember him as Marik One-Hand, and they still celebrate his birthday. The street near my house was named for him."

Mefini shuddered. "That's an ugly story. What's it have to do with us?"

"Much," said Trav, rising smoothly to his feet and pointing with his left hand at the crate where Mefini's doll lay. In the shadows, something like a large spider scuttled to the doll and embraced it. "You see," said Trav, bringing the stump of his right arm from behind his back, "I am Marik One-Hand, and I hold your life in my palm."

The two magicians stared at each other. The air in the basement seemed warmer and more humid than it had moments before. At last, Mefini set his hand on the Scroll of Truth and said sadly, "I swear to forfeit my life and my power if ever I meddle in the affairs of Liavek, or let anyone learn from me the secrets of Marik One-Hand, or use my knowledge in any way to harm Marik or Liavek. Will that suffice?"

"I could require more," Trav said. "But it will do."

"What of my students?"

Trav laughed. "My front door let them into a maze of mirrors. My cats have been amusing themselves by chasing your students through it for the past hour."

"Your cats?"

"Chaos and Disorder. They are a lioness and a tiger, at present."

"I…see." Mefini frowned. "Aren't the names redundant?"

"You have never kept cats." The Magician stepped to the crate where Mefini's doll was still in the severed hand's grip. As he fitted his right wrist to the hand, he glanced toward a door at the rear of the room and called, "Gogo!"

The door opened. Mefini's' eyes grew wide as his students stumbled through it with two great cats snarling at their thighs. The hall beyond was brightly lit and seemed to be made of glowing diamonds set under glass. A short woman in a white tunic stood smiling in the doorway.

Trav told the cats, "That's enough," and they quit chasing the students in order to rub against his legs. "You can stop being affectionate; I'll feed you soon enough," he said. The cats continued, which almost made him fall several times as he carried Mefini's doll to the sorcerer. "It is hard to have cats and dignity."

"I…suppose so," Mefini agreed, accepting the doll. The Magician's right wrist was ringed with a tiny scar, but otherwise appeared normal.

"Our powers didn't work in there!" one student gasped.

"No," Trav agreed. He glanced at Mefini. "I assume you'll be leaving Liavek soon?"

"Yes."

"Give my greetings to your colleagues in the Guild of Power."

"If I do, they'll guess that you were responsible for my leaving, no matter what I may or may not say."

"Yes," Trav said. "Farewell, Chiano Mefini." He stepped into the bright hall with his cats, and the short woman kissed him, saying, "Hi, Baldy," as the door swung shut.

Mefini and his students stared at the basement door for several minutes. At last, the tall woman said, "Shall I?"

Mefini nodded. The woman went to the door and cautiously opened it. The dusty stairs to their embassy lay beyond.

In the long hallway of many doors that was sometimes found in The Magician's house, Gogo said, "You know, you might as well have declared war on Tichen's sorcerers."

"Yes," Trav answered.

"Good. Just so you know. What'll you do when the children come tomorrow?"

"I doubt the boy'll return. When Mefini's memory spell fades, the boy'll go to the embassy for payment. Once he learns that the ambassador left suddenly for Tichen, he'll stay far away from Wizard's Row for some time, I suspect."

"And the girl?"

"I only agreed to *seek* the doll."

"Trav…"

"Maybe we can make her a doll that looks like the one she lost?"

"She lives on the city streets, you know. With no more friends than that boy, who will probably abandon her if he can think of no more schemes in which to use her."

"There is the Levar's Orphanage, Gogo."

"I was thinking of Tel Jassil on the Street of Old Coins. He's kind and he has no children. If you made her adoption a part of the price for the S'Rian coin—"

"He'd pay me half its value, then!"

"Yes." She kissed him. "Poor Trav."

As they stepped into his study, he said, "I will never be rich."

Gogo laughed and put her arm about his waist. "But you'll live well."

Read what Will has to say in his introduction to "A Happy Birthday," and substitute "first Liavek anthology" for "second." A series has to start somewhere, and this seemed like a good spot.

—Emma

Badu's Luck

Emma Bull

The Tiger's Eye was neither the richest nor the largest shop in Liavek, but its many customers agreed that it was one of the most interesting. It was two stories high, stucco-flanked in blinding white, with door and window frames painted bright rust and teal blue. Along the side of the building, on the Street of the Dreamers, firethorn grew to the roof, and at its feet peonies bowed like perfumed courtiers.

Awnings in the intricate patterns of Ombayan weavers shaded the front windows, and by extension, bits of Park Boulevard. But it was the contents of the windows that told the shop's character. There, depending on the whim of the proprietor or her assistant, one could admire a Saltigan crystal decanter threaded with gold, or a flintlock pistol and dagger with matching lapis inlay so handsome that their deadliness went unremarked.

If one were to push open the brass-studded door and make the porcelain bells above the lintel sing like spirits, one would find the promise of the windows richly fulfilled. The door opened on an airy, high-ceilinged room, enticingly scented. Vivid textiles, glassware and ceramics, metalwork, leatherwork, the arts of gunsmiths and blade-crafters, jewelers and cabinetmakers—all these were represented in the wares of the Tiger's Eye. There were children's toys and antique amulets, embroidered slippers and Zhir hammered-harps, and, shining on the back wall like a lamp, an oval mirror framed in silver and sapphires.

The proprietor, whose name was Snake, was hardly less exotic than her goods, though she was a native Liavekan. She was tall, which was power at the Freeladen ships' auctions and the meetings of the minor merchants. And her dress was often foreign, from the loose ankle-length abjahin of the desert nomads to the sleeveless linen tunic and tight trousers of the Ombayan lancers. Her mother had said, in a fury long past but never forgotten by either party, that she dressed like "a brawling caravaneer." It was not true; or at least, it was only true when she drove a caravan.

Not the least exotic of her attributes was her skill with the long whip of the caravan drivers. Unlike the dress, the tool came with her when she left the trading routes. But away from its natural place, the whip became a tool of a different sort, and when asked about it, Snake would turn the subject.

Snake was slouched in one of the two wicker chairs near the little tile-fronted fireplace that warmed the Tiger's Eye in the cooler months. A low brass table next to her held a painted porcelain pot of kaf. Her hands held the matching cup. "Isn't it beautiful?" she said, and not for the first time. The object of her gaze and her approbation was the silver-framed mirror.

"Yes, very," said Thyan, also not for the first time, and with even less inflection than the last. Thyan was Snake's assistant, fifteen years old, and Tichenese. "And you're the only importer in Liavek fool enough to bring a mirror all the way from Ioros Jires by land."

"No, my little raisin. With vision enough."

"Vision. All I see in the thing is myself, and I look the same in any hand glass."

Snake smiled, leaned back and closed her eyes. "You have the soul of a Zhir marine."

"So who will pay you what it cost to transport?"

"Thyan, Thyan, there's more to our business than squeezing a half-copper till your fingers meet in the middle. There's beauty. There's art."

"There's camel dung by the shovelful," muttered Thyan. She applied herself to dusting the glassware, chanting the purchased spell that sent little dust-devils flying across the shelf.

Snake only smiled, sipped her kaf, and looked at the mirror. The detailing wasn't clear from where she sat, but she remembered it. The oval frame told a story in pictures, cast and sculpted of silver: A merchant, leading an ass heavy-laden with fruit, stopped to rest beneath a coconut palm. Two monkeys in the tree began to pelt him with nuts. But as the nuts struck the ground, they became sapphires, large as the merchant's head, and he left the ass behind and fell to his knees to gather the gems. The monkeys descended on his unattended fruit and carried it up the palm. The ass found himself untethered and ran off. When the merchant turned, his possessions were gone, and worse, the sapphires in his arms had turned to hairy coconuts once again. In the leaves above, the wizard-monkeys clutched their bellies and laughed.

It was, Snake reflected, an old lesson, but the elegance of the work, the sense of loving humor, and the sheer singularity of the thing elevated it beyond craft. She would find someone who saw that when he looked at the mirror, who could likewise afford to own it. Then Snake would have the satisfaction of her customer's pleasure. Until then, the pleasure was her own.

"Ah, I have caught them in sloth and self-indulgence," said the woman who stood in the doorway of the Tiger's Eye. She was tall as an afternoon shadow, hard-edged as marble, and dark as a ripe black plum. Her hair was cut close to her head, which made her eyes seem even larger and brighter than they were. She was beautiful and terrible as any goddess, and her laughter made the hangings sway and the porcelain chime.

"Badu," Snake said, smiling, and Thyan regained control of her slack jaw and whooped, "It's Badu!"

"Indeed," said the tall woman, as she stepped into the shop and swung her pack up onto the counter in front of Thyan.

"And what's self-indulgent about dusting?" Thyan said.

"I have heard you say, oh, many times, that to pay for such a spell when the work can be done by hand for free is a costly indulgence."

"Only when it's Snake's turn to dust," Thyan explained.

Badu laughed. "Perhaps, little woman, you should spend less time in the study of magic, and apprentice yourself to a Council member. *Do you continue to study?*"

"Lessons three times a week."

"Ah, but do you learn from them? Recite to me, something recent."

"Now?" Thyan said piteously.

"What good is magic if it will not come when you call? Now."

Thyan sighed and squeezed her eyes shut, and after a moment, began.

> Sweet Illusion's balm for weary heart
> And potent season for the jaded eye.
> Transformation feeds the hungry mouth
> With wood and stone made flesh and fragrant fruit.
> But nowhere is there wizard with the will
> Or wit to make, where nothing stood before,
> A thing, a true Creation, that will last

When wizard and his power both have passed.

Thyan's shoulders dropped with relief, and she grinned. "Splendid!" cried Badu, and Snake applauded.

"But surely," Badu continued, "that's none of Silvertop's teaching. There's too much of humanity there, and too little of theory."

Snake stood and stretched. "I asked Marithana Govan, the healer, to teach her, when she and Silvertop, ah, had a difference of opinion."

Badu turned to Thyan with an expression that would have daunted a roomful of large adults. There was no sign that it worked on Thyan. "Indeed?" Badu was forced to say.

"He was making a spell-web that he said would keep itself working without any attention from him, but all I could tell that it ever did was stink till the neighbors complained. And I told him so."

"Which, of course, he appreciated," Snake muttered.

But Badu shook her head and looked solemn, and put her hands over Thyan's where they lay on the counter's polished wood. "Woman-child, there is no room for your wayward ways in this. What you study is magic, not sewing or gardening where all that is at risk is a seam or a melon-vine. Will you have a lesson now from me?"

Thyan nodded, her eyes very round.

"Then my lesson is this. Until you have learned enough to invest your luck, you will be a student, and no magician, for your magic will come to you only on your birthday, in your birth hours. Yes, I know you know this already. It has made you impatient, and so has placed you in danger."

"Danger?" Thyan squeaked.

Badu nodded. "Know this of investiture, child. You have been told it is hard, and that those who fail that first attempt die, for those who free their luck cannot live without it. But on the birthday when you make your try, you will call up the luck out of you, to place it in the vessel of your choosing. And you will find that you have called an angry sea, a shark-pack, a mountain to fall on you. Untrained luck is a wild force, stronger than you will ever believe until you summon it into your hands and find out for yourself. When you do, you will need all your training, not just what you find it convenient to remember. You will need discipline, to set your will as an inflexible barrier around the luck you've called. And you will need patience, for all that you do must be done again and again. Investiture is a battle of many hours, and a novice must use every moment of it if she is to cheat death and end a magician."

Thyan studied the floor for a moment more, then raised her head and grinned, and said, "All right."

"All right?"

"I'm scared enough to make my stomach bounce, and I promise to be as patient as…as you."

"Oh, flattering girl. Open my pack, then, and take your reward for learning your lessons."

Thyan untied the pack eagerly. Ten peaches, fuzzy and golden, rolled out and jostled themselves into an untidy line on the counter. They were as ripe and unbruised as the day they were picked, in spite of the long, hard journey they'd made, and more beautiful than any other peaches in Liavek; for they were from Ombaya, where farming was a high art. Their fragrance was intoxicating.

"Eat one," said Badu, and one of the peaches leaped into Thyan's palm.

"Eeek. I'm not sure I can, now." But of course, she did, and was plainly delighted with it.

"That was also a bit of bribery," Badu continued sheepishly. "You see, I must ask Snake to send you away."

"What?" chorused Snake and Thyan, both quite shocked.

"Oh, not far, and not for long—only until tomorrow."

"Tomorrow?" said Thyan, implying by her tone that she did not consider the word "only" to apply in this case.

Snake added, "Why?"

"I…can't say." Badu shot a look of great significance at Snake. Snake frowned, since, for all its weight, the look explained nothing.

It was Thyan who responded. She cocked her head, stared hard at Badu, and said at last, "Magic and politics." Badu looked surprised. "And since I don't know the one yet, and don't care for the other, I'll go. Marithana will let me sleep on her roof."

"You are a woman of kindness," Badu said seriously.

Thyan turned at the hanging that curtained the back door of the shop, her arms full of peaches. "But if this has anything to do with *adventure,* I'll never forgive you." They heard her thump up the stairs.

Badu collapsed into one of the wicker chairs, poured fresh kaf into Snake's cup, and gulped it. "Ah, Name of Herself," she sighed, resting her head against the chair back, "would the child call this an adventure?"

"As long as she didn't have to get up early for it. What's got you in such a state?" Snake said, as she dipped water from a sweating jar into an earthenware cup. She offered this to Badu, who smiled sheepishly, poured a few ceremonial drops on the hearth, sipped, and handed it back to Snake. Snake did the same, and emptied the cup. "Did you walk all the way from Ombaya?"

"I came on a walleyed camel of abominable disposition. My first act in Liavek was to go to the market and sell the monster, and I can only hope that he was promptly boiled down into soup."

Thyan thundered down the stairs again, and poked her head through the curtain. "Is midday tomorrow late enough?" she asked.

"Excellent," said Badu.

"Okay. I'll go out the back door."

Snake called, "Take a peach!"

"I took two!" Thyan's voice drifted back, just before the back door thumped closed.

"Now," Snake said, turning back to Badu, "are you going to try to tell me that a camel is the source of all this fuss?"

"No, I think not." Badu sprang from the chair and began to stalk through the store like a restless panther. "My fancy runs to shopping. What have you that's new, and small?"

Snake stared at her. "Do you want me to humor you, or call a doctor?" she said at last.

"Humor, please." Badu fingered a silk sash, then shook her head. "Too fragile. Jewelry would be wiser." She crouched and peered through the glass that fronted a display case.

Snake sighed, went behind the case, and pulled from it a tray and several boxes. She snapped one open and pushed it forward. Inside was a brooch in the shape of a dragon, made of silver and peridots. Its finny tail seemed to flap with the winking of the yellow-green gems, and silver waves licked at its belly.

"Splendid," said Badu. "The sort of piece I would expect only at the Crystal Gull. But too rich for this application."

"If you would *tell* me—" Snake began, but Badu silenced her with a wave and a frown.

"What's in this one?" she said as if to herself, and opened the lid of a box of carved wood.

It contained a pair of earrings of gold-plated brass, set with teardrop-cut emeralds of respectable quality. Snake was consequently startled when Badu flinched away from them.

"No," said Badu. "Too much nonsense in these already. I'd sell them soon, were I you."

"So buy 'em."

"Not I. Ah—" and Badu's hand hovered over the tray. "May I?" Snake shrugged, and Badu lifted a hammered gold leaf, delicately veined, from off the velvet. "Perfect. It suits me, it goes with everything, and it does not catch the eye."

"Why, by Herself, do you want to wear jewelry that doesn't catch—" Snake suddenly thought of a purpose for unobtrusive jewelry, and let her sentence fall.

"So, how much will you ask for the bauble?"

"Nothing," Snake said, watching her. "I think I'm making you a birthday present of it."

Badu smiled hugely. "Your quick wits more than make up for your flaws."

To Badu's clear disappointment, Snake ignored that. "You're finding a vessel for your luck. That means your birth hours are near, when your luck has to be reinvested. But you're looking for a *new* vessel. Two possible reasons for that. Either your old one was destroyed, which would rob you of your magic until your next birthday—and those peaches wouldn't have wandered so freely around the counter—or someone knows what your old vessel is. Even that wouldn't matter, if the someone didn't wish you ill. Boil that, and what floats to the top is: you're in trouble."

"Well, yes," said Badu.

"And, since you told Thyan she could come back at midday, you must be expecting the worst either this afternoon or tonight."

"Both, in fact."

"So you've brought the whole poisonous mess to my doorstep, with the assumption that I will help you deal with it."

Badu nodded.

Snake grinned and pressed both palms to her forehead in salute. "I'm honored."

"I thought you would be," said Badu.

They sat at the little brass table, and Snake poured kaf for both of them. "Aren't you even a little worried about me knowing your luck time?"

Badu shrugged. "Who else do I trust so?"

Snake looked at her cup. "I *am* honored."

"We've saved each other's lives a few times. We're neither of us so wasteful that we'd want the other dead now."

"It's a killing matter, then?" Snake asked, alarmed.

"It may be. If they're wise, they would see me dead, and some other blamed. Their last best chance is tonight, for I meet with the Council representative tomorrow."

"Would you mind terribly starting from the beginning?"

Badu did not mind. "Among the Matriarchs of Ombaya, there is a faction alarmed at Ka Zhir's growing strength and recklessness. Zhir pirates have crossed the Sea of Luck to plunder the little coastal towns to the south of Ombaya. These I speak of, among the Matriarchs, know that only fear of Liavek and her navy keeps the Zhir from striking for control of the whole of the northern seacoast.

"These Matriarchs seek to forge a military alliance between Ombaya and Liavek. The Zhir would hesitate to harry our settlements if they knew that Liavek helped defend them."

Snake poured herself more kaf. "What does all this have to do with reinvesting your luck?"

"Patience, patience, dear friend. You did ask for the beginning, after all. I have many times served as go-between for traders in various lands, who needed a fair negotiator in business matters. My skill in such things brought the Matriarchs of the alliance faction to me. They wish me to establish contact with the speaker for a like faction in the Levar's Council. It seems that certain Council members have independently reached the same conclusions and would seek a military agreement with Ombaya. Liavek, they reason, needs Ombaya's exported grain, livestock, and lumber—and more particularly, would suffer if Ka Zhir controlled them in Ombaya's stead. Such an alliance could also better protect the farmsteads, both Liavekan and Ombayan, on the western plains."

"You sound convinced," said Snake.

"Only, perhaps, convincing. I cannot, in honor, choose a side until my role in this is done." Badu frowned down at her long fingers. "And there is, indeed, another side. In the Levar's Council, there are those who say that Liavek has enough to do, keeping the Zhir shark from her own coast and shipping—there is no strength left to offer Ombaya. In the Matriarchy, many hold that if the Liavekan military is free to move in Ombaya, it will overrun her, in however peaceful a fashion, and Ombaya will end as nothing but a chick to Liavek's hen, like Saltigos and Hrothvek." Badu shook her head at Snake's look of mild outrage. "Can you say, my friend, and believe it, that Liavek would never do such a thing? She is a fair city, as moral and honest as any that ever was—but she is a living city as well, and like all that lives, her first concern is to keep it so. To annex Ombaya...will you not eat a trout, though the trout may have thought itself your equal while it lived?"

"Hmph. Thank you, at least, for not calling the cursed fish 'she.' "

"When I speak Liavekan, I find my thoughts seduced to Liavekan ways," Badu laughed.

"So, you suspect that one opposing side or another is trying to stop you from making your contact?"

"It could be that. It could also be the Zhir themselves, who would fear a Liavekan-Ombayan union, did they know of it. It might be the pro-alliance factions, one or both, who fear that I am not so neutral after all. It would be a clever ploy, could the alliance's opponents trick those I serve into thinking that I secretly work against them. It might even be that Tichen is alarmed by the possibility of Ombaya and Liavek united and strong to the south of her. In short, I have the spectres of countless enemies, and the substance of none."

"Then how do you know you have any?" Snake asked.

"Ah, forgive me. I do have a substantial foe, but still a faceless one."

"Now we're getting to it."

"It was *you* who asked for the—"

"—beginning, I know," sighed Snake. "Go on, before I foam at the mouth."

Badu steepled her fingers under her chin. "The first was at an inn, a day's ride from Ombaya. I had stayed the night, and was preparing to ride out, well before dawn; my camel was brought from his stall, and I had strapped my pack to the saddle-frame and mounted. Then one of the strap buckles broke off and rolled across the stable floor and into a crack. My annoyance distracted me—I had to make the beast kneel again, so that I could dismount and fetch the buckle. Then I would have to wait for the stable-master to mend or replace the strap. I could foresee hours of delay. What I failed to see was the ready way in which an irregularly-shaped buckle had made its way across the rough floor, and the secure stitching that had held it only minutes before, when I had fastened it.

"So I dismounted and thrust my right hand into the crack where the buckle had gone. Immediately, my fingers were seized in a grip so fierce I thought the bones would break. Then I forgot my pain. For the ring that holds my luck was being drawn from my finger."

Badu raised her right hand. Three of the fingers were ringed, but she tapped one, a gold band set with black stones. "I called fire to my fingertips. I heard a gasp, and my hand was freed. I ran from the stable and around the side, but quick as I went, I was not in time to catch my attacker, and with the dark and the distance, all I saw was a figure in many robes, the muffling garb of the desert folk."

Snake took advantage of Badu's pause to weigh the details of the story. She knew Badu well; she did not need to question her observations. If a strong grip and loose clothing were all she described, then they were all the identification that could be had. "You said the first. There was another attack?"

Badu nodded. "Last night, on the Farmers' Road. The first attempt had made me wary, and I spent little time in posting-houses and inns. Last night I camped in the lee of a hill, off the road, and lit no fire. Perhaps it was the same person. If it was another, then he knew of his partner's failure, though I travelled as fast as ever I have. I had set guarding spells, and placed a few warnings of more humble nature. He avoided the magic and all but one of my other warnings."

"A good one, then."

"Very good," Badu agreed. "And clever, or well-instructed. Instead of falling on me immediately, he began to work a spell to stop my breathing from within. I would have seemed to die in my sleep, unmarked, and no one would connect my death with the alliance proposal. Had I still been asleep, he would have succeeded. But I countered his magic. At that, he switched to a physical attack, and we wrestled. I seized the opportunity eventually to throw him over my hip, and he fled into the night."

Snake frowned. "You say 'he' this time. Are you sure of that, or are you only thinking in Liavekan?"

"Language may seduce my thinking, but not so much as that! I have wrestled with men and with women, and though it's true that I might have been fighting a well-muscled woman with very little fat, I suspect still that my attacker was male. And there were other indications. I have rarely met a woman so big-boned in the wrists, and when I threw him, he threw like a man, as if the center of his weight was high on his body."

"Was he armed?"

Badu rose and went to her pack. From it she drew a felt bundle, which she unwrapped. The contents gleamed softly on Snake's counter: a long knife, slightly curved, its hilt wrapped with many bright colors of leather. The weapon was particular, though not exclusive, to the nomadic tribes of the Great Waste.

"This one also wore desert gear," Badu said. "And his face was covered, so that I could be sure only that he had two good eyes of uncertain color."

"Unfortunately, there are a great many men with two good eyes. When are your birth hours?"

"From four-and-a-half hours after midday, until a quarter-hour into tomorrow."

"And you think someone will try to strike at you here, tonight."

Badu smiled wolfishly. "He would be a fool not to, and I would hate to think I am hunted by fools."

Snake rubbed her forehead. "So my job is to keep you safe while you invest your luck?"

"That's more succinct than I would be, but yes."

"The entire Society of Merchants is more succinct than you'd be. Any hope of some help from you, or is it to be my strong right arm and nothing else?"

"Until I have invested my luck, I cannot help you. As I told Thyan, investiture requires complete concentration. Nor can I supply you with magical defenses, for when my birth-hours begin, all my luck will return to me, and any spells that I have made will disappear."

Snake looked down at her right arm. "Just you and me against the hordes of evil," she said. Then she turned again to Badu. "You can use the living quarters upstairs, anyplace you're comfortable. I'm going out, but I'll be back before you have to begin. Set a warding spell or something around the place until then."

Badu smiled, gathered up her pack, and made her way upstairs.

Snake took her caravan driver's whip from behind the counter and hung its coils over her left shoulder. Then she set out the "momentarily closed" sign and headed for Silvertop's.

Silvertop lived on Street of the Dreamers, which Snake had always taken as proof that the Universe was well-ordered. She met the caretaker on the stairs, and they each touched their foreheads in greeting.

"Ah, Madame Snake," the little man beamed. "You visit your Farlander friend?"

Snake nodded. "Is he well?"

"I think he is never not well. And all else is much better, for there is not anymore the smell."

"Ah," said Snake faintly. "I'm glad to hear it."

"Have the good visit," he said, and trotted down the stairs.

Snake knocked on Silvertop's door and received, as usual, no answer. She went in cautiously.

The room had been intended by the builder as a parlor or sitting room. Its present function would not have been completely described by any word that Snake knew in any of several languages. One wall supported shelves untidily filled with bound books, papers, and scrolls. A badly-stuffed peacock was hung from a beam by one brittle foot. The center of the room was crowded by a long table. Its scarred top was cluttered with objects: feathers, broken pen nibs, a goblet on its side (indications were that it had tipped over and spilled its contents some time ago and the fact had yet to be discovered), a ball of string the size of a small dog, and other things less easily recognized or coped with.

Silvertop sat hunched over this intricate chaos, on an upholstered stool from which stuffing leaked intermittently. He was small and slight and bleached-looking, with his pale Farlander skin and silvery blond hair. When Snake cleared her throat, he glanced up from a random-seeming construction of brass wire, bits of wood, and strips of fabric.

"Oh, it's you," he said cheerfully, and returned his concentration to the table. "Come hold this, will you?"

"Not for the Levar's own treasury," Snake replied. She spotted the back of a chair, resolved to excavate its seat, and moved parchment, boxes, and sheets of copper until it was unearthed. She sat down.

"Have a seat," said Silvertop.

Snake didn't bother to respond.

Silvertop frowned at the ill-assorted mess before him. "Up," he said to it, and the whole thing rose, trembling, to a handspan above the table. From out of an empty space in the middle of the object, a curl of smoke rose. Suddenly every knot and weld and wrapping seemed to give way, and wood and brass wire and fabric strips showered the tabletop.

"Beautiful!" said Silvertop, and turned grinning to Snake. "Did you see that? Beautiful!"

"I'm, ah, glad to find you in such good spirits," Snake said weakly.

"Yep, the best. What can I do for you, Snake?"

All of this made Snake not a little dizzy. Silvertop coherent *and* accommodating? There was not a moment to lose. "I need a guardian spell, for the Tiger's Eye."

He blinked. "I thought you only bought housekeeping spells and things that kept sparks from getting out of the fireplace."

"Special occasion."

He turned and began to scoop through the mess on the table with both hands. "D'you want to keep out everything?"

"No," Snake said, trying not to notice the mummified orange that rolled mournfully off the table in front of her. "I want a spell that will keep anyone from entering the shop by magical means."

He looked disappointed. "That's been done before."

"Yes," Snake sighed, "but not for me."

"Wouldn't you rather have—"

"No."

"Oh, all right. Ah, perfect!" Silvertop held up an old grey glove with all the fingertips worn through. "How long do you want it to last?"

"Make it ten hours," Snake said.

Silvertop held the glove under his nose and began to mumble at it, scowling fiercely. He traced the seams of the glove with a fingernail as he chanted; when he came to the glove's missing finger-ends, his tracing continued, as if to fill in the missing lines of stitching. He groped among the table's contents for a moment without raising his eyes from the glove, bumped into a little stoneware dish and pinched something out of it. (Snake wondered if he had any idea what it was he'd grabbed.) He dropped the powder into the palm of the glove, folded it over, and scrubbed the surfaces together. Suddenly he flung the glove into the air. It glowed blinding blue for an instant, then dropped back into his hands, as grey and gnawed-looking as before.

"There you go," he said, and held it out to her. "Tack it up over the front door, inside."

"And hope no one looks up," Snake muttered. She took it by the cuff, gingerly. It was stiff with age and dirt. "Well, thank you. How much do I owe you?"

"It was pretty easy, that specific and that short a time. Call it a half-levar."

Snake pulled out the pouch and counted a half-levar plus a little, which she knew Silvertop wouldn't notice, into his hand.

"Can you bring the glove back when you're done?" he asked her at the door.

"I wouldn't think of keeping it," Snake said fervently.

"Oh, and—" he said, and stopped.

"Yes?"

"Um, tell Thyan that the…um, the spell didn't work. And I guess you should tell her she was right, too."

Snake laughed. "If I don't, she'll say it herself."

"And it's okay if she wants to come back." He looked embarrassed.

"I'll tell her."

"Thanks, Snake. G'bye." And he shut the door behind her.

Out in the street, she steeled herself and tucked the obnoxious glove in her sash. Late afternoon pedestrians eddied past her. Food cart owners hawked meat rolls, fruit tarts, and stuffed dates to tide their patrons over until dinner. From somewhere around the corner she heard street musicians, fiddle and baghorn and drums. A red-headed woman selling half-copper scandal sheets shouted her tease, which mentioned the names of a famous nobleman and a notorious artist in interesting conjunction. There was something encouraging, Snake found, in the way that Liavek ignored her incipient crisis. She strode back to the Tiger's Eye feeling strengthened.

The shop door opened to her pull, and she felt a sudden fear. Badu hadn't barred it behind her. She stepped forward—and thumped painfully against a barricade of perfect transparency and Badu-like contrivance. "Ouch," Snake said. "It's me."

The barrier began to change at once, from iron to pudding to, finally, air, under Snake's hand. She rubbed her nose and went in.

Badu was in the parlor upstairs. The room occupied most of the front half of the second floor, which made it more or less square. The walls were panelled in scrubbed pale pine to about hip-height; above that was rough whitewashed plaster, relieved by a very few carefully chosen woven hangings and other bits of art. Badu sat on the red patterned rug at a low table, setting out sausage, golden cheese, and two of the peaches.

"The last of the travel food," she said with a wave at it. "Have you any bread?"

Snake fetched it from its box in the little kitchen and settled down across from Badu for a hasty picnic. "Anyone come calling while I was out?"

"Either two people, or the same one twice. The first very nearly did what you did, at the front door. The second tried the latch on the back."

"You didn't get a look either time?"

"It didn't seem prudent to stick my head out the window."

"Mmm." Snake gathered up a second helping of everything to take downstairs. "Here's my plan. I assume you'd be better able to do what you were hired for if you didn't have to dodge assassins while you did it."

Badu nodded.

"Then I'm going downstairs and opening the shop. I can't catch the fellow if we barricade him out."

Snake had made sure to say this when Badu's mouth was full, and she ignored the resulting strangling noises that followed her down the stairs.

As she nailed the revolting glove to the lintel next to the bells, she considered her chances. She was not as confident as she had given Badu to think; still, the assassin would very likely underestimate her and her preparations when he found she'd opened the shop. If she simply kept him out for the night, he would make another attempt on Badu's life soon after, and Snake did not care to live with the burden of unpaid debt that would be hers if he succeeded.

And reasoned arguments aside, she felt a stubborn unwillingness to bar the doors and hide in her own house. Had she wanted to live as a cloistered woman, she would have moved to Ka Zhir and bought a veil.

When she stopped hammering, the noise continued. Someone was pounding on the door. Her whip was still over her shoulder, and she judged the hammer in her hand a nice touch. She unbarred the door.

"Your pardon, sir," she said to the man on the other side, and dipped him a shallow but formal bow. "I was closed for…repairs. Be pleased to honor my shop."

He was shorter than she was, but if he found her height disconcerting, he showed no sign. His features, as well as Snake could see, were Liavekan. He had a thin, high-bridged nose, prominent cheekbones, and

clear, penetrating black eyes; in combination they reminded Snake of the
eagles that swept down on occasion from the Silverspine. The lower half
of his face was hidden by a short black beard that looked, somehow,
unintentional, as if its owner were not quite aware it was there, or hadn't
yet decided what to do with it. He was deeply tanned, and creases fanned
from the outer corners of his eyes. Snake found him handsome and immediately suspect.

He wore a high-necked, long-sleeved blouse and loose trousers the
color of sand, and over these a sleeveless coat that reached to mid-calf
made of black felt richly embroidered. Snake recognized the clothing as
bits and pieces from several nomadic tribes in the Great Waste. She specu-
lated on the weapons that could hang from his belt under the coat.

His step over the threshold managed to convey disdain. Snake wondered what he would think if he looked up and saw the abominable glove.
"I wish to see Badu nolo Vashu," he said in tones of polite command.

Snake heard the little clock on a shelf behind her chime mid-hour,
and realized it was half-past four.

She tilted her head to one side. "I beg your pardon?"

"Badu nolo Vashu," he repeated, and frowned at her. Snake had the
irksome feeling that she was being taken for a servant.

"Very sorry. She's not here."

He raised one eyebrow. "I'm afraid I don't believe you." His voice was
chilly.

"What a pity."

"I'm prepared to see for myself, Madame…"

"Snake," she said with a polite smile and a little nod. "And you, sir?"
She was suddenly and perversely reminded of her presentation party at
the age of fifteen.

His eyes narrowed, and he seemed to study her face. She returned the
stare. "Koseth," he said at last. Snake smiled in what she hoped was a
skeptical fashion. It was a fairly common surname. "May I sit down?" he
added.

"I thought you were about to push past me and search the house."

"I changed my mind."

"Good." She stepped aside, and he went to the hearth and sat in one
of the wicker chairs.

"Can I help you find something?" Snake asked, gesturing vaguely toward the merchandise.

Koseth, narrow-eyed and smiling, leaned back in the chair until the wicker creaked. "So, you say Badu nolo Vashu is not here?"

"I said that."

"Does that mean you're here alone?" he said softly.

"Why do you ask?" At half-past four, Badu had begun the rite of investiture. Could magicians sense these things? Was Koseth a magician? Snake wished mightily that she could ask Badu.

His reply, however, was simply, "To find out how you'd answer. The reason behind any question. And I think I shall be satisfied with 'Why do you ask?' "

Snake wished that he would do something decisive, if he was indeed Badu's nemesis. If he wasn't, she wished he'd quit behaving suspiciously and go away. "I'm sorry, sir, but if you've come neither to look nor to buy, you can go to a cafe to sit. I've work to do."

"No doubt." Clearly, he was not easily provoked.

But she was so startled by his next words that she almost forgot Badu. "Did you know Siosh Desoron, before he died? He had three sons and two daughters. The sons learned their father's trade, which was the out-fitting and managing of caravans, out of duty. But he taught his youngest daughter, Galeme, as well. It was said that she could bring a 'van through the Waste in midsummer, with robbers thick as flies in a barn, and never so much as a broken goblet in all the load.

"Now all that is said of someone named Snake, and the Desorons claim that Siosh had only one daughter. Are you, perhaps, *that* Snake?"

Snake replied, with corrosive emphasis on every word, "What business is it of yours?"

He shrugged.

"There's no secret of it, however much my mother may wish there was. But 'Snake' is quicker to say, so for your convenience, you may leave the Desorons out of it."

He rose and made her a bow. There was a great deal of self-congratulation in his smile, and she felt a surge of anger, at him and at herself. Why had she taken his bait, and what possible good could he get out of it?

She stepped out into the aisle, placing herself where he had to confront her or turn toward the door. He chose the latter. So they both saw the flash of gilded red swoop toward the opening. It was a finch, one of the multitude that lived half-tame on the city's accidental bounty, bright fluttering ornaments on roof peaks and windowsills. It was nearly within the doorframe before it beat its wings furiously, veered, and was gone upward and out of sight.

The face that Koseth turned to her was bland and unreadable; but she had caught a glimpse of it before he'd turned, and his look had been black as the bottom of the sea.

After he left, the shop had a breathless quiet about it. The finch, Snake knew, could have been quite ordinary. She'd had to catch birds before that had gotten in a door or open window and forgotten how to get out. Its sudden change of direction might have come when it saw the two humans blocking the doorway.

Or it might have been a magician, wearing bird-shape to enter the Tiger's Eye, who'd discovered the effect of Silvertop's glove. (Which made her wonder, what *was* the glove's effect? Was it a barrier, like the one Badu had made? Did it return a disguised magician to his true shape? Snake wished she'd asked.) If it was a magician, was it an ally Koseth had summoned, or was it the true danger, and Koseth no threat at all?

The third possibility Snake liked even less: that Badu had two enemies.

It was Snake's custom to keep the Tiger's Eye open until seven o'clock on business days. She managed to hold to that, though seven had never seemed so late. The traffic was lively as people came in to browse before continuing on to their dinners. Many ascended to the status of customer: a young man with curly black hair bought a coverlet woven in a rare antique pattern called "palm leaf shadows," known only to an old woman who lived on the Street of Trees; an elegant-looking man in his thirties knocked over a fat little brass bowl and bought it by way of apology; and a shaven-headed ship's captain, who laughed often and without humor, bought herself a large copper earring.

The little clock chimed seven times, and Snake slumped forward over the counter. Her vigil, she knew, was far from finished. But now she could bar the door and make the Tiger's Eye a fortress. She felt a fleeting longing for previous visits from Badu, when at seven o'clock Snake and Thyan would go upstairs and make dinner, and Badu would entertain them with Ombayan gossip.

Or further back, when Snake was sixteen, and she and Badu had been herd guards one summer in Ombaya... It was dangerous work, and the two of them had worked and fought well together. Snake wished Badu could be at her back now.

She had just slid the bar home when she heard a sound behind her. She turned.

The elegant man, the one who had knocked over the bowl, stepped from behind a tall mahogany cupboard. In his hand was a flintlock pistol, its single barrel pointed unwavering at Snake. He cocked it ostentatiously.

"And now," said Snake, "I suppose you're going to tell me all about how you did it."

He flung back his head and laughed. "I confess, that was my intention. Would you prefer me reticent?"

"Not at all," said Snake. She leaned against the door, trying to look off-balance. "Would you mind starting with who you work for?"

"Ah, no," he said sadly, "I cannot oblige. If you knew that, I would have to kill you. As it is, if you will stay sensibly out of the way, you need take no harm from this at all. My business is with the Ombayan woman upstairs."

"I'm nothing if not sensible," Snake nodded. The whip was heavy on her left shoulder. "So, how did you get in?"

"Just as you saw, when I came in as a customer. Your spell kept me out in bird-form—yes, that was I, and quite a setback you gave me then, too." Snake looked at his red-and-gold-patterned half-robe. The finch had been a reasonable match. "I made other, more subtle attempts, and found that the spell was proof against them all. I was driven at last to make a dangerous experiment. I came in and, after a suitable time, knocked down the charming brass bowl. Your attention was drawn away from me for barely long enough. I was able to duck behind the cupboard and leave an illusion of myself in my place, which then went through the motions of buying the bowl, and left the shop. Had that most excellent spell worked both ways, allowing no magic to cross the boundaries of the house, my illusion would have melted in the doorway, and my last hope for subtlety and stealth would have been gone."

"At the very least, an aesthetic defeat," murmured Snake.

"Now I must ask you to unbar your door, if you please. A representative of…my employer will be along presently to verify the fulfillment of my commission." He spoke as if the words tasted bad. "Those without honor assume everyone else to be without it, as well."

"How true," said Snake absently. Inwardly, she rejoiced. The man who stood before her was only the arrow; the archer was on his way. And it was the one who drew the bow that she wanted to trap. She turned and pulled the bar back, keeping her hands always in sight of the man with the flintlock.

"I don't believe we've introduced ourselves," she said when she turned back.

He looked startled, but made her a sketchy bow. "You may call me Yamodas, Madame, if it please you."

"Not your real name, I assume."

"Alas, no."

"My name is Snake," she said, and began to uncoil the whip from her shoulder.

He frowned. "Madame—Snake—as I told you, you have nothing to gain and your life to lose by opposing me."

Snake smiled and flicked the whip hissing along the floorboards.

Yamodas pulled the trigger.

Into the silence that resulted, Snake said, "I once lost a valuable piece of porcelain in an accident involving a drunken Scarlet Guard and a pistol. I then found that a spell can be bought that will prevent small quantities of gunpowder from igniting. It takes a long time to prepare, and only works in an enclosed space, but the cost is really quite reasonable. I have it renewed annually."

Yamodas sighed, looked regretfully at his pistol, and thrust it into his belt. "I suppose you have a surpassing skill with that whip."

"I do. I could put your eyes out with it, or break your wrist, or strangle you. But I'd rather extend to you the courtesy you offered me. If you swear to give up your present, ah, commission, effective immediately, and if you follow the instructions I'm about to give you, you'll go free and unharmed."

He looked at her measuringly. "I am an honorable man, and I am under a previous agreement."

"Mmm. I'd hate to have to shame an honorable man in the sight of so dishonorable a slug as your employer sounds. But if you don't cooperate, I'll truss you like a chicken and hang you from the ceiling to greet him when he comes in."

"On the other hand, I *have* been paid in advance…"

Not long after, there was a harsh knocking at the door of the Tiger's Eye. Yamodas opened it and bowed low to the man who crossed the threshold. The newcomer had the meaty fatness of a wrestler, insufficiently disguised by a saffron yellow robe and a long blue overvest with a pleated back. He wore an abundance of jewelry—necklaces, pins, bracelets, and earrings—and even sported a gold fillet that bound his red-dyed beard just under his chin.

"Have you killed the Ombayan?" he snapped at Yamodas.

"I have not. I was delayed with the shop owner."

"Hah! The deadly Yamodas, tussling with a shopkeeper?"

"She was rather more than that. I should have been warned."

"We knew nothing about her. If you can't do your own research, you're not worth your price."

"Enough. The Ombayan has had no warning. We will go upstairs now, and you may have your proof first-hand."

The fat man snorted. " 'We' will go nowhere. You were hired to take the risks, and you will take them. I will come nowhere near the Ombayan until she is dead. Go up and do what you were hired for, and call me when you're done."

"As you will," said Yamodas, and went to the back of the shop and through the curtain.

From behind that curtain came a muffled thump, as of a door closing, and the fat man's eyes narrowed with suspicion. He hurried toward the back of the shop.

Snake rose up from behind a display case and snapped out with her whip. It coiled around the fat man's neck and bit deep when she pulled it tight.

He grabbed at the whip with both hands, and Snake prepared to resist his pull. It didn't come. Instead, the leather began to writhe and twist under her hands, and the hard, heavy butt end flexed and fastened itself to her forearm with a many-fanged lamprey mouth.

The fat man uncoiled the lash end from his neck, showing a wine-red angry line where it had cut. He whispered to the end he held and tossed it casually toward Snake. It lashed itself around her knees and clung there.

Laughing, he walked toward her. Snake's hands were still clenched together around her animated whip; she swung them like a club at his temple and connected hard. He staggered back against the display case, which tipped over, spilling jewelry and her attacker onto the floor with a crash. Snake grabbed a small bronze fencing shield off the back wall next to her and jumped at him, hoping to bring the edge down on his throat. But before she could reach him, he raised his arms and shouted. A hail of jewelry pelted her face. The shield was wrenched from her hands.

He pulled her up by her hair, which was painful, until she was standing. "You sow!" he screamed at her. "You are the offspring of a goatherd and his favorite nanny!"

"Make up your mind," Snake said through clenched teeth. If she lived through this, she would have to see if Silvertop knew a charm to keep anyone from ever again enchanting her whip. It had let go its grip on her forearm and twined itself around her wrists. She was beginning to lose the feeling in her fingers.

"You have turned my assassin away from his target, and you have marked me—" Here he jerked her head around, and she could see, in the beautiful silver-framed mirror set with sapphires, his face behind hers. His left cheek was cut open and bleeding, probably from the edge of the display case. "You shall watch yourself die, and know that the Ombayan woman will die next, and you could not protect her!"

He began to chant. Snake cursed at him, struggled, tried to kick and would have bit, had there been anything before her but the silver mirror. She could not break his concentration. He raised his right hand before her face, the little finger delicately extended. The fingertip began to shine like a polished knife. She watched in the mirror as he set the fingertip to her throat and began to draw it across the skin with creeping slowness. A drop of blood welled where the finger touched and trickled down, and the fat man's face behind her, shining with sweat and blood, beamed.

Behind him in the mirror she could see the Tiger's Eye, its precious contents glowing like a loving portrait in the lamplight, the front door open on the empty indigo darkness of Park Boulevard. She couldn't scream—probably part of the fat man's chanting. She hoped Thyan would take good care of the shop.

Then from behind them, where the mirror showed empty air, a voice said, "Ahem."

The fat man dropped her and spun to look, and got Koseth's fist in his face, with the rest of Koseth behind it.

Snake's whip suddenly became a whip again, and fell to the floor around her feet. The fat man, his nose bleeding and his face contorted with fury, flung both arms around Koseth and lifted him off the floor.

Snake vaulted over the fallen display case and rammed both her heels into the fat man's kidneys. He went down. Koseth rolled clear and squatted on the floor, clutching his ribs and looking pale.

"Watch him," he gasped. "He's not done yet..."

Koseth was right. The fat man half-rose and gestured fiercely, screaming something. Snake turned and found the silver-and-sapphire mirror flying off the wall at her. She caught it without bending or breaking the fragile silverwork frame, but it continued to press forward, forcing her slowly toward the fat man.

Then at the edge of her vision she saw Koseth stagger to his feet, raise both hands above his head, and begin to whistle. A ball of black smoke formed between his palms. He flung it at the fat man, and it streamed out like a veil from his hands and wrapped around the fat man's head. The fat man cursed and gestured, and the smoke became a veil in truth, made of black gauze which tore easily in his fingers.

All the force went out of the silver-framed mirror. Snake looked from it, inert and shining in her hands, to the fat man, who had begun to chant at Koseth, and felt hot fury begin to rise in her. He couldn't be troubled to defend himself against her? She set the mirror down against the wall, snatched up the broken-off leg, long as her forearm, from the display case, and advanced upon the fat man.

He was chanting steadily at Koseth, who had dropped, white-faced, to his knees. The room smelled of lightning. Snake jabbed the man in the ribs with the leg. "Hey," she said. He turned.

She clubbed him, and he slid gently to the floor.

After a few moments, she heard Koseth clear his throat. "Not a moment too soon. Oh, I hurt. Did you kill him?"

Snake knelt and rolled the fat man over. There was blood in his hair, but he was still breathing. "No. What shall we do with him?"

"Disarm him." Koseth stood up slowly and limped over to Snake. "Help me strip him."

"Strip him?"

Koseth nodded at the man on the floor. "Something he's wearing or carrying is the vessel of his luck. Do you want him to wake up with his magic to hand?"

They stripped the fat man and piled his clothing and jewelry in a heap in the middle of the shop. Koseth bent over it and began to sing. With one finger, he traced a circle around the pile; when the circle was closed, he straightened up and clapped his hands. With a crack! and a rush of air, the fat man's belongings were gone.

Snake said, "Where—"

"They're on your roof," said Koseth. "I'm afraid I didn't have the strength to send them any farther, but that should keep them the necessary three paces away from him."

"My roof." She shook her head. "Come on, let's tie him up."

Once they had, Koseth ventured out into the night and returned with four uncommonly deferential soldiers of the Levar's Guard and a donkey cart. It took all six of them to hoist the unconscious assailant into the cart.

When the soldiers had gone, Snake went back in the shop and dropped into one of the wicker chairs. She looked up, and found Koseth watching her closely.

"No hysterics?" he said.

"The time for that was when he was killing me."

"I find that's exactly when there *isn't* time for them. I like to have mine later."

Snake laughed weakly. "Let me know when, and I'll join you."

"I would be honored," he said, and bowed.

"Now, make kaf and tell me who you are."

Snake watched him dip water from the jar and set the kettle heating on the hearth brazier. To her surprise, she didn't resent the easy way that he found and used her things—she was content, for now, to sit quiet and be catered to, and Koseth seemed content to cater.

When he at last sat down across the brass table from her, he said, "I didn't lie to you, you know. My name is Lir Matean Koseth ola Presec."

She blinked at him in dawning comprehension. "Which means that you're…"

"The Margrave of Trieth," he finished apologetically.

"The Desert Rat," she said, then added quickly, "Sorry, Your Grace."

He laughed. "Well, I am—or was, until I had to take my seat in the Levar's Council. That was when I became involved with a group of councillors who favored alliance with Ombaya."

Snake sat up in her chair. "Are you telling me you're the person Badu was to meet?"

"I beg your pardon? Oh, yes. I am."

"Why, in the names of any of a hundred gods, didn't you just *say* so?"

"Don't shout. We knew there was opposition to the proposal in the Council. We also suspected that one of those opponents was spying for the Zhir, but we had no way to be sure. I was chosen as the contact, since I wasn't yet publicly associated with the pro-alliance group, and was thus least likely to lead the spy to the Ombayan emissary, or to be a target for him myself."

"You haven't answered my question."

"Madame," he said, exasperated, "how were we to know you weren't in the pay of the spy?"

Snake stared at him. "I think I'm insulted."

Koseth—or the Margrave of Trieth—shrugged. "Oh, when I realized who you were, I knew you were no spy. But by that time, I had other things to think of."

"The finch?"

"Exactly. But I could do nothing except keep a watch on the shop front, and as far as I could tell, all was quiet. Until our fat friend strolled down the street and knocked at your door."

"When you very kindly followed him in and got me off his hook. But why didn't you show up in the mirror?"

"Once, in my misspent youth, I tried to creep up on someone who was standing in front of a mirror. It's made me wary. I cast an illusion, causing the mirror to show everything in the room but me. That's a loophole in your guardian spell, by the way—though you can't enter the house by magic, you can cast illusions back and forth through the doorways."

"I know," Snake said, grinning.

He raised an eyebrow, but went on. "And I needed the element of surprise. I'm no match for the likes of Borlis in a head-to-head duel."

"Borlis?" she hinted.

"Our fat friend is Borlis iv Ronwell, the Count of Seagirt, and a Council member high in the opposition movement."

Snake nodded slowly. "And a Zhir spy," she said.

"Exactly. You smoked out our rat. With my testimony, and yours, if you're willing, the opposition will be discredited, and the alliance proposal will be approved by the Council and sent to the Levar."

The kettle began to rumble on the hearth, and he fetched it back to the table. He poured boiling water over the ground beans, fine as powder, and the thick brown smell of kaf rose into the air between them as it brewed. Then he filled two cups and offered one to her. His hands were large and brown, clean, but calloused and broken-nailed—very much like her own, she realized, after a trading trip.

He looked at her over his cup. "And I suppose that Badu *is* upstairs."

"Mmhm." He opened his mouth, and she continued quickly, "And if you're going to ask why she didn't come down when she heard the fight, the answer is, 'None of your business.' "

"Oh," he said.

"I suppose she'll want to know why we couldn't have saved her life a little more quietly."

He stretched his legs out before him. "A good question. An insightful question. Why couldn't we?"

"If all I sold was rugs, I'm sure we'd have had no problem," Snake said, eyeing the smashed display case ruefully.

"Would it be at all helpful," he said, studying his cup, "if I were to stay around—to help you explain it all to Badu?"

Snake shot a look at him. She rather thought she recognized that tone of voice. "To leave before then, in fact, would be unforgivable," she said at last.

He smiled. "Then I'll be courteous and stay." He lifted his cup. "To a remarkable woman," he said, watching her face.

She smiled. "To a charming rescue."

The porcelain cups chimed like bells.

For the second Liavek anthology, we needed a story that would introduce the world to readers who hadn't seen the first volume. I got the job. This was the result.

—Will

A Happy Birthday
Will Shetterly

Early one morning in the month of Fruit, The Magician stood on a tower that rose over Liavek's Old Town. A late summer breeze bore the smells of the sea, and mingled with a tang of brine were the traces of smoke from cooking fires, the aroma of pot-boils simmering and bread baking in brick ovens. The breeze also brought the cries of seagulls and a healthy murmur of conversation, curses, greetings, laughter, bits of song—all the noises that a successful center of trade and art should produce in early morning. The City of Luck gleamed in sunlight reflected from tiled roofs and painted plaster walls. A slight smile touched The Magician's youthful features. If there was something of wistfulness in that smile, there was contentment too.

A new sound came from behind him, of light footsteps on the stairs. A new smell joined those of morning: a hint of copper and jasmine. Then a woman's body pressed against his back, and her arms embraced him. He felt her stand on tiptoe to kiss his neck, then heard her say, "You're being rather flashy this morning."

He shrugged, a little embarrassed. "I've never seen Liavek from this height."

"I thought you were advertising for clients. Liavek's never seen a tower on Wizard's Row."

"Well, not in a few generations, anyway. Besides, it's only visible to magicians."

He felt the woman nod. "It's beautiful."

"The tower?" The golden cylinder was half-again as high as Mystery Hill, usually the highest point in Liavek.

"No, my vain love. The city." She moved to his side, and he put his arm around her. After a moment, she lifted a hand and said, "Here." She held a box wrapped in silver cloth.

He raised an eyebrow.

She smiled. "Don't pretend you'd forgotten, Trav. You just felt like waking well before noon. You just felt like expending Rikiki knows how much power raising a tower that only people like us can see. Right." Slightly off-key, she sang:

> On each birthday, for the hours
> Mothers labored giving birth,
> Folk receive from unknown powers
> Luck, a gift of unknown worth.
>
> On each birthday, wizards wrestle
> With their birth luck to invest
> Birth luck's power in a vessel
> Granting magic on request.
>
> On each birthday, sad folk wander
> Hoping luck will change their fate.
> Happy folk who will not squander
> Happiness stay home and wait.
>
> Happy birthday, happy luckday,
> May kind fortune follow you,
> Luck's capricious, luck loves patterns.
> May my gift shape luck for you.

She thrust the box at him. "Happy birthday."

With a laugh, Trav set the box on the wall and quickly unwrapped it. Her present's nature was obvious when the first corner of the box was revealed. The sides and bottom were teak, but its top was a tessellated inlay of ivory and rosewood. "It opens?"

She nodded, and her wiry bronze hair bounced about her face.

"Thanks, Gogo. How?"

With a smirk, Gogo slid one of the side panels. "Watch this." The game board tilted up, and shah pieces lay beneath it in felt-lined beds.

Each had been carefully carved and painted, so their living models were easy to identify. One set of pieces stood on bases of enameled Liavekan blue, and the other on Tichenese yellow.

Trav moved his finger across the rows. He touched the figure of a small girl in long robes. "The Levar, dressed as she was on her last official birthday."

"Who else for shah of Liavek?"

He tapped another, a middle-aged man in the red robes of the Faith of the Twin Forces. "And His Scarlet Eminence, the Levar's Regent."

"Of course. Who else for sultana? His reach extends to the limits of the board. I think he'd be flattered."

"I do, too." Trav touched two others, one of himself and one of an old woman who wore her white hair braided about her head. "The Ka'Riatha and me. That's very flattering, but you could've used yourself for a wizard."

"I could've used half a dozen folk. But you've been The Magician for nearly three hundred years; you have to be there. And Granny's the link between the old city of S'Rian and the new one of Liavek."

Trav's finger brushed over the two Liavekan towers, one being the Levar's palace and one Fin Castle, and rested again by a stocky, older woman in a gray uniform and a blue cloak, sitting on a racing camel. "City General D'genli for one warrior." He touched a man astride a white horse. The man's red cape helped identify him, as did two flintlock pistols in his sash, as did two dark scars on either side of his face. "And dear Count Dashif for the other. An interesting choice."

Gogo wrinkled her lip, then said, "Admiral Tinthe would have been more appropriate, but a ship would've taken too much space on the board."

The soldier pieces were a miscellany of Liavekan inhabitants: a ship's captain with a shaven head, a white-robed priest of the Church of Truth, a red-haired Levar's Guard, a gaudily dressed entertainer of indeterminate sex, an elegantly dressed noble carrying a walking stick, a street musician playing a cittern, a slender girl in clothes too large for her, and a tall, attractive woman with a whip coiled about one shoulder. Trav paused by the last. "That's the woman from the Tiger's Eye? Who are the rest?"

"Just folk who caught my eye."

Trav nodded as he scanned the other pieces. "The Emperor of Tichen for the opposing shah; his daughter for sultana. I agree. For wizards, the

Guild of Power's Old Teacher and Young Teacher." He touched the latter. "Someone new has taken the Young Teacher's part."

"Yes. Djanhiz ola Vikili. They say she's more impetuous than Chiano Mefini, but more powerful, too."

Trav laughed suddenly, and pointed. "King Thelm and Prince Jeng of Ka Zhir for Tichenese soldiers! You do have a wicked wit, my love."

She grinned. "Just because they don't know they're pawns—"

"It's a little frightening to see Liavek's opponents laid so neatly out."

"Isn't it consoling to see our defenders?"

"Not really. Well, I suppose." He kissed her and said, "Thank you. I suppose we should go below before my magic fades." In spite of his words, he made no move toward the stairs. "I wonder who'll take part in the next game between Liavek and Ka Zhir?" He glanced at the figure of the Levar's Guard, then looked from the set of playing pieces to Liavek below them. "And I wonder if Tichen's Old Teacher has a similar shah set?"

Bejing Ki, Old Teacher of the Guild of Power, flew over the sands of the Great Waste in the belly of a large red bird made of wicker and painted cloth. Her apprentice, a nomad boy named Chiba, sat before her, peering through the red bird's eyes and guiding its flight with levers that controlled the angle of its wings and tail. Bejing's power had lifted the bird into the air above Tichen, but the former Young Teacher, Chiano Mefini, had designed it so well that Chiba's power was sufficient to propel it forward. The Old Teacher's thoughts were free to drift or plan as the Old Teacher pleased. She tried to anticipate her actions in Liavek, and found she could not.

A cluster of images continued to return to her. She heard Chiano whisper his story, and she saw him gasp and die when he finished. She thought of The Magician, and how weak he would be in less than an hour. Chiano had said that today was The Magician's birthday, when the thing called power by the Tichenese and birth luck by the Liavekans would flee whatever vessel Trav had invested it in and return to his body. And while he labored to reinvest his luck before his birth hours ended, he would have no magic to use on other things. Every spell he had ever cast would have failed. Trav, The Magician of Liavek, would be as defenseless on this day as any wizard can ever be.

A very small girl in a clean, unbleached tunic ran through the Canal District of Liavek's New Town. No one chased her, and she did not seem to chase anyone else, so most people smiled and stepped aside for her. A few frowned and muttered about "children today."

Far ahead of her, two men in the gray of the Levar's Guard walked toward the municipal hall. Both wore light wool capes of Liavekan blue, thrown back from their shoulders since the morning had already begun to grow warmer. One was a tall, stocky man with his hair tied at the nape of his neck; the other was slimmer and shorter with reddish hair, though his complexion was as dark as any Liavekan's. The girl's black eyes widened when she saw them, and she tried to yell, but she was too tired and too far away. Her calls of "Rusty! Rusty! Wait for me, Rusty!" disappeared in the sounds of the street.

The two were about to turn onto the Street of the Dreamers when a dog ran into the red-haired man's legs. He tripped into a rack of costly clothing set beside a shop called Master L'von's. An old man ran from the shop at the sound, then stopped. "I suppose you're trying to flush some damned Zhir counterfeiter from the ladies' undergarments, Lieutenant?"

"No, I—" Rusty pointed toward the dog, but it was gone. "I tripped. Sorry."

" 'S all right." The man and the Guards set up the rack and brushed dust from the clothes. "Nothing hurt but the reputation of the Gray Guards, eh?"

Rusty winced and shrugged. As the man went back into his shop, Rusty said, "Two days counting baubles in a ship that stank like a dragon had died in its hold, just because the Navy's too incompetent to sink a captured pirate. Then our replacements relieve us an hour late. Now this. I swear I—"

The girl ran up to him. "Rusty, Rusty! You gotta come help!"

Rusty squatted to catch her in a hug. "Sessi! What's happened?"

"I was playing ball, and the ball rolled into a street, and it disappeared!"

He laughed. "That's odd, little sister, but it's hardly a catastrophe."

"Yes, it is! It was Kolli's favorite ball, and he won't like me anymore if I've lost it."

Rusty nodded. "All right, Sessi. We'll go find it. Where'd the ball disappear?"

"The ball didn't disappear, Rusty. The street disappeared."

The two Guards glanced at each other. The stockier one scratched his scalp. "Wizard's Row, huh? Want some help, Rusty?"

"No. It's probably there now." He stood, touched his forehead in salute to his friend, and began to walk away with the girl. Suddenly, he spun and said, "Stone! What's today?"

"I dunno. Rainday, I think."

Rusty nodded. "Lost track on that inventory job. Tell Captain Bastian I'm taking the day off!"

"She won't like that."

"Tell her it's my birthday present. I'm going to help Sessi find her ball, then I'm going home to hide for the next five hours."

At mid-morning, 17 Wizard's Row was a square, two-story structure of yellow brick. Its front door was oak, with brass fittings which included a large gargoyle's head with a lolling tongue. Two very dark men and a very tall woman approached wearing dusty, hooded robes of the clans of the Waste. One reached to pull the gargoyle's tongue, and it snapped at his hand. The man stepped back, glancing in surprise at his companions.

The gargoyle said, "Go away. We're busy today."

The man hesitated, then said nervously, "We've traveled far. We want to see The Magician."

"Want all you will," the gargoyle said. "But want somewhere else."

The shorter man, who stood to one side, moved suddenly for the handle. The gargoyle's head swung toward him. It began to step out of the oak as though it had only been lying in a pool of water, but the woman touched the gargoyle's neck with a carnelian ring. The gargoyle halted immediately, a bas-relief of a beast with its chest and front claws lunging from the door.

"How long will that hold him, Young Teacher?" said the shorter man.

"Long enough," said the woman, tugging on one of the gargoyle's paws. The door swung silently open.

A dark hall lay beyond, with light splashed at the far end from another room. Djanhiz ola Vikili, Young Teacher of the Guild of Power, remembered what she had learned when she had invaded this house under Chiano Mefini's direction: 17 Wizard's Row was inhabited by the guard they had just passed, two cats, and two humans: Trav The Magician and Gogo. The guardian at the door, whether demon, god, or eccentric magician, was now trapped by a spell which could check earthquakes and tidal waves. Protective spells hid the three intruders from the cats' senses. The hours of The Magician's birth had begun, so all of Trav's power and training were turned to reinvesting his birth luck before those hours ended. Only Gogo remained to face the combined skill of three sorcerers of the Guild of Power.

The taller man completed a simple illusion so that passers-by would see The Magician's door closed. Djanhiz nodded her approval. The shorter man said, "Done," and Djanhiz felt a mystical tether about her waist, linking her to the street like a diver or a climber. If the house suddenly traveled away from Wizard's Row, her companion's spell would snatch them out of it.

Rumor held that others had entered this house uninvited. None had left of their own choice. Some, it was said, had not left at all. The three Tichenese walked slowly down the hall, using every sense to search for traps. Djanhiz found many, and since The Magician's would have failed when his birth-time began, these had to be Gogo's. The Young Teacher's respect for her increased with each guardian spell she unravelled. Half of The Magician's reputation might have come from Gogo's efforts.

At the end of the hall, Djanhiz peered into the open door of a small office. A short, slender woman in a green shift sat facing a slim man who lay on a wicker couch, his body covered with a light sheet for warmth or ritual purposes. The Magician's eyes were closed, as if he slept or medi- tated. Gogo's lips moved as though she were singing, and her gaze re- mained focused on The Magician. Neither gave any sign that they were aware of the three intruders.

The shorter Tichenese whispered, "Why is she here? Investiture is private."

Djanhiz said in her usual speaking voice, "You don't see it?"

"No," the man admitted, with a hint of shame.

"How old is The Magician?"

"Two centuries, at least."

"And does he have some artifact of power to keep him alive when his age returns to his body with his birth luck?"

"He must, if he has lived—" The short man glanced at Gogo, who still chanted silently. "He trusts her? Another magician?"

The man's voice went loud with surprise, and Djanhiz laughed. "Ob- viously. Perhaps he pays her so much that he thinks she cannot be bribed. Perhaps she is so powerful that he does not expect an enemy's spell to bend her will to learn his weaknesses, and perhaps she is so determined that he thinks torture could never break her will. Perhaps they love each

other so much that they trust each other without other considerations. It
is very romantic, isn't it?"

The taller man spoke for the first time. "Yes."

"And it is a shame that they are our enemies," said Djanhiz. "Yet Liavek's
growth must be at Tichen's expense. So we must check that growth with
a few careful prunings."

She touched Gogo's back with the carnelian ring.

As Rusty walked up Healer's Street with the girl's hand in his, he said,
"You play up here often?"

"Uh huh."

"You shouldn't."

"Uh huh."

" 'Course, I suppose that's why it's so much fun."

"Uh huh. Look! It's there now! Wizzer's Row!"

"Of course. If you'd gone back on your own a little later, it probably
would've been there."

"Uh uh. It's 'cause you're in the Guard, Rusty."

He laughed. "Right, kid."

This section of Old Town was never as busy as other districts of Liavek,
for most of the trade was across the Cat River in New Town, by the docks
and in the Merchant's Quarter. Old Town's life centered on Temple Hill
and Mystery Hill, and in the bustling old market between them, the
Two-Copper Bazaar. But Wizard's Row almost always seemed deserted,
or so Rusty thought. It was never the same, but it was usually quiet, often
mysterious, almost always awesome. Some of the buildings were so common as to be unnoticeable. Others were constructed in impossible ways,
and some of impossible things. One house seemed to be made of living
birds who flew about in a pattern that always shaped a house, though the
style and size of the house shifted with the flight of the birds.

"Where's the ball, Sessi?" He wondered if his nervousness carried to
her.

"I dunno." She began walking down Wizard's Row, peering into every
yard. "Maybe it went to see someone."

"I doubt that." He spotted a battered white ball in front of a gate
midway down the street. "That it, Sessi?"

"Yayyy, Rusty!"

He released her hand, and they ran for the ball. He laughed again, forgetting his nervousness. As they came close to it, Sessi said, "Rusty, look!" He glanced where she pointed, at a house unharmed by the flames that surrounded it. His foot came down on the ball. He fell, barely catching himself, and the ball scooted into the nearest yard. Looking up from the ground, Rusty saw a brass gargoyle on the door and the number seventeen above the lintel.

"I been here before," Sessi whispered.

Rusty set his hand on her shoulder. "Yes. The Magician's. He sent you to live with Mom and Dad, thinking they had no children."

"I like him. He's got cats."

"I suppose so," he answered, and the conversation suddenly seemed very strange. "Well. Let's get the ball and go, hey?"

"Sure, Rusty." The girl ran along the flagstones. She reached for the ball, then straightened up, leaving the ball where it lay. "Something's funny about the door."

"I'm sure it is, kid." He grabbed the ball.

Sessi stood before the brass gargoyle. She reached out to pat its nose, and before Rusty could stop her, her hand passed through the illusion. She gasped. "Something's wrong, Rusty!"

"I know," he said carefully, moving toward her. "It's my birthday. I should be asleep in my own bed. I should be reading a good book at my apartments. I should not be on Wizard's Row, trespassing on The Magician's lawn. Let's—"

Sessi stepped through the illusion of The Magician's door.

"I hate kids," Rusty whispered. He breathed deeply, touched his short sword with the back of the hand holding the ball, and entered 17 Wizard's Row.

For Trav, several things happened so quickly that he could not place them in order. His thoughts were of investiture, of coercing his birth luck into his favorite vessel. The birth luck struggled against his will, as it always did, but he felt himself close to success. Then Gogo seemed to start, or maybe her abrupt cessation of motion only seemed to have begun with a tiny movement, the slightest anticipation of surprise. Her words ceased, and so did the flow of power from her spell of youth. The sky fell upon him, as if it would crush him into the sofa. His attempt at investiture collapsed. The birth luck returned to his helpless body, but he did not have the strength to try to use it.

The light in the room grew dimmer, then disappeared just as three shadows seemed to appear. His mouth fell open, but he could not speak. He lay motionless. Something in his mind shrieked in fear. Something else said, *This is death. Accept it.*

In the crowded office, the three Tichenese sorcerers looked at the withered thing that was The Magician. "He still breathes," said the short man.

"For a while," Djanhiz said.

"He has all his teeth," the short man said. "I'd think that he would lose his teeth."

"He took very good care of them."

"Ah." They listened to Trav's slow breaths. "I could smother him," the short man offered.

"No," the tall man said.

"No," Djanhiz agreed. "We are not murderers."

The short man looked at her in surprise, then covered his surprise and said nothing. The tall man spread his fingers wide before them. "Our hands are hardly clean."

"No," Djanhiz agreed. "Nor am I proud of this. But I will be proud of success." She glanced at The Magician. "I wonder if he still lives because his birth luck is within him? Or if it is only that death has not yet recognized its opportunity?"

"Does it matter?" said the smaller man.

Djanhiz shrugged. "No. He cannot live much longer. We will wait."

The hall was dark, lit primarily by light reflected from a far room. The illusion of the closed front door remained inside the house; either the magic that created it also blocked light, or it preserved the illusion *very* thoroughly. Rusty walked in, wanting to tiptoe in hopes of leaving undisturbed and wanting to stomp so the residents would know he did not come as a thief or an assassin. He opened his mouth to call Sessi's name.

Movement toward the middle of the hall proved to be the girl, huddled against a door. Her motion was the bringing of her finger to her mouth for silence. In spite of himself, he obeyed as he came up to her. He reached for her shoulder to grab her and take her away when he heard Tichenese voices from The Magician's study.

That was not odd. Many Tichenese lived in Liavek, and many visited for reasons of politics or trade. The Tichenese embassy was not far from here. Rusty had spent a year in Tichen; he respected the people and their culture. He also knew enough of their language to be surprised when a woman said, "Chiano Mefini failed the Empire, but we will not. Indeed, The Magician's death restores glory to his name."

"Perhaps," a man said. "What of the woman?"

"We will let her live. Perhaps she will inherit The Magician's title. It will be good for the head witch of this little nation to have known failure at Tichenese hands."

"And now?"

"Now we wait. I've completed a spell to ensure privacy. No one, wizard or other, will be able to enter the house until one of us leaves."

Happy birthday to me, Rusty thought.

Danger or caution or surprise had left him unable to do more than listen. Still considering the implications of the woman's words, Rusty mimicked Sessi's gesture and prayed she would understand to be silent. He tugged Sessi's shoulder. She shook her head, but when he tugged again, she began to follow.

Halfway to the door, a floor board creaked under his sandal.

Three people in bulky robes raced into the hall. One whirled, pointing back into the study and saying to another, "Very well. Kill The Magician."

Rusty pushed Sessi toward the door. "Run!" Would anyone's departure cause the woman's spell to fail? If so, Sessi could bring someone back... Rusty felt her ball still in his hand, so he flung it hard down the hall at the head of the Tichenese returning to The Magician's office. It hit, and the man fell, and Rusty praised his birth luck.

Rusty spun to flee, and something seemed to envelop his legs. Sessi stopped before the door, crying, "Rusty!"

"Go on!" he shouted at her. He drew his sword, knowing that steel was useless against wizards. "Run, Sessi! Get help!" The woman who seemed to be the Tichenese leader walked toward him. She smiled grimly as she raised a carnelian ring.

He slashed at her hand. She dodged, laughed, and said something quickly, and his sword arm was caught in whatever held his legs. Watching the ring approach his chest, he yelled again, "Run, Sessi! Get out! Get help!"

At the edge of his vision, he saw Sessi leap through the illusion of the closed door. Too many people had passed through it, or perhaps it was meant to fade when someone left the house. The spell dissolved, and the hall brightened with admitted sunlight.

The tall male Tichenese caught Sessi halfway down The Magician's walk. She screamed and kicked in his grasp, and he carried her back with difficulty.

The Tichenese woman turned her hand to touch Rusty's chest with her palm rather than the ring. "What have you gained, Liavekan? A moment of time, and nothing more." Casually, she tapped Sessi with the ring as the tall man passed, and the girl stiffened in his grasp.

"Damn you—"

"No," the woman said, touching his lips with her finger. "You've been nuisance enough. I'll restore my spell about this house, and then—"

A small red bird glided through the open door.

The Magician wrestled with the question of what had happened to him, to his house, to Gogo, to Gogo, to Gogo… Something in him said, *Live! For her, live!* And something answered, *How? I'm old, old—* He tried with one supreme effort to raise himself, for no reason that he could think of, and he felt pain in his chest.

He relaxed then, and the voice that said, *Die now, Trav, die gracefully, for it's time,* was pleased. It said, *Yes. Accept this. It's been a good life.* And the voice that said, *Live, Trav! Live for her, for yourself, for your city!* was pleased. It said, *Yes. Don't struggle. Save your strength. Relax. Breathe shallowly. Be still. Think. You are The Magician of Liavek, Trav Marik. Survival is success. Survive.*

As Rusty watched, two tiny things leaped from the stiff red bird. They landed on the hall tiles, becoming an old Tichenese woman and a nomad boy, both dressed in dark blue robes. The boy immediately ran to pick up the bird, which seemed to be a toy of lacquered paper. The three Tichenese in desert robes bowed very low to the old woman, the tallest man first placing Sessi carefully on the floor. Rusty thought the old woman must be their leader, come to view their success.

He began to wonder if this was true when the young Tichenese woman said, "Teacher, this is not your concern. I—" The old woman gestured for silence, then turned slightly away to accept the toy bird from the boy.

As it began to shrink even smaller in the old woman's palm, the young woman snapped her carnelian ring toward the old woman's side.

Rusty grabbed the young woman's wrist with his free left hand. She exhaled loudly, almost a bark, in frustration or annoyance that she had forgotten he was not completely bound. The old woman placed the red bird in her pocket and smiled at them both. For a moment, Rusty wondered why he had acted when he was not sure of the players, and whether he had done the best or the worst he could do by acting.

The old woman flicked her hands as if flinging water from them. The three Tichenese in desert robes disappeared. Tiny things like black beads lay where each had stood. The nomad boy gathered the three beads and presented them to the old woman. She nodded to Rusty, and suddenly his limbs were free. "Thank you," she said. Before he could reply, the woman and the boy entered The Magician's office.

Power coursed suddenly about Trav, as though he were immersed in a pool of the raw essence of magic. His eyes opened. Cool air filled his lungs. He smelled foreign scents, of perfume and sweat. He sat up, starting to reach out about him to learn where he was, and then he could see. Shapes resolved themselves in instants. Gogo sat before him with an expression of desperate relief.

He caught her, or maybe he threw himself into her arms; he could not tell. After a moment, he looked around his office and saw they were not alone. An old woman watched with something like cold approval on her face. She wore a silk robe of a blue that seemed darker than black, and after a second, Trav recognized her. He released Gogo to lean forward in a deep bow, bringing the fingers of both hands to his forehead. "Bejing Ki, Old Teacher of the Guild of Power. I would never have expected mercy from you, though I thank you for it."

The woman's face wrinkled into a smile. "Trav The Magician. This is not mercy; this is an attempt to restore honor. You must forgive me."

"If you will explain what has happened," Trav said carefully, "I think I will forgive anything."

"Explanations later," Gogo said. "We have an investiture to complete."

The old woman lifted both eyebrows. "You hope to succeed, with so little time remaining?"

"He is The Magician," Gogo replied.

Trav set his hand on Gogo's. "And I have friends."

In the hall, Sessi suddenly leaped up, crying, "Rusty, what—" He caught her. " 'S all right, Sessi. I think. C'mon, let's—"

A short, scowling, dark-haired man in a green tunic stood by the front door. The man touched both hands to his forehead and bowed low. "He says you're owed an explanation, too. I don't think so. Come."

"Who's he?" Reluctantly, Rusty sheathed his short sword.

"The Magician, of course. Owes me an explanation first. No matter. Come."

The man opened one of the many hall doors, gesturing them into a sitting room, then brought refreshments and left again. Sessi whispered, "That's the door thing."

"The servant?"

She nodded with certainty, then began to feast on honeycakes and lemonade. A gray and white cat hid under her chair, as though it had not decided whether it approved of these visitors. A cream-colored cat climbed onto Rusty's shoulder, where it purred contentedly, occasionally drooling.

The sullen man opened the hall door again, and the old Tichenese woman and the boy entered. Rusty stood to salute in the southern fashion, and the two bowed. "An explanation soon," the woman said. The gray and white cat brushed against her ankles, and she smiled.

Half an hour passed, while Rusty and Teacher Ki talked of Tichen and Liavek and the importance of free trade. Sessi and the boy found a shah set. Ignoring the board, they improvised some game with its pieces, and bits of their conversation occasionally interrupted that of the adults: "An' the whip lady says, 'Hi, Master Emperor, I like sausages and beans a lot!'"

Trav, Gogo, and the scowling man returned. Trav made introductions: "Mistress Gogoaniskithli and Master Didieskilor…"

"Gogo and Didi will suffice," Gogo said.

"For her," said the scowling man.

"…Lieutenant Lian Jassil and his sister by adoption, Sessi Jassil…"

"Hi," said Sessi.

"…Mistress Bejing Ki, Teacher of the Guild of Power, and Chiba of the Tilandre clans."

The Old Teacher nodded. "I owe all of you an apology, I fear." She opened her hand, showing three dark beads. "These hold the souls of my

Young Teacher, Djanhiz ola Vikili, and two of her aides." She glanced at Trav. "How much shall I tell before these outsiders?"

"Enough to explain what has happened."

"Very well." The three beads disappeared, and the woman laced her fingers in her lap. "Some time ago, the previous Young Teacher, Chiano Mefini, laid a trap for The Magician. It failed, but in the course of events, he learned several of The Magician's secrets. The Magician allowed him to live, after he took a vow on his life and luck never to reveal those secrets."

"A vow which he seems to have broken."

"Not by choice, Trav The Magician. There are factions in the Guild of Power, as there are factions in any group. Djanhiz led the most radical of those. When Chiano returned to Tichen in disgrace, he gave up the title of Young Teacher, left our Guild, and turned his attention from the study of magic to the study of science. Djanhiz had accompanied him to Liavek, and she knew that he had learned more about The Magician than he had said, so she forced a spell of compulsion upon him, and he told her all he knew."

"It was not his fault, then."

"Perhaps not. Perhaps he thought if he had been more careful, he would not have been trapped by her. He escaped from the trap she had left him in, and came to me. After he told me what had happened, he willed his death."

"I am sorry."

"As am I. Still, I came to preserve our honor, if I could. You needn't worry about your secrets, Trav The Magician. My apprentice and I have both taken the same vow that Chiano took. So long as Liavek and Tichen are rivals, we will be your opponents, but we will not use Chiano's knowledge against you."

The Magician nodded. "Thank you. What of the three who attacked us?"

"I will take them to Tichen, where they will have a choice. They will each bind their luck forever into a thing of my choosing, and they will accept a magical compulsion to never tell what they know of you. If they do not, I shall transform them into beads again, and throw those beads into the ocean."

"I see."

Rusty said, "You both seem rather trusting, for enemies." All the magicians in the room stared at him, and he said, "Um, I mean—"

Trav said, "Please. Rivals."

Bejing Ki laughed. "You are not a magician, Lieutenant Jassil. You wonder what honor is among magicians? I will tell you this. We may have too much power for any human to wield. Even young Chiba could, with time and great effort, call tidal waves or hurricanes. There are not many in the world of our power, but there are enough. If wizards did not accept constraints, a war of magicians could destroy the world. You understand?"

Rusty nodded slowly.

"I can think of no proper reward for your part in this, Lieutenant Jassil," the old woman said. "But gold is usually appreciated." She drew a purse from the pocket of her robe and gave it to him. "As for your adopted sister, you may tell your parents that Bejing Ki will sponsor her at any of Tichen's universities, when she is of age."

"Thank you." The explanation seemed to be at an end, so Rusty stood and took Sessi's hand. "I don't think we deserve your gifts, or if we do, it's only because I was too stupid to stay in on my birthday, but—"

"Your birthday?" The Magician said.

"Yes. Every fourth of Fruit. Thank the Twin Forces the next is a year away."

"Today is the third."

Rusty stared. "But all the coincidences!" He hesitated, then said, "The secret that these people learned was that today is your birthday."

The Magician nodded.

"I won't tell anyone."

"I know."

"Then I was affected by your luck, not my own? That's incred—"

"No," said Gogo. "I can still feel birth luck in this room, and Trav's birth hours have ended."

Rusty looked at every face in the room.

Sessi smiled shyly. "Do I get a present?"

No, I haven't the faintest idea why Liavek should have inspired me to write a Georgette Heyer novella. But I'm very pleased that it did. This may be the only Regency romance I'll ever do.

— *Emma*

The Well-Made Plan
Emma Bull

The year was waning graciously, as years will in Liavek. Out of a jewel-box of seasons, late autumn brought a rich cascade of topaz mornings, carnelian afternoons, and opulent sapphire-blue evenings. On just such an evening early in the month of Fog, Lir Matean Koseth ola Presec, Margrave of Trieth, was strolling south on Park Boulevard, bound for the Tiger's Eye.

He was full of contrary, contradictory urges, and they fascinated him. His pace, for example: He had no appointments and the twilight was pleasant, almost narcotic. Yet he had to shorten his step constantly, or he would have been striding down the wide street, his embroidered black coat swirling around him in a self-made breeze.

The whitewashed walls of the Tiger's Eye were aglow with the last reflected light of the sky, its two front windows and open door golden with lamplight. The sight conjured its own set of contrary impulses, and these, too, he examined. Here was his destination, and it called to him as his own townhouse never did. Yet he also wanted to turn and saunter away, to come back tomorrow, perhaps. Now, why? Simple contrariness, perhaps, the desire to prove his independence to himself. But if that was all, why was there a school of darting minnows in his stomach?

At the door, he smelled a rich waft of jasmine, and envisioned suddenly what he might find inside—the shop's proprietor, back from her long buying trip, unpacking perfumed oils or incense and stacking them neatly on shelves. Her hair would still be bound in a scarf to keep the road dust out of it, but a strand would have escaped into her eyes, and she would brush it aside with the back of her wrist...

Koseth stepped into the doorway and saw, with a wave of irritation, nothing of the kind. Thyan, the shop assistant, was scooping dried jasmine from a jar into a cone of paper. There was none of the commotion and clutter that attended a return from a buying trip, and, most telling, no proprietor.

"She's not back yet?" he asked, to be sure.

Thyan frowned judiciously at the level of jasmine in the cone and said, "Hullo, Your Grace. You mean Snake?"

"Yes, I mean Snake."

"Not yet, but I expect her back any day."

"You've said that since last Rainday." Then it was his turn to frown. "She's not overdue, is she?"

Thyan looked at him oddly, and twisted the paper cone closed. "No. She's doing a route through the Waste, and there's a lot that can come up."

He knew that, of course. He had spent years in the desert that lay between Liavek and Tichen, before the title came to him and he had to return home and tend it. What he felt, he decided, was restlessness brought on by the season's change, the loose-ended feeling of being between the Last of Wine and Festival Week.

"Hullo!" called a large, rough-edged male voice from the back of the shop. The back door boomed, the cotton hanging on the back wall swept aside, and Silvertop, the young wizard who tutored Thyan, poked his head in. Silvertop seemed never to have grown into his voice; he was small and slender, white-skinned and pale-haired, with narrow shoulders and features as delicate as a court lady's. But his voice, at least, was a magician's.

"*Most* people use the front door," Thyan scolded at him, but she smiled, too. Koseth was amused at the shyness that seemed to bloom suddenly in her. Surely he'd never seen Thyan shy with anyone else?

Koseth could tell nothing from Silvertop's behavior, but then, he never could. Away from his magics, Silvertop never seemed to know where to put his hands and feet. Now he shrugged, and said, "I was coming from Cat Street, so the alley was closer. Your neighbors are having lamb for dinner."

"Well, I'm having sausages, so if you want to eat here, get that wistful note out of your voice," Thyan replied.

"Oh, good. I let the stove go out again at my place."

Thyan rolled her eyes, and Koseth coughed to hide his smile. It was no use to suggest Silvertop get someone in to keep house for him—he would complain that strangers got in the way of his work. And—Snake had told Koseth the story—the cookshop a few doors down from Silvertop's lodgings refused to deliver his meals anymore. Thyan, as Silvertop's emissary, had explained that the elephants had only been an illusion, and a mistake at that, a spell that Silvertop had forgotten to undo that had been brought to life when the door was opened, and the hall light met the light from the window. But the cookshop would not deliver.

And when, Koseth wondered with a start, *did I grow so close to these people?*

Until he'd coughed, Silvertop hadn't seemed to notice him, or at least, hadn't noticed that he was Koseth. Now he turned his pale gray gaze up and said, "Glad you're here."

Koseth raised his eyebrows.

"That is, I was going to come to see you tomorrow. About…about clothes."

"Clothes." Koseth had never seen the least sign that Silvertop thought about clothing, beyond recognizing that he should wear some.

"Yes. I wanted to ask you, um, where you get yours made."

Koseth opened his mouth to ask Silvertop what in the name of luck he was playing at. Then he remembered Thyan's sudden shyness, and stopped. Romance had a way of changing a man's habits, and it wasn't impossible that Silvertop should want to impress Thyan with his elegance. And Silvertop was regarding him with such a curious mixture of intensity and dread.

"A lot of places, actually," Koseth said at last. "But not many that are…moderately priced."

"What about Bright Needle?" Thyan spoke up. "And they're not far from you, on Street of the Dreamers."

Silvertop shot her a quick, blind look, as if he'd forgotten she was there. "Maybe," he said, turning back to Koseth, "if I could…describe the coat to them. Do you mind if I, well, study it?"

Koseth blinked. No, this was all too odd to be put down to young love. Silvertop was up to something. But whatever it was, Thyan was clearly not in on it. Better, perhaps, to pry it all out of Silvertop out of her hearing. He nodded, and Silvertop stepped around Koseth to stand behind him.

"You've got something in your hair," Silvertop said. "Hold still."

Koseth felt something stir the hair at the base of his skull; then Silvertop came around his other side and handed him an olive leaf. Koseth raised an eyebrow. The young magician's eyes met his, but not comfortably.

"I'll see you tomorrow," Silvertop told Thyan, heading for the door.

"But you just—I mean, dinner!" Thyan wailed.

Koseth, too, made for the door. But once in the street, Silvertop had begun to run, and Koseth didn't care for the idea of chasing him like a City Guard after a thief. He turned back into the Tiger's Eye.

"If he does come back tomorrow," Koseth said sternly, "tell your young man that I'd like to speak with him."

"My young man?" squeaked Thyan. She cleared her throat. "He's no young man of mine. I mean, not if that's what you mean. He's a bubble head. And I wouldn't have him if he *was* interested. So there." She turned, abruptly, to fuss with the contents of a shelf.

He smiled. "There's an old S'Rian proverb: A long 'no' is the surest 'yes.'"

She shot him her fiercest scowl.

"All right, I'll go," he laughed, and raised his hands as if to ward her off. "If Snake comes back, tell her I was here."

He strode out and back up Park Boulevard, humming softly. The stars were out, thick as frost on a mountain meadow, and the wind was fresh. He paused just inside the Levar's Park to listen to two women playing cittern and wooden whistle, and to leave them a few coins. The path along Lake Levar was empty and silent, and for a moment he felt a wary itch between his shoulder blades. He ambled around a blind corner, faded quickly back into an oleander hedge, and waited. But he heard no footfalls, and saw no shadows moving but those of the leaves that tossed gently on the sea wind.

He shook his head and smiled at himself. He'd spent too many years as the Desert Rat, it seemed, to settle easily into the peaceful life of the Margrave of Trieth. He walked the rest of the way to his townhouse, just off Gold Street on the Boulevard of Summers Past. His butler opened the door before he reached it, his coppery face pleated with a hundred wrinkles by his smile.

"Welcome home, Your Grace," he said, and pressed his palm to his forehead. "There is a gentleman to see you."

It was late, but not unconscionably late, for company. "Has he been waiting long?"

"No, Your Grace, only a few minutes. I made him comfortable in your study."

"Thank you, Maseka. Will you bring us tea there, please? The Crown of Suns blend?"

"Certainly, Your Grace." Maseka touched his brow again and left him, crossing the courtyard to the kitchen archway with a stately tread.

Koseth shook his head and smiled. *There's more gracious nobility bred into Maseka's big toe than into all of my scruffy self,* he thought. The leathery leaves of the sweetbay rustled over his head, an appreciative audience. The night sky was blue-black, and the three sides of the house and the front street wall made it a square-cut dark jewel splashed with sparkling highlights of stars. *Scruffy or not,* he smiled up at the sweetbay, *I wouldn't change places with anyone in the world tonight.*

The study was on the ground floor of the left-hand arm of the house, with windows on the street and the courtyard. The latticed inner shutters had been closed over all of them for the evening, and the room was rich with the light and smell of the lamps burning scented oil.

The man who rose and bowed deeply to him was in his early twenties, his bearded face very dark. He wore a long cinnamon-colored robe, drawn up and tucked under his sash on one side for easier walking. Beneath that were full black trousers, tied at the ankles on the outside of his soft, low-heeled boots.

Koseth returned the bow. "You bring grace to my home," he said in the shared language of the watering places in the Waste. "I am the Margrave of Trieth. How may I serve you?"

The young man gave a little shake of his head; then he crossed the floor quickly, took Koseth's hands, bent, and pressed his forehead to them. He looked up, smiling. "Great Lord," he said, "you already have."

Koseth laughed and slid back into Liavekan. "Unless you're not what you seem, there are no great lords in this room." The young man looked startled. "Sit, and tell me your name." Koseth dropped into an ebony chair, and the young man sat carefully on its mate.

"My name is Hama, Great L—I am sorry, Your Grace, is it?" Koseth nodded. "And I think you will always be a great lord to the clans of the northern Waste."

Koseth studied his visitor's face more closely. Yes, his features showed the mixture of clan and Tichenese blood that was sometimes found on the northern edge of the Great Waste. But shared blood was no symbol of peace there. Tichen claimed much of the Waste for its empire, and it was the northern clans that most often brought the opposing viewpoint to the provincial governors, usually with fire and steel.

Hama looked down at his twined fingers, then turned his solemn stare on Koseth. "I was fifteen when you led the Casoe and Longfinger clans against the garrison at Well of White Flowers."

It was a pretty name when translated, as Hama had, into Liavekan. Koseth had once thought it pretty in Tichenese, too. "I don't know what seven years of songs have done to the truth," Koseth sighed, rubbing the space between his eyebrows. "But that was not a night of heroism and honor."

Hama looked startled again, before his face closed up completely. "My father died that night."

"I hope he was an exception. The garrison commander treated the clans like a horse he meant to ride to death. Once the clansfolk were inside the fortifications…" Koseth found his eyes drawn by the flames in the grate. "They had too many scores to settle," he finished softly.

There was a gentle knock at the study door, which made Hama jump. "My butler," Koseth said, "with tea."

Maseka brought the tray in and set it on a little round table between them. The pot and handleless cups were the pale azure-green of a summer morning's sky. When Maseka had gone, Koseth poured for his guest.

Hama accepted the cup and sipped hesitantly. "Whatever may be the truth of that night, I and mine have owed you a debt since then. I came here only to tell you that I will pay it back."

"A long way to come to pay a debt."

"The turning of luck has only now brought me to Liavek. Could I have come sooner, be sure I would have."

Koseth smiled. "You owe me no debt. Or if you do, pay it by getting rich and helping your people."

"Perhaps," he said, almost to himself. He set down his cup and rose gracefully. "It is late. I am trying your hospitality sorely."

Koseth shook his head, stood, and bowed. "Come again as your heart bids or luck wills it," he said in the trade language of the Waste.

The young man bowed and left.

Koseth sat for what seemed a long time, staring into the fire, before Maseka knocked and came into the room again. "Olduv has your dinner ready, Your Grace."

"Thank you, Maseka." Yes, easier to be the Margrave of Trieth. No one would have waited dinner for the Desert Rat. "I'll eat in here."

"Very good."

"Oh, and I won't be going out again tonight. Tell the staff to take the evening off."

Maseka beamed and touched his butler's rod to his forehead. "Thank you, Your Grace. I shall."

Koseth woke the next morning to wholesale discomfort and the conviction that he didn't know where he was. For a moment he wondered if he'd fallen asleep on the low couch in his study.

Then he realized he could see the ceiling above him, and knew he was nowhere in his townhouse. Olduv would have taken his own life before he let a cobweb reach such a size. And Koseth was sure that no one in his household would keep a rather plucked-looking stuffed peacock hanging upside down from a crossbeam.

He felt—not weak, precisely, but fragile. He reached to rub his eyes, and stopped, horrified, when his hand came into view.

It was the wrong color.

He sat up, and a wave of dizziness made his vision fold in the middle like a sheet of paper. He clutched the edge of the—probably cot—he lay on, waited for the vertigo to pass, and dismissed explanations as quickly as he thought of them. Drugs, illness, madness—none of them could explain the sight of his hand made small and slender and pale as milk. Pale as...

He looked down at himself, stretched out on a cot, covered with a worn wool coverlet. He pulled that back. The body that reason said was connected to his head was also small, slender, and pale, with a surprising quantity of white-gold hair on the torso and legs. He took very little comfort from knowing that he was still male. In fact, it only fed a growing suspicion.

This time he sat up slowly, and swung his feet onto the floor. With each minute that passed, he was less wobbly and ill. But his body felt like a bad fit; every motion reminded him of it.

The room before him also fed his suspicion. It was in the most complete disarray Koseth had ever seen, and he had seen a caravan encampment after a bandits' raid. Much of the mess seemed to be paper—bound books, scrolls, single sheets—piled on the long work table in the middle of the room, and on chairs, the floor, and any relatively flat surface. There were dirty dishes; old clothes; two sharibi puzzles, both dismantled; a pectoral of beaten copper and coral; an assortment of glass bottles with various colors of murky liquid in them; and other things that made Koseth want to rub his eyes. None of the other things, inconveniently enough, was a mirror. But he saw what looked like a polished tin tray on the seat of a chair. He stood slowly up and made for that.

It reflected his image well enough for what he wanted. For a moment he stared at his suspicion proved true. Then a white-hot fury rose up in him, and he began to curse aloud, until the sound of Silvertop's voice speaking Koseth's words, the sight of Silvertop's face twisted with his anger, made him trail off into befuddled silence.

He sat staring into the bottom of the tray until he realized that his stupefied expression didn't sit well on Silvertop's features, either. He put the tray down.

The little bastard had done it in the Tiger's Eye, of course. Walking all the way around him, the touch on his hair—had he only touched him, or had he left something there? Koseth reached up to feel the back of his head and realized only as his fingers touched the fine pale hair that this was, of course, the wrong head. That prompted another fit of cursing.

So, he decided, once he'd started thinking again, *if I'm in Silvertop's body, then is he in mine? For his sake, I hope he is. If he's in any other body, I'm going to break its arms.* Then he looked down at Silvertop's delicate hands and realized that arm-breaking was not one of his options.

He thrust his hands through his hair, found the wrong hair once again, and went, muttering, in search of clothes.

Koseth's heart plummeted at the sight of his townhouse. It was neat, quiet, and two of the Levar's Guard were posted at the front door. He found two more at the kitchen entrance. What *had* Silvertop done? Koseth had been sure, at first, that this was just another of Silvertop's experiments, done purely in a spirit of magical inquiry. Had Maseka spotted the imposture, and called the Guard?

He started up the low stone steps to the front door, and the two gray-clad guards drew together before him. The one on the right, a lean woman with broad shoulders, nodded. "Pardon, master, but may I ask your business?" She was polite, but not conciliating, and Koseth scented trouble.

"I wish to see—" he couldn't help it; he stumbled over his own name, "—the Margrave of Trieth."

"I must ask you why."

"I have something of his I'd like to return," Koseth smiled. He wondered what effect a Silvertop smile had, and hoped it was reassuring.

"Wait a moment, please," the guard said with a frown, and turned to wield the heavy bronze knocker. Her companion kept his eye on Koseth.

Maseka opened the door, and Koseth saw the expression that usually met his guests. Or at least, something close to it; Maseka was gracious and dignified, but there was a canted look to his brows, and the slightest air of hopeful appeal about his features. This dissipated as soon as his gaze fell upon Koseth.

Before he could speak, the lean guardswoman asked Maseka, "Is this man known to you?"

"No, mistress."

"You're certain? You've never seen him before?"

"Not to the best of my knowledge." Maseka turned to Koseth and touched two fingers to his forehead with grave politeness. "May I be of assistance, master?"

"Not now," the guard said firmly. "We'll want to ask this man a few questions." At this, the second gray guard detached himself from the doorpost and took Koseth, as politely as possible, by the arm.

Maseka cloaked himself in the icy and impenetrable dignity that he employed only in the face of the most awful transgressions of etiquette. "The gentleman has come seeking hospitality of the Margrave of Trieth. Which of you will tell His Grace, when he returns, that you mauled his guests on his very doorstep?"

Returns? thought Koseth.

"Do you think we're standing here for the air?" snapped the guardswoman. "Damn it, man, we're dealing with a *kidnapping!*"

"We're dealing with a what?" said Koseth, and the second guard's hand tightened on his arm.

The woman turned and scowled at him. "The Margrave of Trieth was kidnapped last night, and if you don't stay out of this, I'll arrest you out of sheer annoyance."

"Maseka, is this true?" Koseth said.

Maseka blinked. "Your pardon, master?"

Koseth remembered that he didn't look like anyone Maseka knew. "May I come in?"

"No!" said the guard, and, "Certainly, master," said Maseka.

Koseth looked at the guard. "I...may have some information that will prove useful."

"Then you can give it to me, here or at the nearest City Guard post."

Koseth frowned. It would be a daunting look on his own dark features, but he suspected it wasn't of much use on Silvertop's. "Maseka, *I'm* Trieth. I'd prefer not to explain it here. How can I prove it to you?"

The guard protested, but he paid no attention. He was watching Maseka's face, where disbelief and hope chased each other across the copper-colored features. The butler drew a deep breath, let it out, and studied Koseth. At last, he said, "If you really are His Grace...tell me in what object His Grace has invested his luck."

Koseth stood stunned for a moment before he found his voice and roared, "I'll see us all in jail first! I'd as soon print it in the *Cat Street Crier* as tell it to these two lumps of dung—and it wouldn't do you a damn bit of good, since I've never told it to you!"

The change that came over Maseka was astonishing. He beamed, he glowed, he seemed close to weeping. "Welcome back, Your Grace," he cried, "oh, welcome back!"

Surprise seemed to root both guards to the stone steps, and loosen the grip on Koseth's arm. He stepped through his front door, and Maseka closed it firmly behind him.

When they stood in the cool tile-paved front court, Koseth asked, "Maseka, what, by the Levar's future...womanhood, possessed you to ask me that?"

Maseka's air of pleasant dignity had returned; he nodded and smiled gently. "I am sorry, Your Grace, but I could not be certain we shared any...privileged knowledge. I could only ask a question that would elicit a characteristic response. And if you will forgive me, your response was very much characteristic."

"I...see," said Koseth. "I think. Now, where was I kidnapped from?"

Maseka raised his eyebrows. "Then you *were* kidnapped, sir?"

"This is not an illusion, Maseka—it's someone else's body. I'm assuming the someone else has mine. I'd like it back. If he, and it, are not here, then I have to start looking for them somewhere."

"Yes, Your Grace." Maseka looked taken aback. "Well, you were…he was…the kidnapping occurred in your bedchamber."

On the way up the curve of stairs to the second floor balconies, Maseka added what he knew. He had, as instructed, given the staff the night off after dinner, and retired to his own quarters behind the kitchen. He'd sat down to work on the household accounts. He could remember the popping sound of pottery breaking, and scraps of a succession of ugly dreams. At dawn Maseka woke slumped over his writing table, his ledger stopped in mid-entry and ink dry on the pen. When he searched the house and found Koseth missing, perhaps three-quarters of an hour ago, he called the Guard.

"How did you know I hadn't simply left the house early?" Silvertop, after all, would never have thought to tell the servants he was going out.

"I'm familiar with your wardrobe, Your Grace—you'll pardon me if I say that it is not extensive. All that was missing was your dressing-robe."

No, not even Silvertop would have left the house in a dressing-robe. The bedchamber, the rearmost of the rooms in Koseth's private suite on the second floor, was undisturbed, except for the unmade bed. There was no sign of a struggle or a search. If it hadn't been for Maseka's familiarity with Koseth's clothes, the disappearance might not have been recognized until hours later.

"Have the City Guard brought in a magician yet?"

"Yes, Your Grace. The magician came immediately; the inspector has not yet arrived to do a physical search."

"Find anything?"

"Unfortunately, the trail seems to be rather cold. He could tell that magic had been used both here and in the servants' quarters, but could not identify a spell or its maker."

Not, then, any great outpouring of magic, such as rendering Silvertop—or Koseth—immaterial and whisking him out through a second-story wall. That would leave a trace that could linger for a day or more. Koseth doubted that he could do better than a Guard magician, but he had to try. "Maseka," he said, "brew some kaf for me, would you?"

Maseka looked startled for an instant, then nodded. "Yes, Your Grace." He touched fingers to his forehead and went away. Koseth waited until he heard Maseka's steps on the stairs. Then he went to the marble-topped washstand near the bed and opened a drawer.

For an instant he felt a disorienting lack of something. Then he realized what it was, and a drowning terror seized him. His luck was gone. He felt for its hiding place anyway, but without hope; he was well within three paces of where his invested object should be, and there was none of the comfortable resonance he'd grown used to, his particular manifestation of the bond between magic and its owner. Could the kidnappers have known what his luck was invested in, and taken it, too? But if they thought they had Koseth, they would have done better to leave it where it was, much too far away for their victim to draw upon it. Unless they'd destroyed it…

At the back of the drawer, in its crevice, his fingers met the soft leather of the coin pouch that held his invested luck. He pulled it out and stared at it. It was the same one: thin, glossy black leather, a little scarred with use, drawn closed with a red silk cord. He could feel the weight of the polished ball of rose quartz inside, but he could feel no magic. He rolled the tassel between his thumb and forefinger—

His pale-skinned thumb and forefinger.

The thing was brimming with invested luck, ready to be tapped…but not by Silvertop, and not by Koseth in Silvertop's body. Perhaps he could use Silvertop's invested object, but finding it in that disaster that passed for Silvertop's living quarters would have meant playing a grown-up version of Hot and Cold for hours.

Koseth tucked the pouch into his heavy cotton sash and began to examine his bedchamber. Perhaps familiarity would give him an edge that the Guard, searching later, would lack.

The grillwork over the window was painted wrought iron. He looked for scratches in the paint or flakes of rust on the sill, and found none. They hadn't taken the grill off, then, and hadn't gone in or out that way. The bedclothes were rumpled, but clean. Nothing had been taken from the dressing table or the ornate cedar-lined clothes press except, as Maseka had said, his dressing-robe.

There was no sign of a struggle, which probably meant that Silvertop had been drugged. Maseka's account indicated that *he'd* been. Maseka had also said that he'd heard crockery breaking. Koseth left his chambers, went to the top of the stairs, and shouted, "Maseka!"

The butler popped out the arch from the kitchens. "Yes, Your Grace?"

"You said you heard something breaking, last night?"

"It seemed so to me, Your Grace—not a shattering sound, but a sort of pop, like a cup breaking."

"Did you find anything broken this morning?"

Maseka shook his head. "I looked, Your Grace, after I called the Guard."

Koseth went back to his bedchamber. It was a maddeningly tidy crime, difficult enough to solve without the raveled end of his and Silvertop's identity switch. Had the kidnappers intended to take Koseth? Or had they intended to take Silvertop in Koseth's body? His only route to the kidnappers' identity was motivation, and without knowing who they thought they were kidnapping, he couldn't determine that, either.

Since they hadn't come in the window and hadn't used any great magic, they must have gotten in downstairs and come in the sitting room door. Koseth sighed and got down on hands and knees to study the polished ebony floor and the carpets. He followed a straight route to the bed, ranging a few feet to either side in his search. When he reached the bed, he lifted the nearest bed curtain and shook it out, then raised the bed skirt. Nothing on the floor under the bed. Then his eye was caught by a reflection in the folds of the hanging on the other side of the bed. He scurried over and lifted the other bed curtain.

What rolled out was a piece of broken stoneware. It seemed to be a rough cross-section fragment of a jar, with some lip on one end and base on the other. The outer glaze was a glossy green painted with the outlines of clouds and birds in black and gold. Koseth cupped it in his hands for a moment, then, very delicately, sniffed the inside surface.

The smell, faint as it was, was associated in his mind with being dizzy and falling down, and he was a little surprised when the floor didn't tilt beneath him. Oil of green satinbark, mixed with some volatile liquid and sealed in a breakable jar, would produce a sort of narcotic gas bomb. A very small spell could make a patch of window immaterial, just long enough to levitate the jar through. When the magic was withdrawn, the jar would fall to the floor and break, and the vapors would do their work quickly and be gone, and leave no clue.

But here was the piece of jar. Koseth scowled at it. Had he been meant to find it, or had the kidnappers really overlooked it when they gathered up the rest of the fragments? The chemists and apothecaries of Ka Zhir used such jars, stoppered with porcelain and sealed with melted wax, to hold volatile liquids and oils, and herbs that deteriorated quickly in air or sunlight. Koseth was not certain how he came to the resolution, but he acted on it at once. He pulled a large square of silk from a drawer of the dressing table, and wrapped the bit of pottery in it. Then he went headlong down the stairs and into the kitchen.

Maseka raised his eyes from a neatly arranged tray and blinked. "Yes, Your Grace?"

"I may have found something. Tell whoever shows up from the City Guard that they should meet me at the Tiger's Eye."

"Very good, Your Grace," Maseka sighed. As Koseth swung out the back door, he saw Maseka shaking his head over the pot of kaf.

The ride to the Tiger's Eye was neither long enough nor fast enough to work the fidgets out of his horse. The chestnut was inclined to make the entire journey sideways. Koseth was past the Levar's Park before he remembered that the horse thought he was a stranger—and he felt like one. Silvertop's thighs began to ache almost immediately from their unaccustomed grip on the saddle, and his slender hands threatened to blister under the chestnut's nervous pulling at the bit. When Koseth slid out of the saddle at the door of the Tiger's Eye, his legs quaked with weariness.

He was inside the shop before he realized that Snake was home.

She was surrounded by bales and baskets of things, very much as Koseth had imagined she would be. She was not, however, still in riding clothes. Her hair was freshly washed and still damp. It was pulled back from her face and bound high on the crown of her head with an enameled gold ring, from which it fell to her shoulders in a cascade of tiny black braids. One long gold earring hung from her right ear. She wore a sleeveless calf-length tunic of persimmon-colored wool that pleated and draped from a beaded yoke as if it were no heavier than fine linen. Beneath the tunic she wore a tight-sleeved blouse and narrow trousers of heavy bronze silk. Her slippers were black leather painted with morning glory vines.

She looked up at him and smiled, her face full of gentle amusement, and he realized that he'd been standing dumb struck since he'd seen her.

"Don't tell me," she said in that kaf-with-honey voice, sharp and sweet at once, "you came to elope with Thyan, and my presence has sunk the whole scheme."

"What?" he said finally. He had out-bargained the Tilandre horse breeders, but the sight of this tall, elegant woman in her shop reduced him to unprecedented stupidity.

"It was a joke," Snake said patiently. "Hello, Silver. What can I do for you?"

"I'm not Silvertop," he said, and his words sounded bald, foolish, and completely unbelievable. "I'm Koseth."

Snake nodded and stroked the bridge of her nose thoughtfully. "And I am His Scarlet Eminence."

"Blast it, Snake, it's true!"

"Is this Thyan's idea?"

"It's the sort of crack-brained thing Thyan would think up, but she gets no credit for this one. I'm not joking. It's a vile tangle, but I *am* Koseth."

Snake propped her elbows on the lid of a waist-high basket, and her chin on her knuckles. "I may be over-cautious…but I've lived with Thyan for six years, and it's ruined my disposition. Prove it."

Had he been thinking coolly, he would have been able to summon up any number of more temperate ways to prove himself. As it was, he stalked scowling over to Snake, took her face in both his hands, and kissed her with ferocious intensity.

When he drew back, he was certain for an instant that she'd boxed his ears; he felt as disoriented as he had when he woke in Silvertop's body. Snake blinked and gave her head a quick shake.

"Well!" she said, a little gruffly. "I'm convinced."

"You are?" said Koseth.

Snake grinned. "It didn't feel at all like you, of course. But you're the only person on this side of the Sea of Luck who would do that and expect me to leave his skull intact."

"I seem to have a lot of…singular characteristics. I must remember to thank Silvertop when I see him."

"How is it," Snake said with a tip of her head—a question mark personified—"that you haven't seen him, if you're wearing his skin?"

Koseth flung himself down in one of the wicker chairs that Snake kept by the hearth for guests and leisurely customers. "A fine question. I woke up this morning in Silvertop's body, in his rooms. I assume he woke up in my body. Some poor fool certainly did."

"You haven't checked?"

"I tried. Someone seems to have kidnapped me."

Snake's dark eyes grew round as half-levar pieces. Then she frowned, bit her upper lip, and said, "Why?"

Koseth nodded; it was like Snake to ask the most important question first. "I don't know. It depends on whether they thought they were getting me, or Silvertop in my body."

"Why would they think that?"

Koseth shrugged. "The body-switch was Silvertop's doing. If I knew why he'd done that, it would be a help. Could he have known that someone planned to carry me off, and thought, for some luck-bereft reason, that it would be better if they got him instead?"

"No," said Snake after a thoughtful moment. "Not Silvertop. His sort of silliness is in inaction: forgetting to eat, or not coming in out of the rain. Active silliness is not his style."

"Silliness? To leap heroically forward and take a blow meant for me?" Koseth clutched at his chest. "I'm wounded."

"Silly for Silvertop to do it. Now had it been me, instead..."

Koseth warily raised an eyebrow.

"Well," said Snake with a bat of her lashes, "they'd be shocked, wouldn't they, to find that their victim *could* fight his way out of a flower bed?"

"May your linens mildew and your glassware crack."

Snake grinned. "Start at the beginning, my dear, and tell me the whole of it."

He did, trying to be thorough. When he was finished, Snake said, "Show me the piece of the jar."

"That's partly why I came here," Koseth said, gesturing vaguely at the collection of ceramics on one wall. He pulled the parcel out of his coat pocket, unwrapped it, and handed it to her. She carried it to the window and peered at it closely all around, rubbing her thumb over the inner and outer surfaces and holding it up to the light.

"It's Zhir work," Koseth offered.

"Umm. The shape and the ornamentation are unique to Ka Zhir." She looked up, frowning. "But that isn't where this was made."

"But if it's unique—"

"Come look," Snake said, and he obeyed. "See the foot-ring on the bottom? Zhir potters cut the foot-ring on their pots with a square-edged tool, and you get a sharp angle where the foot meets the pot. This was cut with a rounded edge. Liavekan potters sometimes cut the foot-ring like this, but the ring is usually thicker when they do, and much higher."

Koseth shrugged. "A Zhir pot with impure foreign influences?"

"I don't think so." She put it in his hands, and pointed. "Look at the spots in the interior glaze, where the oxides in the clay have leached through. Zhir stoneware is very clear, almost as clear as porcelain. The combination of this and the foot-ring suggest that this pot is Tichenese."

After a moment, she said, "You're staring again."

"Tichenese?"

"Probably."

"Fascinating. Tell me, why do you think I found a piece of a Tichenese forgery of a distinctive Zhir jar on my bedchamber floor?"

Snake's eyes got wide again. "Because you were supposed to?"

"No—because whoever searched my bedroom after I disappeared was supposed to."

"What I meant."

"And whoever found it wasn't supposed to know it was Tichenese."

They stared at each other over the fragment for a few long moments. Koseth knew that Snake was fitting the facts together in her mind; it was, after all, what he was doing.

"Tichen would love to see Liavek and Ka Zhir hacking pieces out of each other again," she said. "I'll wager they weren't pleased to see Calornen's Stone returned so peacefully."

"And the apparently Zhir kidnapping of a Liavekan noble would certainly toss a cat into the hen yard."

"Do we go to the Guard with this?"

Koseth scrubbed his face with his fingertips. On Silvertop's face, it was more distracting than refreshing. "When the inspector from the Levar's Guard gets to my townhouse, Maseka will direct him here. Whether he'll come straight here or not, we don't know." Koseth drummed his fingers on the window frame. "Damn! If the kidnappers find out they only have half of me, what are they likely to do? How much danger is Silvertop in?"

"That depends. Half of you is quite enough to rouse Liavek against Ka Zhir."

"Unless they don't mean to hold him hostage at all."

Snake understood him immediately, and paled. "Let's go after them, then," she said quietly. "I'll roll Thyan out of bed and tell her to tend the shop. I won't tell her about Silvertop; better she should have her hysterics when we bring him back."

"We can't go after them. Which direction would we go? They could have gone anywhere, curse them, including out to sea." He paced the short distance the crowded shop allowed. He'd been wrong the night before, it seemed; his life as the Margrave of Trieth was going to be remarkably like his life as the Desert Rat. He remembered his visitor, Hama, and the memories the young man had forced upon him of the battle for Well of White Flowers. Chaos and butchery, revenge in the name of justice. The twisted features of the garrison commander...

And the way they mingled with the features of the commander's clanswoman wife in the face of their son, barely come to manhood, beardless then. What had Hama said? *"My father died that night."*

"Get ready to ride," he said to Snake. "I know where they've gone."

He looked down at the fragment of pottery in his hand. It was in two pieces now.

Snake's possessions did not include a fast horse, so they rode double back to Koseth's townhouse and he provided one from his stables, a big black gelding with an ugly head and long, powerful shoulders. Koseth gave Maseka their probable route, and told him to direct the Guard after them.

They rode as quickly as they could through the streets above the Levar's Park and out the Drinker's Gate. Then they turned north and east, onto a road that ran through the bleak western foothills of the Silverspine. Once, when they'd stopped to rest the horses, Snake asked, "If they're bound for Tichen, why this route? Why not through Trader's Town?"

"Too well-traveled. Hama is no cold-blooded professional, to drive a wagon at a leisurely pace down the highway with his captive tied up in the back. He's a young fool bent on revenge. He'll do it on horseback, with perhaps two henchmen and his captive thrown over the saddle bow. Harder on the captive that way, too. So he'll have to stay on the byways until he gets to the Waste."

"And then?"

Koseth shot her a bleak look. "If he gets that far, he can take any damn route he pleases. We'll have lost him."

"Well then," Snake said, getting to her feet and pulling her ash-gray cloak around her, "we'd best not let him get that far."

The only comfort he had, he realized as they rode, was that if Silvertop opened his silly mouth and convinced Hama that he wasn't Koseth, Hama almost certainly would let him live. It was Koseth that Hama wanted, and he wanted *all* of him. And the young codhead wouldn't realize that killing Silvertop would be the best revenge of all: Koseth would be tormented with guilt for a friend's death, and cursed to wear the friend's body to keep the guilt fresh.

At least, Koseth *hoped* that Hama wouldn't realize that.

The sun was setting wound-red in the dusty air over the plains when they sighted their quarry.

Snake shaded her eyes with a gloved hand. "You were right. Four horses, three with riders, what looks like badly-made panniers on the fourth. That would be our wandering lad." She looked at Koseth. "They've turned west, toward the Waste."

He swore gently and flexed Silvertop's cramping hands. "They must have discovered that I'm not all there."

"No surprise for your friends."

"I *gave* you that one."

"Just because it's free, I should turn it down?"

Koseth grinned reluctantly. "That's enough. Well, now it's a matter of the quality of our horses against the quality of theirs."

Snake checked the thong that tied her caravaneer's whip to her saddle. "We've been traveling at a harder pace than they have."

"Mm. But if those are the same horses they rode south on—and they may be, if he's bent on secrecy—then they weren't well-rested to start with."

"Let's find out." The black gelding leaped forward, and Koseth gave the chestnut his head.

They gained several yards undetected, simply by staying among the brush and scrub trees along the road for as long as they could. When they broke out into the sparsely-grown lower foothills and into the sight of the Tichenese, they were galloping.

The rearmost rider of the party turned in the saddle, then shouted something. The Tichenese horses began to run.

It seemed to Koseth that he had been stretched out along the chestnut's lathered neck for hours. The thundering of hooves might have been the noise of a waterfall, or his own blood roaring in his veins. The chestnut's nose drew even with the last Tichenese horse's flank. He slid his saber from its scabbard.

Then Snake's whip curled out with a sound like the sky tearing, and the Tichenese horse shied. The battle-trained chestnut leaped forward at a signal from Koseth's knees and hands, and slammed against the other rider's mount. Koseth's saber rang against the blade of the Tichenese woman.

She was a smart and savage fighter, and Koseth thought later, when he could turn his attention from wielding Silvertop's untrained muscles, that she might have been recruited from the Tichenese cavalry. She would not return to it. Her weary horse stumbled, her guard fell for an instant, and Koseth took her in the throat.

He turned to see the second Tichenese, his lance falling from his hands, yanked from the saddle at the end of Snake's long whip. He landed hard and lay still. Snake rode toward the fallen rider, coiling her whip.

"Desert Rat!" Hama's voice spat out, and Koseth wheeled his horse.

Hama had ridden his smoke-tailed gray up to the packhorse and held it there with his knees. In his right hand he gripped the man-shaped bundle by its wrappings at what looked to be the head. His left hand held his long Tichenese blade. The steel was gory red, and for a moment Koseth stopped breathing; but it was only the reflected sunset.

"Killing in cold blood won't please your father's ghost, Iesu Hama."

"Keep well back, and keep your companion back, too—more than the length of her clever whip."

At the corner of his vision, he saw the black gelding sidle nervously, back and to the left.

"If you kill him, Hama, we'll tear you to pieces and water this slope with you."

The young man grinned fiercely. "Ah, but I will have had half my revenge. What will I have if I surrender?"

Koseth shook his head. "That's the wrong half of your revenge. The fool who let your father die is in this body."

Hama's eyes narrowed. "You think I will believe you did not want my father dead?"

"I wanted justice done. I was twenty-eight years old, Iesu Hama, and if possible, even more of an idealistic idiot than you. The Longfinger and Casoe clans had been treated like domestic animals for a generation, yet I thought they would be wise and noble human beings if I only put freedom in their hands. No, I did not want your father dead."

Hama was silent, watching Koseth. The Tichenese sword continued to press against the wrappings of the packhorse's burden.

"At least my country never used my idealism as yours has," Koseth went on. "How did they find you, Iesu Hama? Who came to you and sharpened your hate like an arrow point? Who set you in his bow and fired you at Liavek, with no more care for your life than a wealthy archer cares for a lost arrow?"

Hama's face warped in a snarl, and his right hand twisted in the cloth wrappings. At precisely that moment, the black gelding reared.

In the space of scrub before the packhorse, something hissed and twisted through the sand in serpentine curves. The packhorse screamed and plunged forward. Hama's tightened grip on his captive yanked him out of the saddle.

Koseth dug his heels into the chestnut. As the horse leaped over the fallen Tichenese, Koseth flung himself off, onto Hama's chest, and swung the hilt of his saber down on Hama's temple.

Silvertop's remaining strength was not sufficient to knock Hama unconscious, but he was dazed enough to lie still when Koseth kneeled all of Silvertop's weight on his chest.

"You had it backwards, damn you," Koseth panted down into Hama's face. "It was I who owed a debt to your father, not you. I will pay it now."

A little tongue of fear flickered in Hama's eyes, before his jaw clenched and he stared bravely back.

"Idiot. At Well of White Flowers, I learned a bitter lesson in human nature. I also learned that blood makes bad currency—the rate of exchange is lousy." Koseth backed off him slowly, holding the tip of his saber to the young man's throat. "Stand up."

Hama did, though he looked a little dizzy.

"Now," Koseth continued, "you're going to get on your horse and ride toward Tichen. We're going to stand here and watch until you disappear over the horizon. If we ever see you again after that, you'll get to find out what we really think of you."

Snake was coming toward them, leading the black gelding and the packhorse and shaking sand out of the coils of her whip. Silvertop sat unsteadily in the pack saddle, wrapped in Koseth's crumpled dressing-robe, clutching the tie-down horns in front of him. Looking at himself in a mirror and seeing Silvertop had been disorienting; watching himself riding toward himself made him want perversely to laugh.

"I'll take care of his assistants," Snake said, and stalked off, a length of thong in her hand.

Hama looked at Koseth, then jerked his head toward Silvertop, in Koseth's body, on the packhorse. "Yes. This pale little body would fit that one."

"He's a good man. His death would have lessened both of us." Hama looked down. "Mount up," Koseth said finally.

They watched as Hama rode north, his back very straight. His surviving henchman rode with him, swaying wearily, his hands tied to his saddle bow; the woman Koseth had had to kill lay over her saddle, wrapped in the cloth that had bound Silvertop.

The Tichenese were only a dark blur when Koseth said, "Silvertop, I hope you have an explanation of rare beauty for all this."

"Gently," said Snake.

Silvertop shook Koseth's head. "No. I mean, this shouldn't have happened. Not the kidnapping, though I suppose that shouldn't have happened either—that we switched bodies, I mean."

Koseth found it very odd to hear his own voice through someone else's ears. "And what should have happened?"

"I…what it was…listen, I'd rather not say, all right?"

Koseth swung around and rested his fist rather firmly on Silvertop's knee. "No, it is not all right. I have had an unpleasant day, Silvertop, and while I realize that yours has not been particularly restful either, I will consider it an insufficient penance. Unless you tell me something to change my mind."

Silvertop's blush tinted Koseth's sharp features. "It's…it's not even really a spell of transference. It was supposed to duplicate in me some of—" Here Silvertop descended to mumbling.

"Speak up."

Silvertop gazed at him rather desperately. "You…know so much about the world. And the way you talk, and move, and the way you think fast when you have to—I thought if I could do some of that—" he stared hard at his hands on the pack saddle, "—then Thyan would like me more," he whispered.

For a long moment, Koseth and Snake stared. Then Snake turned her face against the black gelding's side, and her shoulders began to shake.

Koseth covered his eyes. Finally he looked up at Silvertop, who was turning Koseth's face alternately pale and flushed. "That was all you wanted? You codhead. Snake, tell him."

Snake rolled over against the horse's flank. She was speechless with laughter, and tears rolled out the corners of her eyes and cut through the dust there. At last she gasped, "Too late! She already loves you!"

"She does?" Silvertop gaped unattractively.

"And for only as long as I've known her," Koseth said sourly. "Why should I have thought you would have noticed?"

"Oh," said Silvertop.

"'Oh,' indeed. Do you think you could switch us back?"

"I'm not sure. Something interfered with the spell I did, so I don't know how big a job it would be to straighten it all out again. And I don't have my luck object, anyway."

"It wouldn't do you any good," said Koseth. "In your body, I can't use my invested object. But it may be that in my body, you can." He pulled the black leather pouch, heavy with the polished quartz ball inside, from his sash and handed it to Silvertop.

Snake gave him a long look, and he shrugged. "It's almost my luck day anyway."

"Hah," she said.

Silvertop held the pouch for a moment, then shook his head. "It doesn't work. I don't feel anything."

Koseth groaned, and Snake patted him on the back. "Happy birthday, Koseth," she said.

"What's happy?"

"This," Snake said, and pulled out her own coin purse and jingled it at him. "I may have enough money to pay The Magician to switch you back."

Koseth looked rather sadly at the coin purse. "Surely someone a little cheaper would—"

"—Be able to undo Silvertop's work?" Snake spared a wink at Silvertop. "I wouldn't bet money on it."

"The Magician explained what had happened after he got us back in the right bodies," Silvertop told Thyan, who was listening raptly. They were all, Koseth and Snake, Silvertop and Thyan, sitting in the second floor living quarters of the Tiger's Eye, watching evening settle over the

City of Luck. "I'd put my spell on Koseth, which was supposed to work slowly over the course of the night. Then the Tichenese fellow used a spell that would keep Koseth where he was, and serve as a sort of beacon for their magic, just in case he discovered them and tried to misdirect their spells. A spell of association, y'see, works as a sort of binder on the physical body—"

"Get on with the story, and give me the theory later," said Thyan, but she was smiling.

"Huh. Anyway, the two magics mingled, since mine was still in flux when the second one was laid on, and so instead of getting some of Koseth's characteristics, I got his whole physical self, and he got mine."

Koseth leaned over to Snake and said softly, "We've heard this before. Want to go sit on the roof?"

She pursed her lips. "Colder up there."

"Snake..."

"All right," she grinned.

As they climbed the ladder, they heard Thyan say, "The only thing I don't understand is, why did you put the spell on Koseth in the first place?"

Snake murmured, "I can't bear to watch," and hurried up the last few rungs.

The sky was clear, and the moon, though waning, was still close enough to full to wash the flat roof with silver. Snake kept a little garden here: an acacia tree in a huge tub, some fancifully-trimmed flowering shrubs, a collection of late-season vegetables and herbs. Koseth sat on the edge of the acacia's tub, and Snake sat on the wall.

"So do you forgive him?" Snake asked.

"I think so. He's got blisters, saddle sores, aching muscles, and sunburn. That seems like enough revenge."

Her laugh was strong, and seemed to bubble up out of her like clear water. Koseth shivered.

"I was waiting for you to get back," he said. "Silvertop's and Tichen's little interruptions distracted me."

He saw her head tilt to one side, and imagined what he couldn't see in the dark—her eyebrows raised, her mouth a little puckered. He reached out for one of her hands, and stroked the long calloused fingers.

"I've decided to ask you if you'd marry me, you see. Don't fall off the roof, in the name of luck!"

She steadied herself by taking his hand in both of hers. "Why, pray tell, do you want to marry me?"

"What do you mean, why? Haven't I ever told you that I love you?"

"Yes, of course, but you told me that for the first time two months ago. What's different about it now?"

"Do you suppose it would help if I gave you a good shake?" sighed Koseth.

"No, I'd fall off the roof. I can't marry you, dear. You're the Margrave of Trieth. It would make my mother deliriously happy."

"Oh, luck forbid you should make your mother happy."

"Well, that's what I thought. I'll keep the Tiger's Eye, you know."

"I should hope so. I need something to fall back on after I run heedlessly through my inheritance."

Snake made a rude noise. "You never spend anything. I tell you what— I'll make you a partner in the business. With my knowledge of buying and selling and caravaning, and your money and familiarity with the Waste, we'll have the largest piece of the northern trade in all of Liavek."

"Snake, I'm proposing a marriage, not a merger."

"Same thing." She leaned forward and kissed him, long and intoxicatingly, on the mouth. "I adore you, Lir Matean Koseth ola Presec."

"So what," he grinned, and returned her kiss.

Emma and I discovered that editing anthologies cut into our ability to write for them, so we did not do stories for the third or fourth Liavek volumes. We concluded the series with the fifth. Emma decided she did not need to say anything more about Snake (though I keep reminding her that she has mumbled about writing about Snake's wedding). I wanted to say farewell to Trav. I still liked him, because he'd served me well in the first volume, but I was also annoyed that I had created a series character who was essentially a superhero rather than an ordinary person caught up in unusual events. Some of that annoyance had crept into "A Happy Birthday." I decided to unleash my ambivalent feelings about the super-powerful guardian of the city with this, his final outing.

—Will

Six Days Outside the Year

Will Shetterly

Divination Day

In the middle of a cool and sunny morning, on a palace balcony high above the noise and bustle of the harbor of Ka Zhir, Prince Jeng spooned iced cream with hazelnuts from a yellow porcelain bowl. "How is my father?"

"He woke with a toothache a few minutes after midnight." The old slave's wrists were enclosed in gold manacles to display his position and his worth. A hand's length of iron chain dangled freely from each manacle to show that Advisor L'Vos could be bound again. "The dentist removed the tooth."

Jeng clicked his tongue against the roof of his mouth before taking another bite of the sweet cream. "Though his pain ends, his bite is weakened. A good sign on Divination Day, or a bad?"

L'Vos shrugged. "He says he is an enlightened despot. To believe that the events of one day may shape the course of the next four years is foolish."

"My father and I are remarkably alike." Jeng's voice changed subtly. "Does he suspect?"

"The King always suspects. His recent illness only reduces his ability to act on his suspicions."

"And he still favors my cousin."

"Your cousin ended the island revolts—"

Jeng grunted and waved his hand for silence. The grunt must have sufficed; the Prince remembered too late that while Advisor L'Vos's vision encompassed the future of nations, his eyes had been replaced with black marbles after an attempt to escape.

Jeng turned away from the sightless gaze. Far below, sailors and slaves and officers and overseers worked within view of the palace of King Thelm of Ka Zhir, every Zhir's overlord. A steam-driven cart rolled along one pier, bringing bags of coffee and sugar to a freeladen ship that flew Liavek's blue pennant from its highest mast. "Twenty-three years of peace," Jeng said, not caring whether L'Vos understood what that meant to him. Twenty-three years since Liavek's navy had destroyed Ka Zhir's at the Battle of Gold Harbor. "My cousin would reinforce our friendship with Liavek. More fool he."

Jeng licked his spoon clean, tasting sweet cream and cold silver, and turned back to L'Vos. "What does the King think I'm doing?"

"What you wished. The wood is for a summer house. A careless messenger allowed a letter with architectural plans to be seen by a spy; I've been assured that the house would be beautiful, should you decide to build it. The cloth is for tents to be erected there, for a festival when you surprise the King with the gift of the house. Your Thunder Fist Marines have been brought inland for training on unfamiliar ground, and will display their new skills to His Majesty in the spring, undoubtedly when you give him the palace."

"And the water-gas manufactory?"

"I think he thinks your magicians seek to build a new sort of bomb, and your hired Tichenese have come to work with them."

Jeng laughed, and placed another spoonful of iced cream on his tongue. The dessert was very good; he would try it with mango this evening. The dock workers scurried below. Could they suspect that Ka Zhir's harbor would, within a few years, no longer be the only mouth of a hungry nation, that the eldest surviving son of King Thelm had begun to wrest the nation's dependence from the untrustworthy clutch of the sea?

Jeng turned from the palace window. "The King thinks these are all parts of a gift from a loyal son."

"Yes, Prince Jeng."

"But he believes that the loyal son is preparing a revolution."

"Suspects. None of your plans occur near the sea. You cannot hold the capital without the navy, and the navy is loyal. He sees the beginnings of a pattern and waits to know its final shape." The old man paused, then added calmly, "His assassins wait, too."

"If I feared the Black Cord, I would not be worthy of my father. How do the tests go?"

"Very well. If the winds permit—"

"The winds will permit. Haven't my magicians ensured that the winds will permit?"

"Of course."

"Good." Prince Jeng's thoughts were no longer on his plans, for there was nothing more for him to do. His part had ended when he ordered it begun. His people would succeed, and he would be his father's favorite by the end of Grand Festival Week. Perhaps three bites of the cream and nuts remained. He could taste each, thick and cool and sweet in his mouth. "Hold out your hands."

The iron chains rattled as L'Vos obeyed. Jeng set the porcelain bowl into the slave's palms. "Eat." The Prince's voice held no hint of his smile as L'Vos fumbled for the spoon, then brought a dollop of cream and hazelnuts into his mouth.

"It's good," L'Vos said, with no more feeling than the Prince.

Jeng laughed. "My dessert," he announced, rewarding L'Vos with the knowledge that he had not been poisoned. "You may finish it."

"Thank you."

Jeng looked up at the king's balcony. "What will my father think," he asked, "when I give him Liavek?"

Across the Sea of Luck in the Canal District of the city of Liavek, beside the steps to a gray windowless brick building, a single blue flower of Worrynot grew in a small terra-cotta pot. The presence of the contraceptive plant was the only suggestion of the nature of the business practiced behind the bland face of the house named Discretion.

A young man with plain brass bracelets on each wrist drew the bell chain. After a moment, the door opened, admitting him from a cool and sunny street that smelled of fish and salt and hickory smoke and a distant baker's fresh bread, into a warm and dark greeting room that smelled of frankincense smoke and jasmine perfume. A slender woman in black silk trousers and blouse touched one finger to her forehead in a mockingly affectionate greeting. "I would not have expected you today, Master Magician."

He did not know if she knew his name; he had not cared to learn hers. She always addressed him with the same amusement, as though they knew each other's weaknesses. Perhaps they did: she served Discretion, and he visited it.

"Oh?" he said. "No one spends Divination Day here, hoping twenty-four hours will guarantee four years of pleasure?"

The woman laughed, the sounds of her amusement surprisingly husky from her narrow chest. "Not one. The superstitious fear a day within these walls will ensure that the next four years' pleasures all bear an exorbitant price." She indicated a door carved with scenes of the Kil making love and war beneath the sea, which led to a spacious sitting room with thick carpets and low couches. "Are you superstitious, Master Magician?"

"I do not need to be."

She raised an eyebrow. He had not meant to brag, and he did not care to think about what he had truly meant. "Aychiar," he requested.

"No one is expected to be available today." The woman, opening a low rosewood cabinet to reveal cloudy bottles filled with liquids and powders, reached for an amber Hrothvekan wine that he had drunk on his last visit to the house.

He shook his head. "Aychiar is here?"

"I could see." She stepped toward the hall.

"I would appreciate it." When the woman glanced over her shoulder, he set a stack of gold ten-levar pieces on a delicate mahogany tea table.

He could not tell if she counted the coins in that glance, but her smile became, if anything, more cruel or, perhaps, more pitying. "I suspect he is in," she said. "Will you wait in the sea room?"

"Of course." He knew the way and went, wondering only if she had left him alone as an act of trust or of kindness, or if the House was so very shorthanded on the first day of Grand Festival Week.

The sea room was painted in pale blues and aquamarines. The beams of the ceiling were bare cypress, and the floor had been sprinkled with white sand. Two oil lamps burned in niches carved into either wall. The oil smelled of cinnamon. The bed was a thick mattress covered with sheets the color of hyacinths or bruises.

He waited for several minutes, standing motionless in the center of the room, telling himself to leave the House and making no effort to do so. When the door opened, a bare-chested youth in loose blue trousers entered. The boy's expression might have been boredom, or he might have just woken. His hair was a mat of black braids; his skin was as pale as a Farlander's or a dead man's. A pack of tattooed cats raced up his left arm and around his thin shoulders. "You," he said. It might have been the boy's usual greeting, and not a sign of recognition.

The man opened his robe, letting it fall. He kicked it aside with a sandaled foot. Then he kicked off the sandals and waited, wearing nothing but a black silk loincloth.

"What this time?" the boy said.

The man could not make himself answer. Far away, in another room or in another world, someone plucked lazily at a cittern, spilling notes at the farthest edge of the man's hearing.

The boy demanded, "What?"

The man lifted his chin, a tiny beckoning gesture.

The boy, smiling, reached into a fold of his baggy trousers and withdrew a black pearl-handled flick-knife banded in burnished steel. When his wrist twitched, the knife opened as quietly as a book, its blade the length of a human hand. The boy crouched, the flick-knife low before him, his body twisted away in a fighter's stance, and smiled again and stood erect.

The man nodded.

The tip of the knife cut an inch into the man's left shoulder and separated skin and muscle in a diagonal line from his collarbone to a point near his navel. In spite of his resolve, the man grunted. He and the boy looked at the wound, watching flesh part like butchered meat. Naked bone glistened for the instant before blood filled the cut.

The distant cittern played the first seven notes of "Rag Woman's Luck," then repeated them.

"I wouldn't do this on Divination Day," the boy said.

"The advice is a little late."

The boy shrugged.

"We earn our luck," the man answered, thinking the words sounded true and not sure what he meant by them.

The boy nodded and lifted the knife. "How much?"

"Until I fall and cannot stand."

The knife leaped out, a kiss that traveled from the man's right cheek to his chin, slicing the corner of his lips in its passing. "And then?"

The man tasted his blood. Speaking heightened the pain, so he enunciated extravagantly. He tapped the skin above his heart. "Kill me."

The cittern notes raced each other, a mountain folk reel played for unseen, insane dancers.

Birth Day

Rangzha Fon did not enjoy intrigue. He enjoyed comfort, and he enjoyed wealth (for that was the best way to ensure continued comfort as a citizen of Ka Zhir). He enjoyed living in lands far from King Thelm's court (for that was the best way to ensure continued wealth as a citizen of Ka Zhir). If Rangzha Fon's idea of comfort had not included the amenities of a prosperous city, he would have sought a post as an ambassador to a trading town like Gold Harbor, where Zhir diplomacy was a matter of blatant threats and more blatant bribes, or to the inland matriarchy of Ombaya, where Zhir diplomacy was politely ignored. But Rangzha Fon's idea of comfort included fine restaurants, fine theaters, fine magicians, and fine courtesans, so he had come as the Zhir ambassador to Liavek in the hope that its uneasy peace with Ka Zhir would endure.

The presence of the slender woman standing before his desk assured him that it would not.

"You recognize this." On her thumb was a ring with an ebony stone inlaid with a white bird of prey.

He nodded; that was all she expected, so he would give her as much. This philosophy had served him for the forty-seven years of his life. Through his office window came the aroma of a street vendor's roasting almonds and a beautiful Liavekan song about fate, beckoning him to loiter outside on the curb where he could hum off-key while sharing nuts with the embassy guards and the passersby.

He rested a hand on his belly, sighed inaudibly, and gestured toward several thin cotton cushions. "Please. Be seated."

"My name is Djanhiz ola Vikili. You do not know me?" The woman crossed her legs and sat gracefully. She was very dark and very tall; though he had three cushions and she two, she remained taller than he. Her hair was a cap of tight gray coils cut close to her skull, and her face bore a light tracing of weather or age. If she was a magician, she was not vain in the ways he understood.

"No," Rangzha Fon replied. In Liavek, Djanhiz was conspicuous for her height and her skin's hue; since she could hide neither, she used them in her disguise. Travelers from many nations came to trade and study and live in the City of Luck. During his twenty years here, Rangzha Fon had been visited by his short, swarthy, and rather sullen Zhir countrymen in their bleached cotton tunics and trousers, by very dark and excessively courteous Tichenese in long brocaded robes of sea-green or saffron or indigo silk, and even by ghost-white, round-eyed Farlanders in high-collared wool jackets and heavy boots. He had never been visited by any of the tall, ebony-skinned women of Ombaya, but he had seen them striding through Liavek's streets in their hooded linen tunics and tight trousers. In her green-and-gold tunic and her tan trousers, Djanhiz would pass as a comparatively short and pale Ombayan, a people who had never been Liavek's enemy, and never be recognized as a tall and dark Tichenese, a people who had never been Liavek's friends.

When she smiled at him, he added, "You wear the Ombayan clothing like a native, but not the accent." He kept his tone courteous. Djanhiz frowned, and her glance carried a new weight of respect or suspicion. "Speak with more sibilance," he suggested. "Perhaps a lisp—"

"Thank you."

Her voice said he had gone too far, so he nodded and waited, wondering why a Tichenese woman in Ombayan clothes came to Liavek with the ring of Prince Jeng of Ka Zhir.

Djanhiz looked around the pleasant clutter of his office, the shelves of books that filled one wall and the collection of masks from many cultures that covered another. "I need your help."

He could not deny her, whatever she asked, but he was grateful that she had not ordered him. "I am your slave," he answered in Zhir.

She lifted an eyebrow and said in Tichenese, "We are the hands, another is the mind."

"What does my prince require?"

"We must capture The Magician of Liavek before Festival Night."

Rangzha Fon kept his smile while he nodded. The muscles of his stomach tightened to check his fear in case the woman was making a joke. The muscles of his face tightened to check his amusement in case she was not.

"The Magician's house is on Wizard's Row," Rangzha Fon said gently. "And Wizard's Row is never to be found during holidays. If we did find it, the house is guarded—"

The dark woman shook her head once. "I have encountered The Magician before. That is why your prince accepted my aid in this matter."

"Ah." And why you offered it, Rangzha Fon thought. Her expression disconcerted him, and he glanced at the wall of masks. The painted leather Casoe god of sandstorms and murder watched the world with the same mad serenity.

Djanhiz reached across his desk to center his letter opener, a knife of chipped jade, on top of an unfinished report to King Thelm. "Fortunately, we do not need to find The Magician. We only need to find one of his friends."

"What use is magic?" a woman asked, and The Magician stopped to listen. The speaker, small and boyishly slim in multicolored cotton trousers and a maroon silk shirt, stood with legs wide and arms akimbo on a boulder in the Levar's Park. Her head, shaven as clean as a ship's captain's, reflected the afternoon sun. A small crowd of people eddied at her feet, waiting to see what entertainment she offered.

"What will magic profit you?" she called, and The Magician smiled, knowing she knew her audience.

"Who would hire a magician?" The bald woman grinned. "Only the very wealthy. Only those who need a service that will last no more than a few hours or a few days. Certainly not those who need a service that will last a year or more."

He knew too well the limits of his trade. The intricate rhythms of many drummers came from a crowded open-air restaurant, accompanied by the laughter of dancers and the smells of cinnamon Festival cakes and spiced apple wine. The Magician began to walk on.

"Who would become a wizard?" the bald woman asked. Again she paused, and so did he, telling himself that he stopped to watch a fleet of toy sailboats racing across the Children's Lake.

"Spend years studying magic when you might be studying life? Knowing you're as likely to die as to live when you finally try to invest your birth luck in some object to become a magician?"

On the little lake, a schooner as large as a swan took the lead. On the far shore, a small girl jumped and cheered. On the near shore, a red-bearded man waded knee-deep in the water, awaiting the schooner's arrival. Most of the toy ships had sails or pennants of rich Liavekan blue, but a sloop bearing the yellow of Tichen closely followed the schooner, and a Zhir warship raced aft and starboard of the Tichenese sloop, so close together that they threatened to collide.

"You must love power much and life little, to risk everything to become a magician."

The Magician glanced back at the speaker. He wanted to ask her what she knew of life and power, but he did not care to call attention to himself today. He touched his left hand to the bracelet on his right wrist, and felt his birth luck throbbing there, ready for any use he might find for it.

If he could find a use for it, he would not be wandering the Levar's Park in search of entertainment.

The red-bearded man who cheered the schooner seemed familiar. The Magician imagined him with a shaven chin and wearing a blue sash over his gray tunic, and recognized Lieutenant Lian Jassil of the Levar's Guard. Did that mean the girl— He glanced back at her. Sessi Jassil had grown a head taller since she and her brother came to 17 Wizard's Row, and her dark hair had been cut short. People changed so quickly when they remained in the world.

"But you do not need magic!" the bald woman cried. "You do not need magicians! With every year, we learn to harness the natural forces of the world—" The race had attracted several of her listeners, so she pointed it out to the rest. "Like those boats, powered by the wind. Like the trains of the Levar's railway, powered by steam. Like the airships that will soon ply Liavek's skies, lifted by great bags of water-gas and powered by small engines—"

"It's Featherlake's Folly again!" someone yelled from the audience.

"The engines are new, and lighter—" the bald woman replied. The Magician saw where her speech was going, and saw also that she had lost the crowd's interest. The Margrave of Featherlake had built an airship twenty years earlier. It had risen from a field outside the city walls like a newborn calf struggling to its feet, then sagged and burst into flame. Some said the fault had been the engines, some said the design, some blamed poor construction, others claimed the magicians had acted to keep their monopoly on the air.

"Adding a big balloon to the Festival fireworks?" someone else yelled.

"Wait!" the bald woman said. "Soon you'll see the *Luck of Liavek* fly over this park!"

"Fly to pieces!" another called.

The bald woman shook her head. "The Tichenese have designed an airship that will carry one hundred people or more. Will Liavek be kept to the seas while Tichen rules the sky?"

A new boat, modeled after the Farlanders' razored galleons, threatened to steal the lead from Sessi Jassil's schooner. The girl put one hand to her necklace and made a tiny gesture that only a wizard might recognize. The sails of her schooner filled with a sudden wind. The Magician smiled, thinking that was appropriate; the purpose of magic was to cheat: to cheat nature, to cheat death. Then he laughed, for the schooner listed in the wind, toppling toward the razored galleon, and the Tichenese sloop and the Zhir warship both rammed its stern. The razored galleon escaped the tangle, only to veer off course. A simple fishing boat, probably carved by a parent or a grandparent from Minnow Island, took the lead. It reached a small, delighted boy, and a group of congratulators surrounded him.

Atop her boulder, the bald woman still talked about the chance to buy shares in the Luck of Liavek Airship Company, but most of her audience had wandered to newer diversions. The red-bearded man was wading out to fetch the capsized schooner; his sister was walking around the small lake with her head bowed, as though her muddy toes fascinated her. Someone had stretched ropes across Lake Levar, and two acrobats began a comic act on them. A young wizard created illusions of fanciful, improbable, exquisite flying creatures. A troupe of people in brightly colored gauze danced in complex patterns for the patrons of the open-air restaurant. There was nothing entertaining in the Levar's Park. The Magician turned to leave.

Sessi Jassil looked up, catching his eye. She threw her arms wide and ran toward him. "Master Trav! Master Trav! It's me, Sessi!"

He could hurry into the crowd as though he had not heard. He could disappear in smoke or rise into the air, and let her wonder if he had heard her. Instead, he smiled. "Hello, Sessi. I remembered that you raced boats every Birth Day."

"Oh?" She stopped before him and let her arms come to her side. "I cheated."

"I saw. You're coming along. I hadn't invested my luck until I was twice your age. Don't worry; most first-year magicians trying that trick would've blown every boat up into the trees."

"Well." She glanced down again. "Cheating and winning would've felt wrong, anyway."

"Ah."

"But cheating and losing feels really stupid."

The red-bearded man approached with the toy schooner in both hands. "Master Marik," he said.

The Magician nodded, acknowledging another of his names. " 'Lo, Rusty. How's Hell Week so far?"

"Someone burned down Cheeky's yesterday. A temple or a tax collector's, anyone could understand, but a good tavern should be sacred."

"You'd think—" Trav Marik let the sentence die. On the boulder, the bald woman pointed in triumph. From over the trees and rooftops came a cylindrical bag as long as one of the Levar's triremes. Beneath it hung a wooden platform shared by a bulky engine and a single pilot.

"The *Luck of Liavek!*" the bald woman called. "We'll dock here for the rest of Festival Week. Interested investors may ride…"

The Magician felt the air for unusual magics, but there were none. The *Luck of Liavek* came on, ponderous and ugly, no faster than a landsailer, as remorseless as the future, driven by a grinning girl who sat in a cage of levers and cords. The crowd cheered, seeing nothing more than another Festival Week novelty. Trav Marik felt his throat grow thick with a feeling he did not recognize. Unnoticed by Rusty or Sessi, he turned to go, certain that the bald woman was right. The age of magic had ended.

Procession Day and Remembrance Night

The Pardoners had always been Sessi's favorite of the many religions who marched in the Procession of Faiths. They danced and sang in the streets in comradely chaos, with no apparent intent to display their devotion to any other gods than those of celebration. Several Pardoners parodied priests of other faiths: A man draped a wine-stained white sheet about his shoulders and announced, "All is illusion!" "Oh?" said a woman in a red blanket. "Then I'm not doing this." She slapped the man, and he spun about, whirling his arms and saying, "Uh, n-n-no, I guess not." "Or this," said the woman, giving him a loud kiss while yanking his moneybag from his sash and tucking it into her own. "Well, n-no," said the man in white, rolling his eyes, and all the spectators cheered. "Or this," the woman said, kicking the man in the rear. He jumped high, grabbing his buttocks. Sessi held her arms around her stomach and laughed as though she could never stop.

"Ah, the subtleties of Liavekan humor," said a woman behind her.

"Well, if you knew a little about the Reds, the Faith of the Twin Forces, and the Whites, who're the Church of Truth—" The man's voice reminded Sessi of the Zhir sailors who frequented the docks and the Canal District.

"Is there any reason why I should?"

"Probably not," the man said.

Perhaps forty people in golden robes came next in the procession, singing gentle, ecstatic, wordless notes. They were interrupted by something like firecrackers exploding at the far end of the street. Before Sessi could look, someone behind her touched her bare neck. She gasped; the touch stung like a wasp. She could not hear her own voice in the concatenation of explosions or the babble of the crowd. She started to turn, to confront the foreign couple to tell them that she didn't think this was funny at all, but the street had begun to whirl as if the world was a tornado and she stood at its eye. Then she was not standing. Someone caught her shoulders. Someone said, "Poor dear's had too much excitement. She'll feel better when she's safe at home." Someone lifted her and added, "We all will."

"Night leaps upon the unresisting body of the day," said a moustached man in black evening clothes, "much as I shall leap upon you, my dear."

His companion, a handsome woman whose scarlet jacket and tight trousers were a subtle mockery of the man's, laughed delightedly. "With twenty seconds of enthusiasm followed by an hour of drunken apologies?" Her amusement emphasized her exotic features, the small nose and high cheekbones characteristic of mixed Liavekan and Tichenese ancestry. Her face had been powdered as white as a corpse's.

The couple strolled arm in arm through Liavek's oldest graveyard, a place of urns and mausoleums and high marble beds littered with leaves and human bones. Directly before them lay a glass case containing a perfectly preserved old woman, plump and coiffed and dressed in an elegant, archaic fashion. Glowing letters at the woman's feet proclaimed, "Kaelin Marik, 2906–3013. 'All things considered, I hope I'm dead.' "

The woman in red, sipping a black liquid from a green glass skull, pointed, sputtering, "Ari, look!" A drop of her drink dripped from the corner of her mouth, leaving a dark path on her powdered face. She winced, dabbed at the drop with her sleeve, then drank from a ruby vial that the man gave her.

He rested both hands on a silver-topped cane and studied the old woman's body. "She is surely an artistic piece now, the creation of her own life and her embalmer's skill. But it's the whole of the presentation, the audacity of the setting, that truly makes…" His words trailed off as he looked up at the neighboring mausoleum, a miniature fortress with walls of gray lava.

The woman followed his gaze. A young man in a green robe, apparently immune to the evening breeze, sat cross-legged on the slate roof.

"Forgive us for intruding," the woman said. "We were—" She shrugged. Her embarrassed smile hinted that a blush lay beneath her white powder.

"Remembering the dead," said the young man. "What could be more natural on Ghoul Night?" He swept his hand wide to indicate the dark graveyard or, perhaps, Liavek beyond. The air smelled of dried leaves and mold. A nighthawk pirouetted in the sky, streaking the twilight with the white bars under its wings.

The man in black reached for the woman's arm as if to lead her away, but let his hand fall and addressed the seated man. "Haven't we met? At a party—"

The young man touched both hands to his forehead. "Indeed we have, Aritoli ola Silba. I am The Magician of Liavek."

"I think he's drunk," said the woman. "Whoever he is."

"I am The Magician!" the man cried. "The woman you admire was my first wife."

"I meant no disrespect," Aritoli said softly.

"Of course not." Trav smiled at the woman. "He admires so many wives. How is your husband, Countess ola Klera?"

"We should go," the woman whispered.

"Please, no." Trav, still cross-legged, floated down from the mausoleum and bobbed in the air before them. His robe was stained and torn. "It is a Remembrance Night party. Surely you'll share drink and conversation with an...old friend? No, old acquaintance, but new friend." Extending his legs to the ground, he added, "Never drink and fly."

"I shall try to remember that," said Aritoli. "There was a notice for you in this evening's *Cat Street Crier.* Have you seen it?"

"I'm not in need of clients." Trav laughed. "You have not asked me about Gogo. You remember Mistress Gogoaniskithli?"

Aritoli nodded. "A charming creature."

"Indeed," said Trav. "When she intends to be, and when she does not. Did you know that we lived together for almost two hundred years?"

"No," said Aritoli. "I considered living with someone once. For an entire week, I considered it. Ah, the mad passions of youth."

The nighthawk cried, and they all glanced at the sky.

Trav shrugged. "My apologies, ola Silba. I had not meant to bore you. What're you drinking?"

"Green God's Nectar," said Countess ola Klera, lifting the heavy glass skull in her right hand. "Ari and I began with a drop a day to build up a tolerance. We still need the antidote after every drink." She indicated the ruby vial in her other hand. "A taste of death, a taste of life—"

"Ah, something new. Delightful." Trav held out both palms. "May I?"

The Countess glanced at Aritoli, who shrugged. She gave Trav the skull. "If you want a sip..."

Trav raised the skull to salute each of them, and then held it toward the dead woman in the clear coffin. Putting the skull to his lips, he drained half of the contents.

Aritoli said, "You are a damned fool, Magician."

"Thank you." He gave the skull to the Countess. "I began my study late in life, but I am a clever pupil." His last words rasped from his throat.

"Drink this!" The Countess held out the ruby vial.

Trav shook his head. Sweat burst out upon his brow.

"Even if your magic keeps you alive," Aritoli said, "you must feel a terrible burning."

Trav nodded. He reeled about, grunted something that might have been pain or farewell, and staggered away. High above, the nighthawk cried again, a brave and lonely sound in the darkness.

Bazaar Day and Beggar's Night

Lieutenant Lian Jassil raised his fist to pound upon the naked wood of the front door to 39 Beach Drive. A gleaming brass gargoyle's head rose from the oak beneath his hand like a swimmer surfacing in a pool. Its teeth glistened like fresh-forged daggers as it said, "Dawn is vastly overrated. Consider carefully before you decide to share it with us."

"My sister is missing, Didi."

The head retreated, and the door swung wide, revealing a dark hallway. Gas lights lit themselves when the lieutenant stepped within. Small orange flowers grew in a pot on a wall shelf, scenting the air with a smell like tangerines.

Two kittens, one tiger-striped and one beige, ran in to circle his boots. The first backed away to watch from under a corner cloak rack. The tan one stood with its hind legs on the toes of Rusty's boot as though it intended to climb him, so he stooped to stroke it.

A small woman with hair like a cloud of copper coils came barefoot down a stairway, tying the sash of her short white robe as she walked. An incoherent voice called querulously from behind her. She answered over her shoulder, "A friend! Go back to sleep, Vay!"

Rusty stood and touched the fingertips of both hands to his forehead. "Mistress Gogoaniskithli."

The woman shook her head, and her hair bounced as though in water. "I said a friend, Rusty. What's happened?"

He held out a creased scrap of rice paper. Gogo scanned it once. He knew the words perfectly: *If you value Sessi Jassil's life, have The Magician come alone one hour after sunset on Beggar's Night to the gate where a Liavekan captain surrendered his pistol to three sorcerers.*

"That's the Tichenese embassy," Gogo said. "But it would not be like them to kidnap a girl. Or to leave a note directing the kidnappers there."

Rusty nodded. "It's a meeting place, nothing more. But without The Magician…" The kitten bashed its head against his ankle, so he picked it up and stroked it, trying not to think of how much it would delight Sessi.

Gogo lifted the note. "Who brought this?"

"A girl from a dockside inn. She said a tall woman paid her to deliver it. No reason to doubt her. The description wasn't very helpful. Middle-aged woman. Dark skin, gray hair. An accent that the girl described as 'funny.' No one else in the inn remembered the woman. During Festival Week, that's not surprising."

Gogo handed back the note. "I could disguise myself as Trav. Illusion's a simple spell."

Rusty took the note in his left hand because the kitten had gone to sleep in his right. "It's a simple spell to detect, I hear. We'd use a Guard magician, if we thought that'd work. I don't like involving Master Marik, but I'm afraid for Sessi."

Gogo set her hand on his upper arm. "I'm sorry. If there's anything I can do—"

"The Magician. That's all."

"No one knows where he is. His house has not been on Wizard's Row for months. He's The Magician. He could be anywhere."

"Wizards can't find him, either? I thought he had duties as the Magician of Liavek—"

Gogo released his arm. "His spells are intact. The entire community of magicians will know well in advance if Liavek's attacked by magic, or if armies come by land or sea. But this is…a private matter."

Rusty rubbed his brow with his free hand. Something like a headache wanted to settle on him, but he could not let it. He had slept several hours in the last few days; that had to be enough. "My parents put notices in all of the half-copper sheets, asking him to find us, asking people to tell us where he might be. There's no response, so far. I hoped he might tell a friend where he was."

"I consider him a friend, but he doesn't consider me one." Rusty glanced at her, and she added, "I tried to help. I tried until I realized that I was the only one trying, and he was content for things to remain as they were." She moved her chin, indicating the upstairs. "So I moved in with Vay, and Didi joined us. We're happy now. Is that wrong?"

He made a sound that she could interpret as she wished. "There's no one else he might see?"

"There's Tenarel. The Ka'Riatha. But I doubt he'd go to her. She'd tell him what she thinks of the way he's been behaving."

Rusty nodded and handed the kitten to Gogo. He would return to his parents' home and wait with them, before he had to go back on duty. A Guard should be very good at waiting.

"He's given up, Rusty. I would've seen it a century ago, if I hadn't loved him so much. I don't know why. Maybe he's retreated too far from the world. Didi and I were falling with him. That's why we left the Row, finally."

"You don't have to explain—"

"I'm not making excuses! I'm trying to warn you!"

He blinked, realizing that he had not been listening for the meaning behind her words. "We won't find him?" He shook his head. "I can't stop looking."

Gogo's hand rose for a gesture of emphasis that she did not complete. She let it return to stroking the sleeping kitten. "It's all you can do. So do it. I'll try to find him, too. But you should worry less about finding him and more about whether he'll care to help you, if you do find him."

"I see." Rusty scratched the kitten's head, then turned to go. "Thank you."

"Wait!" Gogo held a red playing card in her hand. "Take this. Vay and I're going away for a few days. We might be back by Festival Night. If you need me before then, tear this card, and I'll come."

Rusty woke to a pounding that could only be Stone's fists on his door. His first thought was that Captain Bastian would lecture him for being late. As he opened his eyes and saw the plaster ceiling of his mother's living room, he forgot Bastian and Stone. He sat up from the wicker couch, saying, "Has anyone heard—"

His father shook his head and opened the front door. Stone stood in the hallway, clutching his blue beret in one huge hand. "Master Jassil," he said. "I'm sorry. Really, I am." Tears fell from his eyes. "We looked everywhere. We talked to everyone."

For some reason, his parents and Stone turned to stare at Rusty. He sat on the couch and began to pull on his boots, saying, "We keep looking." He smelled hot kaf and buttered toast in the kitchen, but he wanted to act, not to eat.

His mother's face was very grim, so he added, "The Magician likes her. He'll help." What point was there in repeating Gogo's warning?

"The Magician likes money," his father said. "Little else."

Not even that, anymore, Rusty thought. He repeated more firmly, "He likes Sessi. He'll help us find her."

"I've got a hundred and twenty-one levars saved," Stone said. "He can have that."

"Oh, gods," said Master Jassil, slumping into his chair and covering his face with his hands. Mistress Jassil put an arm around his shoulders and said very calmly, "She's not dead."

"We'll find The Magician," Rusty repeated, and Stone followed him out the door.

The streets were a maze of carts and spread blankets at midmorning on Bazaar Day. What was not offered freely was sold for its cost, or so every seller swore. Within a few feet of the Jassils' door, a tailor invited passersby to feel embroidered silk robes to appreciate their quality, a baker gave out bits of warm brown bread and honey cake, a woman and a man in garlands of Worrynot kissed anyone who sought an embrace. A girl offered rides on her camel, and three identical boys sang a song that stated that every purchase was an exchange of gifts.

Through this bustle, an unshaven young man in a green robe strode toward Rusty and Stone without a glance to either side. "I can understand advertising in *The Liavekan Herald*," he called. "But did you really think I read *The Old Town Inquisitor?*"

Several Tichenese guards in quilted yellow robes stood with shouldered muskets at the gate to their embassy. Golden Festival lanterns hung from the walls and on poles beyond them as though a sea of moons swayed restlessly in the night.

Trav stepped beneath one. He wore a blue cotton robe, low boots, and black trousers; his hair and his skin still smelled of peppermint soap. He smiled, knowing this would be a good place to attack him, and he had done all he could to be a fine corpse.

A small boy ran up to him with a folded bit of rice paper in both hands. "Are you Master Spider?"

Trav coughed something like a laugh. "I think I'm Master Fly tonight." He touched one hand to his forehead and bowed.

The boy squinted. "The letter's for Master Spider."

"That's a courtesy or a mockery. But I'll be Master Spider." He gave the boy a silver coin and ignored his thanks. The note said: *Shall we meet in the rear gardens of the Zhir ambassador? Walk briskly, and you will arrive on time. Do not travel by any other means or route, and do not dawdle. There are a thousand ways in which you can fail in your mission, and only one in which you can succeed.* It ended, *You're still a magician. Destroy this.*

The message seemed to confirm what the earlier note's reference to a Liavekan captain's pistol had suggested. Djanhiz ola Vikili had returned to Liavek. Knowing the identity of one of his opponents told him surprisingly little. Djanhiz ola Vikili had twice failed to capture or kill him; her second failure had resulted in the permanent loss of her magic. Whether she came now as a Tichenese agent or for her own revenge made no difference, though he wondered if the Zhir played a major part in this, or if Djanhiz simply preferred embassy grounds, where Liavekan officials could not interfere.

At his nod, the note ignited in his hand.

He hurried through crowds of laughing beggars, many of whose sores were paint and whose tatters were velvet and otter or artfully shredded silk. He wondered if Djanhiz ola Vikili had expected the Festival to impede his progress through the city. He could not tell if he was followed, and did not care. He would play the game fairly, and by doing so, he would win. Sessi meant nothing to Djanhiz, so she would be freed. And he meant everything to Djanhiz, so he would finally die.

The Zhir embassy was a large whitewashed building, noteworthy only for decorative iron bars on every window and a high stone wall that enclosed it. The embassy's inhabitants had gone to sleep or had left for the more exciting quarters of Liavek; every barred window was dark. Two Zhir musketeers stood at the front gate. "I believe I'm expected," Trav announced.

"I believe you're invisible," one guard answered, stepping aside so Trav could pass.

He followed a brick path around the building to the only source of light, a three-legged iron brazier that had been placed in the center of a tiled patio. When Trav came near, Djanhiz ola Vikili stepped from under a tree and began snapping her fingers, setting a moderate, steady tempo. She recited, "You will not speak or so disrupt in any way this little song. Four verses tell what you must know. The girl dies if you interrupt."

He nodded, pleased that Djanhiz expected him to trick her and wondering what he might have done if he had intended to try.

"A man and she wait somewhere near. He watches while you hear me speak. If my lips pause at any point, he'll cut her throat from ear to ear."

Trav glanced at the quiet windows of the embassy and saw no signs of anyone's presence.

"You need not wonder if I lie. I know the vessel of your luck. Discard it now and back away, or leave and let your small friend die."

Centuries of habit made him reluctant to expose and abandon the container of his power; this amused him when he considered his resolve. His smile grew, and he wondered how Djanhiz interpreted his humor.

"The final verse must now be said." Her voice might have quavered as she began the line, but her expression preserved infinite confidence.

Trav rested his left hand on the bracelet around his right wrist and felt his birth luck pulsing there. He could do anything now, except kill himself. Anything he did would result in Sessi's death. Yet the power tempted him. A last magical feat that Liavek would remember forever…

"The watcher's knife is at her throat. In sixteen syllables—"

He tugged at his wrist, suddenly sure that he had waited too long, that the knife in the hand of Djanhiz's hidden companion would part Sessi's throat before Trav could comply.

"—we'll learn if you prefer—"

He felt his vessel sliding free in his left hand.

"—her live—"

He dropped the vessel onto the patio and hurried backward.

"—or dead." Djanhiz smiled. "I congratulate you on your choice."

His right hand lay on the flagstones. As he took his fourth or fifth step away from it, he felt his magic dwindle and disappear, lost to his senses and his control.

Djanhiz picked up the hand by the tip of its little finger. It dangled like a small, dead animal. Djanhiz glanced at Trav, as if about to speak, then smiled and threw the hand onto the coals of the brazier.

He started forward without thinking, moving close enough that a shadow of his birth luck caressed him.

Djanhiz said, "Remember the girl!"

Trav nodded and backed again. The brazier had darkened when his hand fell into it. As the hand began to smoke, Trav gasped and dropped to his knees. His birth luck whirled about him, wild and strange, a storm that he perceived as silver light and tamarind scent and something like burning honey. Then his birth luck fled, freed from the prison that had been his severed right hand. Every spell that he had ever made dissolved in that instant.

His sight left him, and so did his balance. He fell forward, bruising his left hand and his right stump on the tiled patio, then vomited.

Djanhiz sighed. "I suppose it was too much to hope that your own magic kept you young. You still trust Gogo with your life, though she left you? Or another? It is a weakness, Magician."

His vision returned, though there was nothing he wished to see. He wiped his chin and rose unsteadily, sneering as he said, "It'll keep me alive until I invest my luck again." He and Gogo had always used their magic to keep each other alive during their birthdays, when their magics failed as their birth luck returned to their bodies. Gogo had left Trav at the end of the month of Fruit and found or hired someone else to help her through her next birthday. Without telling him, she had renewed the spell that would keep Trav alive through his. He had cried then, though not since.

Djanhiz said, "Take off your clothes."

He glanced at her and began to undo his sash.

She laughed. "Because I remember when you walked freely into Chiano Mefini's trap, and I would know what preparations you might have with you now."

He stood naked in the night while Djanhiz ran her hands over his clothing and prodded his coin purse. Frowning, she stepped closer to him. Her eyes narrowed, and she reached out, touching a thin pink slash across his chest. He almost grabbed her hand, then remembered the knife at Sessi's throat. She said, "It would've been easy to heal that entirely. It must itch—" Her fingers moved to a shorter reddish line just beneath his sternum, a puckered line as wide as two fingers.

She held his gaze. After a moment, he nodded and glanced away. She prodded the wound with her fingers, and he cried out, bringing his left hand and the stump of his right wrist up to cover his chest.

"You disgusting—" Her full lips curled, but found no words. He waited, wondering if she could understand, or if her loathing would help him understand himself.

"I'd planned to kill you quickly," she said softly, "if another's magic kept you young. I couldn't decide between water and fire, whether to sink you in the sea and let the fish clean the living flesh from your bones, or to close you in an oven until even your bones were ash. I doubt anyone's spell would keep you alive then. But now I suspect that keeping you alive would be the crueler thing to do." She smiled again. "We've nine months before your birthday and the return of your luck. That's sufficient time to decide."

"No!" Trav drove his left fist toward her face, forgetting everything for a moment. Her smile disappeared, but her left arm came up in the smooth movement of the experienced martial artist. Her right hand knifed into his solar plexus. He fell again and lay on the ground, hugging himself. When air returned to his lungs, he began to cry.

Djanhiz touched her ring to his bare arm. He felt the bite of a needle, then nothing. As the world retreated, Trav wondered if that had been an act of convenience, or of kindness.

Festival Day

His mother met Rusty at the door to her apartment. "Here," he said, thrusting a folded scrap of rice paper at her. "Where's Dad?" He glanced past her and saw that the apartment had been hung with small blue lanterns and sashes. A blue glass chipmunk sat behind a bowl of candied cashews, Sessi's favorite Festival treat.

"Sleeping." The hollows of his mother's eyes were dark, and he hoped he had not woken her. She took the note. Sessi's abductor had written, *The Magician has arrived. Expect Sessi Jassil on Restoration Day. She will be healthy and unharmed.* "Bastards," she whispered.

"She's all right."

"You believe that?"

He glanced at the blue glass chipmunk. "Why would they send the note, if she wasn't?"

"To gain time to escape, my son, the Guard lieutenant." When he winced, she said, "Why not send her home now?"

"My best guess? Because she knows something that would hurt them. Something that won't matter tomorrow. Who they are, maybe how they'll leave the city. The Guard is still watching for her, in case she's not in the Zhir embassy."

"Can't a magician verify that she's there, at least? Just knowing whether she's alive—"

Rusty shook his head. "The Zhir aren't the most sophisticated wizards, but every Guard magician says they outdid themselves in laying blankets of secrecy spells on their embassy. Four of our wizards are trying to find a path through. I asked if Gogo could help. They say it's not a matter of power, but of patience. Let Gogo enjoy Festival Week. Someone should."

His mother sighed and touched his cheek. "You should be resting."

"I can help Sessi as much on duty as off. 'Sides, the Guard needs everyone during Hell Week. Sessi's kidnapping isn't our only case."

"Sessi will never forgive herself if The Magician dies for her."

"We're looking for him, too. Bastian's agreed to tell the Zhir that we followed Marik to their embassy, but she's not hopeful. Any search that the Zhir allow us will be a joke. They'll move their captives from room to room ahead of us like a damned shell game. If we really press them, they'll kill Sessi and Marik and bury them in the cellar. So we wait."

His mother nodded. "Don't sneak in by yourself."

"Mom! You don't think—"

She smiled and shook her head. "You're in the Levar's pay. It'd be an act of war. It was enough to stand by while The Magician sacrificed himself. Don't expect me to let my son throw away himself and his city."

Rusty bit his upper lip, then said, "What do you expect of me?"

"What you expect of me." She hugged him. "We wait."

Ceramic dolphins swam from chandeliers and wall lamps in every room of the Zhir embassy, excluding the basement and the south guest room. Rangzha Fon stood in the doorway of the south room and wondered why he had always thought it so beautiful; he would repaint it when his visitor left. He said carefully, "It's dangerous to keep The Magician alive."

"Would you kill him? You're welcome to try." Djanhiz adjusted the front of her bright yellow Festival gown. "You could chop him into tiny bits. Would each bit continue to live, do you think, no matter how small you cut it? You could fill a tub with lye and lower him into it. Would that amuse you?"

Rangzha Fon shuddered.

"We are safe," said Djanhiz. "If your tour did not convince the Guard that only Zhir are in these walls, it did convince them that they could not find the girl or The Magician without occupying the building. We've nothing to fear from The Magician so long as he's drugged. Liavek's remaining wizards are celebrating Festival Night in their various ways. By the time anyone learns of your prince's plans, it will be too late. Now we only wait to see if his plans display genius or madness."

"Why do you drug The Magician? The Guard won't return until Festival Week's over and Jeng has...acted."

Djanhiz turned to him and grinned. He flinched when she extended a long-fingered hand toward him. Smoothing the front of his Liavekan evening jacket, she said, "You're off to hear speeches, see fireworks, light a Festival lantern or two, and celebrate like any of the Levar's most honored guests. Do you really enjoy worrying?"

Rangzha Fon nodded again.

Djanhiz laughed. "Then let me tell you a bit of esoteric magical lore. If a master magician—and The Magician is certainly that—does not invest his luck or has his luck freed—and we have done that for Master Marik—he still has access to his power during the nine minutes or so of each day that correspond to the moments of his birth."

"May Thung feign mercy!"

Djanhiz shrugged. "So we keep Trav Marik unconscious. Tomorrow we can convince him to reveal the exact time that he was born, and then ensure that he never has a chance to use his birth-moment magic." Djanhiz glanced out the window at the dying light of the day. "He should be coming to, soon. Can you feed him his dinner without me?"

Sessi sneezed into her hand, wiped it against the wall, and wrapped her wool blanket more tightly around her. The Magician remained unconscious on the other cot, where the fat Zhir and the old Titch had thrown him the night before.

She knew her windowless cell very well after two days. Two walls were cool, damp stone, telling her that this room was probably in a basement. Two walls were thick wooden planks. Iron rings hung from the ceiling beams; Sessi did not want to know their purpose. The only light came through the narrow bars set into the door. When she stood on tiptoe and peeked through the bars, she could see an iron lamp standing close to their door, and a shadowy hallway lined with more sturdy doors like theirs. She hoped those rooms were normally used for storage. A guard always waited at the end of the hall, but the only people who ever entered the cell were the fat Zhir and the tall Titch.

Something blocked the light, and the door rattled open. The fat Zhir, wearing evening clothes, entered with a tray holding two bowls of soup and two mugs of water. Placing the tray by The Magician's cot, the Zhir locked the door with a key that hung around his neck and said, "He hasn't stirred since lunch?" The Magician, semiconscious, had been spoonfed by the Zhir and the Titch, and then had gone back to sleep.

Sessi shook her head. Wanting to test a suspicion, she reached for the bowl and cup that were closest to The Magician.

The Zhir slapped her hand. "No! The Magician's has a special medicine. It's only for magicians. It'll help him rest."

The Zhir lifted The Magician's head, and he groaned. "Wha— Where?"

"Shush," the Zhir said kindly. "Drink." He held the cup to The Magician's lips. "You'll feel better."

Sessi tried not to watch the Zhir feed The Magician. She made herself finish her own bland dinner, thinking that food was strength and she would need hers, if a chance came to escape. The Zhir helped The Magician with the nightpan, then set it and their dishes into the hall. Sliding a clean pan back in the cell, he said, "Rest well," and fled.

Sessi counted to twenty-five to be sure that the Zhir had gone. She reached across The Magician's bed to grab his far shoulder, then turned him onto his side. His eyes flicked open once, and he said, "Uh?"

As his eyes closed, Sessi whispered, "Please don't bite," and stuck her fingers down The Magician's throat.

Trav woke on his back in a dark room to the sensation of something damp and scratchy moving across his face. He reached for it, and a child said, "Oh, thank the Twin Forces! I thought you'd never wake up!"

He rolled over, tangling himself in a rough blanket. Someone had taken his clothes. Feeling for the edge of the bed, he remembered that someone had taken his hand, too. The room smelled of vomit, and the taste in his mouth told him whose.

"I saved some of my drinking water," the child said. "Go on. They didn't need to drug me." He could not see her face clearly, but she was small and short-haired, wearing a flowered tunic and a braided necklace. She had been holding a blanket, which she dropped.

"Sessi?" He sipped from her wooden cup. There was only a taste of warm water, enough to tell him how very thirsty he was. His head ached and his chest felt hollow. "Drugged?"

"Yes. I don't know what, but it's something to keep you unconscious. I made you throw up. It was really disgusting."

"Sorry."

"And it still took hours for you to wake up. We've got to get out of here!"

"They destroyed my luck piece." Trav knew that he should care, but he could not.

Sessi whispered, "They didn't destroy mine." She touched the pendant of her necklace, a blue stone chipmunk. "Didn't think a little kid could've invested her luck yet, I guess. But the only magic I know is wind and orange smoke and an illusion that looks like a kitten if you turn your head sideways and squint."

"Not terribly helpful."

"No," Sessi agreed.

Trav let himself fall back onto the cot and draped his arm over his forehead. He might have a fever; he could not tell. "Then we stay here."

"We have to try something! The Zhir are attacking Liavek tonight!"

He squinted at her. "That's ridiculous."

"It's true! When I woke up after they captured me, they were talking about airships and the Levar and Festival Night and marines and holding the palace and like that." She nodded to herself. "We have to do something, Master Trav."

"Yes." Trav closed his eyes. "Let me rest." All of Liavek would be celebrating Festival Night. Gogo would be celebrating too, in her new home, with her new friends. Would she miss him? He might have been celebrating, too. He tried to remember what had become of his friends and his life. He knew a city's worth of dead people.

She shook him. "You're The Magician! The Levar depends on you."

He laughed. "Hardly. There's the Guard for worldly troubles, and half the inhabitants of Wizard's Row to deal with magical ones." But the inhabitants of Wizard's Row vacationed like other Liavekans. How many of Liavek's greatest magicians were in the city? How many of those looked for danger during Festival Week? They all knew—

They all knew that the Levar's Regents had paid The Magician very well for a web of spells that would detect any magical threat that came to Liavek, or any mortal threat that came by land or sea.

He thought of the smoking ruin of his right hand. Every spell that he had formed had dissipated when it burned in Djanhiz's brazier.

His loss did not matter to Liavek. The city's officials were not fools. Other magicians had been hired to set magical defenses around Liavek, too; the city's fate could not depend on one person's well-being. More magicians had added their own spells out of love of Liavek and the Levar. Sessi's fears were ludicrous.

"Master Trav?" Sessi said hesitantly.

He twitched his head for silence. Something besides his headache and his weakness nagged at him. "If any worldly threat came by land or sea," he said, remembering the *Luck of Liavek*, bulky and slow and carrying no more than a passenger or two as it floated quietly over the Levar's Park. A thousand of those would fill the sky. What wizard would think to set spells to watch the air for dangers that did not come by magic? How many experienced soldiers would be needed to seize the palace and the Levar, if they could arrive without warning in the middle of the chaos that was Festival Night?

"The Zhir and the Titch didn't say anything about land or sea," Sessi whispered. "They said airships."

"The entire idea's ridiculous," Trav answered. Then, wrapping the blanket tightly around himself, he stood and began to study their prison.

Fek Zhang dreamed of being a boy in his mountain village near the city of Ka Zhir. When he woke, his first thought was relief that he would not have to explain to his mother how the goat's milk had spilled. His apprehension returned when he realized that he had fallen asleep at his post in the basement of the embassy in Liavek, and smoke and screams came from the prisoners' room.

Something must have knocked over the hall lamp (for surely no wind could have blown in this closed place). Fek Zhang grabbed a fire bucket and ran to scatter sand over the flames. He looked all around the narrow hall, wondering how a cat or a dog could have crept past him while he slept.

"In here!" the girl prisoner called. "It's burning in here!"

Fek Zhang could not see within the cell; smoke and darkness hid the room from him. Drawing his pistol from his sash and bringing its hammer to full-cock, he unlocked the door. "Come out! There're buckets—" Orange fumes billowed from the open door, as if driven by wind. Fek Zhang coughed and blinked, and something leaped for his face. Through his watery, half-blinded vision, it seemed a demonic caricature of a kitten.

Fek Zhang screamed and fired his pistol. The kitten disappeared with the sound of his shot. Fek Zhang gasped deeply and watched for the thing's return.

The Magician of Liavek, naked and filthy, stepped from within the smoky cell. Fek Zhang lifted the pistol, and The Magician smiled. "Hello. Don't you wish you had time to reload?"

Fek Zhang tried to club the man with his flintlock's barrel, but The Magician blocked the blow with his right forearm and drove his left fist into Fek Zhang's stomach. Within a minute, the fight had ended. For the rest of his life, Fek Zhang maintained that he would have beaten the one-handed man, if only the misshapen kitten had not returned in the form of a girl-demon that climbed on his back and clawed at his eyes.

Though Rusty's shift had ended and he should be somewhere asleep, he waited in the alley across from the Zhir embassy. A dark woman had left early in the evening, and the ambassador had departed soon after. He did not know how many servants remained, and wondered whether he should ignore his mother's warning and enter. Near midnight, he saw a slim man in ill-fitting Zhir trousers and tunic leave by a side door. Rusty nodded to Stone, and they both moved forward. When Sessi stepped into the street behind the man, Rusty and Stone began to run.

Rusty caught Sessi in a hug and, laughing, whirled her around. Only then did he notice that her one-handed companion was The Magician, and The Magician was walking quickly away.

"Master Marik!" Rusty called. "Thank you! What happened—"

"Alert the Guard," The Magician answered. "The Zhir may invade this evening. Protect the Levar."

"You're sure?"

"Not at all. Do it anyway. Look for Djanhiz ola Vikili. Sessi can describe her. A Tichenese woman who was once a wizard. You'll want the Zhir ambassador, too, I think." One of the new pedicabs wheeled by, and The Magician called, "Taxi!"

"Wait!" Rusty yelled after him. "Where're you going?"

"For a ride on an airship. Beautiful night for one, don't you think?"

"Faster!" he called from the padded bench of the pedicab, though they took a corner on two of the cab's three wheels and he had to grab the side of the seat to keep from falling. He wished he knew the time. He wished he had calculated the exact minute when his birth-moment magic would return. He feared his luck would come too soon to be of any use to Liavek, if there was any substance in Sessi's mad suggestion.

"That's a joke, right?" the wiry driver answered without looking back. "You want to pump the oak till it's broke? Or you want to let me?"

His strength was half of hers, after his stay in the Zhir embassy. "Sorry. It's important."

The driver laughed. "I'm getting you to her as fast as I can."

Festival lanterns hung at every pole and window, transforming the City of Luck into a city of light. Each major intersection was blocked with revelers who danced to bands playing music from every culture of the known world. Liavek's avenues were impassable, so they raced through alleys and back streets until the cab rolled into the Levar's Park.

Trav found a coin purse in the Zhir guard's trousers and tossed it to the pedicab driver. "Thanks, Master!" she yelled as he leaped from the bench and ran toward the *Luck of Liavek*.

The airship shifted at its mooring in the middle of the meadow like a lazy tethered elephant. Trav saw no one near it. The fireworks had begun across Lake Levar, attracting most of the people who passed Festival Night in the Levar's Park. A rope ladder hung from the netting around the pilot's platform, so Trav scrambled up it, snatching at its wooden rungs with his one hand. Midway up, he heard the bald woman call, "Who comes? I'm armed!"

"A passenger! I'm not!"

"It's the middle of the night!"

"Do tell?" He gained the platform, wondering if she would kick him off.

"Oh, luck of a chipmunk. We need the money." She took his elbow with a firm grip and helped him over the low wall of netting. She wore wool trousers and a leather jacket; a blanket had been spread near the pilot's chair, which was built into the front of the wood-and-wicker platform. "When and where do you want to go?"

"Up. Now." A wave of dizziness rolled over him, surely the effect of his haste.

"Right." Her gaze inventoried his cheap, badly fitting clothes, and perhaps his desperation, too. "Come back tomorrow, when you're not drunk or stoned. If you're just stupid, don't come back."

"Now. I'll pay—" He patted empty pockets and wondered how much money he had given the taxi driver. Fireworks exploded above the lake. He told himself that the glow before his eyes was only their reflected light.

The woman shook her bald head. "No crew to launch us, no crew to bring us in. The field isn't lit for landing. Come back tomorrow."

"I'm The Magician. Going's vital for Liavek's safety."

"I'm the captain. Staying's vital for my safety."

"Oh, gods." He doubled over, feeling the world grow bright as though the sun shone for him alone. His nose filled with the scent of cinnamon. The captain set her hand on his shoulder. "Puke over the rail if—"

Trav straightened up, as strong and as clear-headed as if he had never been captured by Djanhiz and the Zhir. "Take the controls."

"Don't speak—"

A fireball appeared at each of his fingertips. "I'm The Ma—"

She hit his hand, destroying his concentration. "Damn it, man! Water-gas is inflammable."

"Sorry." The flames imploded silently. "Take us up."

"No."

Trav imagined the mooring cords untying themselves like restless snakes. "Take the controls."

The captain dropped a hand to the long knife at her hip. "Never."

"I'd rethink that." He pointed. The brilliant lights of Festival Night sank slowly beyond the platform rail. The *Luck of Liavek* drifted toward Lake Levar and the fireworks beyond.

"How'd—" She ran to the engine at the rear of the platform and began to crank it. "Grab my bedding!" she called. On the fourth turn, the engine's explosive protests became a rough roar. "Stuff the blankets in that locker!" As she took her seat, she pointed at a chest built onto the platform. "And haul up the ladder!" The ship's wooden propeller turned faster and faster behind them. "You damned fool!" she shouted. "You endanger my ship!"

"Sorry!" Trav shouted back. "I'm The Magician."

"I know you're a magician! Didn't I say you're a fool?" The *Luck of Liavek* turned lazily toward the south. "You toy with a ship I've spent my life building as if it was a bauble conjured out of dreamstuff—"

"I'm sorry."

"As though the rest of us had no—" She glanced back at him. "What?"

"I'm sorry. And I'm a fool. Please, don't land."

"Land?" The captain laughed without humor. "Not till dawn. Not even then, if we can't find a sober landing crew."

"You'll be paid well, whatever happens. This is the Levar's business. Please. Take us higher. Over the sea."

She studied him, and he thought he had failed. Then she nodded. "All right."

At least two minutes of his magic were lost. "Can we go faster?"

"Engine and fuel and the two of us make a lot of weight. You could jump."

"Ah, no, thanks." He pictured the platform and its load, then thought of feathers. The city of Liavek dwindled more quickly beneath them.

She opened her mouth, closed it, and said, "You did something?"

He nodded. "What else would speed us?"

Surprise and delight came to her face. "An engine of the finest steel, twice as large as this one. A propeller to match. A larger gas bag, long and sleek like a rigid eel. And twice the fuel!"

He nodded again, then grabbed the low wall of netting to keep from falling as the transformed airship surged forward. Its nose lifted until the captain did something with the dangling cords around her seat; the platform became level again. The engine seemed smoother and louder, a beat for tireless dancers, and the wind whipped at Trav's borrowed clothes. He realized he was cold, and glanced at the captain. She'd turned up her leather hood. He made himself a jacket to match hers.

She grinned at him. "I've dreamed of a ship like this. But why do you want an airship when you could magic up something that didn't care how the natural world wanted things to behave?"

"Because my power will be gone in four or five minutes. And I need to concentrate on something besides staying in the air."

"Ah. Let my ship's true weight return slowly, then, not all at once. Even so, I'll be playing tricky games with the controls to keep us aloft when the *Luck* reverts."

He nodded, noting that and ignoring it. He probed the skies around him, casting intangible nets for humans in the air. He found gulls and owls and nighthawks, and then, a mile away, two people high above Liavek. He smiled grimly, thinking he had found Sessi's Zhir invaders a few moments before they would act. His smile changed when he realized that two magicians were celebrating Festival Night in their own way, then changed again when he realized who they were.

"Be happy, Gogo," he whispered.

"What?" the captain called.

"Nothing. Be quiet." Catching her scowl, he added, "Please. There's no—" And then his nets found the Zhir, perhaps thirty miles away. Not a fleet of small airships, but three leviathans of the air, each carrying ninety soldiers. He thought of fireworks, and knew how easy it would be to imagine skyrockets within the explosive water-gas bags of the Zhir's huge ships.

Would the explosions be visible from Liavek? Three balls of fire would hang in the sky like exploded stars. Would the flames consume the Zhir soldiers? A passing sailing ship might find flotsam that hinted at alien vessels and unknowable calamities. Would the Zhir soldiers die screaming as they fell onto the hard, green waves of the Sea of Luck? Would the fall to the sea kill the burning airmen, or save them? The passing sailing ship might find charred swimmers who dared not speak of their mission or their fate.

Trav touched one Zhir's mind, and discovered impatience after twelve hours in the air and a fear of leaping from the airship at night to circle down on a fragile glider onto a strange city; the hope of landing safely in the bright, confused streets, of being one of those who made it to the palace to seize the Levar and close the palace gates before any semblance of resistance came against them; the hope that his parents would be proud of him...

A minute or two of Trav's birth magic remained, at most. He remembered the captain's warning and commanded the *Luck of Liavek* to begin its return to its original weight and form. He thought he could see three dark dots on the southern horizon, though they might have been imagination.

He pictured a tiny, turbulent fist of air over the Sea of Luck that beat itself into a spiral of wind. Something resisted his will; weather had its own desire and its own momentum that he must master or coerce, if he could. He imagined the spiral whipping faster, driving itself against the night breezes, becoming a storm between Liavek and the three Zhir airships. He wrestled with the raw stuff of the sky, shaping a hurricane to protect the city he loved.

His birth-moment magic ended without warning. He sagged against the netting, weary and cold, then made himself stand.

If he'd succeeded, the effects of the storm would continue, and the winds would drive the airships southward, away from Liavek. One or all might crash, but he could think of nothing better that he could have done for the Zhir or for his conscience. If he'd failed, a battle would be fought in Liavek's streets. Whether Liavek endured or fell, he would share in each death on either side.

"Didn't expect that," the captain said, throwing a bag of sand over the netting and pointing. A small dark turbulence built in the distance like a wall between them and the southern stars. "Thought it was going to be a nice night."

Trav glanced at her, then laughed at himself. "It's going to be a great one."

She shrugged. "If you say so. Mind if we head back? I don't want to be caught if that comes our way."

"No, not at all." His teeth chattered, but he did not care.

"Take one of my blankets." She moved around her seat to open the locker. "Sounds like you could use it."

"Thank you." He looked away. The black clouds hid the southern stars. Though the storm grew larger, it did not seem to be approaching them. Moonlight rolled over the waves of the Sea of Luck below them. To the north beyond the harbor islands, Liavek beckoned, a city etched in light.

"Fortunately," the captain said, passing him the blanket and reaching again into the locker, "I keep a few refreshments on board for special occasions. Happy Festival Night." She lifted out a bottle and two glasses, then smiled, and Trav laughed for no other reason than joy.

Restoration Day

Rangzha Fon returned to his embassy with his evening clothes stained and rumpled. He wore a mask of a blue chipmunk around his neck and sang a Liavekan love song that he had learned from a desert tribesman who did not understand the words. Between them, the lyrics had become "Dippa didi wokka wie," which seemed to express all that Rangzha Fon wished to say. He carried a large teak box in both hands.

"You are drunk," Djanhiz ola Vikili told him as he entered his office.

"Excellent." Rangzha Fon placed the teak box in the center of his desk, hung the new mask among the others on the wall, then fell into his chair. "Would've been a shame to waste all that wine."

"A Gold Harbor ship came into Liavek this morning with many ship-wrecked Zhir marines aboard."

"Poor shipwrecked Zhir. Missed Festival Night."

"The ship that was wrecked was an airship."

"Oh," said Rangzha Fon, and when Djanhiz ola Vikili seemed insufficiently pleased, he repeated it. "Oh."

"The Prince's ships were caught in a storm."

"Well." Rangzha Fon waved his hand, still smiling, but realized from the demands of his stomach that the wine's quality had been less than it had seemed. "Storms happen."

"There should not have been a storm last night. If The Magician had not escaped, there would not have been a storm, don't you think?"

Rangzha Fon burped.

"How elegant," said Djanhiz ola Vikili. "Several of your shipwrecked countrymen have asked for asylum in Liavek. Their story has perplexed the Liavekans. Messages have traveled between Liavek and Ka Zhir."

Rangzha Fon nodded. "You're a very smart person, Mistress ola Vikili."

She slammed the palm of her hand against his desk. "I am a captive in this embassy, Rangzha Fon. And so are you! The Liavekans will arrest us if we step outside. Jeng will not help us, because we have failed him. What will we do?"

"A very smart person," Rangzha Fon repeated. "But you worry too much. Don't worry about the Liavekans outside."

She raised an eyebrow.

"I invited them in." Rangzha Fon clapped his hands.

Two Liavekan Guards in gray and blue stepped into his office, led by a red-bearded lieutenant with weary eyes. When Djanhiz ola Vikili reached toward the jade letter opener on Rangzha Fon's desk, the lieutenant drew his pistol and aimed it at her heart. He said, "My part in this business has been to watch and to suffer and to do nothing at all. I would be most grateful if you attacked me."

Djanhiz's hand remained over the jade knife, then drew back. She stared at Rangzha Fon, making him feel almost sober, and he reminded himself that her magic had been destroyed years ago. "Why?" she said softly.

"I'm the ambassador," Rangzha Fon answered. "King Thelm had his magicians send a gift to the ambassador to present to the Levar." As Djanhiz glanced at the teak box, he fumbled in his robes. "A scroll, too. But I think I'll give his gift to the Levar's Regents, and let them give it to the Levar, if they want." He met her glance. "Go ahead. Look."

Djanhiz ola Vikili reached out with both hands and lifted the hinged cover, revealing the head of Prince Jeng of Ka Zhir.

"Scroll says, 'Accept this proof of Ka Zhir's friendship with Liavek. Though Thelm's bite is weakened, his pain ends.' "

Every year, Sessi dreaded the arrival of Restoration Day. It meant the end of Festival Week, the end of celebrating life and the return of living it. Yet every Restoration Day, she decided this was really her favorite day of the year.

The Street of Old Coins bustled with people, mostly its inhabitants but also visiting friends and family, ostensibly cleaning up after the excesses of Festival Night but actually sharing gossip and leftover holiday food. The littlest kids picked up trash and the older ones swept and scrubbed, and no one minded that their work was interrupted by impromptu games, like now: Sessi and six friends chased each other with straw brooms, swatting and laughing. Her mother usually did chores that she had wanted to do for months; today she was in the front yard, painting their shutters a joyful blue. Her father usually napped in a chair on their balcony, claiming the day's best use lay in restoring himself, however that was done. Neither of her parents seemed to be devoting themselves fully to their pastimes. Now and then, they would glance at her or at each other and smile.

As she chased the cute boy from the next block, determined to swat him twice as many times as he had swatted her, a hand fell on her shoulder. She gasped and spun, flailing with the broom.

The Magician stood still, letting her hit his shoulder, and said, "I'm sorry, Sessi. I didn't mean to startle—"

"Master Trav!" She hurtled into his arms. He caught her awkwardly, then she felt his grip grow tighter for a long moment.

When he released her, he said, "I wanted to say thank you, and I wanted to say good-bye."

"You're going away?"

"For a little while, anyway." He laughed, and she laughed too, because she had not seen him really happy for the longest time. "I'm going to build and design airships. Remember the captain of the *Luck of Liavek*? We'll be partners. Each day when I've got my birth-moment luck, I'll create and test a new design. Next year, we'll build a proper manufactory and start producing ships that won't disappear when my magic does. Want a ride on the first?"

She nodded. "Who'll be The Magician, then?"

"Gogo. She'll keep giving you magic lessons, if you want them."

Sessi nodded again.

"Listen," he said, squatting so they were alone in the crowded street. "It's all right if you're scared sometimes. Do you have nightmares?"

She gave the tiniest nod.

"Me, too."

"You're The Magician." She looked at his face and said, "Were."

"When you're The Magician, you'll have nightmares, too. Different ones. Don't let them rule you, and you'll be better for it."

"Me? The Magician?"

He laughed and nodded. "If you work hard. If you don't let the bad things scare you too much. If you remember that luck is something to share. If you never give up, no matter how pointless it seems." He stood up. "That's probably a good exit line. I should go."

She touched his sleeve, the empty one where a hand had been. "There's Festival cake. With almonds and cherries and chocolate sauce."

He looked away, destroying their moment of privacy in the street. Sessi's friends still chased each other. A little kid had fallen and begun to cry, but his older brother was already picking him up. An old woman in a wheelchair played a game of shah with the university student who lived across the street. A group of singers made a merry hash of "Pot-boil Blues." The smell of fresh bread came from the bakery around the corner. Someone hawked the latest edition of the *Cat Street Crier* with surprising enthusiasm for Restoration Day: "Storm destroys Zhir airships! Abducted girl returns safely! Beautiful weather for Restoration Day! All the news of Liavek for only half of a copper!"

"Well," said the man who had been The Magician. "There's more to life than a good exit line. A slice of Festival cake would suit me very well indeed."

When War for the Oaks *appeared in print, I was very happy, but I still kept looking over my shoulder, figuratively speaking; I was still waiting for someone to notice that I'd snuck into the club of People Who Write by rapidly waving my membership card for the club of People Who Think They Can Write. They do look a little alike, after all. Then Diana Wynne Jones asked me if I'd contribute a story to her anthology* Hidden Turnings. *I realized that one of the high-ranking officers of that most desirable club had examined my credentials and offered me a glass of sherry. I wrote this for her.*

It doesn't seem to me, on rereading this story, that I made it up at all. I'm half convinced it was dictated to me by the narrator. Orpheus Coffeehouse was real; I owe it, and Steve Powers, a considerable debt.

—Emma

A Bird That Whistles

Emma Bull

The dulcimer player sat on the back steps of Orpheus Coffeehouse, lit from behind by the bulb over the door. His head hung forward, and his silhouette was sharp against the diffused glow from State Street. The dulcimer was propped against his shoulder as if it were a child he was comforting. I'd always thought you balanced a dulcimer across your knees. But it worked; this sounded like the classical guitar of dulcimer playing. Then his chin lifted a little.

'Twas on one bright March morning, I bid New Orleans adieu,
And I took the road to Jackson town, my fortunes to renew.
I cursed all foreign money, no credit could I gain,
Which filled my heart with longing for the lakes of
     Pontchartrain.

He got to the second verse before he stopped and looked up. Light fell on the side of his face.

"I like the bit about the alligators best," I said stupidly.

"So do I." I could hear his grin. " 'If it weren't for the alligators, I'd sleep out in the woods.' Sort of sums up life." He sounded so cheerful, it was hard to believe he'd sung those mournful words.

"You here for the open stage?" I asked. Then I remembered *I* was, and my terror came pounding back.

He lifted the shoulder that supported the dulcimer. "Maybe." He stood smoothly. I staggered up the steps with my banjo case, and he held the door for me.

In the full light of the back room, his looks startled me as much as his music had. He was tall, slender, and pale. His black hair was thick and long, pulled into a careless tail in back, except for some around his face that was too short and fell forward into his eyes. Those were the ordinary things.

His clothes were odd. This was 1970, and we all dressed the way we thought Woody Guthrie used to: blue denim and workshirts. This guy wore a white t-shirt, black corduroys, and a black leather motorcycle jacket that looked old enough to be his father's. (I would have said he was about eighteen.) The white streak in his hair was odd. His face was odd; with its high cheekbones and pointed chin, it was somewhere out beyond handsome.

But his eyes—they were like green glass, or a green pool in the shadow of trees, or a green gemstone with something moving behind it, dimly visible. Looking at them made me uncomfortable; but when he turned away, I felt the loss, as if something I wanted but couldn't name had been taken from me.

Steve O'Connell, the manager, came out of the kitchen, and the green-eyed man handed him the dulcimer. "It's good," he said. "I'd like to meet whoever made it."

Steve's harried face lit up. "My brother. I'll tell him you said so."

Steve disappeared down the hall to the front room, and the green eyes came back to my face. "I haven't forgotten your name, have I?"

"No." I put my hand out, and he shook it. "John Deacon."

"Banjo player," he added. "I'm Willy Silver. Guitar and fiddle."

"Not dulcimer?"

"Not usually. But I dabble in strings."

That's when Lisa came out of the kitchen.

Lisa waited tables at Orpheus. She looked like a dancer, all slender and small and long-boned. Her hair was a cirrus cloud of red-gold curls;

her eyes were big, cat-tilted, and gray; and her skin was so fair you should have been able to see through it. I'd seen Waterhouse's painting *The Lady of Shalott* somewhere (though I didn't remember the name of the painter or the painting then; be kind, I was barely seventeen), and every time I saw Lisa I thought of it. She greeted me by name whenever I came to Orpheus, and smiled, and teased me. Once, when I came in with the tail-end of the flu, she fussed over me so much I wondered if it was possible to get a chronic illness on purpose.

Lisa came out of the kitchen, my heart gave a great loud thump, she looked up with those big, enquiring eyes, and she saw Willy Silver. I recognized the disease that struck her down. Hadn't she already given it to me?

Willy Silver saw her, too. "Hullo," he said, and looked as if he was prepared to admire any response she gave.

"Hi." The word was a little breathless gulp. "Oh, hi, John. Are you a friend of John's?" she asked Willy.

"I just met him," I told her. "Willy Silver, Lisa Amundsen. Willy's here for open stage."

He gave me a long look, but said, "If you say so."

I must have been feeling masochistic. Lisa always gets crushes on good musicians, and I already knew Willy was one. Maybe I ought to forget the music and just commit seppuku on stage.

But you can't forget the music. Once you get the itch, it won't go away, no matter how much stage fright you have. And by the time my turn came—after a handful of guys-on-stools-with-guitars, two women who sang *a capella* for too long, a woman who did Leonard Cohen songs on the not-quite-tuned piano, and the Orpheus Tin-and-Wood Toejam Jug Band—I had plenty of stage fright.

Then Willy Silver leaned over from the chair next to me and whispered, "Take it slow. Play the chord progression a couple of times for an intro—it'll settle you down."

I looked up, startled. The white streak in his hair caught the light, and his eyes gleamed green. He was smiling.

"And the worst that can happen isn't very bad."

I could embarrass myself in front of Lisa…and everyone else, and be ashamed to ever show my face in Orpheus again. But Willy didn't look like someone who'd understand that.

My hands shook as if they had engine knock. I wanted to go to the bathroom. Steve clumped up on stage, read my name from the slip of paper in his hand, and peered out into the dark room for me. I hung the banjo over my shoulder and went up there to die for my art.

I scrapped the short opening I'd practiced and played the whole chord progression instead. The first couple measures were shaky. But banjos give out a lively noise that makes you *want* to have a good time, and I could feel mine sending those messages. By the time I got around to the words, I could remember them, and sing them in almost my usual voice.

> I got a bird that whistles, honey, got a bird,
> Baby, got a bird that will sing.
> Honey, got a bird, baby, got a bird that will sing.
> But if I ain't got Corinna, it just don't mean
> It don't mean a natural thing.

At the back of the room, I could just see the halo of Lisa's hair. I couldn't see her face, but at least she'd stopped to listen. And down front, Willy Silver sat, looking pleased.

I did "Lady Isabel and the Elf Knight" and "Newry Highwayman." I blew some chords and forgot some words, but I lived through it. And people applauded. I grinned and thanked them and stumbled off the stage.

"Do they clap because they like what you did," I asked Willy, "or because you stopped doing what they didn't?"

Willy made a muffled noise into his coffee cup.

"Pretty darn good," said Lisa, at my elbow. I felt immortal. Then I realized that she was stealing glances at Willy. "Want to order something, now that you're not too nervous to eat it?"

I blushed, but in the dark, who could tell? "PB and J," I told her.

"PB and J?" Willy repeated.

We both stared at him, but it was Lisa who said, "Peanut butter and jelly sandwich. Don't you call them that?"

The pause was so short I'm not sure I really heard it. Then he said, "I don't think I've ever been in a coffeehouse where you could order a peanut butter and jelly sandwich."

"This is it," Lisa told him. "Crunchy or smooth, whole wheat or white, grape jelly or peach preserves."

"Good grief. Crunchy, whole wheat, and peach."

"Non-conformist," she said admiringly.

He turned to me when she went toward the kitchen. "You *were* pretty good," he said. "I like the way you sing. For that last one, though, you might try mountain minor."

"What?"

He got an eager look on his face. "Come on," he said, sprang out of his chair, and led the way toward the back.

We sat on the back steps until the open stage was over, and he taught me about mountain minor tuning. His guitar was a deep-voiced old Gibson with the varnish worn off the strategic spots, and he flat-picked along with me, filling in the places that needed it. Eventually we went back inside, and he taught me about pull-offs. As Steve stacked chairs, we played "Newry Highwayman" as a duet. Then he taught me "Shady Grove," because it was mountain minor, too.

I'd worked hard at the banjo, and I enjoyed playing it. But I don't think I'd ever been aware of making something beautiful with it. That's what those two songs were. Beautiful.

And Lisa moved through the room as we played, clearing tables, watching us. Watching him. Every time I looked up, her eyes were following his face, or his long fingers on the guitar neck.

I got home at two in the morning. My parents almost grounded me; I convinced them I hadn't spent the night raising hell by showing them my new banjo licks. Or maybe it was the urgency with which I explained what I'd learned and how, and that I had to have more.

When I came back to Orpheus two nights later, Willy was there. And Lisa, fair and graceful, was often near him, often smiled at him, that night and all the nights after it. Sometimes he'd smile back. But sometimes his face would be full of an intensity that couldn't be contained in a smile. Whenever Lisa saw that, her eyes would widen, her lips would part, and she'd look frightened and fascinated all at once. Which made me feel worse than if he'd smiled at her.

And sometimes he would ignore her completely, as if she were a cup of coffee he hadn't ordered. Then her face would close up tight with puzzlement and hurt, and I'd want to break something.

I could have hated him, but it was just as well I didn't. I wanted to learn music from Willy and to be near Lisa. Lisa wanted to be near Willy. The perfect arrangement. Hah.

And who could know what Willy wanted?

Fourth of July, Independence Day 1970, promised to be the emotional climax of the summer. Someone had organized a day of Vietnam War protests, starting with a rally in Riverside Park and ending with a torchlight march down State Street. Flyers about it were everywhere—tacked to phone poles, stuck on walls, and all over the tables at Orpheus. The picture on the flyers was the photo taken that spring, when the Ohio National Guard shot four students on the Kent State campus during another protest: a dark-haired woman kneeling over a dead student's body, her head lifted, her mouth open with weeping, or screaming. You'd think a photo like that would warn you away from protesting. But it gives you the feeling that someone has to do something. It gets you out on the street.

Steve was having a special marathon concert at the coffeehouse: Sherman and Henley, the Rose Hip String Band, Betsy Kaske, and—surprise—Willy Silver and John Deacon. True, we were scheduled to go on at seven, when the audience would be smallest, but I didn't care. I had been hired to play. For money.

The only cloud on my horizon was that Willy was again treating Lisa as one of life's non-essentials. As we set up for the show, I could almost see a dotted line trailing behind Willy that was her gaze, fixed on him.

Evening light was slanting through the door when we hit the stage, which made me feel funny. Orpheus was a place for after dark, when its shabby, struggling nature was cloaked with night-and-music magic. But Willy set his fiddle under his chin, leaned into the microphone, and drew out with his bow one sweet, sad, sustained note. All the awareness in the room—his, mine, and our dozen or so of audience's—hurtled to the sharp point of that one note and balanced there. I began to pick the banjo softly, and his note changed, multiplied, until we were playing instrumental harmony. I sang, and if my voice broke a little, it was just what the song required:

The sun rises bright in France, and fair sets he,
Ah, but he has lost the look he had in my ain country.

We made enough magic to cloak *three* shabby coffeehouses with glamour. When I got up the nerve to look beyond the edge of the stage, sometime in our fourth song, we had another dozen listeners. They'd come to line State Street for the march, and our music had called them in.

Lisa sat on the shag rug in front of the stage. Her eyes were bright, and for once, her attention didn't seem to be all for Willy.

Traditional music mostly tells stories. We told a lot of them that night. I felt them all as if they'd happened to friends of mine. Willy seemed more consumed by the music than the words, and songs he sang were sometimes almost too beautiful. But his strong voice never quavered or cracked like mine did. His guitar and fiddle were gorgeous, always, perfect and precise.

We finished at eight-thirty with a loose and lively rendition of "Blues in the Bottle," and the room was close to full. The march was due to pass by in half an hour.

We bounded off stage and into the back room. "Yo," said Willy, and stuck out his right hand. I shook it. He was touched with craziness, a little drunk with the music. He looked…not quite domesticated. Light seemed to catch more than usual in his green eyes. He radiated a contained energy that could have raised the roof.

"Let's go look at the street," I said.

We went out the back door and up the short flight of outside stairs to State Street. Or where State Street had been. The march, contrary to the laws of physics governing crowds, had arrived early.

Every leftist in Illinois might have been there. The pavement was gone beneath a winding, chanting snake of marchers blocks and blocks and *blocks* long. Several hundred people singing, "All we are saying / Is give peace a chance," makes your hair stand on end. Willy nudged me, beaming, and pointed to a banner that read, "Draft Beer, Not Boys." There really were torches, though the harsh yellow-tinted lights of State Street faded them. Some people on the edges of the crowd had lit sparklers; as the line of march passed over the bridge, first one, then dozens of sparklers, like shooting stars, arced over the railings and into the river, with one last bright burst of white reflection on the water before they hit.

I wanted to follow the march, but my banjo was in the coffeehouse, waiting for me to look after it. "I'm going to see what's up inside," I shouted at Willy. He nodded. Sparklers, fizzing, reflected in his eyes.

The crowd packed the sidewalk between me and Orpheus's front door, so I retraced our steps, down the stairs and along the river. I came into the parking lot, blind from the lights I'd just left, and heard behind me, "Hey, hippie."

There were two of them, about my age. They were probably both on their school's football and swimming teams; their hair was short, they weren't wearing blue jeans, they smelled of Southern Comfort, and they'd called me "hippie." A terrible combination. I started to walk away, across the parking lot, but the blond one stepped forward and grabbed my arm.

"Hey! I'm talking to you."

There's nothing helpful you can say at times like this, and if there had been, I was too scared to think of it. The other guy, brown-haired and shorter, came up and jabbed me in the stomach with two fingers. "You a draft dodger?" he said. "Scared to fight for your country?"

"Hippies make me puke," the blond one said thoughtfully.

They were drunk, for God's sake, and out on the town, and as excited in their way by the mass of people on the street above as I was. Which didn't make me feel any better when the brown-haired one punched me in the face.

I was lying on my back clutching my nose and waiting for the next bad thing to happen to me when I heard Willy say, "Don't do it." I'd heard him use his voice in more ways than I could count, but never before like that, never a ringing command that could turn you to stone.

I opened my eyes and found my two tormentors bracketing me, the blond one's foot still raised to kick me in the stomach. He lost his balance as I watched, and got the foot on the ground just in time to keep from falling over. They were both looking toward the river railing, so I did, too.

The parking lot didn't have any lights to reflect in his eyes. The green sparks there came from inside him. Nor was there any wind to lift and stir his hair like that. He stood very straight and tall, twenty feet from us, his hands held a little out from his sides like a gunfighter in a cowboy movie. Around his right hand, like a living glove, was a churning outline of golden fire. Bits of it dripped away like liquid from the ends of his fingers, evaporating before they hit the gravel. Like sparks from a sparkler.

I'm sure that's what my two friends told each other the next day—that he'd had a sparkler in his hand, and the liquor had made them see something more. That they'd been stupid to run away. But it wasn't a sparkler. And they weren't stupid. I heard them running across the parking lot; I watched Willy clench the fingers of his right hand and close his eyes tight, and saw the fire dim slowly and disappear. And I wished like hell that I could run away, too.

He crouched down beside me and pulled me up to sitting. "Your nose is bleeding."

"What are you?" I croaked.

The fire was still there, in his eyes. "None of your business," he said. He put his arm around me and hauled me to my feet. I'm not very heavy, but it still should have been hard work, because I didn't help. He was too slender to be so strong.

"What do you mean, none of my business? Jesus!"

He yanked me around to face him. When I looked at him, I saw wildness and temper and a fragile control over both. "I'm one of the Daoine Sidhe, Johnny-lad," he said, and his voice was harsh and colored by traces of some accent. "Does that help?"

"No," I said, but faintly. Because whatever that phrase meant, he was admitting that he was not what I was. That what I had seen had really been there.

"Try asking Steve. Or look it up, I don't care."

I shook my head. I'd forgotten my nose; a few drops of blood spattered from it and marked the front of his white shirt. I stood frozen with terror, waiting for his reaction.

It was laughter. "Earth and Air," he said when he caught his breath, "are we doing melodrama or farce out here? Come on, let's go lay you down and pack your face in ice."

There was considerable commotion when we came in the back door. Lisa got the ice and hovered over me while I told Steve about the two guys. I said Willy had chased them off; I didn't say how. Steve was outraged, and Lisa was solicitous, and it was all wasted on me. I lay on the floor with a cold nose and a brain full of rug fuzz, and let all of them do or say whatever they felt like.

Eventually I was alone in the back room, with the blank ceiling tiles to look at. Betsy Kaske was singing "Wild Women Don't Get the Blues." I roused from my self-indulgent stupor only once, when Steve passed on his way to the kitchen.

"Steve, what's a—" and I pronounced Daoine Sidhe, as best I could.

He repeated it, and it sounded more like what Willy had said. "Elves,"
he added.

"What?"

"Yeah. It's an Irish name for the elves."

"Oh, Christ," I said. When I didn't add to that, he went on into the
kitchen.

I don't know what I believed. But after a while I realized that I hadn't
seen Lisa go by in a long time. And she didn't know what I knew, or
almost knew. So I crawled up off the floor and went looking for her.

Not in the front room, not in the kitchen, and if she was in the milling people who were still hanging out on State Street, I'd never find her
anyway. I went out to the back steps, to see if she was in the parking lot.

Yes, sort of. They stood in the deep shadow where Orpheus's back
wall joined the jutting flank of the next building. Her red-gold hair was a
dim cascade of lighter color in the dark. The white streak in his was like
a white bird, flying nowhere. And the pale skin of her face and arms, his
pale face and white shirt, sorted out the rest of it for me. Lisa was so small
and light-boned, he'd lifted her off her feet entirely. No work at all for
him. Her arms were around his neck. One of his hands was closed over
her shoulder—I could see his long fingers against her dark blouse—and
the gesture was so intense, so hungry, that it seemed as if that one hand
alone could consume her. I turned and went back into Orpheus, cold,
frightened, and helpless.

Lisa didn't come back until a little before closing, several hours later. I
know; I was keeping watch. She darted in the back door and snatched her
shoulder bag from the kitchen. Her eyes were the only color in her face:
gray, rimmed with red. "Lisa!" I called.

She stopped with her back to me. "What?"

I didn't know how to start. Or finish. "It's about Willy."

"Then I don't want to hear it."

"But—"

"John, it's none of your business. And it doesn't matter now, anyway."

She shot me one miserable, intolerable look before she darted out the
back door and was gone. She could look like that and tell me it was none
of my business?

I'd helped Steve clean up and lock up, and pretended that I was going
home. But at three in the morning, I was sitting on the back steps, watch-

ing a newborn breeze ruffle a little heap of debris caught against the door-sill: a crushed paper cup, a bit of old newspaper, and one of the flyers for the march. When I looked up from it, Willy was standing at the bottom of the steps.

"I thought you'd be back tonight," I said.

"Maybe that's why I came back. Because you thought it so hard." He didn't smile, but he was relaxed and cheerful. After making music with him almost every day for a month, I could tell. He dropped loose-limbed onto the bottom step and stretched his legs out in front of him.

"So. Have you told her? What you are?"

He looked over his shoulder at me with a sort of stunned disbelief. "Do you mean Lisa? Of course not."

"Why not?" All my words sounded to me like little lead fishing weights hitting the water: plunk, plunk.

"Why should I? Either she'd believe me or she wouldn't. Either one is about equally tedious."

"Tedious."

He smiled, that wicked, charming, conspiratorial smile. "John, you can't think I care if Lisa believes in fairies."

"What *do* you care about?"

"John...," he began, wary and a little irritable.

"Do you care about her?"

And for the second time, I saw it: his temper on a leash. "What the hell does it matter to you?" He leaned back on his elbows and exhaled loudly. "Oh, right. You want her for yourself. But you're too scared to do anything about it."

That hurt. I said, a little too quickly, "It matters to me that she's happy. I just want to know if she's going to be happy with you."

"No," he snapped. "And whether she's going to be happy *without* me is entirely her look-out. Rowan and Thorn, John, I'm tired of her. And if you're not careful, I'll be tired of you, too."

I looked down at his scornful face, and remembered Lisa's: pale, red-eyed. I described Willy Silver, aloud, with words my father had forbidden in his house.

He unfolded from the step, his eyes narrowed. "Explain to me, before I paint the back of the building with you. I've always been nice to you. Isn't that enough?" He said "nice" through his teeth.

"Why are you nice to me?"

"You're the only one who wants something important from me."

"Music?"

"Of course, music."

The rug fuzz had been blown from my head by his anger and mine. "Is that why you sing that way?"

"What the devil is wrong with the way I sing?"

"Nothing. Except you don't sound as if any of the songs ever happened to you."

"Of course they haven't." He was turning stiff and cold, withdrawing. That seemed worse than when he was threatening me.

The flyer for the protest march still fluttered in the doorway. I grabbed it and held it out. "See her?" I asked, jabbing a finger at the picture of the woman kneeling over the student's body. "Maybe she knew that guy. Maybe she didn't. But she cares that he's dead. And I look at this picture, and *I* care about *her*. And all those people who marched past you in the street tonight? They did it because they care about a lot of people that they're never even going to see."

He looked fascinated and horrified at once. "Don't you all suffer enough as it is?"

"Huh?"

"Why would you take someone else's suffering on yourself?"

I didn't know how to answer that. I said finally, "We take on each other's happiness, too."

He shook his head, slowly. He was gathering the pieces of himself together, putting all his emotional armor back on. "This is too strange even for me. And among my people, I'm notoriously fond of strange things." He turned and walked away, as if I'd ceased to exist.

"What about tonight?" I said. He'd taken about a half-dozen steps. "Why did you bother to scare off those guys who were beating me up?"

He stopped. After a long moment he half-turned, and looked at me, wild-eyed and...frightened? Then he went on, stiffly, across the parking lot, and disappeared into the dark.

The next night, when I came in, Willy's guitar and fiddle were gone. But Steve said he hadn't seen him.

Lisa was clearing tables at closing, her hair falling across her face and hiding it. From behind that veil, she said, "I think you should give up. He's not coming."

I jumped. "Was I that obvious?"

"Yeah." She swept the hair back and showed a wry little smile. "You looked just like me."

"I feel lousy," I told her. "I helped drive him away, I think."

She sat down next to me. "I wanted to jump off the bridge last night. But the whole time I was saying, 'Then he'll be sorry, the rat.' "

"He wouldn't have been."

"Nope, not a bit," she said.

"But I would have."

She raised her gray cat-eyes to my face. "I'm not going to fall in love with you, John."

"I know. It's okay. I still would have been sorry if you jumped off the bridge."

"Me, too," Lisa said. "Hey, let's make a pact. We won't talk about The Rat to anybody but each other."

"Why?"

"Well…" She frowned at the empty lighted space of the stage. "I don't think anybody else would understand."

So we shared each other's suffering, as he put it. And maybe that's why we wouldn't have called it that.

I did see him again, though.

State Street had been gentrified, and Orpheus, the building, even the parking lot, had fallen to a downtown mall where there was no place for shabbiness or magic—any of the kinds of magic that were made that Fourth of July. These things happen in twice seven long years. But there are lots more places like that, if you care to look.

I was playing at the Greenbriar Bluegrass Festival in Pocahontas County, West Virginia. Or rather, my band was. A columnist in *Folk Roots* magazine described us so:

> Bird That Whistles drives traditional bluegrass fans crazy. They have the right instrumentation, the right licks—and they're likely to apply them to Glenn Miller's "In the Mood," or The Who's "Magic Bus." If you go to see them, leave your preconceptions at home.

I was sitting in the cookhouse tent that served as the musicians' green room, drinking coffee and watching the chaos that is thirty-some traditional musicians all tuning and talking and eating at once. Then I saw, over the heads, a raven's-wing black one with a white streak.

In a few moments, he stood in front of me. He didn't look five minutes older than he had at Orpheus. He wasn't nervous, exactly, but he wasn't at ease, either.

"Hi," I said. My voice was steady, for a miracle. "How'd you find me?"

"With this," he answered, smiling a little. He held out an article clipped from a Richmond, Virginia, paper. It was about the festival, and the photo was of Bird That Whistles.

"I'm glad you did."

He glanced down suddenly. "I wanted you to know that I've been thinking over what you told me."

I knew what he was talking about. "All this time?"

Now it was the real thing, his appealing grin. "It's a damned big subject. But I thought you'd like to know…well, sometimes I understand it."

"Only sometimes?"

"Rowan and Thorn, John, have mercy! I'm a slow learner."

"The hell you are. Can you stick around? You could meet the band, do some tunes."

"I wish I could," he said, and I think he meant it.

"Hey, wait a minute." I pulled a paper napkin out of the holder on the table and rummaged in my banjo case for a pen.

"What's that?" he asked, as I wrote.

"My address. I'm living in Detroit now, for my sins. If you ever need anything—or even if you just want to jam—let me know, will you?" And I slid the napkin across the table to him.

He reached out, hesitated, traced the edges of the paper with one long, thin finger. "Why are you giving me this?"

I studied that bent black-and-white head, the green eyes half-veiled with his lids and following the motion of his finger. "You decide," I told him.

"All right," he said softly, "I will." If there wasn't something suspiciously like a quaver in his voice, then I've never heard one. He picked up the napkin. "I won't lose this," he said, with an odd intensity. He put out his right hand, and I shook it. Then he turned and pushed through the crowd. I saw his head at the door of the tent; then he was gone.

I stared at the top of the table for a long time, where the napkin had been, where his finger had traced. Then I took the banjo out of its case and put it into mountain minor tuning.

Gardner Dozois and Susan Casper did an anthology on Jack the Ripper a few years ago. John M. Ford told me that they had noticed that most of their submissions fell into one of three categories. I found myself less interested in the Ripper than in the obsession with the Ripper. Jane Yolen bought the story, and Gardner and Sue are still kind to me when we meet.

—Will

Time Travel, the Artifact, and a Famous Historical Personage

Will Shetterly

Jack was everywhere. He pushed a cart past the end of the baking supplies aisle just as Kate reached for a package of enriched flour in Rainbow Foods. He hurried into the Business and Technology section of the Minneapolis Public Library as Kate, on her way to Art and Music, glanced down from the up escalator. He came from one of Dayton's revolving doors and disappeared into the lunchtime traffic as Kate walked toward the post office. He touched Kate's shoulder lightly from behind as she rode a crowded elevator down from a temp job in a law office, said, "Excuse me," and got out on the third floor. His voice was as accentless as a TV announcer's. She watched his back while the doors closed and did not breathe until the elevator reached the lobby.

She never saw his face in these encounters, but she knew him. She knew his height, his haircut, his walk. When she dreamed, she saw him clearly: medium height, medium build, short brown hair—so common-looking that she could never describe him as an individual when she woke, yet knew him. She tried to draw him in her diary, but her sketch was of an awkward, elongated, androgynous figure whose smile was a silly leer. She never showed it to anyone.

She knew his handwriting too. Two postcards written in red ink had come with Hell for a return address. The first had arrived a month ago, shortly before she saw Jack in the grocery store. The second came two weeks later. The postmarks said they came from New York City; she did not know if Jack expected her to think they had been forwarded or if he was making a joke. The first said, "I wil be back as sharp as evre. No need for the trade name, you kno who I am." The second said, "You want to use Jack but Jack is to clevr. I am coming from the devle since you invited me so nisely."

After each sighting, after each dream, after each postcard, she told herself that she was too imaginative. The sightings were of ordinary men, the dreams were signs of her obsession, and the postcards were a misguided joke by someone who had heard of the book and did not know how much the postcards terrified her. She could tell David, but he would only worry.

She tried to describe Jack once. Not to David, who would laugh, ask her if the book was getting to her, then recognize what he had done, apologize, hug her, and never understand that this was not enough compensation for his laugh. She tried to describe him to Kenny, who laughed before she finished, but with delight, not condescension. Kenny slapped his new pink sofa and said, "That's your dreamfuck!"

"I beg your pardon?"

"Mr. Perfect. The Candy Man. Your lean, clean, sex machine."

"Kenny, I—" She heard her annoyance and began again. "My ideal man is Prince grown six feet tall. This guy isn't any taller than I am, and he's just as pale. And I don't want to fuck him."

"He sounds cute."

"Cute. Right, Kenny. If I want him, why am I afraid of him?"

"Because you're afraid to admit that you're tired of David."

"I love David!"

Kenny shook his head, grinned slightly, and tapped his chest with both hands. "Did I say you didn't? *Petit moi?* I said you're tired of him."

"I love David," she repeated.

"What's that got to do with anything? When was the last time you seduced him? When was the last time you wanted to seduce him?" When she said nothing, he added, "Face it, you're tired of being Mom for the boy wonder. You want excitement. You want a lover."

"Not Gentleman Jack."

"Why is this Jack? Somebody shows up in your dreams. He's nice-looking. He smiles at you. He's nothing like David."

"David smiles at me."

"Sexy?"

"Well… Friendly sexy."

"Right," said Kenny. "And this guy in your dreams, there's no friendly in his smile, there's just sex."

"There's no sex, Kenny. Weren't you listening to me? He *scares* me."

"Weren't you listening to you, girl? Why do you think this guy is Jack?"

"Because I know it."

"Has he got a knife? Does he say who he is?"

"He just smiles."

Kenny nodded smugly. "It's because you're putting together an anthology about the Ripper. You're obsessed, so you decide Dreamboy is Jack."

"Right."

"Hey." He put his hand on her shoulder. "I didn't mean to upset you. Maybe I play shrink too much."

"Maybe."

"Maybe you should talk to someone at the U."

"It's not really bothering me."

"Maybe you should talk to David."

"He's too busy. This book's important."

"Maybe you two shouldn't do the book."

"We signed a contract. A lot of stories are in already." She smiled. "We spent our share of the advance."

"Oy," said Kenny. "Then do the book quickly, hmm? And think about leaving David. It might be best for both of you."

"Right, Kenny. You going to do a story for us?"

"Maybe. A gay Ripper, pressured by society… It'd be interesting to portray the Ripper as a victim…" He shrugged.

"A victim." She patted his knee, thinking that Kenny would probably never write the story, and if he did, it would be bad. "That could be interesting."

Walking from Kenny's apartment, she considered leaving David. That would mean moving into her sister's basement in the 'burbs and having to take the bus anyplace she wanted to go. That would mean abandoning the book she and David had planned to write together. That would mean that their friends would be divided into his friends and her friends, because David would not take this well.

She smiled, realizing that she was not thinking about the most important consequences. What of David? His friends had said she was good for him, that since they were together, he was less excitable, he washed himself and his clothes more often, he wrote more than he had in years, he had finally gained some weight. How would David react? Did he already suspect that something was wrong?

As she turned onto LaSalle, she saw Jack drive by in a yellow Toyota. A little black kid on a 10-speed bicycle that was too large for him said, "Hey, lady. You all right?" She nodded and walked on. She wanted to go straight home, but avoiding the mail would be the same as admitting that she was frightened.

There were no postcards in the post office box. There were three manila envelopes. Two were from writers she did not know, and one was from Curt. Delighted, she ripped open the envelope as she walked outside, then sat on the low wall across the street to read the cover letter.

5/14
David and Kate—
    Here's a story after all. Didn't think I'd have time, but when I found a copy of Rumbelow's book on the Ripper, I became a bit obsessed. Hope my story isn't too cute.

Ever so timidly,
Curt

P.S. to Kate: I almost didn't do this. Rumbelow made me realize we aren't talking about Boogeyman Jack, creature of legend, but a madman who killed women in horrible ways. I understand why David's editing this— David would steamroller his grandmother if he thought it would result in a nice metaphor (and sometimes I admire him for that)—but I wonder about your motives. For the last hundred years, Old Leather Apron has probably been the ultimate symbol of violence against women, yet you choose to cash in on his legend?

    That's not fair, and I apologize. Of course the Ripper's a richer symbol than that. He's the upper classes preying on the lower, he's the mad herald of the 20th century, he's knowledge without restraint, he's lust without love, he's the slasher of hypocrisy, he's the dark self in all of us. So I suppose that's how I rationalize writing a story for you. Even if you don't like it, it was fun, I blush to admit.

She stuffed the letter and the manuscript back into their envelope. What sort of hypocrite was Curt to send a story if he felt like that? She walked faster than usual to her apartment. She wanted to return Curt's story unread. His success had come too soon, and he had never learned to behave professionally. His cover letters were smarmy, sloppy, presumptuously intimate. His stories weren't very good either. His characters had no depth, no motivation. Describing his prose as workmanlike was an excess of kindness. She did not need to read his submission. If she rejected it, she could be proud; it would prove that their anthology was constructed on the merits of the stories, not on the writers' names.

If the anthology was constructed on the merits of the stories, she would have to read Curt's. By the time she reached the apartment, she felt calmer. Curt was probably the nicest of David's friends, and God knew none of her friends had perfect social skills. Maybe Curt meant well with his postscript. Or maybe he had rid himself of his doubts by transferring them to her.

Snicker and Doodle met her at the front door. Snicker rubbed against her ankle, meowing as if he had been neglected for weeks. Doodle sat sullenly in the entryway as if annoyed that David was not home, too. Two of David's friends were in town, and he would be drinking with them until the bars closed, talking about writing and not doing any.

Kate closed the thin front curtains. Passersby in the harsh summer light became shadowy figures of unknowable age, race, or sex. She fed the cats and cleaned their box, then began to microwave a leftover slice of Pizza Florentine.

Pouring a diet root beer, she saw a note on top of yesterday's mail, still heaped on the kitchen counter. She began to smile, thinking it was from David. The handwriting was strange. The note was written in red ink. It began: "Boss lady—"

The plastic root beer bottle was cold and slick in her left hand. The Flintstones glass was cool and brittle in her right. If she did not stop pouring, the root beer would overflow. The apartment was very quiet.

The upstairs neighbors should be fighting by now, since this was a Friday. The kid next door should be playing Metallica on his stereo and trying to turn the receiver up to 11. The kitchen counter had several toast crumbs on it, and a coffee splotch to make Rorschach proud.

Jack had left a note in her apartment.

She recapped the root beer and set it beside her glass. She turned around slowly, completely around. She saw no one. The cats behaved normally, for cats that no one could describe as normal. Would the cats behave oddly if a maniac from the nineteenth century was waiting in her home?

The carving knife lay beside the stove. David had probably halved a bagel at lunch. David often halved bagels at lunch. She ran to the knife and snatched it. The rough wooden handle comforted her, and she realized that if Jack—or anyone—was in her apartment, he was not likely to set out a knife for her.

The phone was in the living room. The back door always creaked loudly, and anyone might be waiting on the back stairs. She had come safely from the living room. She should return to it. She could call the police and say— No. If someone was here, she would not be allowed to finish a call. If no one was here, the cops would be less likely to come later, when—if—she needed them. Since she was more afraid of the back door, she went to it first, and then searched the apartment. The doors and windows were locked, as they should be. No one was hiding in the closets or under the bed.

Halfway through her search, she realized that the note had to be from David, the red ink a coincidence, the letters blocky because David had hurt his wrist, perhaps. She returned to the kitchen and touched the note with the point of the knife to turn it toward her.

> Boss lady—
> You wil hear that Saucy Jack is operating tonight.
> Maybe you wil kno it, ha ha.
>
> J.

It was a very bad joke. David had thought it would be funny to scare her. Maybe he hadn't thought that the note would scare her; maybe he expected her to be amused. Notes from Jack the Ripper, ha ha ha. Had David written the postcards, too? Sent them to someone like Curt to mail from New York? Or had Curt created them in collusion with David? She ran back to the living room to find Curt's manuscript.

The envelope had been addressed with the same typewriter that was used for the story. Curt's signature on the cover letter was a quick, graceful scrawl in blue felt-tip.

Someone wrote with a different hand than usual, or perhaps a third person had collaborated with them. Kenny? Was Kenny so desperate to be published that he would help David in a stupid prank?

Curt and Kenny were her friends, and David was her lover. She was being paranoid. Yet the note remained, something frighteningly tangible from something unknown.

The knife remained in her right hand. She realized that her left rested on the telephone. Who could she call? The police? Her sister? Kenny? What would any of them say? You're terrified because of dreams. Oh, and postcards. Who would have your address, then? Hundreds of writers, because you'd put a notice in a writer's magazine that you were in the market for Jack the Ripper stories? It's probably some nut. Why're you so worried about some nut?

Because a note had been placed in her kitchen.

A note. Anything threatening in it? Uh huh. Anything else strange? The cats cut up into little pieces? Your boyfriend in Baggies in the deep-freeze? Intestines strewn decoratively about your bedroom? No? And your boyfriend isn't home? You ought to talk to him, lady, or to your landlord. Not us. We got a job to do.

She giggled suddenly, and Snicker looked up at her. David had done stupid things before, thinking to amuse her.

The pizza was warm, and so was the root beer. She took her dinner into the living room and placed Curt's story on top of the two unsolicited submissions.

Curt's story was not as good as she had hoped nor as bad as she had feared. David would be annoyed, because Curt had done a Sherlock Holmes pastiche in which Holmes realized that he had committed the Ripper murders while under the influence of laudanum. Was that too much like David's story about Robert Louis Stevenson and M. J. Druitt, the doctor who was David's favorite candidate for the Ripper? David had Druitt inspire Stevenson to write the Jekyll and Hyde story. Curt's and David's stories weren't that similar, and what David had completed was certainly better written than Curt's.

The first of the unsolicited stories began:

> "I wish to purchase something that belonged to Jack the Ripper," the American said, his bright blue eyes rolling about the crowded interior of the quaint little London shop.
> "Blimey, sor," the jolly shopkeeper said with twinkles in his eyes. "We 'ave just the thing. 'Is braces."
> "I didn't know there was anything wrong with Jack the Ripper's teeth."
> "Wot you'd call 'is suspenders, guv'nor."

She skipped to the end. The American, wearing Jack's suspenders, killed his girlfriend, and then, anguished by his deed, hung himself with the suspenders. The shopkeeper came into the American's apartment to recover the suspenders and smiled with beams in his eyes, thinking that he was Cain and another unfortunate had fallen to the Curse of Jack the Ripper. Kate decided that David did not need to read this one, tucked it into the writer's self-addressed stamped envelope, and turned to the next.

The cover letter simply said, "I have enclosed a story for your consideration." It was signed J. Noble. The story was titled "Time Travel, the Artifact, and a Famous Historical Personage." Kate began to grin, then frowned. The unsolicited submissions—and a significant number of the solicited ones—fell into three sorts: someone travels to Jack's time or Jack travels to another time; an artifact of Jack has an effect, inevitably gory, on someone; a famous historical person who lived in Jack's time is involved with the Ripper or turns out to be the Ripper. Her favorite of the last sort, already returned to its writer, revealed that Jack the Ripper was Queen Victoria in drag, happily not thinking of England for a few minutes.

Had J. Noble submitted the quintessential unsolicited Jack the Ripper story? Or was this a submission by someone who had heard David mention the kinds of stories they were getting? She looked again at the return address: New York. Curt had mentioned that a friend might send them a story. Curt might have told the friend about the submissions they received.

On the first page, when she discovered that the main characters were two editors who were compiling an anthology about Jack the Ripper,

Kate stopped and looked around the apartment. The carving knife still lay beside her, on the coffee table next to the sofa. Snicker slept on a nearby chair, Doodle on the window ledge. The kid next door played the ultimate self-referential rock song; its lyrics seemed to consist solely of "rock, rock, rock." Wishing they had decided to do an anthology about Mother Teresa or Mr. Rogers, Kate continued to read.

The editors, Spencer and Eileen, had two friends, writers who shared an apartment: Benny, who wrote badly, and Burt, who was fairly successful. The editors received postcards written in red ink, apparently from the Ripper. They then received an anonymous story titled "Time Travel, the Artifact, and a Famous Historical Personage."

Its main characters were modeled after Spencer, Eileen, Benny, and Burt: Fletcher and Lisa were the editors, Lenny was the aspiring writer and Art was the popular one. The postcards received by the editors in the anonymous story were identical to the ones that Spencer and Eileen had received…which were identical to the postcards that Kate had received. At the end of the story within the story, the editors, Fletcher and Lisa, were killed and mutilated by Lenny, the unpublished writer, who then wrote the account of their murders and sold it as fiction for a great deal of money.

After reading the end of the anonymous story, Spencer and Eileen, terrified, went to Benny's house, and killed him when he denied terrorizing them. In their rage, they mutilated his body with the Ripper's trademarks: slashed ears and nose, organs piled beside the eviscerated body, intestines dragged out of the corpse and looped over the right shoulder. Leaving Benny's house, exhausted but finally feeling safe, they met Burt, Benny's housemate, who said, "You guys get my story? Sorry I forgot to include a cover letter."

Kate placed the manuscript carefully on the coffee table. Night had come while she read. She had not drawn the roller shades, which meant that from the street, this bright room was perfectly visible through the thin curtains. She went to the window, telling herself that no one would have been watching her, and if anyone had, he would only have seen her reading. J. Noble's story, she thought, meant nothing. It was an exercise in bad taste on some would-be writer's part. An exercise in bad taste with flawed logic. An exercise—

Jack stood on the sidewalk, studying the number above the door of Kate's apartment building.

She yanked the roller shade down. Knowing Jack would not be there when she looked again, she looked again. He was not there. Someone knocked at their apartment, and she ran to snatch up the carving knife. "Special delivery," Jack called through their door, his voice cheerful and midwestern.

Kate pressed herself against the wall. Pretend no one was home? Sneak out the back stairs? No. She was mistaken. She had to be mistaken. "What is it?" she called.

"Special delivery, ma'am."

"Slide it under the door."

"You have to sign for it."

"Slide the receipt under. I'll sign it."

"Yes, ma'am." The pink slip appeared at the bottom of the door. As she reached for it, she thought of TV commercials for door locks, in which booted men kicked down massive oak doors with ease.

The slip was for something from New York. She had to hold the knife in her left hand to scratch her name in the appropriate box. After she passed it under the door, a thin envelope in U.S.A. colors came through to her. Jack said, "Thank you, ma'am," and she listened by the door until he had walked away.

The envelope held a small note on pink paper, written in red ink:

> Please discard my previous submission. I am revising it. There is a problem that I should have caught: If Burt wrote the anonymous story without intending to terrorize Eileen and Spencer, why would he send the postcards?
>
> In my revision, only Eileen is terrorized by the notes. That is much, much truer to the spirit of the Ripper. In the story which she and Spencer receive, only the female editor is killed and mutilated; the male editor is arrested for her murder; Lenny, the unpublished writer, writes up the story as fiction and sells it for a lot of money. After reading this tale, Eileen waits for Spencer to come home, wanting to tell him of her fears about Benny's sanity. At the end, she learns that the anonymous story and the notes are from Spencer. He is insane, you see, partly from jealousy, partly from frustration. He knows

that his career is over. He knows that she stays with him because of his fame, his connections in publishing, and possibly out of some condescending pity for him. He knows she will leave him when she realizes she has no more use for him. Why is Spencer so obsessed with Jack the Ripper, anyway? Why did Eileen never think of this, before it was too late? Those are her last thoughts, before he kills her.

I think it'll be much better this way.

—J. Noble

Kate sat down with the note between her thumb and index finger. She released it, and it fluttered to the floor. Noble. Jay Noble? Jackie Noble? Noble. Jack. Gentleman Jack?

Her thoughts would not cohere. She was being persecuted by Jack the Ripper, as a punishment for exploiting his legend. She was being persecuted by Kenny, who had some mad idea that this would result in a story that he could sell. She was being persecuted by David, who believed she would leave him. What had she done? She had helped David when he had needed help, and now—

If Kenny was responsible, how far would he go for the sake of a story? If Kenny was Benny was Lenny, the answer included her death. If David? She knew how David behaved in the morning when he had not eaten, she knew what he liked when sex between them was good, she knew how he responded to small children and long-haired dogs, but she did not know if he would terrorize, kill, and mutilate her.

If Jack was responsible, it did not matter what she did.

Curt? Curt was fifteen hundred miles away. In "Time Travel, the Artifact, and a Famous Historical Personage," Burt was not responsible for the killings, nor was Art responsible for the killings in the unsolicited story within the story. Kate nodded. It must be Curt because he was the only one without a motive. She forced a grin, suddenly certain this must be the work of a writer in New York, a real person named J. Noble who probably knew Curt. She checked their phone list, then dialed Curt's number.

"Yo," someone said.

"Curt? Kate here."

"Oh, God." His voice was immediately quiet. "I was going to call, really, then I forgot. The kid lost her bike, and we were—"

"What is it, Curt?" Her fear was forgotten as she wondered if something had happened to someone she knew and liked.

"Did David tell you, or did you figure it out? I shouldn't have agreed, I know, but he thought..."

"Yes?"

"He thought you were getting cold and distant, and maybe you'd come to him if you were scared."

She didn't think she had been cold or distant before, but she knew how her voice sounded now. "You mailed the postcards for Davy."

"Yeah. And the J. Noble things. I shouldn't have, I know, but he promised he'd explain everything the second you seemed upset. He thought it'd be interesting to get your reaction. He's thinking about doing a story about an editor who gets a submission that's obviously inspired by her life."

"Not the Jekyll and Hyde thing?"

"No."

She listened to Curt breathe on the line.

"Kate? You still there?"

"You shit."

"Kate, he begged—" His voice was cut off as she slammed down the receiver.

The phone rang. She waited, counting twenty-two rings, then decided it would never stop, and picked up the receiver.

Jack laughed into her ear.

She slammed the phone down. She held the carving knife in her lap, one hand on the handle, a finger touching the edge of the blade. She had cut herself, so she put her finger in her mouth.

I'll call my sister, she thought. I'll call my mother. I'll call Elise in California. I'll call Kenny...but Kenny might be part of it, too.

She picked up Curt's submission, the Sherlock Holmes story, to throw it across the room, then stared at the cover letter. He had written it, knowing that he was helping David, and never hinted— Had he giggled as he wrote the postscript?

David would come home soon. Would he be expecting to comfort her? Would he come in trying to scare her? She could imagine him calling, "It's yours truly, Jack the Ripper!" then beginning his shrill, self-satisfied laugh. When she did not answer him, the laughter would break off and he would call, "Kate? Sweetcakes?" In the dark and quiet hallway, he would finally begin to be afraid that he had done too much. He would run to the bedroom, not knowing whether she was asleep or gone.

Kate walked through the apartment, turning off lights. One light in the living room would suffice; she would not let herself be afraid. In the mirror at the end of the hall, her reflection was familiar and strange: moderate height, moderate build, short brown hair.

One hundred years of Jack the Ripper, she thought. And now, David, Curt, Kenny… One hundred years of Jill.

In the mirror, Jack smiled.

Terri Windling created the Borderlands shared world series shortly after she had us create Liavek. She did the first volume, and Emma and I were jealous because she hadn't asked us for a story. Then she suggested we come out to Boston, where she was living, to attend a Boskone and visit her. We pleaded poverty. She told us to write a Borderlands story. This trick doesn't always work.

The division of labor is not as clean on this story as it may appear. Yes, Emma created Orient and I created Wolfboy. Yes, we wrote the first draft by passing sections back and forth to each other. But we tinkered with each other's prose and suggested lines and ideas to each other. I'm pretty sure Rico was my creation, but I'm not sure who came up with the Terrible Trio. What can I say? It was a collaboration. We share the credit and the blame equally.

Oh, I had so much fun with Wolfboy that I wrote two Borderlands novels, Elsewhere and Nevernever. That must mean something.

—Will

I don't know that we were jealous, exactly. But the Borderlands are more fun than an unlimited ride ticket on the bumper boats. Will and I wrote this in about a week, spending all day talking out the twists and details, and most of the nights writing. Our niece, Lynda Hoffmaster, proofread sections as we wrote them and egged us on. Thanks, Lynda.

This is the story in the collection that I most want to rewrite completely, because the characters' voices have grown up in my head since, and Bordertown has become a bigger place. But I suppose that wouldn't be quite fair, at least to them.

Oh, and I had so much fun that I wrote Finder, which is, of course, about Orient.

—Emma

Danceland Blood

Emma Bull & Will Shetterly

Friday night started, for me and for all of us I suppose, in the street outside Danceland. I was sitting in the sidecar, waiting for Tick-Tick. She'd parked the bike outside Danceland and made her usual arrow-like way across the street to Snappin' Wizard's Surplus and Salvage ("More Bang for the Buck, More Spell for the Silver").

Snappin' Wizard's is the only other thing on that end of Ho Street that's still lit up late at night. And oh, is it lit. Pre-Change cartop revolving lights flash rude and red in the windows. Between them, will-o-wisps bop back and forth in rhythm. Signs on the window glass, in paint and fairy dust, shout about solar cells and self-bored stones and logic boards and clock spells, and how they're cheap cheap cheap!

The Queen of bloody Faerie couldn't keep Tick-Tick out of there. She'd left with a mumble about being just a minute, and she'd be right back. Or maybe she didn't say it this time, and I only supplied it from the memory of all the other times she had. Whatever. I didn't expect the Ticker back inside half an hour.

I slid way down in the sidecar so I could prop my head against the back padding, and shook an herbal cig out of its box. They're big stuff with the elves, who don't much like tobacco. I think they like them because it makes them all feel like old vid stars, dragging moodily on a cigarette. I'm not poking fun. Why do you think *I* smoke them?

I rolled the coltsfoot-and-comfrey smoke over my tongue like wine and watched the crowd in front of Danceland. People were milling on the sidewalk, waiting for the band to start. Four elven Bloods in poet's red clustered near the doors, looking sharp (and aware of it, I'll bet) against the building's black-patent paint job. A halfie woman with a lion's mane haircut dyed black and white was practicing some synched dance step. She was coached by a black human woman with silver bells in her elflocks. An elf kid had his seedybox balanced on one shoulder, and people were dancing to its music. Four members of the Pack pulled up on two cycles, their jackets trailing bright motley streamers. One of them asked the crowd at large if the music had started. One of the Bloods by the door shook her head, not really friendly but not like anyone expected war, and the Pack kids drove off again.

Danceland's double doors were arched over with row after row of white lights that flashed in sequence and seemed to chase each other forever. "Danceland" was written in script over the doors in pink-red neon—the genuine pre-Change article, but the gas was rattled around now with a spell. (I know this only from the Ticker's explanation. The business of How Things Work is her specialty, not mine.) When I squinted, the whole front of the building became a blaze of bright fog.

It's at the very end of Ho, but it's worth the trip. The Factory is older, the Dancing Ferret is trendier, and the Wheat Sheaf is more exclusive. But Danceland has the *old* magic, the kind you don't have to be an elf to make. The old magic is made with loud music and sweat and colored light. But the best thing about it is that stinging feeling at the back of your head that says *anything* could happen tonight.

Which is, come to think of it, the most pervasive magic in Bordertown. But keep in mind that magic doesn't always work the way you expect in the Borderlands.

"Uh...hi," somebody said behind me, breathy and excited-scared.

I leaned my head back a little more and looked up into big round brown eyes under a heavy thatch of brown bangs. Her skin was tan, too, or maybe just evenly grubby. She wore a gray denim jacket and jeans that weren't ruined yet, and a black cap with a pheasant feather tucked in its band. The cap looked new. The whole ensemble was the quintessential Worldly kid's idea of What They Wear In The Borderlands. You could start a mail-order company selling outfits like that and clean up: Halfie Frankie's Faerie Fashions. I hate runaways. They make me hurt all over, just under the skin.

There's always been places that called to people. Even before the Change, there were cities that shone in the back of the mind like Faerie gold. You knew, *knew,* that if you could just run away to one of those places, you'd become someone else, someone wonderful, and wonderful things would happen to you. I heard a list of those magical cities once. I remember London, Liverpool (interesting name, but a disgusting concept), New York, and something with two words that started with an *S.* I've forgotten the rest.

Then the Elflands came back, and with them came the Borderlands. Suddenly there *was* a place you could go to change your whole life. Not necessarily for the better, mind you, but if you leave the World for the Borderlands, I can guarantee change, if nothing else.

"Are...you elvish?" she asked, smiling and biting her lip.

There's nothing ambiguous about the roundness of my ears, and yes, I'm pale, but it's sallow-human pale because I hate going to sleep as much as I hate waking up. I remember being her age, though, and being about as long in town. I tilted up one lens of my riding goggles, showing her a dark-blue eye, and said kindly, "No, I'm Jewish."

"Oh," she said, crestfallen. I hoped she'd be gone by the time Tick-Tick came back; one sight of the Ticker and the kid would be offering to lick the Genuine Faerie Mud off her motorcycle boots.

"My name's Orient," I told her, as something of a peace offering, and stuck my hand out. She shook it.

"I'm Camilla," she sighed, and wrinkled her nose. "It's a stupid name."

That gave my stomach a little twist. Camilla means "attendant at a sacrifice." There were too many things of value to sacrifice in Bordertown if you were young, scared, and not scared enough.

"That's okay. Everybody in Bordertown has a nickname." She looked hopeful. Oh, I hate runaways. "Yours is..." I thought for a second.

"...Caramel."

She was disappointed, though she tried to hide it. I knew what she'd been hoping for: something like Firebird, or Starwind. The sort of name no one could live with, or up to. So I gave her one of my lopsided grins that Sai says looks rakish even without my eyes to help. I said, "Burnt sugar. Sweet, but smoky, and it's been through the fire."

Okay, it was hokey, but it cheered her up. "I guess that's pretty good," she admitted.

"Where you from?"

"Bellinbroke."

"Pretty far away?"

"Took me nine days to get here, and I got good rides the whole way."

It was too far; she'd never go back home, even if she wanted to. When she wanted to. I dragged hard on the cigarette to loosen the lump in my throat. Coltsfoot is supposed to be good for that.

"Want some water?" Caramel asked me, and there was a coyness in her voice that made me raise both sides of my goggles this time. She held out a beer bottle, half-full of beautiful, translucent crimson. Mad River water.

I took it from her. I wanted to peg the thing into the alley and hear it shatter. But that would be no help in the long run.

"Have you had any of this yet?" A nice, calm voice—I was impressed with myself.

"A little." She was defiant at first. Then a sheepish look crept across her face, and she shrugged. "It tastes kind of gross."

"This is elf stuff, Caramel. To them, it's just water. The sort of humans who drink river water are...not in style." Which was true enough, if you only counted the Wharf Rats. But there were humans and halfies who thought money was a license to be stupid in public, who wore crystal or silver cups on chains or silk cords around their necks. Maybe this kid hadn't seen any of those yet. "I'll make you a trade for this," I said, swinging the bottle a little.

She looked at it, and at me. "What kind of trade?"

I balanced the bottle between us on the sidecar's rim. Then I slid one of the silver bracelets, not the thinnest, off my left wrist and held it out. "I'll give you this for it. On the condition," I added, as she reached, "that you use it to pay your way into there," and I nodded at Danceland. "You can keep the change. Whoever gives it to you, tell 'em Orient sent you, and you want to talk to Goldy. Deal?"

Her eyes were practically rolling, from me to the bottle to Danceland's front doors.

"Straight," I said. "It's just a dance club, and Goldy's just a bouncer." Goldy would disagree, of course. "He's a good guy to talk to when you need to."

She bit her lip—no smile this time—and finally took the bracelet. "Why this Goldy? Why not you, if you're so concerned about me?"

I grinned, which was harder than it sounds. "Because I come and go. But I'll find you if I need you." Which was a joke of sorts, but of course she didn't get it.

She turned to go, and we both saw him at once. You might think he was wearing a full-head mask, a good one of the sort that outfits like the Horn Dance sometimes wear. And once you wrote off the head as a mask, you could come up with something to explain the pelt on the rest of him, too, like a fur suit in spite of the weather. But Caramel was new in town, had never seen the Horn Dance or anything else, and hadn't developed that cynical turn for explanations. She not only stopped when she saw him, she stepped back a pace or two.

"Wolfboy!" I called, and his long nose swung our way. He grinned, which can put you off if you've just met him. He headed toward the sidecar, that long swinging walk earning a jealous scowl from one of the Bloods.

When you get used to it, he looks pretty good, actually. He's lean and rangy and muscle-y, and covered all over with short coarse red-brown fur. He shaved his face once, and we all hated it. I think he decided never to do it again when the Ticker said, "It makes you look so…young." That night he wore a black t-shirt with the sleeves ripped out, tight black jeans and black hi-top sneakers. His ears end in pointed tufts, the lower half of his face is lengthened, and his canine teeth are…well, about what you would expect. He has claws, thick and slate-colored, on his fingers. When he types, he sounds like a dog on a kitchen floor.

"Wolfboy," I said, "I'd like you to meet Caramel."

Give the kid credit; she held out her hand. Wolfboy took it and inclined his head. Pretty courtly for a guy with a dog nose.

"Pleased to meet you," Caramel breathed. She turned and looked at me sideways. "Guess I should go…"

I gave her a nod. "You don't want to miss the first song."

Wolfboy and I watched her go. I said, "Lord, lord. Perfectly nice Friday night, and I have to get pinned down in the street by some little thing with the dust of the World still behind her ears."

Wolfboy chuckled deep in his throat and patted my head.

"Oh, go chase cats." I shook out another cigarette and held it out. I lit it, too, since paper matches are a nuisance for him.

"You been out of town?" I asked after his first mouthful of smoke.

He grinned like a fiend from hell, and pulled a many-folded leather wallet out of his back jeans pocket. With a flourish, he let the folds fall open in a sort of waterfall. Neatly flattened inside and preserved with a bought spell were something like twenty four-leaf clovers.

"Oh my stars and garters," I breathed. "Well, if I need to borrow money I'll sure 'nuff come to you. You gonna sell 'em inside?" I asked him, pointing to Danceland.

He refolded the wallet with a practiced flip, and nodded.

"Offer one to Goldy. He's going to need it." When Wolfboy raised his eyebrows, I said, "I just sent that runaway to him."

He giggled in a voice low enough to make a couple of Packies nervous and shook his head.

"I don't suppose you'd trade one of those little green beauties for the latest copy of *Stick Wizard,* would you?" I squinted speculatively at him.

He looked down at me with an expression that even on his face was easy to read: You've got to be kidding.

I pulled my copy out of the map pocket in the sidecar (after all, what else am I going to use the map pocket for? Not maps, anyway). The stick-figure characters on the cover were block-printed with ink and fairy dust, and moved when you looked at them. On this issue, the Wizard was flying off his beat-up cycle as it hit a trip-wire. At each end of the wire were, of course, his arch-nuisances, Tater and Bert, the cigar-smoking elf delinquents. I could almost see Wolfboy salivating. Tater and Bert are favorites of his. He thinks they should have their own book. I don't know about Wolfboy sometimes.

But he shook his head finally. I didn't really expect him to deal—by the end of the night someone might *give* him a copy. So I smiled and put it away.

"Here's a fine convocation of riffraff," Tick-Tick said behind me.

"Boil me in lead," I cried, and turned. "She's back before morning!"

"Oh, shut up. Hi, Lobo." She smiled at Wolfboy. He smiled back and dropped his gaze. He loves being called "Lobo."

The Ticker was loading a paper-wrapped parcel into the bike's top cargo box.

"Goodies?" I asked.

"Well, not that you'd think so. A little replacement stock, wire connectors and that sort of thing. And a toy or two."

"Or eight or ten," I said, but she didn't rise to it.

Tick-Tick is pure elf, and looks it. Pointed ears, luminous pale skin, shining silver eyes. Slender and almost oppressively tall. She'd never fit in the sidecar, so it's a good thing she owns the bike. She usually dyes her hair dandelion-yellow and wears it short, with a single long lock at the very front and center of her hairline that hangs fine as milkweed fluff to her eyebrows. In spite of her height, she looks delicate as spun-sugar. It surprises people to find that her favorite perfume is Eau de Bearing Grease and Hot Solder.

She was wearing her idea of power dressing tonight: a long gray leather coat and tight pants of the same, low red leather boots, a dark gray suit coat, white shirt, a red leather tie, and three garnet earrings in her right ear. I've tried to tell her that this is *not* what they wear in the boardrooms of the World's corporations, but she points out (and rightly) that I can't be sure, can I, and they might if they had the good taste to think of it, now mightn't they?

"So," she said, "anyone here want to rock the moon down?"

"Me! Me!" said I, and leaped out of the sidecar. Wolfboy, sober lad that he is, let out a yell that made the whole street shudder. I left my goggles in the sidecar, and checked my hair in the rear-view mirror. The Ticker had done my dye job the week before, and I was still nervous about it; the spikes of red around my face showed like lit matches against the natural black of the rest. It's been years since I left the World, but it has its fangs in me yet. There's a limit to how conspicuous I can be and still feel safe.

"Yes, yes, you're just breathtaking," Tick-Tick sighed. "Come along."

The crowd outside had turned into crowd inside, we found. Danceland's insides are all black cinder block walls, from which they wash the fairy dust graffiti every night. "After all," the club's owner, Dancer, says, "this place is supposed to be *different,* for Zeus' sake."

The stage lights were still out, but the band's equipment was set up, and the spell boxes that ran the amps were glowing gently. The Ticker headed for the pool tables to fleece a few unsuspecting Bloods, and Wolfboy and I pushed through to the bar.

Valda was already clunking bottles of beer down on the counter three at a time. "Val, precious Val," I bellowed across three feet of noisy space, "did the coffee come in yet?"

She looked at me as if about to say no, then smiled and said, "You're a lucky boy." I blew her a kiss, and she headed for the other end of the bar to pour me a cup. Not, mind you, that I don't like beer. I adore beer. But I can get that anywhere.

She set the cup in front of me and a bottle of beer in front of Wolfboy. I pried a silver stud out of my wristband—the bracelets are for major purchases—and told Valda, "That's for both," before Wolfboy could pay.

He raised his bushy eyebrows at me, and I shrugged. "So pay me back when you've made your killing in good luck," I said. He winked and hoisted his bottle.

I let the steam and the coffee smell wash over my face for a second before I actually sipped any. Coffee is shortage-prone in the Borderlands, and expensive since most of what passes through is doing just that: passing through to Faerie. But, oh, it's worth the price to me.

Someone tapped me on the shoulder and said in my ear, "Watch that stuff, young man."

I turned and found Goldy shaking his head at me. Goldy is black and not tall, even for a human. But he's built like a pyramid standing on its head. His hair is plush-short and metallic gold—thus the nickname, of course. He was in uniform, which is a green long-sleeved Danceland t-shirt. It's not that conspicuous, since Dancer sells the things, and there are always a few in the club on any night.

"Goldy. What it is. Watch what stuff?"

He narrowed his eyes at my coffee cup. "That's a dangerous intoxicant. You may get high as the Tooth and tear the place up before the night is out."

I rolled my eyes. "Call me Mr. Coffee Nerves."

"Or perhaps I might toss you out now and save myself a bit of trouble. It'd be no more than you deserve."

"Me? Oh, you got my present, then."

"If you mean your runaway, yes, you snot-nosed little mutant, I did. What am I supposed to do with her?"

"Talk her out of doing all the stupid things we did at her age."

"Except for continuing my acquaintance with you, I've never done anything stupid. I assume you found her?"

I could hear the capital *F* he meant to put on "found." " 'Course not. Though I suppose you could say I found her nickname," I mused. I wondered what she would have been called if she hadn't met me.

The colored lights in the ceiling spat and swirled. "Back to the fray," Goldy sighed, and disappeared into the crowd. Then the stage lights came up, and Dancer walked across the stage. I saw the way she did it, sort of lazy, as if there was no audience at all, and I shot a look at Wolfboy. When Dancer introduces the band, it's something special. But when Dancer walks to the mike like that…. Wolfboy gave me the thumbs-up, and we started moving toward the stage.

So did everyone else, but we made it to the middle of the dance floor, at least. Somewhere ahead of us I thought I caught a glimpse of a little black cap, with a feather that vibrated with its wearer's excitement.

Dancer stood at the mike for a second, during which you could hear every breath that was drawn in Danceland. Twice she began to move her hands, as if to preface words that didn't come. Then she threw back her head and laughed, and said, "I give up. Ladies and gentlemen, Wild Hunt!"

The roar of the audience shook those black walls, and I helped. I doubt there was anyone in Danceland that night who didn't know the name. Bordertown had been full of the sound of Wild Hunt all spring. The recordings came out once a week, a song at a time, on mag tape, or in an impression ball, or digitally coded. But there were no pictures of the band. No one had ever seen them in concert, and nobody seemed to know someone who worked in the studio where they'd recorded—you know the sort of thing. So we'd play the recordings, the tearing, heart-shaking music pouring over us, and we'd pretend that we could tell from the sound how they looked.

We were wrong. All of us. They took us by surprise, and she most of all, because all the poets and painters and visionaries in Bordertown could never have imagined her.

It's not that she was the archetypal elf. Strider, the third of the Danceland bouncers, is the archetypal elf, a real flipping Prince of Faerie sort. No, this was the Snow Queen from out of that old tale, the beautiful White Lady of any romantic ghost story.

She was tall, of course, and pale, paler than Strider or the Ticker or any other elf I'd ever seen. Her eyes were the color of silver in the sun. Her hair was white as new snow, or expensive paper, or the fiery-white highlights on silver. Again the word silver—white as she was, she was a rich-looking white, and demanded rich words to describe.

Her hair was clipped close to her head on the left side, lengthening as it went over her head until it looked like a white wave cresting over her right ear. Her left eye was caught up in a bar of light blue paint that ran from her nose to her hairline, where it became a streak of pale blue dye across the short white hair. The dye ended in a curling tail above her left ear. It's difficult for a human to judge elven features—by human stan-dards, there's no such thing as a homely elf, I think—but I would swear that hers was the most beautiful face that Bordertown had ever seen.

She wore white leather leggings and a white sleeveless thing that shim-mered like the silk that comes from the Elflands. She played a Fender Witchfire bass the blue of midnight. Fairy dust swirled in the paint job in galaxies and nebulae, suns that formed and flashed and died as you watched. Light strobed off the rings on her fingers as she chorded and slammed down on all four strings, then scraped her pick down the E. It was the opening riff of "Shake the Wall Down," and suddenly everybody was dancing.

Wolfboy got snagged by an elf-girl with pale green hair, a wicked grin, and a red jewel on her cheek like a birthmark or a tear. He picked her up by her waist, whirled her around, and they were both gone into the crowd.

The hyperharpist played a Fairlight, one of the Sorcerer series judging from the stuff he got out of it. Waveforms so clean you could have eaten off them. The lead guitarist had a topknot of burgundy hair, an eight-stringed axe, and six fingers on each hand to play it with. The drummer was insane, but drummers often are. They just aren't all as precise and tasteful in their madness as this elven woman was. I won't even try to describe what the halfie on elfpipes did with that instrument, but it wasn't anything that an Elflands elf would have thought of, or approved of. The total effect was wonderful and impossible and, all right, magical.

And they sang, of course. All of them, in close, twisting harmony; or just her, the White Lady, with a pure clear voice that made every word a projectile into the head and heart. They segued straight into "Heart's Desire," a modified version that was somehow as creepy as it was driving.

Suddenly Sai appeared before me. She was grinning and shaking her head, and I realized that I'd been dancing by myself, gaping at the band ever since the music started.

"What are you doing, letting your tongue dry?" she yelled at me.

I gave her my best I'm-an-idiot shrug.

Sai is another Danceland bouncer, the middle member of the Terrible Trio. She's a halfie, tall, plump, with a round pink face and rainy gray eyes. She has Oriental hair, uncompromisingly straight, heavy, and black. She wears it shoulder-length to show it off. Not that she liked her father, mind, or even knew him. She just hopes that someday some elven bigot will smart off about it, and she can loosen his teeth. When an elf makes trouble in Danceland, Goldy and Strider let Sai throw him out, whenever possible. It makes her so happy.

"When did Dancer score this coup?" I shouted at her, and pointed at the band.

"Two days ago. She was half-crazy with it, I tell ya. Didn't know whether to bless her luck, or cuss it for not leaving time to do advertising."

"Poor baby."

She shrugged and grinned at the same time. "Word gets around." And it was true that the place was full. Advertising would have only meant the Terrible Trio would have to turn away tourists.

Strider slid gracefully through the crowd and put an arm lock around Sai's neck. She rolled her eyes and pinched his thigh.

"Owoo! Halfie scum," he said affectionately, loosening his grip and giving her a quick kiss behind the ear.

"Pointy-eared creep," she replied in kind, and put her hand in one of his back pockets.

Strider, as I said, is a veritable Lord of Elflands. He has the fine mane of silver hair to the middle of his back, the regal carriage, the elegant long-fingered gestures that melt the hearts of human girls.

Someday I'm going to ask how such an unlikely pair as Sai and Strider became sweethearts. Not anytime soon, mind you—but someday.

"Dance with this jerk," Strider told her, nodding at me. "He looks brain dead standing there by himself."

"I'm on duty," Sai protested.

Strider shrugged. "Nothing's goin' down. Goldy and I can handle it for half a song, girl."

"You can't handle your—"

He stopped her by smacking a kiss on her lips. "You've got the dirtiest mouth on Ho Street."

I didn't hear her response, but I think he blushed. Then he smiled lazily and drifted off through the dancers.

Sai dances well. You wouldn't think, looking at her, that she'd have that elven grace, but she does. She says it comes from her boxing days. I put some effort into trying to match her, and ended the song pleasantly winded.

Wild Hunt swept on into "Running on the Border." It's not really a dance number, but it has too much intensity, too much a sense of head-long motion, to be a ballad. It's a showpiece for the guitarist and lead vocalist. They're out in front for the whole song, weaving in and out of each other's work with only breathing space between verses. People stayed on their feet and on the dance floor, swaying in place and singing along, doing double handclaps just like on the tape.

Then someone pushed past me, so hard that I would have fallen if Sai hadn't caught me. I got a ragged view of him as he went by, and a better one from the back once he was past: an elf, and from the clothes not a Bordertownie. He wore a full-skirted coat that fit close to his waist and stopped at mid-thigh, in a brocade of some magical weave that changed pattern restlessly. His hair was uncolored, and worn in a moon-white braid that reached his waist.

"My, my," Sai said happily. "Weeds of Elfland he doth wear."

I hung onto her upper arm. "Calm down, he hasn't done anything yet."

"Couldn't I just warn him a little?"

"No."

I realized a moment later that Sai might get her chance yet. The elf in brocade pushed his way to the edge of the stage and shouted something at the band. It might have been a name; the Elflands accent throws me off until I get used to it.

Wild Hunt tried to keep going, but you could tell they were all rattled. When he shouted again and pounded a fist on the stage, the White Lady faltered and stopped, and the rest of the band came to a ragged halt behind her.

She turned off her mike, but I could still hear her in the silence that followed the music's death. "Leave me alone," she said. She had the Elflands accent, too, but not as thick.

The elf down front balled his fists and said something furiously in Elvish.

"No! I told you no. I am not—I *will* not go." She was hanging onto the neck of the bass as if she was afraid someone would try to take it away.

Sai had begun moving forward, which was tough. The crowd had pressed itself away from the stage and back toward us, and they were packed as tight as a new brick wall. I followed along behind her as best I could.

More Elvish from the guy in brocade; I recognized the words for "clan" and, I think, "Border."

The White Lady was turning away from him, as if to walk off stage, but she stopped when she heard his little speech. "Are you, now?" she said with scorn that would crack metal. "Well, not me. Maybe all *those* pretty sheep—" and she pointed in the general direction of the Elflands, "—but not me." And this time she did walk away, taking off her bass as she went.

The elf grabbed the edge of the stage, to vault onto it. Then Strider was there, a defending knight in a ragged Danceland t-shirt, as if he'd appeared out of the air. He set those long white hands of his on the guy's shoulders, spun him around, and gripped his lapels.

Suddenly Strider let go and took a step backward. For a moment I felt a dropping feeling in my guts, wondering if he was hurt, if the Elflander had done something to him. But they each took a step sideways, and I could see wariness and surprise in Strider's face, but no pain.

The Elflander had a long, angular face, with thin lips, a high-bridged nose, and slender eyebrows that winged up at the ends. He was looking at Strider as if the latter were something found growing on the floor of a public rest room.

Strider spoke an elvish name, rather cautiously. I won't try to transcribe it.

The Elflander raised his chin a notch, and let his upper lip curl just a little. "You are not permitted to be free with my name," he said.

"You're over the Border now. That name doesn't mean piss-all here." Strider was usually politer than that, especially in a situation like this, where he's supposed to be just doing his job. I don't know whether the Elflander had meant to insult Strider or if the man was naturally arrogant—or naturally foolish. But Strider *always* knows exactly what he's said.

After a quick up-and-down look at Strider's habitual attire—the green Danceland shirt that looked as if someone had driven over it several times (which, in fact, Strider had), the blue jeans that seemed to be held together with patches and optimism—the Elflander said, "Little more than a savage. It is pitiful to know you are an elf."

"Yeah, well, you set a fine example for the race, rich boy. Go make trouble in somebody else's place." Strider took a step toward him, to make his point a little plainer.

The elf drew something from under the skirt of his coat. At first I thought it was one of the retractable metal antennas that the gang members duel with sometimes. But he snapped it to its full length and slashed the tip across Strider's face with one quick motion, and it didn't leave a welt. It left a gash.

In front of me I heard Sai cry out, and I wondered where Goldy was. Trapped in the crowd, most likely. People were scrambling away in that mad, mindless way that happens when something has happened and no one knows what. Strider stumbled back against the stage, blood on the lower half of his face like a bandit's kerchief, and the Elflander pressed the attack grimly. A lunge caught Strider in the upper arm. Another pass sliced his t-shirt through the middle of the Danceland logo. It was too precise to be coincidence. I caught a glimpse of the bloody stripe across the skin beneath.

I was sticking my elbows into people, trying to get through to help. What I intended to do when I got there, I don't know. My motions seemed horribly slow, and the Elflander horribly fast. I had an awful vision of reaching Strider only to find him in bits on the floor.

He was, in fact, on his knees, one arm clutched over his middle, his other hand in a fist. Sai had broken through and was nearly in reach of that damn Faerie blade when Strider gasped, "No."

Sai stopped instantly, to my surprise, and looked to Strider for an explanation. The Elflander drew back a pace and lowered the tip of his blade just a little. Behind him Goldy stepped out of the crowd like a black phantom, ready to nail the stranger if he didn't like Strider's reason for not doing so. He had snatched a baseball bat from under some counter, and it hung loose at his side.

Strider shook the hair out of his face and turned cold, narrowed eyes on the Elflander. "This is an honor fight. Nobody gets this son of a bitch but me."

Sai stiffened and looked as if she would have objected, but Strider ignored her.

"And I *will*," he spat out.

The Elflander turned his back (a fine gesture of contempt, but *I* wouldn't have turned my back on Sai just then, whatever Strider's stated preference was). He saw Goldy for the first time, and was obviously startled. But Goldy smiled evilly and bowed him through the crowd, which parted grudgingly. Every face I saw among them was turned to the Elflander, hard with hate. Strider is not always easy to like, but he's one of *ours*.

Just before the door, the Elflander turned. He had returned his cutter into his gaudy jacket, and he drew himself up with, I'll admit, a certain amount of elegance. Addressing Strider, the stage, or us all, he said, "We shall continue this matter sometime soon."

"Damn straight," Strider grunted.

The two locked eyes. Then the Elflander glanced away and smiled thinly. He bowed as though we had all come to pay court to him, swirled, and was gone.

Sai and I helped Strider to his feet. I remembered the band only then, but they had left the stage. I was glad of it.

Wolfboy was holding the door to the back hall open for us. He looked impassive, even for him. We got Strider into the office and made him sit on the couch, but he refused to lie down. Sai got the first aid kit.

Strider pulled the shirt off over his head, with a fair quantity of teeth-gritting. The Elflander, it would appear, had gotten in a few licks that I hadn't seen. It always looks bad when an elf is wounded; it's the combination of gore on that pale skin and elven blood's tendency to clot slower than human. And of course, it looks worse when the elf is a friend.

I filled a bowl with water at the office sink and brought it, with a couple of towels, to Sai. She started with Strider's face. The water in the bowl changed color quickly. There was a lot of silence, broken only by Strider's occasional swearing. I wanted to say something cheerful. Plenty of things came to mind, all of them abysmally stupid. I kept quiet.

Goldy stuck his head in. "Is it as bad as it looks?" he asked.

Sai frowned, but Strider shook his head. "I'll live. Mostly slashes, and none of them deep. The bastard knew what he was doing." He grinned suddenly, which was almost frightening. "When he drew on me, he'd lost it for a second. But when he started cutting…"

"What was that objectionable little tool of his? Any idea?"

"It's a goddamn dueling toy in the Elflands," Strider replied.

I think we were all equally startled. After Strider's near-silence on the subject of his life in Faerie, a sentence like that one sounded like the whole Alexandrian library.

Sai rummaged in the first aid kit, found the tube of Gold-N-Rod Creme, and began to streak it across the slashes on Strider's skin. Though she was careful, he said some remarkably inventive things, and when she did his face she had to hold him by the hair to keep his head still. I watched the stuff draw the edges of the skin together, appreciating that miracle more than I ever had. In the Elflands, of course, it works instantly and prevents scars from forming at all. That probably explained the Elflander's perfect face, given his habits. But maybe he was just very good with his fencing gadget. Lucky him.

Goldy looked helplessly at Wolfboy and me. We shrugged, about in unison. "Strider, my lad," he said finally, "are you quite sure you don't want me to find him, cut off his pretty braid, and see that he eats it?"

"The hell you will!" Sai said, and her voice made us all jump, even Strider. "If he doesn't want to do it himself, I'm gonna, you hear me? Oh, shit." She turned away and banged her fist against her thigh.

Strider squeezed her shoulder. "Hey, all of you, why don't you take a walk? I don't feel like talking right now. Okay?"

Sai looked up at him.

"Yeah," he said gently, "you, too."

She nodded and stood. Wolfboy and I were already on our way out. Sai came out, closed the door behind her, and we all stood in the hall feeling useless for a minute.

At last Goldy said, "Ah, well. Friday night, a band that will draw half of Bordertown when the word gets out, and only two of us on the floor. Nothing we can't manage, yes?" He looked at Sai.

Sai pursed her lips, then shook her head slowly. She held up one finger.

"Oh dear," said Goldy.

"Please, Goldy? I gotta get out of here. I'd just take this out on some poor jerk out front."

Goldy sighed. "Very well. Don't do anything foolish, will you?"

Sai grinned wearily at him, and went down the hall toward the back door.

As we went the other way, back to the main room, Wolfboy tapped his chest, and Goldy said, "You'll fill in?" Wolfboy nodded. Goldy shook his head. "If there's any more trouble, wait for me, hmm? You may look like Captain Fangs'n'fur, but you're a pussycat in real life." Wolfboy growled at him, and we all felt a little bit better.

Dancer had obviously held things together in the aftermath. The crowd had stayed, the band was on stage powering up and tuning, though the White Lady wasn't back on yet. I wondered how *I* would feel, knowing that someone who'd sliced up Strider with no great provocation was very, very angry with me. I began to wonder if she'd like someone to walk her home...

Tick-Tick met us by the door. "I'll buy," she offered.

"Thank you, but no," Goldy said. "I'm going to need every wit I have left. And as of this moment, all my breaks are canceled." He gave us a little salute and went back to work. Wolfboy glanced at Goldy's back as if thinking how rarely the Ticker offered to buy, then shook his head sadly and left us to get a shirt from Val so everyone would know he was on duty. I think Wolfboy likes playing dress-up even more than the rest of us.

"Well, *I'll* let you buy me something," I said. Maybe I should've offered to watch the place, too, but I look bad in green.

"Good. I refuse to get drunk alone, just now."

We didn't actually get drunk. Valda set dark bottles down for both of us, and let us drink some before she asked, "Is he okay?"

I thought about it. "That depends on your definition of 'okay.' Emotionally, no comment. Physically, he'll be fine in a while, though he'll have a peachy dueling scar."

"Dueling," Val spat. "That wasn't goddamn dueling." She wiped a glass with a furious motion. "He cut up Strider the way you'd cut the head off a weed. And Strider without even a pocket knife on him…"

That was when my body and mind caught up with each other. I found myself tight all over and inclined to shake.

"Drink up," the Ticker said solemnly. "We're all alive, and in a year this'll be nothing but an anecdote."

"Only if something worse happens in the meantime," Valda muttered.

The White Lady came back on stage then, and the band started up. Even Wild Hunt couldn't get me to dance any more that night. But I let the music erode the tension in me, and clear my head a little. Watching that white elven woman helped, too; the very sight of her was like a cold compress to the forehead.

I was halfway through my second bottle before I said, "Ticker?"

"Mm-hm?"

"Why are the Trio the way they are?"

She raised her eyebrows. "Which way?"

I struggled with the answer—I hadn't had quite enough beer to loosen my tongue. "Goldy and Sai have suddenly gone a little bloodthirsty. And Strider, for that matter. If someone cut you up like that, how would you react?"

"I'd lie down and moan for a week."

"Well, of course. But would you…"

"Swear vengeance, and insist that I be allowed first crack at the beggar? I don't *think* so."

"Would you expect me to do it for you?"

"Heavens, no!"

"Good. Though I don't know what I *would* do. And yet, we're as close as Goldy and Strider are."

"Closer." She finished her beer. "Where is all this going?"

I shrugged. "I'm not sure. But I don't like the Terrible Trio's reaction any more than I like what they're reacting to."

Tick-Tick thought about that for a while. "I think it's just steam. They've been playing their parts for so long—you know, Borderland's baddest—and this reminds them that they're mortal." She looked at the empty bottle. "My, two beers do make me profound."

"Chatty, anyway," I beamed at her. She slugged me.

After a minute, I asked her, "You think he knew him?"

She blinked. "Strider and the pretty boy?"

I nodded.

"You think he didn't?"

I hated not knowing what had really gone on out there on the dance floor. I hated worse knowing that I probably never would. If Strider didn't want to talk about it, he wouldn't. I certainly wasn't fool enough to go ask him, not then. He might confide in Sai or Goldy, but for the very reason that they wouldn't repeat it. We all have secrets in Bordertown; I suppose everyone has secrets in the World and in Faerie, but their secrets are smaller—and maybe more desperate. At least we can think of ourselves as—well, what's that line from the song by Locas Tambien? "We're tragic, romantic figures / We're so much cooler than you!"

From then until closing, we did nothing more demanding than listen to the music and spend the Ticker's money.

Wild Hunt came back for an encore, and then had to come back for another one even after Dancer turned the lights on. They finally got people settled down and ready to go home by resorting to a ballad, "Jenny on the Hill." The White Lady put down her bass and sang it, in a style that was brutally simple and wonderfully effective. It took the melodrama out of the ending, and made it seem that lost love and premature death were simply the way of the tragic world. I had to pretend to sneeze when the song was over, so I'd have an excuse to blow my nose.

Tick-Tick went to help herd people out the door.

"Orient!" Valda called.

I turned and found her holding up a push broom. "So you want to stay after closing like the employees?"

"Oh, lord," I sighed, and took the broom. Wolfboy joined me in stacking chairs—all except the one Goldy dropped into and refused to leave.

He looked more drained than I'd ever seen him, and a little tense around the mouth.

"That bad?" I asked him.

"I doubted I'd live to see this moment. I don't suppose you'd be so kind as to fetch me a beer?"

"The dying bouncer's last request," I said, and handed Wolfboy the broom. He snarled at me.

When I came back with the sweating bottle, Goldy said, "Seen your little runaway lately?"

I'd forgotten Caramel, frankly. "No."

Goldy shook his head. "We may have lost her, then. I'm afraid that the events of the evening scared her away."

"Can't blame her for that." I didn't correct Goldy; I knew he wasn't talking about the kind of lost that could be corrected by finding her again, which I knew I could do. I remembered my last sight of her jaunty, foolish pheasant feather. I'd felt a sneaking smug pleasure, one I hadn't admitted to myself then, that thanks to me she'd gotten into what might prove to be the concert of the year. I felt dreary suddenly, and very, very old.

Wolfboy looked up then, and Goldy and I followed his gaze. The White Lady was crossing the dance floor toward us. She was even more of an apparition in the dusty setting of Danceland with the house lights on. Once there were angels, and they must have looked like that.

She smiled, a lovely curving of her carved alabaster lips. "May I sit?" Her right hand moved in a fluid arc toward the stacked chairs, and her rings all flickered.

Wolfboy grabbed a chair and set it out for her with a little bow. "Thank you," she said with a grave smile. I wondered if she'd like one to rest her feet on. Hell, why use a chair? I'd get down on all fours and she could rest 'em on my back.

"You—all of you—were wonderful," I said, and felt like an idiot.

She laughed. She had the kind of laugh that made you want to say a lot of amusing things. "That's very sweet of you."

"And very true," Goldy said solemnly.

She smiled and tucked her chin. It was a charming gesture. "We don't often play in concert, and it's difficult for me—I feel very shy in front of an audience. But everyone here was so excited, so kind to us…" She fluttered her white hands. She had three rings on her right hand, all of elf-silver and sapphires, with only her middle finger and thumb bare of them. She wore none on her left hand; they're hard on the guitar neck. A sapphire swung from each of her earlobes.

"There was a little too much excitement tonight, I'm afraid," Goldy said, "for which I am heartily sorry."

The smile fell off her face, chased away by something that might have been fright. She looked down. "I'm sorry, too," she said softly. "The one who made the trouble…he was my fault, I think."

"Your fault?" I asked. It was startled out of me, I suppose.

"He…we were lovers, for a short time. He is not willing to leave it at that."

So that was half of the night's mystery solved. I felt a little sorry for the Elflander, even as I felt alarmed for *her*. It wouldn't be easy to accept the loss of the White Lady with anything like grace.

We all fell silent, not wanting to pry, but not sure how to change the subject. In Bordertown, even more so than in the World, you tread very lightly around personal matters—your own or someone else's.

The pressure was relieved when Dancer came up to us, Tick-Tick dawdling along behind. "Good show," Dancer said to the White Lady. "Damn good show." Then I realized that she was carrying the bag that held the night's receipts. Business with the band leader, of course. We all scattered to various jobs.

I managed to be the one by the door, though, when the White Lady was ready to leave.

"Will you be all right?" I asked her.

"What? Oh, yes, of course. You mustn't worry about me." She offered me a lovely smile, a little tinged with sadness. I don't care if she *was* half a head taller than me. I felt protective.

"If he's out there waiting for Strider, you could be in trouble."

She shook her head. "He won't hurt me. But I'll watch for him, and be careful." She touched my hand lightly, and added, "You are very kind."

I was struck quite dumb, of course, in both the original and the more corrupt senses of the word.

"Perhaps I will see you again?"

"I'd like that," I said finally, getting my tongue loose from the roof of my mouth. "People around here usually know where I am."

She looked amused. "But who would I ask them for?"

Oh. Right. "My name's Orient."

"Orient. And mine is Linden." She touched me again, a fingertip to my hand, and slipped out into the street and the dark.

I leaned against the door for a moment to catch my breath. Wolfboy was watching me from the bar; he grinned when I met his eyes.

I walked over to him. "I was only asking if she'd be all right," I muttered. He treated me to one of his hair-raising giggles.

Valda called down the counter to us. "Guys? One more favor of you? Can you take the bottles back to the alley?"

Wolfboy spread his hands out, as if to imply that we would do anything for her. I wasn't feeling quite *that* generous, but I wasn't above hauling a box or two.

Val had already loaded the empties into the crates. The brewer would pick them up in the morning from the alley. Wolfboy and I shouldered one each and headed for the back.

The way led past the office door, and I wondered if I should knock, see if Strider was all right. From the way Wolfboy slowed down, I suspected he was wondering the same thing.

"Oh, hell," I said, "why not? If he objects, he'll just break my face, right?" I knocked. There was no answer. I tried again, a little louder, and when nothing happened, I opened the door a little. Then I stuck my head in.

The room was just as we'd left it, but Strider wasn't in it. I pulled my head back out and shut the door. "He must be all right," I said. "He's gone."

Wolfboy thought about that for a second, then shrugged. We went on, through the door at the end of the hall that opened into Danceland's private garage, and through that to the alley door.

All right, it's not really an alley, it's a very small cul-de-sac, with the building's back door located near the closed end. So it's black as the inside of an intestine out there on any night except when the moon was bright. Tonight, unfortunately, the moon was bright.

He was lying in a grotesque parody of ease, hands folded over his stomach, legs straight. He looked like a tomb statue in white marble. It was a long and horrible moment before I realized it was not Strider. Then I saw the braid and recognized it, and knew whose corpse it was in Danceland's alley.

I've been staring at that last sentence for fifteen minutes. I've tried to go on and describe the body, and failing that, to simply recount, in order, who did what. After all, this is why I'm writing, this is the event I'm trying to make some tentative sense out of. But even though I can see, in my mind, the Elflander's body—all too well, in fact, which may have as much to do with why I haven't slept yet as this narrative does—I can't write it down. It makes me shake.

Dancer sent Val to alert the cops, and Tick-Tick to Strider's and Sai's place to warn them. The Ticker came back and reported that they weren't there. Just as we were trying to decide if we were relieved by that, Strider came in the front doors. I wish now that one of us had thought to ask what he'd come back for, but I don't suppose the answer would have been of any use. It's just a loose end, like where he'd gone in the first place, like where Sai had gone when she'd left the club, like whether anyone could swear that Goldy and Wolfboy had been inside Danceland *all* night, like whether Linden was bothered enough by her old boyfriend that she'd want him dead. Even the Ticker's alibi is low-grade. Hell, maybe they all did it. The only person whose innocence I'm certain of is me. And if this goes on, before long I'll be asking people to corroborate my memories.

So the cops arrived, and did all the investigative things we'd done and a great many more besides, and finally took Strider away with them to the lock-up. It was the obvious thing to do, but it didn't make it any easier to watch.

The sun's been up for three hours. I'd forgotten this particular time of day existed. I went back to Danceland after writing the last paragraph. I wanted a cig, and I wanted my damn copy of *Stick Wizard,* because I knew I wasn't going to sleep. Both things were still in the sidecar. The Ticker had parked the bike in Danceland's garage for safekeeping and gone home with Sai, to keep her from being alone and from doing something stupid.

I went to see if someone was around to let me in, or if I could get in by myself. I had to go through the cul-de-sac, of course. I didn't get in the garage, didn't even try, because I found something on the ground near the street end of the cul-de-sac, and it distracted me.

So I don't have my cigs. I have a pheasant feather with a distinctive nick out of one edge, dirty now from lying in the mud. I've been picking it up and twirling it or sliding it through my fingers, as if it's an impression ball, ready to pour out its stored song at a touch. I'll sleep now. I have to, whatever I might dream. But I want to know what it means. Caramel, where are you now?

Doesn't seem right to scribble in Orient's diary. I look at my writing on his pages, and it's like I came to Orient's grave to make a speech (pretty silly idea, huh?) and found myself puking on the funeral flowers. Too late now. Should've tried this in pencil maybe, and erased it if I didn't like it. Sorry, Orient.

I want to say that this is Lone Wolf's writing that you're reading now, but Orient calls me Wolfboy, like most people. Could be worse. Guess I'm grateful I don't have to say it's Dogbreath writing this.

It's not easy. I look at all those pages Orient wrote, and I'm jealous, and I'm sad. He began with last night, but I'll begin earlier. Orient's my friend, or maybe, was my friend. That's why I'm doing this, continuing what he started. Even if my written words aren't much better than my spoken ones. Orient and I are a bit alike, you see, so it's more than just finishing something a friend began.

That looks stupid: Orient and I are a bit alike. But it's true. Maybe he's not as quiet as I am, but he watches more than he talks. He likes to read, 'cause he thinks there's more to living than most people do. He—

I hate writing this. God, I hope he's all right.

He and I, we've both been changed by the Change. I don't know who had it worse. Orient's fey. That means "touched by Faerie." He grew up in the World, and people always thought he was strange 'cause he could find things. Things he'd never seen. All he needed to know was that something existed, and—

Shit. I'm writing about him in the past tense. I won't do that anymore, until we know something. And if he's dead, I'm sorry. This stupid journal will be my tribute to him. Maybe I'll burn it, or throw it in the Big Bloody, or see if I can get it published. Something. If he's alive, he'll get to read this. If he gets to read this, I want him to know that he's a pissbrain and the only reason I wrote this was to mess up his stupid diary. The Human Compass writes about me as Wolfboy. What a pissbrain.

I hope he's okay.

All Orient needs to know is that something exists, and he can find it. He told me about driving through some strange city with his Mom when he was eight. She wanted Greek olives for some reason. Maybe she was taking salad to a family get-together. Orient pointed off in the distance, saying, "There." She laughed at first, but he got mad. I can imagine it: "There, Mom! There!" And she got mad at his insistence. And she followed his directions to prove that he was wrong, 'cause he had never been in this city, he couldn't know where to find Greek olives, he didn't even know what Greek olives were since she had never made this salad before. She would prove her point to him, then she would spank him, and he would never mention this nonsense again.

Orient led her to a Greek grocery that had the most beautiful olives you could imagine. Big, purple—

All right, I'm making that part up. Maybe they were tiny, dried, bitter olives. The point is, they were there.

And the point is, she stared at Orient like he was what he wasn't.

And the point is, that's when he quit thinking of himself as a person and started thinking of himself as a freak.

And he never mentioned that nonsense again.

'Course, that didn't do any good. He couldn't stop finding stuff. People couldn't stop noticing. People don't like what they don't understand. People don't know that the trick is to try to understand what they don't like. Orient was a freak, and in spite of being a handsome, bright kid, he was fey. Everyone whispered it. Some people shouted it. Some people laughed at him. Some people beat him. After a while, he got tired of pretending he didn't hear and he didn't hurt. He did what almost all fey kids do. He ran away to beautiful Bordertown. Just like the kid last night, I imagine, and if it's different, it doesn't matter.

Started off completely differently for me. I wasn't bright and I wasn't unusual and I wasn't fey. I was a little geek with zits who wanted all the pretty girls, and none of the pretty girls wanted me. Not because I was fey. Because I was nothing special. What I would have given then to be fey...

So I did what all kids do who want to be special. I ran away. Just like the kid last night, maybe. And I ran with a couple of gangs in B-town, and I found that one way to be special was to develop a rep for a smart mouth. I was extremely high one night in The Dancing Ferret and some elf woman was talking too loudly about short-lived humans and their habits. So I said, "Yap, yap, yap. What a—" Well, you can guess what I called her by what she turned me into.

She stared at me at first. She obviously expected something more. Even elves forget sometimes about the way magic ebbs and flows in the Borderlands. Then she laughed, and everyone else laughed, even the Packies I had come with. I turned and ran. Loped, maybe. I could see my hands and arms, and I felt my body hurting and changing. I got my life-long wish then. Even in Bordertown, I was no longer like anyone else.

There's a million stories in the big city, and... Nah.

The thing is, Orient and I went through the same things, even if we did them in reverse order, for different reasons. The same past. We both knew too much about being outsiders. Maybe that's part of the reason he became friends with me. Doesn't explain the rest of our friends, or maybe it does. Orient said I liked playing dress-up better than most of our crowd, and that's true so far as it goes. I like feeling a little less like something waiting for a silver bullet and feeling more like part of a community. But I could join any of the thousands of little gangs that form the greater gangs of the Pack, the Rats, the Bloods. Or even one of the independent gangs: Dragonfire, the Horn Dance, Commander X's Kids... I don't want to. Orient forgets that he was the one who once suggested we pick a name for ourselves, and I was the one who vetoed it with a chopping motion.

I'm not writing about it. I ought to. Somebody reading this is going to wonder what the hell happened, so I'll be nice:

The early part of Friday night went pretty much like Orient told it. He was a little more taken with the White Lady, Linden, than I was. I thought she was too fond of playing tricks with her voice, and I've seen elf and human and halfie women who did more for me. I thought the real talent in the Wild Hunt was the drummer and the hyperharpist and the halfie on elfpipe. Big deal. The band's good and deserves its fame.

I heard a little more of the argument between the Elflander and the White Lady than Orient did. I hear a lot better than I did before I was changed. And I know a little more Elvish than Orient, so the argument was clearer to me. The Elflander wanted Linden to come back with him, he wanted her to come back now, it was important, and her life in Bordertown wasn't. I'll bet that really endeared him to her.

I can't add anything else up until the end. Orient went into the alley first, moving awkwardly with three crates of empties. I knew something was wrong first. I smelled blood. I'm not as good as my rep; I didn't know what kind of blood it was. I smelled a lot of things, most of them alley things, and some of them things that the Elflander did as he died. I attributed those to the alley, too, at first.

It was the stupid Fairiecloth coat that tipped me off. It caught the light from the back door. I wondered why the stranger ditched it, then I grinned, thinking someone had swiped it from him to teach him a lesson about SoHo. I was still grinning when I saw that he was still in his coat. I was still grinning when I saw what had been done with him while he was in his coat. I made a grunting sound and set down my load of crates.

Orient turned. Then he saw what I was looking at, and we both stared for a little longer, then he went to the side and threw up. I don't think he left that part out because he was ashamed. I think it wasn't important to him.

The Elflander's coat was in ribbons, like his skin, and the light made him all shiny with elf blood. I don't know why I didn't vomit. Maybe dogs can't vomit for emotional reasons. The Elflander's long white braid had been stuffed into his mouth, and a part of my mind was saying that wasn't very original while another part stared in horror. His dueling toy was still in his hand.

Orient and I went into the back room without having to suggest it to each other. Neither of us wanted to be near the corpse. Orient leaned against a stack of whiskey kegs and brought up both hands to push back his black, red-tipped hair. Or maybe just to massage his temples. He said, "Strider's in trouble."

I grunted.

"Can we cover it up?" That was phrased as a question more out of habit, I think, of being considerate of me. He answered it himself. "No way. Might get Dancer in trouble with the cops, if we wait. Might get Strider in more trouble. Shit." He looked at me then, face pale and controlled. "I'll tell Dancer. It's her alley, after all."

I nodded. I was as happy to pass on the decision. Now I wish to god I'd sat down with Orient and talked about what we saw, him babbling, me scribbling on something. Maybe he wouldn't be missing now if we had.

Having read what Orient wrote, I can guess what thoughts were going through his head as we went to tell Dancer. Strider did it. No, Strider'd meet the Elflander near the river or in a bombed-out house or in a deserted theater, and they'd fight until honor was satisfied or Strider was dead. That's how Strider thinks, the simple git.

Sai did it then, to protect Strider from the stranger who had cut her lover for fun. No, Sai wouldn't jump someone in the alley, and Sai wouldn't go after him until she knew Strider was fine. Then she'd arrange for the stranger to be without his little dueling toy—have some friends surround him, or something. And she'd show him why she was SoHo's middleweight champion for a season and a half, until she decided she was too pretty to stay a boxer. Sai wouldn't kill. Not like this, anyway.

That meant Goldy did it, because he was frustrated that he couldn't do anything else to show he cared for Strider, because he felt that he should have stopped the stranger sooner somehow, because he stepped outside to grab a breath of fresh air and saw the Elflander waiting for Strider— And that didn't work either, because Goldy's not like that, any more than the rest of us are. In fact, Goldy might take a certain delight in tossing the Elflander to the cops for a night in the B-town jail. Wouldn't do that with a local, but with a Faerie lord in a silly coat...

And that left Orient with one last suspect, his White Lady. He wouldn't like that, 'cause he had a crazy crush on Linden. But Orient's smart. He'd weigh the possibility, and it wouldn't work any better than any of the rest. You don't carve up a crazy boyfriend. You just wait patiently until he finds someone else to pester. No wonder Orient seemed so frustrated in his last notes.

We stepped into the main room and Orient said, "The elf that made trouble tonight..." I was the only one who knew why he stopped, but everyone could tell something was wrong.

Val came over and put her arm around his back. "What?" she said.

"He's dead. In the back alley. He's all..." Orient winced. "...cut up."

"Fuck," Goldy said. Goldy never swears.

Dancer and the Ticker went back to look, while Orient tried to describe it to Goldy and Val. His words didn't do much to tell it, but his tone did. I was actually glad I couldn't talk, myself.

"We call the cops," Dancer said when she came back.

"No," Goldy whispered, and I thought there was going to be worse trouble.

Dancer didn't hear, or maybe she's wise enough to know when to pretend she didn't. "Val, go tell Strider and Sai what happened. Tick-Tick will go tell the cops." She glanced at the Ticker. "Better take the avenues to the cop shop, 'cause the short cuts might not be safe this time of night.

And I wouldn't be surprised if you didn't even leave for another five minutes or so. Bikes can be so hard to start, sometimes."

The Ticker smiled a tiny bit, more in recognition than in humor. Goldy nodded, said, "Yes. That's right."

Dancer brewed a pot of coffee while we sat around, not really talking about anything important, people saying things like "Good band," and "Bastard deserved it," and "Fuckin' *hell!*" and no one bothering to answer any of the things. Dancer poured coffee for us all, and I realized that was another first. Not the freebies, 'cause Dancer can be so generous I sometimes wonder how she stays in business. But she never worked behind the counter. Val usually made decent coffee, and Goldy brewed great coffee. Dancer's tasted like she was the one who taught Goldy, but even Orient's "good coffee" seemed perfunctory.

Val came back and said Sai and Strider weren't home. I didn't like that. Then Strider came in. I liked that less. He was pocketing his key to the place and saying, "Anybody seen Sai?" He stopped, stared at us staring at him. "What'd I say?" And when no one answered immediately, he added, "Hey, if my part's crooked, I'm sorry, I lost my comb." His hair, as usual, was a perfect white mane.

Goldy shook his head.

"That's a joke," Strider said, moving toward the bar where we had gathered. Then he stopped and said quietly, "Something happened to Sai."

"No, Strider," Goldy said. "Not that we know of."

"It's that elf," Dancer said. "He's dead back by the empties. Cut up bad, like someone hated him." That was obviously a warning, not an accusation. "Tick-Tick's gone for the cops. I told her to. If I didn't, they'd shut me down."

Strider's pale face went paler, which is some trick. The new scar was like a lightning flash on his cheek. He sat on a stool and whispered, "Oh, to sail a sunless sea." It took me a minute to realize that was a Faerie oath, and before I did, Strider sounded more like himself. "It's all right, Dancer."

"I told her to stall. You could get out—"

He shook his head. "And go where? This is Bordertown. I'm Strider. I don't want anything else."

"Don't be a bigger fool!" Goldy hit the table with the flat of his chocolate-brown hand, and our cups danced.

Strider smiled slightly. "Hey, Goldy, don't give me that. You know."

"Yeah, you bastard." Goldy turned his back on us all. His broad shoulders shook, and no one spoke for a minute or two.

"He's dead," Strider said, not quite asking.

"Yes," Orient said.

"Fine. Then I don't have to see him." He glanced at Dancer. "Coffee, please?"

"Yeah, sure." She slid him a cup.

"Goldy?" he asked, lifting the cup to his lips.

Goldy grunted, sounding like me, I suppose. He didn't turn around.

"Tell Sai I love her. Tell her not to do anything stupid. And don't you do anything stupid, either."

Goldy's bright head bobbed in a nod.

"Got any poems for me, Wolfboy?"

I shook my head. I hadn't written anything in three weeks, but I knew I'd write something soon.

"You're innocent," Orient said, and his voice was accusing and angry.

"Maybe."

Orient looked upwards in exasperation. "You could say so, then."

Goldy said, "He doesn't have to."

"No," said Orient. "I guess not."

Tick-Tick came back with the cops soon after that. I didn't recognize them as cops, not immediately. There's not a lot of law in B-town, and you almost never see the Silver Suits in uniform in SoHo. Law only comes in for important things, like an ugly killing that too many people will hear of. The woman was about Dancer's age. Her hair was a sun-bleached brown with flecks of white, combed straight back from her forehead. Her skin was lighter than Goldy's and darker than Tick-Tick's. She wore a loose cotton jacket cut from a pattern of tropic flowers, black slacks, and black loafers. Her eyes were hidden behind silver glasses, probably Night Peepers. She kept one hand in her slacks pocket, maybe 'cause there was a weapon there, maybe 'cause it made her jacket hang better. The elf was less conspicuous, with his white hair cut very close to his skull and dressed in a sea-green suit.

"Name's Rico," the human said, not smiling. "My partner's Detective Linn. Anyone want to see a copper card?"

"It's all right, Sunny," Dancer said, and Goldy snickered.

"Good," Rico replied, looking at Dancer. "Sorry you're in this." Her head didn't move at all as she asked Goldy, "Something amusing?"

"Yeah," he said. "Sunny." Once we had a talk about why cops were called coppers. Goldy had said that was because you could buy them cheap.

"For my cheerful disposition," Rico said. So far her face hadn't been any more expressive than her silver glasses. "Think it's funny, Walter?"

Goldy didn't answer. At another time, the whole exchange would have been amusing, but it wasn't now. I think Rico agreed. She said, "Everyone stick around, okay? You—" She pointed at me. "—show me the body while Linn takes statements."

I can't say that she did anything more significant than we did. She lit the place with a torch spell, which impressed me until I saw that it only made everything more obvious, and more ugly. Rico whistled a low note as she looked at the Elflander. She walked around and studied things, not touching anything. Then she stood quietly, and I figured she was doing what I was doing: trying to imagine it.

When she was ready to go, I stepped in front of her. I pointed at the body, pointed at the alley, and shrugged. Rico's about my height, so she looked straight at me in that way they must teach at cop school and said, "Aren't I going to do something more? What do you want? I should take fingerprints? I should try a spell to sense what happened here?"

I nodded.

"Right. Look, Lobo—" I realized it must have been the Ticker who told her my name. "—even if we had the murder weapon, we probably wouldn't sense anything more than rage, quick heartbeats, and a real sick pleasure. And that last is a guess, so don't quote me. As for fingerprints, make me laugh. No murder weapon. In an alley, anything else is circumstantial. The whole case would probably end right here, if it weren't for two things." She held the back of her hand toward me and lifted her index finger. "Your friend made some crazy threats in front of three hundred people." She raised the next finger. "Someone killed Tejorinin Yorl."

I tucked my chin slightly, showing her I didn't understand.

"I don't know either," Rico admitted. "Not exactly. Some elf kid who just inherited something important in Faerie. Don't know why he came out here; maybe on vacation or something. But he was rich and important, and we've gotta get someone for his murder."

I almost hit her.

"I don't like it," Rico said. "Not at all. Dancer's told me about most of you, and I asked questions of your friend at my office. Sounds like you're all okay, for B-town kids. But facts are facts, Lobo. If we can find who's responsible, everything'll be fine. If we can't..." She shrugged and headed back into Danceland.

I stood there and thought about it, till she called back, "C'mon, Lobo. I know you write. Linn'll want your statement too."

I just realized one of the reasons Orient might have started writing this account. It's a testimony. I thought it was a diary, or what he said: he couldn't sleep. Then I thought maybe he wanted to publish his version of the story in one of the street papers, maybe try to sell a book to one of the World presses: *I Ran With a Bordertown Gang* by "Orient." Yeah, sure. Orient's smarter than that.

Consciously or subconsciously, Orient was thinking about the same things Rico made me think about. Questions are being asked, and the answers have to go a long way. This Yorl was an Elflander, so there'll be reports going to Faerie at least, and maybe to the World as well. Which means, just maybe, this thing we're writing is going to be read by people who don't know dick about B-town.

I went in and listened to the last couple of stories. The elf cop had a notebook, and he wrote everything in. Strider claimed to have been walking around, just thinking. Goldy was moving around the floor all the time, he said, but the cops knew he could have ducked out for a few minutes while claiming to be in a back room or on the balconies. They wrote down the names of the members of Wild Hunt, but didn't seem too excited about getting anything from them. About the only time no one was watching them was while Yorl was slicing Strider, and Yorl was still alive when the band reassembled.

"What about Sai?" asked Rico.

"She went walking, too," said Goldy, not too happy.

Rico nodded. "It's a houseful of great alibis."

I sat there, scribbling on some paper that Dancer lent me. I could have interrupted the statements, I suppose, but I wanted to write out my theory in full. So I did, and it was short, only a paragraph like the following:

The killing was the work of a gang, three at least and probably more. I saw Yorl when he was cutting Strider on the dance floor. Yorl was good, like he'd studied that dueling gadget for years. He was too good to let himself be carved all over, even by Strider. And this work was done mostly for the fun of the carvers. You saw that. The business with the braid. Even if Strider killed Yorl, Strider wouldn't do that. Yorl had to have been surrounded, and as one kid distracted him, another cut him. Some sickies probably heard talk about Strider and the Elflander and decided to kill an outsider for fun, figuring Strider would get the blame. Everyone on Ho Street had to be talking about what happened in Danceland.

"A gang," Rico said, when she joined me at a table.

I nodded.

"You're the only one with this gang theory."

I nodded again and gestured for her to give me back the paper. When she did, I wrote something like:

Orient doesn't know much about knife fights. He didn't think about the cuts. Or about what it means, doing that thing with the braid to a corpse. You blame him?

I think she smiled a tiny bit, and that was worse than the absence of expression.

"No, I don't. You want to pin this on the Bloods, the Pack, or the Rats?"

I snorted in disgust and wrote:

You think there's only a few gangs here? There are hundreds. There are some really twisted bunches that hide within the bigger gangs. They wear the colors of the Bloods or the Pack or the Rats. They claim allegiance to the bigger gang and act like the rest of that gang is behind them. Could be any of them.

That little smile came back. "Dancer and I ran with the Go-boys when I was your age. We were part of the Pack. So, who do you favor?"

That made me stop, not because of what I wanted to say, but because of the fact I was writing this for a cop. Then I wrote: *You hear of an idiot named Fineagh Steel who styled himself the leader of the Bloods?* Fineagh built a little army of elf morons—they may live longer than us, but they can come just as stupid—then jackbooted around SoHo for all of a week or two. Some kid took him out in a duel. I imagine a few of the bigger Blood gangs would've done something about him if the kid hadn't.

Rico nodded. "I hear he's dead. I hear his gang's scattered. You think this was the work of one of his lieutenants maybe?"

I shrugged.

"Doesn't work, Lobo." She took off her glasses and grinned at me. Her eyes weren't any friendlier than the glasses. "Why carve a strange elf? If they were jealous of him, they'd rough him up and steal his money, that's all. No need to get the cops down on everyone."

I nodded, wishing I had someone better to point at.

Rico folded up the page I'd written on and replaced her glasses. "Nice theory," she said. "No evidence to back it up." When she said that, it was like she'd kicked me, even though her voice sounded kind, for her. "Sorry." Then she tore up my statement and handed me the shreds. I stared at it. She said, "If I convinced anyone that Strider couldn't have done it by himself, we'd just have to lock up a couple of his friends, too." She patted the back of my hand and left me sitting at the table.

I decided not to tell anyone about it until I knew more. Maybe Orient would still be around if I'd showed the pieces of my statement to him.

Rico and Linn left with Strider when a van and a few Silver Suits showed up. The Silver Suits poked around and fingerprinted us all and did some mystical juju that obviously had as much effect as Rico expected, but now their report would be nice and fat. When they were done, one of them said none of us should disappear. Goldy laughed at that, but it's a little ominous, now that Orient's gone. The Silver Suits took away Yorl's body in a shiny black bag, and finally, Dancer said, "To hell with it. Good night, everybody." And we all wandered out into the good night.

It's Sunday. Still no Orient. I woke, went away, heard some interesting news, drank a whole lot of coffee. Now I have to do something while I wait, so I'll keep abusing Orient's journal.

I woke up around noon Saturday and didn't want to get out of bed. I lay there, thinking it was time to change the sheets and wishing I lived with somebody and wondering if maybe Strider did it. Time does that, lets you see things differently, sometimes in ways you wish it didn't. Whether he did or didn't, I like Strider. But what do I know about him? What do I know about myself? Maybe the killing was an accident, and then Strider had to figure out how to cover it up. If you accept that, it's not too hard to imagine him doing the rest, forcing himself to do something so atypical that no one would believe he had killed Yorl. Under normal circumstances, all he would need was a reasonable amount of doubt in the situation and charges would probably be dropped. He may never have known that he'd killed someone as important as Tejorinin Yorl.

Or maybe he knew exactly who he'd killed. What was Strider in the Elflands, before he was Strider?

The day was cooler than the day before, but that doesn't bother me. I found my other jeans and a corduroy jacket and decided not to bother with shoes. There's enough broken glass in B-town that that isn't the smartest thing to do, I suppose, but it makes people think I'm tough. The fact is I tended to run from trouble before I was changed. Now that I'm stronger and more perceptive, I run even faster.

I went to Sai's. She makes great huevos rancheros without the least provocation. And if she didn't feel like cooking for a stray, she might need some company.

She had company. Tick-Tick was there, sitting a little stiffly on a purple beanbag, maybe aware that it clashed with the red leather outfit that she wore. Sai wore a faded man's undershirt and cut-offs. Under her black bangs, her eyes were almost as red as Tick-Tick's leather. I made a little circular motion with my hand, and Sai smiled a tiny bit, saying, "Hi, Wolfboy. C'mon in. The Ticker toasted bagels, but I'm not too hungry."

I suppose I should mention that Sai was almost always hungry, but you probably get the idea that Friday night's events had everyone acting out of character.

Tick-Tick said, "Rico and her faithful elven companion came by earlier."

I nodded and stuffed a bagel in my face.

"They didn't have anything useful to say," she said, and shrugged. "We didn't have anything useful to tell them."

"She said I could visit Strider," Sai said. "You want to come, too?"

I grabbed two bagels and followed. Sai took her bike, a beautiful blue thing that she called the Bat-cycle for some reason. I hopped into Orient's usual place in Tick-Tick's sidecar, which made me wonder where he was. I pointed at the seat and frowned, and the Ticker said, "I haven't seen him around. We were supposed to meet. We can swing by his place after seeing Strider."

The B-town jail isn't particularly better or worse than most jails, I imagine, but I wouldn't want to stay there. Rico had left a note at the front desk, so we didn't have any trouble getting in. I wasn't too crazy about the man at the front desk, who shook his head as he looked at me and said, "You kids are getting weirder every year."

A couple of Silver Suits walked Strider into the waiting room and leaned up against the wall as if they were bored enough to sleep. One was bored by each door, and they both had three-foot sting-rods dangling from straps around their right wrists.

"Nice place," Tick-Tick said.

"You should try their breakfast," Strider answered.

"You're such an asshole," Sai said.

"I'm glad to see you, too, love."

They kissed, and the Ticker and I tried to pretend we were as bored as the guards.

"We're getting you out of here," Sai said quietly.

"No whispering," one guard called. "And no, you aren't."

"He's innocent!" Sai said.

"You're confessing?" the guard asked. Before Sai could say anything more, he said, "Look, kids. Behave yourselves, and we won't bug you."

"Yeah," Strider said, seconding the guard's advice.

"Okay," Sai said. "Okay. But I don't like this, Strider. I want you out of here."

"No chance for bail," Strider said. "I just hope I don't lose my tan."

"Don't be a pain," Tick-Tick said. "You just make it worse for Sai when you act like that."

Sai quickly shook her head. "No. I understand."

"Hey," Strider said softly, and he stroked her chin with his forefinger. "I'm okay. Maybe I'll get a lot of reading done."

"Rico said the charge is Murder One," Sai said. "I don't want you to get that much reading done."

Tick-Tick's elven features were very grim as she said, "You won't get any reading done if they opt for a memory-wipe, Strider. Not until you learn how again. And if they pick death—"

Strider turned away suddenly. "Trial's weeks away. 'Sides, they'll do what they'll do, okay? You guys better leave now."

"No," the Ticker said.

"I can go back to my cell anytime," Strider said.

"You certainly could," the Ticker admitted. "That won't help you, and it won't help Sai. Is that what you want?"

"I want out," Strider said.

The Ticker nodded. "I know. We have to find who did it. The cops need someone to hang for this one. Maybe literally."

Strider glanced at Sai. She looked at her lap, and I suddenly knew why Strider was being so stupid. I suspected it earlier, but I knew it then. He thought Sai did it. He was too stupid to realize that if she had and he'd been arrested, she would've confessed immediately. I wondered if she'd already considered confessing anyway, just to save Strider. I decided to ask Tick-Tick or Orient later. No point in giving Sai the idea.

I pulled out a sheet of scrap paper and wrote out something like what I'd written for Rico about my theory, then added: *Problem is, we don't have anyone likely. Any ideas?*

One of the guards read it before letting Strider have it. Strider read it and his eyes flicked wide from their usual squint. "You sure about this, Wolfboy?"

I held my hands wide, like: Who's ever *sure?* Then I nodded.

Sai and Tick-Tick read the note together. Tick-Tick said, "You should've said something— Oops."

I waved downwards to show I'd let that pass, then grabbed the note back and scribbled: *Rico didn't like it. Where's a suspect? Who'd want to carve a stranger, even one as bad as Yorl?*

"Wharf Rats, perhaps," Tick-Tick mused. "A chance for fun, and a chance to blame someone else."

"Not all the Rats are like that," Sai said. Her brother's a Rat.

"It only takes three or four like that," Tick-Tick said.

"There were five Rats in Danceland last night," Strider said, and we all got very quiet.

"Is it my turn to call you an idiot?" Tick-Tick asked.

"No," Strider said. "Hers." He pointed at Sai.

"I'll save it for later," Sai said. "What about these Rats?"

"They had a table up on the left balcony. Near the women's room. I was watching them before Yorl decided I was a fencing dummy."

I lifted my hand. Tick-Tick glanced at me, then told Strider and Sai, "After you two left, Lobo filled in on the floor."

"Did you see the Rats?" Strider asked, surprisingly hopeful for Strider. "One was a little brown-haired guy with tiny round glasses. Wire rims.

The rest were, well, Rats."

Rats aren't usually distinctive as anything more than Rats. Sai's brother is a nice guy, but he's a River addict like most of them, and he dresses poorly and smells a little funny... I didn't think about any of that. I just shook my head.

"You went by that corner," Tick-Tick said to me, 'cause she likes things very clear. "After Strider and Yorl fought. And the Rats weren't there." I nodded. I'd remember Rats. The Ticker added, "Was this when you and Goldy first made the rounds?" I nodded again. Tick-Tick smiled. "Rico might like your theory a little better, now."

"Yeah," said Strider without any emotion at all. "Some Rats did it. She'll love that."

"Still..." Tick-Tick said.

"We'll find them," Sai announced.

Strider nodded, not particularly hopeful, and said to Sai, "I thought..."

"I know," she said, and the Ticker and I looked away again. We talked for another couple of minutes about nothing particularly promising. When it was time to go, I gave Strider a poem I wrote late the night before. It was a stupid thing about owls flying over dark forests, but he read it and said, "Nice. I'll put it on my wall."

His own damn wall. That was when I could've cried.

Tick-Tick watched me give him the poem, then suddenly began patting her pockets. She came up with the new *Stick Wizard* and passed it on, saying, "From Orient and me."

Sai looked sad. "I didn't bring you anything."

"Yes, you did," he said, and kissed her lightly on the lips. Then his mouth quavered a fraction, and he turned and said to the guards, "Let's go."

Sai watched him leave, then said, "Where to?"

"Orient," Tick-Tick announced.

"He can find a Rat with round glasses?"

"I don't know," the Ticker admitted. "But it's worth a try."

And it would have been, if we could have found Orient. We went to his flat, then to Danceland, where we told Goldy and Dancer and Val what we'd learned. None of them had seen Orient. Val was annoyed because he'd promised to buy her lunch at Taco Hell. We went back to Orient's apartment. The Ticker had a spare key, so we went in and bitched about him being out of anything worth drinking. Then Sai saw this diary open on the kitchen table.

"You shouldn't read that," Tick-Tick said.

"It's about last night," Sai replied.

"Ah," Tick-Tick said, and she read over Sai's left shoulder while I read over Sai's right. Tick-Tick finished first. She moved away and said, "Why didn't he come get me?"

"He didn't want to wake you," Sai said hesitantly. "Maybe he didn't want to wake me."

Tick-Tick didn't answer. She looked out the window, then said, "I'm spreading the word. I'll tell the Horn Dance, I'll tell Scully, I'll tell Commander X's Kids. Somebody must have seen him somewhere."

"I'll go too," Sai said.

"Someone should wait here, in case he returns."

They both stared at me until I volunteered with a nod. I re-read Orient's entry, then began my own. No Orient. I woke this morning on his rug—which needs to be swept or beaten. Goldy came by with a turkey sandwich and a quart of orange juice. He brought coffee beans. (I write that hoping Orient will read this and suffer a little for troubling his friends.) Goldy made a big pot of coffee and told me that the gangs are turning B-town inside out. Everyone was calling in favors. Sai has her brother's friends cruising the wharfs. Goldy talked to a few Pack leaders who hope he'll join their gangs someday. Tick-Tick spread the word among the Bloods; what with the ones who like her and the ones who admire Strider, there'll be a lot of elves in red leather cruising B-town. She even made a run up the Tooth to speak with Scully and some of the Dragon Fire kids. Dancer and Val went to talk with Farrel Din and other old-timers. Goldy says the streets are alive. We'll find Orient and we'll find the Rats who were in Danceland Friday night, and maybe we'll even find who killed the Elflander. Sometimes I'm rather proud of this stupid town.

Reading Wolfboy's entry, I almost felt as if I *was* dead. Are there ghosts? If they walk, do they suffer from the guilty looking-over-someone's-shoulder feeling that I got from Wolfboy's introduction?

There's a lot of comfort, for me, in reading his account of what happened. The knowledge that Wolfboy and the Ticker were at work on the other end of the puzzle and that we eventually met in the middle—it puts everything in context. I wasn't alone, I wasn't isolated; I was helping to solve the larger problem in my own inimitable nitwitted fashion. But that's not what it felt like in that room.

As soon as I'd written, "Caramel, where are you now?" I felt the pull. It's not as if it grids itself out nicely in my head: here's all the compass points marked with little red letters, and here's the dotted line drawn over the street map with the big star at the end marked "You Win!" I'm a finder, not a cartographer.

"Pull" is the best description I have for it. When I'm trying to find something, whether it's running water or someone's glasses, I can feel it drawing me toward it as if I was on the end of a string. The string, unfortunately, can go straight through furniture, buildings, or a dozen feet of solid earth, which is more than can be said for me. I also don't know where the thing is until I've found it, which is why you can't walk across town, knock on my door, say, "Orient, I've lost my pink socks," and expect me to tell you they're on the floor of your closet. But if you ask me to find them for you, I'll feel the pull, and if I follow it, I'll be led eventually to your place, your closet, and your socks. Payment in advance, please.

So Caramel felt like Thataway, and I left the journal and the feather behind and followed my feelings.

I dodged around a lot. The way led through SoHo, where fallen buildings or contumacious gangs will sometimes block off streets or even whole neighborhoods. There are also a few gangs who wouldn't dream of keeping strangers out—the local economy would collapse if they did. I triangulated around anything I couldn't walk through, and ended up near the river.

Caramel was in what remained of a warehouse-loft a few blocks from the wharf. It had been brownstone once, with a frosting of terra-cotta details: garlands and vases and things, and elaborate moldings around the windows. Some of the terra-cotta remained, though much was either scavenged or broken. The whole building had been painted by the simple expedient of getting on the roof and pouring cans of paint down the walls. No one had thought to mask the windows, apparently.

I could hear harsh-voiced bells from a distant boat. I smelled fish, machine oil, and the sweet-and-musty odor of the Mad River. An orange cat slid from a windowsill and into hiding as I watched. Nothing else moved. It was too late in the morning for the fish markets, and too early for anyone else in this neighborhood. Hell, it was too early for me. I was hungry, and raw all over from lack of sleep. I felt as if I'd left my eyeballs in talcum powder overnight. My finding talent, which doesn't turn off and fades only slowly, had begun to feel like a rhythmic yanking, mostly at my back teeth. And, of course, I was solidly in the middle of Wharf Rat territory. My day was made.

I circled the building once, just to make sure Caramel was in it and not in something past it. The possibility that she'd done the murder had crossed my mind. It must have been on its way to someplace else, because it didn't stay long. But it made me nervous to find her in Rat City. It reminded me of that bottle of river water I'd taken from her. The water of the Big Bloody can, among other things, produce multiple personalities in a human being, all with a remarkable talent for disguise. Many of the Rats are raving psychotics in lamb suits.

If she didn't kill the Elflander—which, nervous or not, I wasn't buying—then the evidence pointed to her as a witness. If I could get her out of hiding and convince her to talk...well. I was counting on her clearing Strider. But if she convicted him instead, then that was right, it was justice, and I'd see it done and get the hell out of town because I wouldn't be able to stand the sight of the place anymore.

There was no security on the front door, of course. I followed my talent up the stairs, through a hall whose walls might have been held up by the binding action of the spray paint on them. Then in mid-hallway I stopped, and stepped back into an alcove where a radiator had once stood.

The Ticker would have had my skin, I realized, long before that. She's tried for years to instill a sense of self-preservation in me, and after all her work, it's only rudimentary. In this case, for instance, it kicked in much too late.

Sin Number One: I'd arrived unarmed, unprovisioned, and unaccompanied. I could just hear her. *Orient, my dear boy, we have a body count* already. This is Condition Red. I don't care if you're only going down the hall to take a *leak*...

Sin Number Two: Having already committed number one, I'd compounded it by walking into a strange building in hostile territory without noticing what was, literally, right under my nose.

There are a lot of ways for an inhabited building to smell. Infants. Boiled cabbage. Sex. Disinfectant. Lamb chops. Perfume. Wood stoves. I haven't got the Wolf's nose, but I didn't need it. This building was lived in by a group of people with nasty personal habits. Drinking river water gives human sweat and urine a characteristic odor, and that odor haunted the halls and clanked its chains at me. Oh, I knew those chains.

I stood in the alcove cussing myself out for maybe three-quarters of a minute. Then I continued down the hall. What else could I do? If they had a sentry hidden, I'd already been seen, and there'd be someone waiting for me on the stairs. If there wasn't a sentry, I had nothing to worry about anyway.

There were only two doors in the hall, and one of those was a rusty sliding one for an old dumbwaiter system. My trail led through the wall between them. I put my ear to the clammy plaster and heard voices, but none of them were Caramel.

I heard a sound behind me and turned. I was just in time to see that the rusty dumbwaiter door hid a nice renovated *quiet* lift mechanism, and that the woman stepping out of it had a tire iron. Her first swing caught the wrist of the arm I'd blocked with. Her second landed where the first had been meant to: the side of my head. Lightning flash. And nothing.

Coming back was slow, and I suspect intermittent. That last is hard to be sure of, since I wasn't a reliable observer through much of it. But I know when I woke up more or less in earnest.

I didn't know where I was. I don't mean I didn't recognize it—I'm talking about with my eyes still closed. I couldn't find north. I couldn't find anything.

It was like waking up to discover you're lying on the ceiling. A scream worked its way into my throat and stuck there.

I don't know if it was the vertigo or the blow to the head—I haven't had a lot of experience with being knocked out—but stage two involved being violently sick. I got myself propped up on my elbows afterward, in the process discovering the grinding pain in my wrist. I was cold and sweating and trembling, and I wanted to wash my mouth out with something. I lifted my head, very carefully, and saw what the Welcome Wagon had left.

A big glass jar of water. In red.

A little despairing noise got out of my mouth before I could stop it, and I rolled over and covered my eyes with my good arm. Welcome back, Orient.

I heard a door open; then someone kicked my foot solidly. The little seismograph recently installed in my skull went to the top end of its scale. When I dared open my eyes, I found a brown-haired man in wire-rimmed glasses bending over me. He smiled kindly when he saw I was conscious. All his teeth were bad.

"Hello. Are you feeling better now?"

I felt much worse. He had the gentle voice and sweet manner that I associate with genuine maniacs.

"Good. You know," he said with a birdlike turn of his head, "if you meant to ride in like The Borderland Kid and rescue your little friend, you didn't do a very good job."

His eyes went quickly to the other side of the room, and I got my head up enough to look there. Caramel was sitting hunched in the corner, staring mournfully from under her tousled brown hair. Big miserable brown eyes. I lowered my head. "Thank you. I know," I said. I felt very much like hell.

He smiled meditatively down at me, massaging his fingers. "Well, you'll have to stay here now. She'll pull her weight just fine, once she gets used to things—" and he grinned at the jar of river water next to me. "You—we'll find a place for you too, I'm sure. Make yourself comfortable." He nodded and left the room. The bolt slid home.

I heard Caramel scramble across the floor to me. "Are you—" she began in a whisper. "Oh, shit, of course you're not okay. Can I do anything to help?"

"No. Thanks." I wasn't whispering to keep them from hearing us. I was whispering to keep *me* from hearing us.

A moment later she lifted my head, very carefully, and put something soft under it. "My jacket," she explained.

The cloth smelled like soap and clean cotton. And I'd thought she lived in a building like this?

"When they brought you in… I thought you were dead. There's blood on your face." She paused, then said, "I know you shouldn't drink this stuff, but is it safe to wash in?"

"Yeah. Better wash it now, though, before I get desperate."

"Desperate?"

"Before long we're going to be very thirsty. That's why it's there."

"Should we throw it out, then?"

"They'll bring us more."

She didn't answer that. After a moment I felt damp cloth against my cheek and smelled the water. I opened my eyes finally.

She looked older than she had last night. That's not quite true; she still looked sixteen. It was just an older sixteen. Ah, Bordertown, with its little rites of passage.

"You have a concussion, I think," she said.

"How do you—"

"Your right pupil looks a little bigger than the left. What are you doing here?"

That last sentence sounded yanked out of her. I smiled, sort of. "I told you I'd find you if I needed you."

"How?"

I told her about my talent. It was a little perfunctory, since I felt out of breath the whole time. But when I finished, her eyes were round and wondering.

"That's marvelous!"

"Not always," I said.

She was startled. Then she looked down and seemed very intent on wringing out her scarf. "I guess this is one of those times."

"No!" I reached toward her with my right hand. She was on my left side, so it didn't quite make it. "That's not what I meant."

I now know what a searching look is; she fastened one on me. "You're a nice guy," she said, as if it was not a compliment but a simple observation of fact.

My conscious mind was beginning to go out with the tide. "Not always," I repeated, and went off into the dark again.

Waking up was much simpler the second time. I shifted position in my sleep, and my left wrist hit the floor. I made some noises, some of them profane. I had the good sense to raise my head to look at it, rather than raising the arm. My wrist was plum-colored where the tire iron had connected, and impressively swollen. "Should splint it," I muttered to myself.

"Working on it," Caramel said. She sat down next to me and held up two pieces of wood. "Dividers from the desk drawers," she said cheerfully.

Neither of us really knew how to apply a splint, but I helped by lying still and gritting my teeth. When she was done I felt like a seal with a wooden flipper, but the joint was immobile.

I hadn't known there *was* a desk in the room until then. I got my right elbow under me and checked out the cell.

It had been someone's library once, high-ceilinged, with tall windows and decorative plaster friezes at the tops of the walls. Most of the walls were fitted with built-in shelves, all of them empty now. There were water stains on the plaster from leaks in the roof. One window had been inexpertly bricked up, probably right after the Change. The other window was barred, and the light came dimly through a layer of pea-green paint. There was a fireplace between two tiers of shelves, closed up with a sheet of plywood wedged into the opening. The floor must have been handsome once, but damp and neglect had weathered the planks gray. A heap of what looked like bedding occupied one corner, and the aforementioned desk, one drawer missing, stood in another.

"All the comforts of home," I muttered. Caramel didn't answer.

"Are you okay?" I asked.

She snorted. "Yeah."

"They...didn't hurt you, did they?"

She shook her head, then realized what I was really trying to say. "No. A couple of them thought about it, but I talked them out of it."

"You talked them out of it?"

She grinned. "This is kind of embarrassing."

"I won't laugh. I'm not sure I can."

"Well, I told them something from an old story I heard once. I told them I was fey, and that everybody in my family turned into tigers when they lost their virginity, and ate their lovers. And that I was still a virgin."

I had to laugh after all. "That's really dumb."

"I know." She was laughing, too. "But they were all pretty high. I don't think they'd have swallowed it otherwise." She folded her knees up under her chin. "I hadn't been in here long before they brought you in."

"Did they bring you here?"

She shook her head. "I followed them from Danceland. I managed to get myself locked in the garage downstairs. That's where they found me."

"You shouldn't have followed them."

Caramel fell silent for a little, then said, "They killed that guy."

That was hard to reply to. So I didn't.

"I think they were waiting for him. I saw him turn the corner into the alley, walking with one of them, and when I got to the corner, the rest were there. The guy with the glasses held out something in his hand and said, 'Looking for this?' and the elf went for his sword thing. Then they closed in on him and started sticking him, and...and cut off his braid. And..." She covered her face with both hands. I thought she wouldn't go on, but she said, "The one with the glasses said something about the river, that it was the blood of Elfland. And that if it was good, what would the blood of an elf be like?"

Then she stopped. I was glad of it.

I wanted desperately to know where Wolfboy and Tick-Tick were. Wanting should have been enough to give me a bearing on them. Nothing happened.

The jar of river water was beginning to stick in my thoughts. I wondered how Caramel was feeling. My mouth was dry and still sour-tasting, and my throat scratched a little. When *had* I last drunk something? At Danceland? I'd had coffee and beer there, both good for drying you out eventually.

"Why did you follow them here?" I asked Caramel.

"What was I supposed to do, go home and stick my head under the pillow?" she snapped.

"I would have."

She looked at me for a long moment. "Would you have? When they started splitting up to leave, and you knew you were the only person who could find out where they were going?" She looked like an empty-handed person who wanted something to throw. Then her eyes got wide and a little bleak, and she turned back to me. "You could have done it, couldn't you?"

"What?"

"You could have tracked them down. You could have found them."

"No. Not unless I'd seen them. Otherwise I wouldn't know who I was looking for, and I couldn't do it."

"Really?"

"Really."

She rubbed her face and swept her hair back. She had a very high forehead. "Well," she said. "Well. Like I say, they split up when they left, to cover their tracks, I guess. The guy with glasses had a bike, and he drove off on that. But before he left I saw him put whatever it was he held out to the elf in his saddlebag. So I followed one of the ones who were on foot, and got here. I snuck into the garage, to find that thing. It seemed important, and I was afraid that if I didn't take it, the glasses guy would get rid of it before anyone could get back here. And I found it, and hid it—and then they caught me."

"But you said you hadn't been here long before they brought me in."

Caramel looked rueful. "It took me a long time to get up the nerve to break into the garage."

That made me laugh a little, which made her do the same. "So what was it?" I said. "The thing in the saddlebag."

She nodded and began to unlace one of her sneakers. That puzzled me, until she pulled it off and shook something out into her hand. "I don't think he knows it's gone yet," she said, and held it out to me.

I didn't take it from her. It was temporarily beyond me to raise my hand and reach for it. And such an unassuming little object, however valuable it might be...

It was a ring of elf-silver set with a sapphire.

"Hide it again," I said, when I could. "It's important."

Linden was never offstage long enough to have done it. No, we knew who'd *done* it—Glasses and Friends. But if the deed had been bought...? Oh, I wanted something cold to drink, and I wanted a nice herbal cig with it, and I wanted to bang my head against the wall until all my problems went away. I had a witness, and a missing puzzle piece, and no way in the World or Elsewhere that I could deliver either of them.

The pea-green light grew steadily weaker. I crawled across the room and propped myself against a wall. Caramel took a nap, curled up on the heap of bedding. I looked at the jar of river water. I tried to remember every band I'd ever seen play. I counted the number of times I'd seen Tick-Tick take an engine apart. I looked at the jar of river water. Caramel shifted position. I looked at the jar of...

The door lock made noise, and I tapped Caramel's ankle to wake her up. Glasses came in with a flashlight and blazed it at us. None of the kindly light of a Faerie lamp here. I doubted there had ever been magic in this room, beyond the twisted magic that the river worked on humans.

I couldn't see him in the glare, until he turned the beam on the jar of water.

He made a clucking noise. "Maybe I should leave you some crackers," he said. He turned the flashlight back on us. "It's not so bad, you know.

They'll tell you out there that it's dangerous, but they always say that. That's wisdom in that jar, strength, inspiration. They don't want you to be smart or strong or great. They want to step on you. That's why they're afraid."

I blinked and shook my head, and the light came closer.

"Really?" His sweet voice came out of the flashlight beam. "I'm stronger than you, right now. And you're afraid of me, aren't you?"

I could see him, finally; he squatted companionably next to me. He took my chin in his fingers. Then he drew his hand back and slapped me casually. A lot of little bells rang in my head, and I slid further down the wall.

"Leave him alone," said Caramel, in a surprisingly steady voice.

He looked at me, then toward her, as if considering the merits of her suggestion. Then he got to his feet. "All right, dear, I can do that for a little while. But you can help, you know. Just get him to drink up, and all the unhappy times are over, okay?" He smiled at her, and went out the door.

"D'you think you could knock him out the next time he comes in?" I said thickly.

"Hmm." A moment of silence. "I could hit him with a desk drawer... No, I don't think I could hit him hard enough. I'm not very big."

True, she wasn't. I sat in the dark and remembered what she looked like. Once, in the World, they would have called her elfin. That was before they discovered that the elves were a lot bigger than they'd made them out to be.

I wanted something to goddamn *drink*.

"You want to sleep?" she asked.

"No. I want to talk. What's Bellinbroke like?"

She chuckled a little. Have you ever noticed how much laughter can sound like crying? Bubbles of air coming out, and a little inhalation at the end like a sniff? "I'll get homesick, and it'll serve you right."

But she told me about her father, who taught at the University; and about her mother, private and self-possessed as a feral cat, who left her husband for one of his younger colleagues. Caramel told me how her father seemed to forget that his daughter existed, except when she forced him to remember. There are a lot of ways to forcibly get your father's attention, most of them unpleasant. Caramel had worked her way through, she figured, about half of them before she realized that the effect was never permanent. So she ran away to the Borderlands.

"What about you?" she said at last.

"Me?"

"Yeah, you. Come on, I told you mine."

So I told her, which is a measure of how out of touch I'd become. There was a terrible pain in my head that made all of my thoughts rattle around loose, I didn't know where anything was, and I was so dry I was afraid I'd crack if I moved. No, let's be honest. I was too far gone for witty descriptions. Drink the damn water, I told myself. Drink it now, get out of here, and you can kick it later. I wasn't so fuzzy-minded that I couldn't spot the two basic errors in that sentence.

I told Caramel almost all of it. I told her about the stupid olives, I told her about my mother watching me out of the corner of her eye when she thought I didn't see. Believe me, you can live with getting beat up in the parking lot at school dances. You can put up with opening your locker and finding a dead cat in it. You can even bear it when the next-door neighbor, usually distant but kind, gets drunk one night and tries to run you down with his car. But when you realize that your mother never touches you except when she has to…

I think I was semiconscious some of the time. I discovered that Caramel was holding my hand at one point, and couldn't remember when she'd first taken it.

I didn't tell her all about my early life in Bordertown. I told her I did some pretty despicable things, and left it at that. Safe enough, since I know I've forgotten many of them. The river will do that. It *does* make you feel strong and smart, but only because it takes away all the things you've ever measured strength and smarts by. Everything, even your own well-being, is set at a distance and devalued. You can do the most appalling things and forget them a moment later, because they simply aren't significant. And then even the river begins to slip away and forsake you, and you need more and more of it to make you strong and smart, to make you forget your freakish talent that's the real cause of your fall, not the river, not your own asshole self-pity. That much I remember.

And I remember, after resorting to something stronger than the river, not being allowed to sleep, being stuck under cold running water until I was awake enough to scream and claw, being made to walk, walk, walk with a fierce voice alternately cursing me and bursting into tears.

If we didn't get out of there soon, I would drink that water, I would take my faithless mistress back. In the dark of that room where magic never came, I was certain that this time no one would be there to make sure I kept walking.

I should have told her about some of the good things. I didn't. I fell asleep.

When I woke up, it was still dark. Caramel had her head on my knee, probably napping again. My mind was full of the exquisite clarity that is often the leading edge of hallucination. My mouth felt glued shut.

I thought, reveling in the ability to do so. Escape. Not for me; I wouldn't get a block away in this condition, even if every Rat in the building went to Faerie on holiday. For Caramel. Camilla. Attendant at a sacrifice. In hiding behind Danceland, watching five Rats let the blood out of a fairy tale, for the greater glory of whatever they worshipped. I'd taken away her name, but the destiny seemed to have stuck. Well, she wouldn't have to attend mine.

The door was no good—solid, locked, raving lunatics on the other side of it anyway. Neither of us was strong enough to get the bars out of the window. The floor was old, but in good shape—Glasses had crossed the room with nary a creak. The ceiling was also solid, and fifteen feet away. How to get one small girl out of a second-floor room...

The fireplace. Oh, god, the fireplace.

I shook Caramel awake and pried my lips apart. To her eternal credit, she woke up fast and without a fuss.

"Go see if you can get the plywood out of the fireplace opening," I whispered. Even that made me feel as if I'd been breathing thumbtacks. "If you can't do it without making a racket, come back here and tell me."

I waited alone in the dark while she made scrabbling noises at the other end of the room. "Can't," she said finally in my ear. "Not without a noise."

"Help me over there."

I worked on one end, with my one good hand, and she worked on the other. I felt all my fingernails break and bleed, and kept clawing anyway. Finally I got desperate enough to give the bottom of the plywood a kick. With a scraping sound that nearly made me swallow my tongue, it tilted. We grabbed the now-grabbable top edge and pulled the board free.

Maybe they were all asleep. Nobody came in. I stuck my head into the fireplace opening, trying not to think of all the things that might accumulate in a disused fireplace. Far above me I saw a square of dark blue shot with stars. The flue had rusted and fallen out, along with an ominous lot of crumbling firebrick. Still, if I hadn't been so dehydrated, I would have cried.

"Take a look," I whispered. "Can you get up that?"

She brushed by me; I felt her hair against my face. "I think so."

"Careful. There'll be loose brick. Watch out for a guard on the roof."

It was staccato and disconnected, but I knew I couldn't keep talking for long.

"Where do I go for help?"

I shook my head, which, of course, she couldn't see in the dark.

She grabbed the front of my shirt and hissed, "Where? Come on!"

I didn't know where. I didn't know where anything was. Or anybody. People might be at Danceland; more likely, it was closed. She could try a dozen different places and not find anybody. I couldn't find anybody. Delirium was setting in.

"Please!" I could hear her crying. "I don't know people in Bordertown, and by the time I get help, it could be too late for you. Where can I find help?"

And it came, like a couple of notes from a familiar song, just enough to recognize it by. Thataway.

Not enough. What the hell way was it? Where was north? I felt for it and called for it, until the dark in front of me was shot with colored sparks. That was north. There.

Still not enough. This time I couldn't just follow until I got there. I had to figure it out from here.

I found them all, in the midst of pain and madness—Danceland, Tick-Tick's place, Wolfboy's. They were all too far south to be the trace I'd gotten when Caramel asked me to find help. Then I tried my place. It matched.

I told her. She sobbed, and kissed me on the mouth, and lowered me gently to the floor. Then she scrambled around me and went to work.

I reconstructed it later, with no small quantity of admiration. She piled the bedding up to look as if she was in it, all except a couple of pillows. Those she put in the bottom of the fireplace, so any loose bricks that she dislodged would make no sound when they hit. Then she leaned over me again.

"Can you get the plywood back up once I'm in?" She had a hand on my face, so I could nod in answer. "Okay. Hold the fort, Orient."

I heard her at first in the chimney, until I fought the plywood back into place. I think anyone who was looking for something amiss would find it—but that was my job, to keep anyone from looking. Just long enough for Caramel to get away.

I dragged myself away from the fireplace and let go of consciousness for a while.

I have large, merciful gaps in my memory where the rest of it should go. I remember waking up to find the window an oblong of gray-green in the shadowed room, and discovering that I'd dragged myself most of the way to the water jar. Instinct is a wonderful thing.

I remember Glasses coming in, casting a cursory glance toward the pile of inhabited-looking blankets, and giving me the benefit of his conversation for a few minutes. He drank some out of the jar. I could hear him swallowing, see his throat working. A little of it trickled down his chin and shone there, until he saw me staring at it. He wiped it away very slowly. I tried not to cry until the door closed behind him.

Many gray intervals later, something boomed, not far away. The second time it happened, I identified it as an explosion. It happened a third time.

These, I knew, were significant. I decided to stay awake, on the off chance that I'd remember why.

The gunshot brought me fully conscious, though. It came from the next room. Then the door burst inward, and Glasses stood in the opening, eyes wild. He had a sawed-off shotgun, and he was leveling it at me. The whole scene seemed remarkably clear, and I had time to wonder why, after years of haphazard observation, I should suddenly be able to count the hairs on the backs of my murderer's hands.

I thought the roaring noise was the sound of the shotgun, and me dying. But some of Glasses' chest blew into the room, and so did he. A second later the Ticker came through the door, all scarlet leather and bared teeth, an immense handgun in a two-fisted grip.

She looked to me, saw the water jar, and stooped on it like a hawk. It broke against the wall with a splash, and I whimpered.

"Shh, shh," she said, and held me against her. It was Tick-Tick, you see, who wouldn't let me quit walking and die all those years ago.

I felt her start to shake, and remembered that, for all her skill with things that go boom, I'd never seen her do what she'd just done. "Lobo!" she shouted. "All clear. Get your ass in here!"

He had the water, a cloth soaked with it. They'd known I wouldn't be able to swallow at first. Wolf's brown-furred face was contorted, as if he'd be crying if his tear ducts worked that way. They carried me out between them, through the smell of fired weapons.

Someone had thought to bring a stretcher, and it was waiting in the hall, along with Goldy and Sai and—dear grinning god, was that Scully, from up the Tooth? The wet cloth had given me back the use of my tongue and lips, if not my throat, exactly. I whispered to the Ticker, "How big a party is this, kid?"

She shrugged as best she could, carrying me. "We had to get you back. We've all lost our house keys." And then, for only the second time in as long as I've known her, I saw her cry.

No point in going over the rescue. There are enough pieces of it in Orient's part of the story. It was your basic arrival of the cavalry, I suppose, but none of it was fun. Too much worry about what could go wrong, for us and for Orient, and whether we could free him before the Rats realized that we were there. The worst part was when their sentry spotted us from the roof, right after Tick-Tick's first smoke bomb went off. The Rat had a gun, and we were all pinned down until the Ticker said, "We need to lower the technology level around here." She closed her eyes and mumbled something, and there was an explosion from the roof that was almost as loud as one of hers. She nodded grimly, and we went in. Afterwards, there wasn't much happiness in our success. Orient was a mess, and we all knew we wouldn't have found him at all if Caramel hadn't escaped. Still, we thanked everyone who had shown up and watched the Gathering of the Gangs disperse.

We took Orient home while a couple members of the Horn Dance fetched Doc. Doc cleaned and splinted and bandaged as Orient gasped and winced and looked extremely unhappy. He wrote out a short version of his stay at Glasses' place. I wanted to make a joke about having two mutes in our little group, but I couldn't think of anything funny. People had died. Nobody important enough that the cops would come around, but people nonetheless. Orient drank a lot of water while he wrote it. Then Doc said, "That's enough. You got your story from him, now go away and let him sleep."

"What do we owe?" Tick-Tick asked.

"Ah, forget it. Wasn't interesting enough to charge you for."

I fetched Doc's coat. Next time she puts her hand in her pocket, she'll find seven four-leaf clovers.

We all went out and sat on the steps so we wouldn't disturb Orient. No one spoke. Tick-Tick's face was drawn and tired, almost gray under her dandelion hairdye, and one pointed ear was bruised and slightly bloody. Sai squinted in the distance, her eyes very Oriental and very elven at the same time. She wasn't watching anything that I could see. Goldy rubbed his strong, brown hands over his metallic hair and stared at the sidewalk. It was just after noon of a beautiful day, we'd saved Orient, and I expected us all to pass out from exhaustion.

Caramel stood nearby, looking like she didn't know whether to stay or leave. Sai noticed her and said, "Hey, c'mon. Sit and rest. You could use it. We all could."

"Thanks," Caramel said as she sat cross-legged beside me. She glanced at Sai, then at the rest of us. "What're you going to do now?"

"We're going to talk too much," Goldy said. "As usual."

Tick-Tick nodded. "And maybe we'll figure it all out. What have we got?"

I held up the ring that Caramel had found. A sapphire set in Faerie silver. Orient had winced when he reminded us who wore sapphire and silver rings.

"We have the ring," Tick-Tick said. "And a witness." She nodded at Caramel. "That'll clear Strider."

"It's not enough," Sai said.

"It'll free him," Tick-Tick said.

"It's not enough," Sai repeated with a shake of her thick, black hair.

Goldy nodded. "The singer would've let Strider die for her. The Rats were just Rats, but she's the one who used them."

"We could go to Rico with what we've got," Tick-Tick said. "Maybe Rico could help."

Goldy said, "Rico can't do a thing. Linden will say the ring was stolen by the Rats, and that'll be that."

"Even if we do nothing," Tick-Tick said, "Linden will have to live with it." I wondered if she was thinking about the Rat she shot, or the one whose rifle had exploded in his grip.

I raised my hand, then started scribbling while they waited: *Why the ring? Why was it important to Yorl? Why would Linden kill someone who meant little to her? Why were the Rats at Danceland that night?*

"Very good questions," Goldy said. "But do you have very good answers?"

Why did Yorl come here from the Elflands? Who is Yorl? Who is Linden?

Goldy said, "No, no, no, my friend. Good *answers*."

No one laughed.

"I doubt Linden's in Rico's files," Tick-Tick said. I agreed with a nod. Records in B-town are pretty thin. The cops get reports on runaways sometimes, and they're building a file on people they've arrested, but that's about it. Rico would need a better reason than "we think she hired some Rats" to go through the trouble of tracing a SoHo musician.

Where's Linden? I wrote last, and Tick-Tick shook her head sadly. "We're going to have to wake poor Orient."

Orient woke violently, scattering his bedcovers. Tick-Tick put her hand on his brow and he settled down.

"Sorry, kid," he whispered.

"It's all right. Lobo's got some questions for you."

Orient nodded sleepily. "You guys can't do anything without me." He looked bad, pale enough to be an elf, but he sounded pleased. I was still sorry we woke him.

I wrote: *Where's Linden?*

He closed his eyes, which turned into a wince. After a second he pointed toward the hotel area in SoHo. "Thataway," he croaked.

Then I wrote the tricky one. *Where's an elf named Yorl, a relative of Tejorinin Yorl?*

Orient frowned at me. I wasn't sure he understood, and even if he did, the question might be too vague for him. A worse possibility occurred to me: what if there were as many Yorls among the elves as Joneses among us? But Orient grinned weakly.

"If there's more than one of them, I'm gonna have a migraine, Wolf." He bit his lip and closed his eyes. Then he opened them again, wide. "Same way," he whispered, nodding toward the hotel area. "Same damn way."

We talked a lot more after that, sitting in the street. Everyone liked my theory and no one liked my plan. No one came up with a better one, so finally we scattered to the various bikes. The Ticker stayed with Orient because someone had to—and because she thought this last part was unnecessary, I think. Or maybe she didn't want to get in a position where she might have to hurt someone else. Caramel was willing to play the part I wanted the Ticker to take, so the B-town Players were ready for their first bit of improv.

Finding Linden wasn't hard. We asked at a couple places for the lead singer of Wild Hunt, and somebody said she was staying at the Roses of Elfland. Sai and Goldy weren't happy about waiting in the street, but they agreed. They thought they were there in case the plan fell apart. They were there because I didn't trust them to keep to the script with Linden.

Caramel and I knocked at Linden's door. She answered, opening it enough that we could see sunlight and expensive furniture behind her. The room smelled of herbal cigarettes, perfume, and something tart that was her own scent. She wore a sea-green dress with billowing sleeves. It was cut on one side to reveal golden stockings set with tiny diamonds. Her hair fell over her right shoulder like a moon-lit avalanche of virgin snow. I understood why Orient was so taken with her. I thought she was reasonably attractive, even. "Yes?" she said, and then, catching my gaze with her silver eyes, she said, "You helped pack up after the gig at Dance-land. We appreciated that." She smiled kindly.

I wanted to bow and say something gracious. Caramel and I looked odd in the clean hall of the Roses of Elfland. My jacket and jeans hadn't looked good before this morning's adventure, and Caramel's gray traveling clothes were smudged with grease, mud, soot, and half-a-dozen things less easy to identify. Then I almost laughed, realizing that the clothes were the least of our oddness. Caramel seemed very shy and very young as she stood before Linden, and I was hardly the boy next door. I nudged Caramel, who said, "Uh, we have something you'll want."

"I beg your pardon?" asked Linden.

"A ring," said Caramel, growing more sure of herself. "Belongs to Ms. Yorl. Is it yours?" She showed the silver and sapphire ring. It was almost identical to the three on Linden's right hand.

"No," Linden said, blinking at us. "But it looks just like mine. Your Ms. Yorl and I have remarkably similar taste." When neither of us said anything immediately, she smiled thinly and said, "Good day." She began to close the door.

Okay, it was a stupid plan. I had an impression ball in my pocket, recording since we came up the stairs. Nothing we recorded would be proof, not in court, but I'd hoped we'd get something that would convince Rico to probe into Linden's past. That was shot now.

Then Caramel said, just before the door closed, "So you won't care if we take it to the cops." Something about the way she said it reminded me that she'd watched Tejorinin Yorl get cut up.

The door stopped swinging. Linden's face was framed in it, a porcelain face haloed in sunlight. "Why should I?" she said, sounding suddenly short of breath. I almost felt sorry for her.

"No reason." Caramel stroked the ring between her thumb and forefinger. "What do you think a wizard could learn from this? Betcha one could find its owner at least. Betcha we'd get a good reward."

Linden's lips pressed together, and she shook her head slightly. Silver strands of hair drifted freely, and I suddenly knew we'd won. She said, "What do you think you're doing? What do you want from me?"

I grinned at her. I doubt I could've put my whole face into it. Baring the teeth was probably enough.

"Do you want money?" she said quickly, her voice going up the scale. "Is that it? It is a nice ring." She reached for it, and Caramel stepped back. "I had nothing to do with it!" Linden cried. "Nothing!"

I nodded and looked at Caramel until she asked the obvious question: "Nothing to do with what?"

Linden stood in the doorway and stared as if she was seeing something besides us. Then she slammed the door.

Rico liked the impression ball. Linn preferred the ring—he coaxed all the magic out of it and found not just Linden-as-owner, but a little trick that made it seem that where the ring was, Linden was, too. Just in case somebody being led into an alley should need a little magical reassurance that this was a safe place to go. Combined with Caramel's statement, it made Linden look bad.

Rico looked for female members of the Yorl family. I had wondered why someone with a new inheritance would suddenly come to Bordertown, especially someone who seemed to despise B-town the way Yorl had seemed to. I expected that Yorl had a sister. Rico found that Yorl had a wife who had left him a couple of years before his mother died. Mom's death left him the head of the family and a rich guy. Now that he was dead too, the missing wife stood to inherit a nice piece of whatever it is that elves consider valuable, if only she would reappear in Faerie. There were no photos or fingerprints of this wife; the elves don't seem fond of either. But, amusingly enough, her elvish name translated into English as Linden.

The rest was easy to put together. Yorl must have arrived inconveniently in B-town and insisted that Linden abandon the band and be a proper wife and lady because he had a position to uphold now. When Linden heard that the mom was dead, the temptation must have been too much. So the Rats came to Danceland to meet with her, and during the confusion between Yorl and Strider, she gave them their commission and the Yorl-decoy off her finger. Whose idea it was to do it in back of Danceland to frame Strider, we'll probably never know. Me, I bet Glasses thought the chance was too good to waste.

Today we all went to the Wall to watch a couple of elven Silver Suits escort Linden Yorl through the gate to Faerie. No matter what happened to her there, she wouldn't come through the gate again. Rico told us that she was officially Not Welcome in Bordertown.

We dressed in our best, of course. Orient was up and around, maybe a little too pleased with the effect of his arm in a black sling. And Caramel stayed close to him; Tick-Tick thinks Orient doesn't need any more nursing, but Caramel is very protective of him still.

Linden saw us. We'd meant her to. I saw her give a quick look to Orient, but he didn't move an eyebrow.

As Linden went through, Strider called out something in Elvish.

"What was that?" Sai asked him.

"Jealous, love? Never you mind."

But I know enough Elvish to recognize the proverb. At least, I'd always thought it was a proverb. Now I'm not sure. Loosely, it's "Love wealth above life itself, and starve in splendor." It might be a curse. My other suspicion I don't want to think about: that it might be part of Faerie's penal code.

We went back to Danceland, Goldy made coffee, and Orient found Dancer's lost receipt book. And I wrote this.

I guess this is as close as I'm likely to get to explaining where I get my crazy ideas. To anyone who ever wanted to ask that question: Everybody *gets crazy ideas. Not everybody gets the training, the encouragement, the permission, as it were, to turn them into stories, or paintings, or dances, or whatever. Stop trying to figure out who's talented and who's not, and just take a shot at it, okay? Do some art. Tell anybody who asks that I said it was all right.*

—*Emma*

Wonders of the Invisible World:
How I Came to Write *War for the Oaks*
Emma Bull

I keep getting mail from people I admire, asking, "But why would the high courts of Faerie be living in Minneapolis?" Until now, I've explained that I hadn't imagined them living anywhere, permanently; for the purpose of my plot, they came to the Twin Cities when it became an interesting piece of territory to fight over. But I've never been happy with that answer. So from now on, it's going to be, "Where do you *think* the Seelie Court would live? Manhattan? Berkeley? Give me a break."

War for the Oaks is a contemporary fantasy set in Minneapolis and St. Paul, in which a local rock musician becomes involved in a civil war between elves and bogarts, phoukas and kelpies, brownies and redcaps—the Seelie and Unseelie Courts of Faerie. And nobody from out of town really understands. Why the Twin Cities? Why rock 'n' roll? Why elves? They ought to ask, too, Why a novel?, but they usually don't.

The Twin Cities are something more than the setting of the book, at least for me. They're part of the cast. The characters in a novel ought to be true to themselves; what they do, they do because of who they are and what's happened to them. The plot of *War for the Oaks* goes as it does, I hope, because the characters are in character, but I can't imagine it happening anywhere but in Minneapolis and St. Paul. Minnehaha Falls and Central Park are not interchangeable, in substance or spirit. Walking down Hennepin Avenue on a Friday evening calls up a different set of emotions and attitudes than walking down any given street in Manhattan. And the mix of attitudes and influences—parks and punks, the New Riverside Cafe and 7th Street Entry, a wildly active music scene in well-mannered, well-ordered metropolitan surroundings—only happens here. People outside the Twin Cities may say what they like. I can't think why the high courts of Faerie would want to live anywhere else.

Still, lots of people like Minneapolis and St. Paul; they don't all write fantasy novels about supernatural electric violin players and sharp-dressed elves on the Nicollet Mall. Why did I write *War for the Oaks?*

It all started in the dance club called First Avenue...

In First Avenue, the walls disappear in the dark, and the neon, the overhead lights on the balconies, the reflections, are left to define the space to the eyes. Music defines it to the ears, music that's loud and fast and never stops. I navigate just fine in the space the sound carves out, but I stumble occasionally into walls and railings. That I keep half-seeing things at the edge of my vision doesn't help. When I walk into the ladies' room, there's a woman with Nefertiti's profile putting on lipstick in front of the mirrors. Out on the dance floor, I watch a hollow-cheeked man jumping and shaking with unnatural grace, driving away devils I didn't know were there. The air is thick with dreams—the audience's, the band's—and those dreams are wired up to the high voltage of loud music and colored lights in the dark. I'm sitting at one of the balcony tables when a scene blazes up in front of my eyes, an overlay on my view of the stage. Magic being done in a room so full of its own kind of magic that no one notices. The Queen of Air and Darkness standing on the V.I.P. balcony in First Avenue. On stage, a little blonde woman with a red guitar, armed with music and words, fighting for—what? It will be the climactic scene of the novel, but I don't know that yet. My job is to go home and figure it out...

In the 400 Bar, I stand packed in the audience, looking up at Boiled In Lead onstage. We're all sharing breathing air and sweat, dancing furiously in place, because there's no room to dance but we *have* to. The band melts down "Fisher's Hornpipe" and builds it back up in their own electro-Celtadelic image. I'm full of emotions too big to hold, longing and exaltation at once. The people around me seem to feel them, too. I look back up at the band, and think, "They're making this happen. This is *real* magic." The feeling will evolve, in the dim-lit back of my mind, until it can emerge into the light much later as the spine of my plot. When it does, it's a surprise to me...

One sunny day in fall, I go to Prospect Park, because I want to put the witch's hat tower in the book, though I'm not sure where. As I scramble up the steep side of the hill, the light changes. The sky above me is pearly with overcast. The wind hisses in the young trees, suddenly much colder. At the top of the washed-out path is the tower, with its rust-red door barred and chained shut. I walk around the base and read the graffiti. Names of people, bands, school teams. Somebody + Somebody. Then, approaching the door from the other side, I see a stenciled drawing: two human figures, one with a pistol in the act of shooting the other in the head from behind, and the caption, "BANG YOU'RE DEAD." The tower has always seemed graceful and frivolous to me. But for fifteen crucial minutes, it becomes a symbol of illusions, of confinement, of betrayal. Then the sun comes out again. Those fifteen minutes are a question that can only be answered at home, at the keyboard...

Minnehaha Falls in autumn flood. I go down a flight of stone stairs half-hidden in the wall along the driveway, and the city disappears. At the bottom, at the end of a great green basin of grass, there's a bump of ground topped with two trees, as artificial-looking as a burial mound. Behind it is a wooded hill that rises all the way back to street level. In the folklore of the British Isles, you can get into Faerie through hills like this, if you can only find the door. On moonlit nights, the Sidhe might ride out of it on their legendary white horses, whose manes and tails sweep the ground, and whose necks arch like waves. Or like the tumble of water that rushes down the creek. The sound of the falls rumbles everywhere, and calls me to come see—like a band heard through the open door of a club. Every path through the trees makes the promise that paths always made when I was a kid: This is the one. Follow this one, and you'll find adventure. You'll find magic. I find a willow that stands alone and rustles without wind, and a muskrat that swims the creek and disappears into the bank almost at my feet, and the uncomfortable sensation that Minneapolis is no longer behind me where I left it. But I'm not supposed to be comfortable. I'm just supposed to write it down...

Still, why a novel? Why translate all this experience into fiction, all these true stories into a tissue of lies full of made-up people with assumed names? I ought to write an article or an essay, a personal narrative about... Well, there's the problem. If I wrote a travel article on Minnehaha Falls, how could I include the things I didn't quite see, and the things they made me think about? And if I didn't include them, how could I tell anyone what it was really like at Minnehaha Falls? If I wrote a concert review, how could I talk about that sudden, heightened rush of emotion, the feeling of being connected to the rest of the audience and the band by currents of the heart and mind? And if I didn't, how could I describe what hearing Boiled In Lead was really like that night? And how, in any piece of nonfiction, could I explain that First Avenue makes me see visions?

So to tell a few little truths that I can't manage in any other way, I tell a larger lie. I make fiction. But sometimes, when I'm lucky, I find that in the process of telling that big lie, I tell more truth than I set out to. When I'm luckiest, I tell myself things even I didn't know.

The real world wears a layer of familiarity, like dust, that dulls its finish and blurs its sharp corners. Turning the real world into fiction blows that familiarity away. An essay is about the world we know; and because we already know it, we may not peer so closely at the assumptions involved. Fiction, especially fantasy fiction, can erect a whole new set of assumptions, and by doing so, turn a reader's notions of what the real world looks like inside out. But the writer, in the course of telling a story, becomes a reader, too; his first audience is himself. When you write, you're telling a story you haven't heard yet. No matter how much you've outlined and plotted and planned ahead, you can't really know how it will turn out until you've written it. Another Minneapolis writer, Steven Brust, has said, "If the process of writing a book doesn't teach me something or make me examine what I believe, then I've done something wrong." Yeah—your own story can jump out at you and shake you up, and ought to.

When it happens to me, it's because of the autonomy the book has in my head. I usually imagine the characters first, and often in a way that makes me feel as if they're defining themselves, and I'm only taking dictation. Scenes play out in my mind like previews of a movie that someone else is making, characters exchange a whole page of dialogue, in whatever style they insist is theirs, that reveals to me the heart of the relationship between them. It seems wasteful bordering on immoral not to write it all down.

Those easily-come-by pieces are a trap and a snare. They aren't a novel; they're only the clues that lead to one. The rest of the process is the hard part, and not nearly so interesting to talk about, except with another writer. And when two writers find themselves talking about writing, maybe it's a sign that they ought to quit talking, go home, and get back to work. If the world were logical and rational, that would be it. The story would begin and end on the printed page, and stay out from under foot when the author and the readers returned to the business of day-to-day life. But this is the world that prompted me to turn the Seelie Court loose in Minneapolis in the first place. You don't dare turn your back on a world like that.

I'm in a band again, Cats Laughing, the first since I wrote *War for the Oaks*. We'd been together for several months when Bill, the rhythm guitarist, said to me, "I re-read your book last night."

"Oh," I said, feeling, as I always do when someone says that, inexplicably guilty.

"You know, some of what's in there, the parts about the band, are a little...prophetic."

That wasn't the sort of word I'd expected at the end of that sentence. He didn't tell me more than that, and I hesitated to ask. But I'm beginning to understand what he meant. It's not the details—reality is too rich to have to copy the details of fiction. It's something to do with the atmosphere, with all those things I almost see at the edge of my vision. It's another story set in Minneapolis, that couldn't happen anywhere else.

Emma Bull

Novels

War for the Oaks, Ace Books, 1987.
Falcon, Ace Books, 1989.
Bone Dance, Ace Books, 1991.
Finder, Tor Books, February 1994.
The Princess and the Lord of Night (picture book), Harcourt, Brace, 1994.

Short Stories

"Rending Dark," *Sword and Sorceress* (M. Z. Bradley, editor), DAW Books, 1984.
"Badu's Luck," *Liavek,* Ace Books, 1985.
"The Well-Made Plan," *Liavek: The Players of Luck,* Ace Books, 1986.
"Danceland" (with Will Shetterly), *Bordertown* (Terri Windling, editor), Signet, 1986.
"A Bird That Whistles," *Hidden Turnings* (Diana Wynne Jones, editor), Methuen, 1989; Greenwillow, 1990.
"Silver or Gold," *After the King: Stories in Honor of J.R.R. Tolkien* (Martin H. Greenberg, editor), Tor, 1992.

Non-Fiction

"Wonders of the Invisible World: How I Came to Write *War for the Oaks,*" *New North Artscape,* October-November 1988.
"Why I Write Fantasy," *Pulphouse* 6, Pulphouse Publishing, 1990.

Recordings

Cats Laughing, *Cats Laughing* (Spin Art, 1988; re-released as *Reissue,* 1992).
Cats Laughing, *Another Way to Travel* (Spin Art, 1990).
The Flash Girls, *The Return of Pansy Smith and Violet Jones* (Spin Art, 1993).

As Editor (With Will Shetterly)

Liavek (anthology), Ace Books, 1985.
Liavek: The Players of Luck (anthology), Ace Books, 1986.
Liavek: Wizard's Row (anthology), Ace Books, 1987.
Liavek: Spells of Binding (anthology), Ace Books, 1988.
Liavek: Grand Festival (anthology), Ace Books, 1990.

As Publisher (SteelDragon Press)

Fiction in hardcover:

To Reign In Hell by Steven Brust.
The Time of the Warlock by Larry Niven.
Merlin's Booke by Jane Yolen.
Saint Mary Blue by Barry B. Longyear.

Comic Books:

Captain Confederacy #1–#12.
SteelDragon Stories.
Ant Boy #1–#2.
Captain Phil and the Intergalactic Space Pals.

Emma Bull was born in 1954 in Torrance, California. Two of her favorite childhood memories are of typing out nonsense words on her parents' black Royal manual, and watching the neighbor mow the lawn. She went to Beloit College (Wisconsin), where she earned degrees in English Literature and Composition, read lots of wonderful books, and learned that novels were written by real human beings and that she could write one, too.

She moved to Minneapolis in 1976, where she worked as a freelance journalist and as an editor and graphic designer. She and her husband, Will Shetterly, founded SteelDragon Press in 1983 to publish comic books and limited edition quality hardcovers.

Emma's first novel, War *for the Oaks,* is a contemporary fantasy set in Minneapolis, in which the high courts of Faerie recruit a local rock musician to take part in their civil war. It was a finalist for the Mythopoeic Society Award. Her second novel, *Falcon,* is a science fiction book that's part political thriller and part coming-of-age story. Both books were named by the New York Public Library as being among the 300 best books for young adults in the years of their publication. She describes her third novel, *Bone Dance,* as "a fantasy for technophiles." It was nominated for the Nebula, Hugo, and World Fantasy Awards, and received the Philip K. Dick Award second honors. Novel number four, *Finder,* will be published by Tor Books in early '94, and her first book for children, *The Princess and the Lord of Night,* will be coming out from Harcourt, Brace around then, too, as part of the Jane Yolen Books line.

With her husband, she edited the Liavek fantasy anthologies, featuring stories by Gene Wolfe, Jane Yolen, Patricia C. Wrede, Steven Brust, Barry B. Longyear, Alan Moore, Megan Lindholm, and others.

Emma and Will have been part of the Interstate Writers' Workshop, aka The Scribblies, since its founding in 1981. The Scribblies is arguably one of the most successful fiction writers' groups in Minnesota; none of its original seven members had sold fiction when the group was formed, and by 1985, they all had professional sales. Emma and Will were instructors for the St. Charles Science Fiction Society's annual science fiction writing workshop in St. Louis in 1988 and '89, and taught Clarion West in 1991.

Emma is also a musician; she's a member of Cats Laughing, a psychedelic folk-rock band that released its second album in 1990, and is half of the Flash Girls, a duo performing contemporary and traditional folk music. She says that musical improvisation and writing have a lot to do with each other.

Will Shetterly

Novels
Cats Have No Lord, Ace Books, 1985.
Witch Blood, Ace Books, 1986.
The Tangled Lands, Ace Books, 1989.
Elsewhere, Harcourt Brace, 1991.
Nevernever, Harcourt Brace, 1993.
Dogland, Tor Books, 1994 (forthcoming).

Short Stories
"Bound Things," *Liavek,* Ace Books, 1985.
"A Happy Birthday," *Liavek: The Players of Luck,* Ace Books, 1986.
"Danceland" (with Emma Bull), *Bordertown* (Terri Windling, editor),
    Signet, 1986.
"Six Days Outside the Year," *Liavek: Festival Week,* Ace Books, 1990.
"Nevernever," *Life on the Border* (Terri Windling, editor), Tor Books,
    1991.
"Time Travel, the Artifact, and a Significant Historical Personage,"
    Xanadu (Jane Yolen and Martin H. Greenberg, editors), Tor
    Books, 1992.
"Oldthings," *Xanadu 2* (Jane Yolen and Martin H. Greenberg, editors),
    Tor Books, 1993.
"Dreamcatcher," *The Armless Maiden* (Terri Windling, editor), Tor
    Books, 1994 (forthcoming).

Comic Books and Graphic Albums
Captain Confederacy #1–#12, SteelDragon Press, 1986–1988.
"In Charge," *Grimjack* #39, First Comics, 1987.
"Home is a Hard Place," *Open Space* #3, Marvel Comics, 1990.
Captain Confederacy #1–#4, Epic/Marvel Comics, 1991.

As Editor (With Emma Bull)
Liavek (anthology), Ace Books, 1985.
Liavek: The Players of Luck (anthology), Ace Books, 1986.
Liavek: Wizard's Row (anthology), Ace Books, 1987.
Liavek: Spells of Binding (anthology), Ace Books, 1988.
Liavek: Grand Festival (anthology), Ace Books, 1990.

As Publisher (SteelDragon Press)

Fiction in hardcover:
>   *To Reign In Hell* by Steven Brust.
>   *The Time of the Warlock* by Larry Niven.
>   *Merlin's Booke* by Jane Yolen.
>   *Saint Mary Blue* by Barry B. Longyear.

Comic Books:
>   *Captain Confederacy* #1–#12.
>   *SteelDragon Stories.*
>   *Ant Boy* #1–#2.
>   *Captain Phil and the Intergalactic Space Pals.*

Nonfiction

Articles in *The Utne Reader.*
Articles in *Artpaper.*

Awards , Education, and Employment History

1976	B.A. in English Literature from Beloit College.
1979	Actor, New York City. Played Sloane in film, *Toxic Zombies,* and Nureyev in *Little Blue Stars,* an Off-Off Broadway play.
1980–present	Writer, editor, and publisher.
1992	*Elsewhere* received the Minnesota Book Award for Fantasy and Science Fiction.

William Howard Shetterly was born in Columbia, South Carolina, on August 22, 1955. He presently lives in Minneapolis, Minnesota, with his beloved wife, Emma Bull, and his tolerated cats, Chaos and Brain Damage. With Emma Bull, he is the publisher of SteelDragon Press, a tiny publishing house specializing in fantasy and science fiction comic books, trade hardcovers, and collectors' edition hardcovers. It really isn't worth watching *Toxic Zombies* to see his very brief appearance in a very bad movie.

Editor's Acknowledgments

Our proofreaders were Ann Broomhead, Gay Ellen Dennet, Mark Hertel, Merle Insinga, Rick Katze, Tony Lewis, Mark Olson, Priscilla Olson, Davey Snyder, and Tim Szczesuil. Our final proofreader was the irreplaceable George Flynn. Our contracts were drawn up by Peggy Thokar and Rick Katze. Thanks also go to David Dyer-Bennet, Merle Insinga, Rachel Insinga, Mark Olson, and Ben Yalow for their assistance and support. Special thanks go to Patrick & Teresa Nielsen Hayden for the introduction, Nicholas Jainschigg for the great dust jacket illustration, and SteelDragon Press (Box 7253, Minneapolis, MN 55407) and the authors, for having their work available on disk—and for being such a delight to work with!

Aron Insinga, Editor
Nashua, NH
December 18, 1993

This book was designed and set by Aron Insinga in Adobe Garamond, Adobe Post Antiqua BE, and Adobe Wood Type Ornaments 2, using Microsoft Word and Aldus PageMaker on a Macintosh IIsi, and printed on Neutral pH 60# Natural Smooth paper by BookCrafters of Fredericksburg, Virginia, from camera-ready copy generated at 115% on an HP LaserJet 4M printer.